The Founders of Geology

CONTENTS

CHAPTER I

CHAPTER II

CHAPTER III

CHAPTER IV

CHAPTER V

CHAPTER XIII

CHAPTER XIV

CHAPTER XV

CHAPTER I

IN science, as in all other departments of inquiry, no thorough grasp of a subject can be gained, unless the history of its development is clearly appreciated. Nevertheless, students of Nature, while eagerly pressing forward in the search after her secrets, are apt to keep the eye too constantly fixed on the way that has to be travelled, and to lose sight and remembrance of the paths already trodden. It is eminently useful, however, if they will now and then pause in the race, in order to look backward over the ground that has been traversed, to mark the errors as well as the successes of the journey, to note the hindrances and the helps which they and their predecessors have encountered, and to realise what have been the influences that have more especially tended to retard or quicken the progress of research.

Such a review is an eminently human and instructive exercise. Bringing the lives and deeds of our forerunners vividly before us, it imparts even to the most

A

abstruse and technical subjects much of the personal
charm which contact with strenuous, patient, and
enthusiastic natures never fails to reveal.   Moreover,
it has a double value in its bearing on the progress
of those who are engaged in original research.   A
retrospect of this kind leads to a clearer realisation
of the precise position at which they have arrived,
and a wider conception of the extent and limits of
the domain of knowledge which has been acquired.
On the other hand, by enabling them to comprehend
how, foot by foot, the realms of science have been
painfully conquered, it furnishes suggestive lessons as
to tracks that should be avoided, and fields that may
be hopefully entered.

   In no department of natural knowledge is the
adoption of this historical method more necessary
and useful than it is in Geology.   The subjects with
which that branch of science deals are, for the most
part, not susceptible of mathematical treatment.   The
conclusions formed in regard to them, being often
necessarily incapable of rigid demonstration, must
rest on a balance of probabilities.   There is thus
room for some difference of opinion both as to facts
and the interpretation of them.   Deductions and
inferences which are generally accepted in one age
may be rejected in the next.   This element of
uncertainty has tended to encourage speculation.
Moreover, the subjects of investigation are themselves often calculated powerfully to excite the
imagination.   The story of this Earth since it became
a habitable globe, the evolution of its continents,
the birth and degradation of its mountains, the mar-

vellous procession of plants and animals which, since the beginning of time, has passed over its surface, —these and a thousand cognate themes with which geology deals, have attracted numbers of readers and workers to its pale, have kindled much general interest, and awakened not a little enthusiasm. But the records from which the chronicle of events must be compiled are sadly deficient and fragmentary. The deductions which they suggest ought frequently to be held in suspense from want of evidence. Yet with a certain class of minds, fancy comes in to supply the place of facts that fail. And thus geology has been encumbered with many hypotheses and theories which, plausible as they might seem at the time of their promulgation, have one by one been dissipated before the advance of fuller and more accurate knowledge. Yet before their overthrow, it may often be hard to separate the actual ascertained core of fact within them from the mass of erroneous interpretation and unfounded inference that forms most of their substance.

From the beginning of its growth, geology has undoubtedly suffered from this tendency to speculation beyond the sober limits of experience. Its cultivators have been often described as mere theorists. And yet in spite of these defects, the science has made gigantic strides during the last hundred years, and has gradually accumulated a body of well-ascertained knowledge regarding the structure and history of the earth. Few more interesting records of human endeavour and achievement can be found than that presented by the advance of this science. Little more than a century ago geology had no generally acknowledged name and place in the circle of human studies. At the present day it can boast a voluminous literature, hundreds of associations all over the world dedicated to its cultivation, and a state organization in almost every civilized country for its systematic prosecution. I propose to trace some of the leading steps in this magnificent progress. Even speculations that have been thrown aside, and theories that have been long forgotten, may be found to have been not without their use in promoting the general advance.

If all history is only an amplification of biography, the history of science may be most instructively read in the life and work of the men by whom the realms of Nature have been successively won. I shall therefore dwell on the individual achievements of a few great leaders in the onward march of geology, and indicate how each of them has influenced the development of the science. At the same time I shall trace the rise and progress of some of the leading principles of the science, which, though now familiar as household words, are seldom studied in regard to their historical development. Thus, partly in the life-work of the men, and partly in the growth of the ideas which they promulgated, we shall be able to realise by what successive steps geological science has been elaborated.

The subject which I have chosen, if treated as fully as it might fitly be, would require a full course of lectures or more than one printed volume. Within the limits which I have prescribed to myself, I can only attempt to present an outline of it. Instead of trying to summarize the whole history of geology, I think it will be more interesting and profitable to pass somewhat briefly over ancient and medieval time during which geological ideas were crudely taking shape ; to dwell rather fully on the labours of a few of the early masters, who, by actual observation of nature and deduction therefrom, laid the broad foundations of the science, to touch only lightly on the work of some of their less illustrious contemporaries, and to do little more than allude to the modern magnates whose life and work are generally familiar. I have accordingly selected for fullest treatment, in this volume, what has been called the Heroic Age of geology, or the period which extends from the middle of the eighteenth to the earlier decades of the nineteenth century, an interval of about seventy years. A few later conspicuous names will require some brief notice in order to fill up the general outlines of our picture.

The most casual observation is now-a-days sufficient to convince us that the surface of the earth has not always been as it is to-day. At one place sheets of sand and gravel point to the former presence of running water, where none is now to be seen. Elsewhere shells and other marine organisms underneath the soil show that the dry land was formerly the bed of the sea. Masses of sandstone, conglomerate and limestone, once evidently laid down in horizontal layers on the sea-bottom, but now hardened into stone, disrupted, placed on end, and piled up into huge hills and mountain-ranges, prove beyond all question to our modern eyes that stupendous disturbances attended the conversion of the sea-floor into land.

A few of the simpler and more striking of these features might attract notice even among the earliest and rudest tribes.   But still more would the elemental forces of nature arouse the fears, excite the imagination and stimulate the curiosity of primitive man.   Wind and lightning, rain-storms and river-floods, breakers and tidal waves, earthquakes and volcanoes would seem to be direct and visible manifestations of powerful but unseen supernatural beings.   Nor would the more obtrusive features of landscape fail to add their influence—mountains with their clouds, tempests and landslips ; crags and precipices with their strange grotesque half-human shapes, ravines with their gloomy cliffs and yawning chasms between.

It is not difficult to conceive how from these con-current materials there would spring fables, legends and myths, long before the spirit of scientific observation and deduction was developed, and how such fables might continue to satisfy the popular imagination long after that spirit had arisen among the more reflective few. The earliest efforts at the interpretation of nature found their expression in the mythologies and cosmogonies of primitive peoples, which varied in type from country to country, according to the climate and other physical conditions under which they had their birth.   Geological speculation may thus be said to be traceable in the mental conceptions of the remotest pre-scientific ages.

The popular beliefs continued for a time to influence, in a greater or less degree, the speculations of the philosophers who began to observe the operation of natural processes and who, though their deductions were often about as unscientific as the myths for which they were substituted, may yet be claimed as the earliest pioneers of geology. The first stages of advance in theoretical opinions on these subjects may best be illustrated by a brief survey of the geological ideas to be found scattered through the literature of Greece and Rome.

Among the poets allusions abound to the popular interpretations of geological phenomena, wherein the influence of gods and heroes in altering the face of Nature became the subject of legend and myth. It is interesting to note the progress of the decay of these ancient superstitions and their replacement by more natural explanations, based upon actual observation of the present order of things. As an example of this transition, reference may be made to the various attempts to account for the remarkable defile of Tempe, which was one of the marvels in the scenery of Greece. The wide mountain-girdled plain of Thessaly was popularly believed to have once been covered with a lake which was ultimately drained by the kindly intervention of Poseidon, who himself split open the gorge in the encircling rocky barrier, whereby a passage was given for the escape of the stagnant waters to the sea. Later generations attributed the friendly act to Hercules. By the time of Herodotus, however, (B.c. 500) the supernatural had given way, in the minds of reflective men, to a natural interpretation of such features. Yet the Father of History, as was natural to his pious and reverential spirit, does not scornfully reject the long established belief. " That the gorge of Tempe," he says, " was caused by Poseidon is probable ; at least one who attributes earthquakes and chasms to that god would say that this gorge was his work.   It seemed to me to be quite evident that the mountains had there been torn asunder by an earthquake." [1]

By the beginning of our era, supernatural interpretations of geological features had still further gone out of fashion among the writers of the day, and it was now thought unnecessary even to allude to them. Strabo (B.C. 54—A.D. 25) simply refers the Vale of Tempe to the effects of an earthquake, as if its origin were so manifest as to offer no reasonable ground for any doubt.   In no respect do the writings of this geographer differ more conspicuously from those of Herodotus than in their attitude towards the myths of the olden time.   The difference no doubt marks the general progress of public opinion on the subject in the course of five centuries.   Strabo usually passes over the legends in silence, and when he takes occasion to refer to them, it is not infrequently to reject them with contempt.   He will not believe the story that the River Alpheus flows under the sea and rises again to the surface as the fountain of Arethusa at Syracuse, and the reasons which he gives for his refusal are such as a modern man of science might use.[2]   Referring to a statue at Siris, in Southern Italy, which was alleged to have been brought from Troy after the siege and to have closed its eyes when certain suppliants were forcibly dragged away from its shrine, he sarcastically remarks that some amount of courage is required to believe this tale, and also to admit that so many statues

[1] Book vii. 129.   [2] vi. ii. 4.

could have been brought from Troy as were so reputed.[1] He states that while at the Memnonium at daybreak, he certainly heard a noise, but whether it came from the statue or was made by some of the company, he could not tell, though he was disposed to believe anything rather than that stones themselves emit sound.[2] He even carries this critical spirit into his account of alleged historical events, as where, in ridiculing the statement that the Cimbri were driven out of their territory by an extraordinarily high tide, he appeals to the known regularity and periodicity of the tides, as a natural, harmless and universal phenomenon, which disproves such tales.[3]

In considering the opinions of the Greeks and Romans relative to the origin of the various features of the external world, it is well to note that the nations gathered together in the vast basin that drains into the Mediterranean Sea were placed in an exceptionally favourable position for having their attention drawn to some of these features. In particular, this region displays with remarkable fullness the operation of various natural agencies whereby the surface of the earth is altered. It reveals also in a striking manner to the observant eye proofs that these agencies have been at work from a remote antiquity, and have in the course of ages profoundly modified the distribution of sea and land. Thus the countries situated within its borders have been and still are subject to continual shocks of earthquake. For many thousands of years probably not a month has passed without a concussion in some part of the region, usually slight enough to

[1] vi. i. 14.　　[2] xvii. i. 46.　　[3] vii. ii. 1.

alarm without doing much damage, but ever and anon
as appalling calamities that have prostrated cities and
destroyed thousands of their inhabitants.   Moreover
another phase of subterranean energy has from time
immemorial been conspicuously developed in the same
region.   Two distinct and widely separated volcanic
centres exist in the Mediterranean basin, and have had
their eruptions chronicled by poets and historians from
a remote antiquity.   One of these centres lies in the
Aegean Sea, where the isle of Santorin still remains an
active volcano.   The other and much the more important area extends from the Phlegraean Fields around
Naples to beyond the southern coast of Sicily, and
includes the great cones of Etna and Vesuvius, besides
other smaller but active vents.   From the dawn of
history the inhabitants of Greece and Italy have witnessed the awe-inspiring eruptions of these volcanoes
which notably coloured some parts of the old myth-
ology.

Again, the Mediterranean region contains within its
limits a remarkable diversity of climates, and consequently a varied and abundant development of all
those geological processes over which climate exerts a
controlling influence.   The mountain chains, from the
far Pyrenees on the one hand to the distant Caucasus
on the other, with their snow-fields and glaciers, their
cloud-caps and storms, display the extremes of winter
cold, and of rainfall, tempests and landslips.   On the
southern side of the basin lie wide tracts of country
with little or no rain, and passing inland into vast
sandy deserts of almost tropical heat.   From the
mountains innumerable torrents gather into lakes and

rivers, which water the plains and bear the drainage out to sea. Drought and inundation succeed each other, and the same river which at one time carries fertility all over its valley, at another time, swollen into an impetuous flood, spreads across the plains, sweeping away farms and villages, and burying the soil under sheets of sterile gravel and sand. The operations of such streams as the Rhone, the Po, the Tiber, the Danube, the Achelous and the Peneius were not only watched by the inhabitants along their banks but became the subjects first, of widely diffused legendary tales, and afterwards of philosophical discussion. On the south side of the great sea, the Nile, with its mysterious sources and its unfailing annual rise, furnished an inexhaustible source of wonder and speculation.

Further, all round the basin of the Mediterranean the younger geological formations, upraised from the sea, now underlie many of the plains and rise high along the flanks of the hills. In these deposits, shells and other remains of sea-creatures have been preserved in such vast numbers as could not fail to arrest attention even in the infancy of mankind. Since the organisms are obviously like those still living in the neighbouring sea, the inference could readily be drawn that the sea had once covered the tracts of land where these remains had been left. This conclusion was reached by some of the earliest Greek philosophers, and there can be little doubt that it led to those wide views of the vicissitudes of Nature which were adopted in later centuries by their successors.

Our retrospect of the growth of an intelligent appreciation of the geological phenomena so well developed in this long inhabited region need not take us further back than the time of Aristotle, the true Father of Natural History, (B.C. 384-322) who besides his own original contributions to science, supplies valuable references to writings of his predecessors which have not come down to us. His treatises furnish an admirable exposition of the state of natural knowledge in his time. When he wrote, the geocentric view of the universe was still publicly accepted without question. But he had firmly grasped certain truths regarding our globe, which, though taught long before by some of his predecessors, were not yet generally admitted. Thus he recognized that the planet possesses a spherical form, which is the most perfect of all, and he pointed in proof to the round shadow cast by the earth upon the moon during a lunar eclipse. He showed also by the difference in the aspect of the stellar heavens, as we move but a little way from north to south or south to north, that the mass of our globe must be relatively small. "The size of the earth is nothing," he says, "absolutely nothing, compared with the whole heavens. The mass of the sun must be far greater than that of our globe, and the distances of the fixed stars from us is much greater than that of the sun."[1] Accepting the common belief that the world consisted of four elements, he looked on these as arranged according to their relative densities. "The water is spread as an envelope round the earth ; in the same way, above

[1] *Meteorics*, i. viii. 6 ; xiv. 18.

the water lies the sphere of air, while outside of all comes the sphere of fire."[1]

With regard to the surface of the planet, Aristotle had formed some sagacious conclusions, though mingled with certain of the misconceptions that were prevalent in his time. In trying to gain a general impression of the manner in which geological problems were treated by him and the succeeding naturalists and philosophers of antiquity we may find it convenient to consider them under the three sections of (1) Underground processes ; (2) Surface processes ; and (3) Evidence of geological changes in the past.

1. *Underground Processes.* As Greece, from its special geological structure, has from time immemorial been subject to frequent earthquakes, the attention of the more réflective men in the country must have been early drawn to these subterranean disturbances and to a consideration of their possible cause. Aristotle has devoted a portion of his treatise on *Meteorics* to a discussion of earthquakes, and has quoted the opinions of some earlier philosophers in regard to them. He tells us that Anaxagoras (B.C. 480) accounted for these disturbances by the descent of the surrounding ether into the depths of the earth ; that Democritus (B.C. 460–357) thought they were caused by the bursting out of the mass of liquid within the earth, especially after heavy rains ; and also, after the earth had become desiccated by the great commotion arising from the fall of water from the full spaces into those that were empty ; and that Anaximenes (B.C. 544) supposed

[1] *Op. cit.* II. ii. 5. The sphere of fire, the "flammantia moenia mundi" of Lucretius, was the region of the stars and planets.

them to be produced by the disruption of mountains
when the earth, at first full of water, dries up; for
he remarked that they take place chiefly during
droughts and also during excessively wet seasons,
because in the one case the earth is dried and splits
up, while in the other, it gives way on account of
being saturated with liquid.

Rejecting the explanations of his three predecessors
just cited, Aristotle remarks that if some of their
views were true, earthquakes ought gradually to grow
less abundant and severe, until at last the earth should
cease to shake, but that as this diminution has not been
observed, another interpretation must be sought. He
accordingly proposes one of his own which is a curious
and memorable instance of imperfect observation and
inaccurate generalisation. Earthquakes are due, he
thinks, to a commingling of moist and dry within the
earth. Of itself, the earth is dry, but from rain it
acquires much internal humidity. Hence when it is
warmed by the sun and by the internal heat, wind is
produced both within and without its mass. Wind,
being the lightest and most rapidly moving body, is
the cause of motion in other bodies; and fire, united
with wind, becomes flame which is endowed with great
rapidity of motion. It is neither water nor earth
which causes an earthquake; it is the wind when
what is vaporised outside returns into the interior.
Remarking a relation between the frequency and
violence of earthquakes and the state of the weather,
Aristotle admits with Anaximenes that they occur most
abundantly in spring and autumn, during the seasons
of heavy rain and of great drought, but he thinks

that the reason of this relation should be sought in the fact that during these seasons there is most wind.[1]

Aristotle regarded earthquakes and volcanic eruptions as closely related phenomena. He states that it had been observed in some places, that an earthquake has continued until the wind from the interior has rushed out with violence to the surface, as had then recently happened at Heracleia on the Euxine, and before that event at Hiera (Volcano), one of the Lipari Isles. At this latter locality the ground rose up with a great noise and formed a hill that broke up and allowed much wind to escape from the fissures, together with sparks and cinders which buried the whole of the neighbouring town of the Liparans. The shock was even felt in some of the towns on the opposite mainland of Italy.

Aristotle was further led to propose an explanation of the great heat that forms part of the volcanic phenomena. " The fire within the earth," he remarks, " can only be due to the air becoming inflamed by the shock, when it is violently separated into the minutest fragments. What takes place in the Lipari Isles affords an additional proof that the winds circulate underneath the earth." [2]

This idea that volcanic action was mainly due to the movement of wind imprisoned within the earth obtained wide credence in antiquity. Aeolus, the god of the winds, was believed to have his abode under the so-called Aeolian Isles, which are all of volcanic origin, and among which eruptions have been taking place since before the dawn of history.

[1] *Meteor.* II. vii., viii.   [2] *Op. cit.* II. viii. 20.

Aristotle in his wide survey of the organic and inorganic kingdoms did not omit to consider the nature of stones, metals and minerals, and to offer his suggestions as to their possible origin. He supposed the existence of two exhalations which play a notable part in nature both inside and outside the earth. One of these, the smoky or dry exhalation by burning substances, gives rise to minerals and other kinds of stone which are insoluble in water. The other or vaporous exhalation produces the metals which are fusible or ductile. Aristotle's favourite pupil, Theophrastus (B.C. 374-287) took up this subject in a much more practical way in his tract on *Stones*, which describes the external characters, sources and uses of the more familiar rocks and minerals. Interesting as a narrative of what was known and thought in his day in regard to the mineral kingdom, it may be claimed as the earliest essay in Petrography. His treatise " On Fishes " contains a reference to remains of fishes found in the rocks of Pontus and Paphlagonia. The philosopher thought that these fossils were developed from fish-spawn left in the earth, or that fishes had wandered from neighbouring waters and had finally been turned into stone. He also expressed the idea that a plastic force is inherent in the earth whereby bones and other organic bodies are imitated.

Lucretius, whose great poem, *De Rerum Natura*, appeared about half a century before the beginning of our era, states with his characteristic force the explanations then in vogue to account for the phenomena of earthquakes. The interior of the earth, he declares, must be full of wind-swept caverns, with lakes, rivers, chasms and cliffs, as above ground. The fall of some of these vast mountainous rocks, undermined by time, gives such a shock as to send gigantic tremors far and wide through the earth. Again, wind, collecting in these subterranean cavernous spaces, presses with such enormous force against the walls towards which it rushes as to make the earth lean over to that side, and to topple down buildings above ground. Sometimes the air, either from outside or from within, sweeps with terrific whirling violence into the vacant spaces underneath, until in its fury it cleaves for itself a yawning chasm in the earth by which it escapes to the daylight. Even when it does not issue at the surface, its violence among the many underground passages sends a tremor through the earth.

The poet stating that he will explain how volcanic eruptions, such as those of Etna, arise, declares that the mountain is hollow within and that the wind and air inside, when thoroughly heated and raging furiously, heat the rocks around. Fire is thus struck out from these rocks and with its swift flames is swept by the air up the chasms, until it issues from the mountaintop, hurling forth ashes, huge stones, and black smoke. From the sea-floor caverns reach down into the depths of the mountain, and the water that enters there, mingled with air, rushes out again in blasts of flame with showers of stones and clouds of sand.[1] We are not definitely told, however, by what process the heat inside is engendered, whether the explanation

[1] *De Rerum Natura*, vi. 535-702.

of Aristotle was favoured, or the common belief in subterranean accumulations of sulphur and other combustible substances.

Coming down to the beginning of the Christian era, we turn to the pages of Strabo, who besides availing himself of the labours of his predecessors, more particularly of those who wrote in Greek, travelled over a considerable part of the ancient world, with observant eyes as to what he himself saw and a critical judgment as to what he heard from others. Though his great work is mainly a description of the topographical and political geography of his day, it is interspersed with acute observations and reflections regarding the physical features of the various countries, and the natural processes whereby these features have been produced or altered. His *Geography*, therefore, contains not a few important statements of fact in regard to the general effects of subterranean energy. Thus he cites a number of earthquakes by which chasms in the ground were formed, thousands of people were destroyed and cities were swallowed up. He also gives some information regarding volcanic eruptions which had taken place within the historical period in the Mediterranean region. In his time Mount Vesuvius was not only quiescent, but was not known to have ever been active. His quick eye, however, detected the true origin of the mountain. From the aspect of its summit, he inferred that it was once a volcano, with live craters which had become extinct on the failure of the subterranean fuel, and he compared its slopes to the ground around Catania, where the ashes thrown out by Etna have formed an excellent soil for vines. He recognised the truly volcanic nature of the whole district from Etna to the Phlegraean Fields, under which Typhon, as Pindar sang, lay crushed on his burning bed.[1] In his excellent account of the ascent of Etna, Strabo compares the molten lava to a kind of black mud which, liquefied in the craters, is ejected from them and flows down the sides of the mountain, cooling and congealing in its descent, until it becomes a motionless dark rock like millstone.[2]

Strabo, however, made no advance on his predecessors in regard to an explanation of the nature and cause of volcanic action, which he continued to attribute to the force of winds pent up within the earth. He alludes to the connection between the state of the weather and volcanic energy at the Lipari Isles, already noticed by previous writers—a connection which, so far as it exists, doubtless tended to confirm the popular attribution of the eruptions to the escape of subterranean wind. The most important remark of this geographer in regard to volcanic action is undoubtedly his obser-vation that the district around the Strait of Messina seldom suffers much from earthquakes, whereas formerly, before the volcanic orifices of this region were opened up, so as to allow of the escape of the fire smouldering within the earth and of the im-prisoned wind, water and burning masses, the ground was convulsed with frightful earthquakes. The doctrine that volcanoes are safety valves, which was once thought to be a modern idea, is thus at least as old as the beginning of the Christian era.

[1] Book vi. i. 5.   [2] vi. ii. 3, 8.

Strabo cites examples of wide-spread and also local sinkings of land, as well-known historical events, such as the catastrophe that submerged the town of Helice in Achaia, together with an extensive surrounding district. He believed that to earthquakes and similar causes were due the risings, slips and other changes which at various times affect the surface of the earth, and he held that deluges, earthquakes, eruptions of wind, and elevations of the bottom raise the level of the sea, which on the other hand, is lowered when the bottom subsides.[1]

The numerous islands in the Mediterranean Sea occupied much of Strabo's attention. He appears to have believed that their insular character arose from two causes. Some he supposed to have been torn from or joined to the mainland by such convulsions as earthquakes, while others were obviously thrown up by volcanic agency. Those which lie off headlands he was inclined to attribute to the former cause; but those which stand in the middle of the sea seemed to him to have been most probably thrown up from the bottom. He does not appear, however, to have had any settled grounds of belief upon this question, for in one passage he speaks of Sicily having been broken off from the mainland of Italy by earthquakes,[2] while elsewhere he thinks that this island " may have been thrown up from the bottom of the sea by the fires of Etna, as the Aeolian and Pithecusan Isles (Ischia, etc.) have been."[3] He refers to submarine eruptions among the Lipari Islands that had given rise to islets or shoals of hard rock

[1] Book I. iii. 10.   [2] vi. i. 6.   [3] I. iii. 10.

—an interesting observation in connection with some events in the recent history of this volcanic district.[1]

The philosopher Seneca, besides the treatises and plays by which he is chiefly known, wrote towards the end of his life a tract in which, under the title of *Natural Questions,* he discoursed largely of the heavenly bodies and of meteorological phenomena, and discussed also, more fully than any previous writer whose work has come down to us, some of the more important geological processes of nature. He was born a few years before the commencement of our era and met his tragic fate in A.D. 65. As the tract in question refers to events which had happened some time before, in the spring of A.D. 63, it is probably his latest work. Seneca appears to have been familiar with all the literature of the subject up to his own time, and he quotes and criticises the opinions of many of his predecessors. Especially interesting are his disquisitions on the flow of water at the surface and below ground, and on the results and origin of earthquakes. From his treatment of these matters he can be seen to have been a shrewd observer and sagacious reasoner, though still unable to advance much beyond the opinions prevalent in his day, and still holding to some of the most erroneous popular beliefs. Yet he clearly recognized that the system of Nature is no capricious series of events, liable at any moment to be interrupted and changed by the fiat of some irascible divinity. "Though the processes below ground," he remarks, "are more hidden from us than those on the surface

[1] vi. ii. 11.

of the earth, they are none the less equally governed
by invariable laws."

Seneca appears to have been much impressed by the
earthquake which did so much damage in Campania on
5th February A.D. 63, for he refers to it again and
again, and furnishes from the lips of eye-witnesses some
interesting particulars regarding it.   Thus he tells how
a flock of 600 sheep were killed in the district of
Pompeii, a fate which he attributes to the rise of
pestilential vapours from the ground.   He was informed by a most learned and serious friend that when
he was in the bath the tiles on the floor were separated
from each other and were then driven together again,
while the water at one moment sank through the
opened joints of the pavement, and thereafter boiled up
again and was jerked out.   The philosopher's account
is the earliest detailed description of an earthquake,
which has come down to us.   The recentness of the
event, the serious nature of the damage done, and the
abundant narratives of those who had been in the midst
of the calamity led him to consider the effects and
causes of earthquakes more at large than had been done
before his time.

After giving a graphic picture of the terror of the
human mind when the ground beneath our feet is
convulsed, and the one thing in the world that seemed
securely fixed gives way beneath us, he ridicules the
action of those who from fright deserted Campania and
vowed they would never return.   Where, he asks, can
they promise themselves to find a more steadfast soil?[1]

[1] Little did he realise the volcanic nature of the ground and the
potential possibilities of destruction which were to be manifested

We run the same risks everywhere, for no part of the wide earth is immovable. He then proceeds to enumerate the various explanations that up to his day had been proposed to account for the phenomena. Among these he cites that of Anaximenes as to the collapse of subterranean portions of the earth. But he himself adheres to the view which had now been adopted by the majority of authors, including those of most weight, who supposed the cause to lie in the movements of wind imprisoned beneath the earth. He offers a long disquisition on the manner in which he conceives that the subterranean wind acts. Nothing known to us, he states, is more powerful or more penetrating than air in motion. Without its aid none of the other forces in nature, even those which are most energetic, are of any avail. As beneath the earth there are abundant hollows, with rivers, lakes and large bodies of water, which have no exit above ground, so in these dark caverns and recesses the heavy air is pressed down and by its motion gives rise to currents of wind. The force of these currents is increased in proportion to the impediments in the way of their escape, until they find a vent to the surface.

Seneca distinguishes between the up-and-down movement (*succussio*) in earthquakes and the oscillatory movement (*inclinatio*) like that of a ship at sea. He thinks that even a third kind of motion should be recognised, that of trembling or vibration. He

only sixteen years after the Campanian earthquake by the outbreak of Vesuvius in A.D. 79, and the overwhelming of Pompeii and Herculaneum.

believes that each of these motions arises from a different cause. Thus the trembling or vibratory phase, like that produced by the passage of a heavily-laden wagon, or like that arising from a landslip, may be due to the collapse of the sides of subterranean cavities, when the rocks fall with great weight and noise into the recesses below. These catastrophes may sometimes be aided by the abrading power of the overlying rivers, and the constant action of water in widening and weakening the fissures of rocks. When the concussion is so great as to shake down the walls by which the roof of one of these underground empty spaces is supported, the whole ground will give way and sink into the abyss, carrying down large tracts of the surface and even entire cities.

This philosopher recognized the local character of earthquakes, and connected the limitation of their extent with the restricted dimensions of the subterranean caverns where the wind is developed. If it were not so, he remarks, wide tracts of country would be agitated and many places would totter at the same time. But the movement never extends beyond a distance of two hundred Roman miles, and he points once again to the recent example that had filled the Roman world with its renown, yet did not itself travel outward beyond the bounds of Campania.

Volcanoes form the subject of some interesting remarks in Seneca's treatise. He refers to various eruptions in the Italian and Greek centres of volcanic activity. In speaking of two outbreaks at Santorin he remarks that an island rose out of the sea by protracted eruptions from below, and he notes that the internal fire is neither extinguished by the weight of the superincumbent depth of sea, nor prevented from rushing to a height of a couple of hundred paces above the water.[1] He speaks of Etna having sometimes abounded in much fire, and thrown out a great deal of burning sand, day being turned into night, to the terror of the population. On such occasions, thunder and lightning are said to have abounded ; but these came from the concourse of dry materials, and not from ordinary clouds, of which probably there were none in such a raging heat of air—a shrewd anticipation of the modern distinction between ordinary atmospheric electric discharges and those evoked during the ejection of vapours, gases, dust, and stones from a volcanic orifice.[2]

Following the general opinion of the learned men who had preceded him, Seneca had no doubt that volcanic eruptions, like earthquakes, were due to the struggles of subterranean wind to break out to the surface. It is evident, he says, that underground there is a great store of sulphur, and of other substances not less capable of combustion. When the subterranean wind in seeking an outlet has whirled itself through these places, it must in so doing set these inflammable things on fire by mere friction. The flames spreading, in spite of the somewhat sluggish air, make way with vast noise and force, and find at last their escape to the surface, as at Etna and elsewhere. There are fires covered up within the earth, some of which occasionally burst forth ; but a vast number are always burning in

[1] Book ii. xxvi. 5.　　　[2] ii. xxx. 1.

concealment.[1]   As the result of these subterranean
commotions, new mountains are raised and new
islands are placed in the midst of the sea. " Who
can doubt, for instance," the philosopher asks, " that
wind gave birth to Thera and Therasia, and to the
younger island which even in our own time we have
seen spring up in the Aegean sea ? "

Another work of Seneca's time deserves mention
here—the voluminous *Natural History* of the Elder
Pliny, in which so vast a mass of miscellaneous notes
has been compiled regarding the plants, animals, and
minerals known to the ancients, and the earthquakes,
volcanic eruptions, inundations and other natural
events which had happened within the times of
history.[2] Though rather a chronicler of other men's
opinions and experiences than himself an original
observer, he must have been imbued with a keen
interest in every department of Nature, as he certainly was endowed with portentous and unwearied
industry in gathering together all the information
that could be ascertained from every source.   The
graphic picture which we have of him in his nephew's
letters to Tacitus shows him as the eager and
enthusiastic naturalist, keenly interested in every
phenomenon, ready with his tablets to make a note
of all that he saw or heard or read, and strictly
methodical and austerely temperate in his habits of

[1] Book v. xiv. ; ii. x. 4.

[2] Those who are interested in such matters will find a useful
compendium of Pliny's remarks on minerals, rocks, earthquakes
and volcanoes in Dr. H. O. Lenz's *Mineralogie der Alten Griechen
und Römer*, Gotha, 1861.

life. It must always be remembered that it was in
the pursuit of scientific knowledge that he lost his
life by venturing too near the scene of the disastrous
eruption of A.D. 79, which overwhelmed Herculaneum
and Pompeii. If the tradition be correct that Empe-
docles met his death by approaching too close to the
edge of the crater of Etna, this philosopher may
perhaps be claimed as a victim to the desire to
explore the mysteries of volcanic action. But in the
case of Pliny there is no uncertainty. He is enrolled
for all time as the first definitely recorded martyr to
the cause of geological science.

After referring to the opinion of the Babylonians
that earthquakes and all allied phenomena are to be
ascribed to the influence of the stars, Pliny remarks:
" My own belief is that they are caused by wind.
They only occur at times of complete calm, when
the wind, having sunk down into the subterranean
chasms, breaks forth once more."[1] He enumerates
a number of earthquakes of note, and in discussing
the phenomena that take place in connection with
them on land and sea, he states that towns with
numerous culverts and houses with cellars suffer less
than others, and that, for example in Naples, those
houses are most shaken which are built on hard
ground. He likewise recounts instances of volcanic
eruptions and the appearance of new volcanic islands,
but without throwing any light on the causes of
these disturbances.

It thus appears that during classical antiquity no
perceptible advance had been made in the investigation

[1] *Hist. Nat.* II. 81.

of the nature and cause of earthquakes and volcanoes. The idea that both of these manifestations of hypogene energy arise from the action of air imprisoned within the earth and struggling to escape continued to hold its ground, the heat and fire of volcanoes being regarded as probably due to the action of the internal wind in setting fire to sulphur, bitumen or other combustible substances.

2. *Processes at work on the surface of the earth.* Among the geological agents which alter the face of the land, rivers have naturally occupied much of the attention of mankind in all ages. Herodotus during his visit to Egypt was greatly interested in the Nile, and he devotes some space to a discussion of the remarkable characteristics of this stream. He enumerates and criticises the various explanations which had been given of its annual rise, but without venturing on any definite conclusion himself. He recognises however the significance of the yearly deposit of silt on the surface of the country, and concludes that "Egypt is the gift of the river."

Aristotle discusses the phenomena presented by rivers, and shows considerable acquaintance with the drainage system on the north side of the Mediterranean basin. He criticises previously expressed opinions as to the source of rivers, particularly ridiculing the suggestion of Plato that all rivers flow directly from a vast mass of water under the earth. He appears to have held the opinion that just as the vaporised moisture in the atmosphere is condensed by cold and falls in drops of rain, so the moisture beneath the earth is similarly condensed and forms the sources of rivers.

He states that the mountains, by their cold temperature, condense the atmospheric moisture and receive
a vast quantity of water, so that they may be compared to an enormous suspended sponge. He shows
by geographical illustrations, drawn from Asia and the
Mediterranean basin, that the largest rivers descend
from the loftiest ground, where the water accumu-
lates in numberless channels. He admits the possible
existence of underground lakes from which rivers may
issue, and alludes to the disappearance of some streams
into subterranean channels.

Aristotle, moreover, reflected profoundly on the
geological operations of rivers. Recognising the
truth of the observation that the plain of Egypt had
been built up by the deposits of the Nile, he also
noted that along the shores of some parts of the
Black Sea the river alluvia had increased so much
in sixty years that the vessels in use there had to
be much smaller than formerly, and that in this case,
as in so many others, the silting up might go on
until the marsh-land became dry ground. Similar
changes were then in progress on the Bosphorus.
The contemplation of these and other vicissitudes led
the philosopher to some striking generalisations as to
the past and the future of the surface of our globe,
to which reference will be made on a later page.

To Strabo we are indebted for some sagacious
observations on the hydrography of the Mediterranean
basin. He points out that, like the Nile, the other
rivers that enter this sea form extensive alluvial
deposits at their mouths, as well as inland over the
low grounds, and he specially instances the plains of

the Hermes, Caÿster, Mæander and Caïcus as having
been formed by the streams that flow through them.[1]
The deltas vary, he thinks, according to the nature
of the regions drained, being most developed where
the country is large and the surface rocks are soft,
and where the rivers are fed by many torrents. He
remarks that these accumulations are prevented from
advancing further outward into the sea by the ebb
and flow of the tides.[2]

Strabo believed the outflowing currents of the
Mediterranean Sea, as well as that of the Bosphorus,
to be due to the escape of the surplus water that
drains into the basin. In the course of his narrative
he is led to discuss the question of the opening of
a connection between the Black Sea and the Mediterranean, and between this latter and the outer
ocean. He expresses the opinion that we should not
be surprised if the Isthmus of Suez were to be disrupted or to subside, so as to allow the Mediterranean
and Red Sea to be joined together.[3]

In his philosophical survey of Nature and its problems, Seneca found room for a consideration of the
water-circulation of the globe. His reflections on this
subject show that in one important respect he had
not advanced beyond the position of Aristotle. In
his essay already cited he discusses at some length
the various kinds of terrestrial waters, noting their
tastes, temperature, uses, effects and other features.
He speaks of himself as a diligent wine-grower,[4] and

---

[1] Book xv. i. 16.   [2] i. iii. 7, 8.   [3] i. iii. 6, 7, 17.

[4] Seneca evidently used his eyes to some purpose in the country.
He calls attention to the remarkable power of vegetation in displacing

in this capacity he had noted that the heaviest rain does not moisten the earth for more than ten feet downward, most of it flowing off into the beds of streams. He gives his opinion, therefore, that rain may make a torrent or help to swell a stream, but that it cannot of itself be the source of a river flowing with an equable course between its banks. If he is asked whence, then, does the water of rivers come, he replies that the question is as inept as it would be to demand where air and earth come from. Water being one of the four elements forms a fourth part of nature. Why then should we be surprised if it can always keep pouring out? He knows that just as in the human body there are veins which when ruptured send forth blood, so in the earth there are veins of water which are found even in the driest places, at depths of two or three hundred feet below the surface, and which when laid open issue in springs and rivers. The water at these depths, so far below the limits to which rain can moisten the earth, is not regarded by him as of atmospheric origin, but living water (*aqua viva*), for as all things are contained in all, the earth, water and air can pass into each other. The earth contains water which it presses out and also air which, by the cold of winter, it condenses into moisture ; the earth itself is also resolvable into moisture.

Coming to the consideration of water at the surface, he is on sounder ground when he discusses the regime of rivers. He can see no more reason why

stones and destroying monuments, even the most minute and slender rootlets being able to split open large rocks and crags, II. vi. 5.

we should wonder at the changes of volume in rivers than we do at the regular succession of the seasons. After an excellent account of a flood on the Danube, of which we may believe him to have been an eye-witness, he enters upon a discussion of the rise of the Nile which he describes as it appears at Philae. In rejecting the popular opinion expressed by the tragedians that the cause of this annual phenomenon is to be sought in the melting of snow on the mountains of Ethiopia, he repeats the arguments of Herodotus (whom however he does not cite) but with the interesting addition, which he may have derived from the explorers sent by Nero to the south of Egypt, that in Ethiopia no hibernating animal had ever been found, and that the serpent may be seen there in winter even on the open high grounds.[1]

The effects of floods in destroying woods, houses and flocks are described, and the philosopher, in his characteristic way, turns from a contemplation of these events to moralise over the destiny of mankind. He asks in what manner, when the fatal day of the deluge shall arrive, will a large part of the earth's surface be destroyed by water, whether the great ocean will overwhelm us, or ceaseless torrents of rain, or prolonged winter, pouring deluges from the clouds, or rivers swollen into floods, and torrents rushing from newly opened sources, or whether it will be by no single agency, but when all will conjoin together; when rains will descend, rivers will overflow, the sea will issue from its depths and all will sweep in one fell array against the human race.[2]

[1] Book iv. ii. 7-30.   [2] iii. xxvii.

3. *Proofs of geological changes in the past.* Throughout the Mediterranean basin the profusion of well-preserved marine shells in the upraised younger formations which underlie the lowlands and crop out along the sides of the hills, must have attracted the notice of the earliest inhabitants. Accordingly we find in Greek literature frequent allusion to them and to the inference deduced from them that many tracts of land had once lain beneath the sea. Xenophanes of Colophon (B.C. 614) is recorded to have written concerning sea-shells found among the inland hills in Malta and elsewhere, and to have concluded from them that they prove periodical submergences of the dry land, wherein man and his dwelling-places have been involved. Xanthus the Lydian (B.C. 464) is quoted by Strabo as having seen shells like cockles and scallops, far from the sea, in Armenia and Lower Phrygia, and having inferred, from this evidence and that of scattered salt-lakes, that these regions had once been submerged beneath the sea.[1] Herodotus noticed petrified sea-shells in the hills of Egypt, especially those near the oasis of Jupiter Ammon, and he too concluded from them, and from the saline crust on the ground, that the sea had once spread over Lower Egypt.[2] Some centuries later these observations were confirmed by Eratosthenes (B.C. 276-196) who noted vast quantities of marine shells 2000 or 3000 stadia from the sea and for a distance of 3000 stadia along the road to the Ammon oasis, together with beds of salt and saline springs.[3] Strato (B.C. 288) also is quoted by Strabo as having come to the

[1] Strabo, 1. iii. 4. [2] II. 12. [3] Quoted by Strabo, *loc. cit.*

conclusion that the temple of Jupiter Ammon was once near the sea, which then spread over Egypt as far as the marshes, near Pelusium, Mount Casius and the Lake Sirbonis.   He speaks of salt being dug in his time in Egypt under layers of sand mingled with shells, as if the whole region had formerly been covered by a shallow sea that stretched across to the Arabian Gulf.[1]

No writer of antiquity has expressed himself more philosophically than Aristotle regarding the past vicissitudes of the earth's surface.   Having studied so carefully the operations of the various agents that are now modifying that surface, he recognised how greatly the aspect of the land must have been transformed in the course of ages.   His remarks on this subject have a strikingly modern tone.   He contemplates the alternations of land and sea and furnishes illustrations of them, much as a geologist of to-day may do. "The sea," he says, "now covers tracts that were formerly dry land, and land will one day reappear where we now find sea.   We must look on these mutations as following each other in a certain order, and with a certain periodicity, seeing that the interior of the globe, like the bodies of animals and plants, has its periods of vigour and decline, with this dif-

[1] *Loc. cit.* Strabo narrates his own experience as to fossils in the rocks of Egypt.   When standing in front of the Pyramids he noticed that the blocks of stone that had been brought from the quarries contained pieces which in shape and size resembled lentils (*nummulites*) and he was told that these were remnants of the food of the workmen turned into stone—an explanation which he rejects as improbable, though he cannot suggest a likely origin for them. xvii. i. 34.

ference, however, that while the whole of an organism flourishes and then dies, the earth is affected only locally.

" These phenomena escape our notice because they take place successively during periods of time, which, in comparison of our brief existence, are immensely protracted. Whole nations may disappear without any recollection being preserved of the great terrestrial changes which they have witnessed from beginning to end. So too the increase in the area of habitable land is brought about so imperceptibly in the course of long ages that we can neither tell who were the first inhabitants to settle in such new tracts, nor in what condition they found the land." After quoting in illustration the early history of Egypt and of the territories of the Argives and Mycenians in Greece, he remarks that what had transpired in a little district appears to take place in precisely the same way in more extensive regions and over entire countries. He then proceeds to consider how these vicissitudes of topography are to be accounted for.

" The cause to which such terrestrial mutations are to be assigned may perhaps be that just as winter regularly recurs among the seasons of the year, so a great winter, lasting through a vast period of time, may arise, bringing with it an excessive rainfall. Such a precipitation would not always affect the same countries. Decalion's deluge, for example, only extended over old Hellas which lies near to Dodona and the river Achelous, which has often shifted its course. Land that is lofty and has a cold temperature gives rise to and retains an abundance of water which keeps it perpetually moist, while lower grounds, especially where the rocks are porous, are the first to be dried up. In course of time one area becomes more or less desiccated, until a fresh return of a great period of inundation." [1]

As geographical proof of the probability of these suggestions, he refers again to the early condition of Egypt. Herodotus had long before announced his belief that the Nile had filled up with its sediments the tract between Thebes and Memphis, once an inlet of the sea, and had continued to push out its silt so as to form the delta. Aristotle, enlarging on the statements of the historian, declares that Egypt was evidently at one time covered by a continuous sea, and that the Nile, with its annual burden of sediment, has shallowed this expanse of water, turning it first into marshes which by degrees became entirely dried up. He concludes with these remarkable words : " It is clear that, as time never stops and the universe is eternal, the Tanais and the Nile, like all other rivers, have not always flowed ; the ground which they now water was once dry. But if rivers are born and perish, and if the same parts of the land are not always covered with water, the sea must undergo similar changes, abandoning some places and returning to others, so that the same regions do not remain always sea or always land, but all change their condition in the course of time." [2]

Though Strabo was more intent on recording geographical facts than indulging in geological speculations, he could not refrain from sometimes intercalating a

---

[1] *Meteor.* i. xiv. 1 *et seq.* 20.   [2] *Op. cit.* i. xiv. 31.

pregnant remark as to the connection of the present with the past. In regard to the interchange of land and sea in former periods he held firmly to the doctrine so clearly expounded by the earlier philosophers. "Every one will admit," he writes, "that at various periods a great portion of the mainland has been covered and again left bare by the sea." "All things are continually in motion and undergo great changes, much of the land being turned into water, and much of the water changed into land. Some parts of the earth now inhabited by man once lay beneath the sea, while some portions of the bed of the sea were once inhabited land." [1]

The poet Ovid (B.C. 43-A.D. 18), who flourished about the same time as Strabo, in a well-known passage in the 15th book of his *Metamorphoses* represents Pythagoras as himself expounding his view of the system of Nature. This philosopher's doctrines have only come down to us reported and perhaps distorted by others. As Ovid introduces into Pythagoras' discourse allusions to some incidents which took place long after the philosopher's death, the narrative cannot be regarded as historically accurate, or as more than a digest of what, in the time of Augustus, was believed to be the Pythagorean philosophy. The sage is represented as maintaining that the world is eternal and consists of the four elements—air and fire above, water and earth below. "Nothing in this world perishes but only varies its form ; to be born is merely to begin to be something different from what we were before, and to die is to cease to be that same

[1] Book xvii. i. 36.

thing.   In spite of all transformation, the sum of
everything remains constant."   The vicissitudes of
the earth's surface are then enumerated, and historical
examples of some of them are given.   They may be
summarised in the subjoined paragraphs.

What was once solid land is now covered by the
sea, and new lands have been made out of the deep.
Sea shells have been found far inland, and the anchor
on a mountain crest.

Former plains have been carved into valleys by the
descending waters, and thus mountains have been
washed down into the sea.

Ancient lakes have been turned into tracts of burning sand, and dry ground has been changed to stagnant
marshes.

Nature has opened new springs in some places, and
elsewhere has closed up the old ones.

By former earthquakes many rivers have been made
to spring forth, or to sink down and disappear.

Places that were once islands, like Antissa,
Pharos and Tyre are now joined to the mainland,
and, on the other hand, tracts of once continuous
land are separated by sea-straits like the island of
Leucadia.

Cities have been submerged beneath the sea, as in
the case of Helice and Buris of which the walls, still
standing inclined beneath the waves, are pointed out
by the sailors.

Plains may be turned into hills, as happened at
Troezene where the violence of the winds, imprisoned in their dark caverns within the earth and
unable to find egress, heaved up the ground like

a bladder and made a prominent hill which still endures.[1]

Waters vary in temperature, some being cold during the day and warm at morning and evening. Others (accompanied with petroleum or inflammable gas) can set wood on fire. Some have a petrifying quality, and others have varying effects on the human body and mind.

Islands once floating have become fixed, like the ancient Ortygia which is now Delos, and the Symplegades, which once terrified the Argo, but are now anchored, and firmly defy the tempests.

Etna which now glows with its sulphurous furnaces will not always be a burning mountain, and there was a time before it began to burn. Whether the earth is an animal that lives and breathes forth flames from many vents; or winds pent up within the earth break out and cast up stones and flame until the caverns are emptied and cooled; or some bituminous mass has taken fire and burns until it dies away in faint fumes of yellow brimstone; a day will come when the fires within will die out for lack of fuel.

From this sketch of the knowledge possessed by the ancients regarding geological processes it appears that while some sound observations had been made and a certain amount of correct information had been gathered together, speculation as to the causes of things was much more cultivated than the patient collection and comparison of facts. The same fanciful

[1] An account of this eruption is given by Strabo (i. iii. 18) and its effects have been described by the late Professor Fouqué of Paris, *Compt. rend.* lxii. pp. 904, 1121, and by other later writers

hypothesis was accepted and reiterated for centuries, without apparently any effort being made to test or verify it by actual observation of nature. Certain vague and more or less obvious inferences were drawn as to ancient changes in land and sea, and some of these changes were correctly referred to the agencies that produced them. Yet the epigene forces of nature were but partially comprehended, while the hypogene activities were entirely misunderstood. Not even the faintest suspicion had yet dawned on the minds of men as to the long succession of events in the great terrestrial evolution which geology has revealed. In short nothing in this department of knowledge had yet been accumulated to which the name of science could be applied.

In one important respect, however, a momentous forward step had been taken in the intellectual progress of mankind. The primeval belief that Nature was governed by impulsive and capricious divinities, interfering continually with the sequence of events, had for centuries disappeared from the creed of all reflective men, though it still found rhetorical expression among the poets. In its place had come a more or less definite recognition that the world is regulated by laws which, invariable and impartial in their operation now, had been at work from the beginning. The spread of this more enlightened conception was happily untrammelled by any active opposition either from a jealous priesthood or from popular animosity. Each philosopher was at liberty to hold and to express the views which he chose to adopt, and while the old religion of classic paganism slowly lost its hold on the people, the rise of Christianity at first offered no impediment to the freedom of philosophical inquiry. The fate of the Roman Empire and the inroads of the barbarians arrested for centuries the progress of natural history investigation. When this progress was resumed towards the end of the Middle Ages, a new spirit of intolerance had arisen from which Antiquity had been free.

CHAPTER II

Growth of geological ideas in the Middle Ages—Avicenna and the Arabs : Baneful influence of theological dogma. Controversy regarding the nature of fossil organic remains. Early observers in Italy—Leonardo da Vinci, Falloppio, Steno, Moro. The English cosmogonists—Burnet, Whiston, Woodward. Robert Hooke, John Ray, Martin Lister, Robert Plot, Edward Lhuyd.

During the centuries that succeeded the fall of the Western Empire such learning as survived in Europe was to be found only in the monasteries and other ecclesiastical establishments. But it concerned itself little with natural knowledge, save in as far as this was contained in the works of the writers of antiquity. From about the middle of the eighth century onwards for some five hundred years, the Arabs kept alive the feeble flame of interest in researches into the secrets of Nature. With great labour and at large cost, they procured as much as they could obtain of the literature of Ancient Greece and Rome, and studied and translated into their own language the works of the best writers in philosophy, medicine, mathematics and astronomy. They were thus able to some extent to enlarge the domain of these subjects. One of the most illustrious of the Arab authors was the famous Avicenna (Ibn-Sina, 980-1037), the translator of Aristotle, whose views he largely adopted. But if the volume " On the conglutination of Stones " be truly ascribed to him, he expressed, more clearly than his Greek master, opinions regarding the origin of mountains and valleys which show a singular forecast of modern geology. " Mountains," he says, " may arise from two causes, either from uplifting of the ground, such as takes place in earthquakes, or from the effects of running water and wind in hollowing out valleys in soft rocks and leaving the hard rocks prominent, which has been the effective process in the case of most hills. Such changes must have taken long periods of time, and possibly the mountains are now diminishing in size. What proves that water has been the main agent in bringing about these transformations of the surface, is the occurrence in many rocks of impressions of aquatic and other animals. The yellow earth that clothes the surface of the mountains is not of the same origin as the framework of the ground underneath it, but arises from the decay of the organic remains, mingled with earthy materials transported by water. Perhaps these materials were originally in the sea which once over-spread all the land."

With the revival of learning in Europe, attention was once more drawn to the problems presented by the rocks that form the dry land. More particularly did the occurrence of fossil shells, far distant from the sea, arouse inquiry. We have seen that in the days of ancient Greece and Rome the questions suggested by these objects did not wholly escape attention, and that while, in general, no doubt was cast upon their organic origin, the natural conclusion was drawn from them that they proved the sea to have once overspread the land.

This deduction was likewise adopted after the revival of learning. But by this time the Church had gained such an ascendency over the minds of men that no opinions were allowed to be promulgated which appeared to run counter to orthodox beliefs.   If therefore an observer who found abundant sea-shells imbedded in the rocks forming the heart of a mountain chain ventured to promulgate his conclusion that these fossils prove the mountains to consist of materials that were accumulated under the sea, after living creatures appeared upon the earth, he ran imminent risk of prosecution for heresy, inasmuch as according to Holy Writ, land and sea were separated on the third day of creation, but animal life did not begin until the fifth day. Again, the overwhelming force of the evidence from organic remains that the fossiliferous rocks must have taken a long period of time for their accumulation could not fail to impress the minds of those who studied the sub- ject.   But to teach that the world must be many thousands of years old was plainly to contradict the received interpretation of Scripture that not more than some 6000 years had elapsed since the time of the Creation.

To court martyrdom on behalf of such speculative opinions was not a course likely to be followed by many enthusiasts. Various shifts were accordingly adopted, doubtless in most cases honestly enough, in order to harmonise the facts of Nature with what was supposed to be the divine truth revealed in the Bible. A favourite mode of escape from the difficulty consisted in denying that the fossils ever formed part of living creatures. The old notion, first suggested by Theophrastus, was revived, to the effect that there exists within the earth a plastic force by which imitative forms are produced, resembling those of true organisms, but in reality as inorganic in origin as the plant-like forms made by frost on window-panes. The fossils were regarded as simply mineral concretions, and were described as *lusus naturae*, mere freaks of Nature, *lapides sui generis*, *lapides figurati*, "figured" or "formed" stones.[1] Some writers, unable. to detect the action of any such formative agency in the earth itself, supposed that the occult influence came from the stars.

There were many observers, however, who could not gainsay the evidence of their own senses, and who recognised that either we must believe that the minute and perfectly-preserved organic structures in the fossils could only have belonged to once living plants and animals, like those which possess similar structures at the present day, or that the Creator had filled the rocks of the earth's crust with

[1] The earliest account of these objects accompanied with illustrative plates was that of the distinguished Conrad Gesner (1516-1565) *De rerum fossilium, lapidum et gemmarum figuris*, 1565. He had no very clear idea as to the origin of these objects, some of which he thought might be remains of plants or animals, while others he regarded as more probably produced by some inorganic process, as minerals and ores are formed.

these exquisitely designed but deceptive pieces of mineral matter, with no apparent object unless to puzzle and disconcert the mind of frail humanity.[1]

If they refused to accept the latter alternative, they found themselves face to face with the dogmas of the Church and the consequences of professing disbelief in them. The only escape from the dilemma which then presented itself to such orthodox minds was to have recourse to the Deluge of Noah. This event was at that period regarded as having been a world-wide catastrophe when, according to the sacred narrative, " the fountains of the great deep were broken up, and the windows of heaven were opened." For those writers especially who had little or no personal acquaintance with the actual conditions of the problem, who did not realise the orderly manner in which the fossils are disposed, layer upon layer, for thicknesses of many thousand feet in the solid rocks of the land, the doctrine of the efficiency of the Flood offered a welcome solution of the difficulty. They had no conception of the physical impossibility of accumulating all

---

[1] It is almost incredible how long some of these ignorant beliefs lasted, and what an amount of argument and patience had to be expended in killing them. I have been told that even within the last century a learned divine of the University of Oxford used to maintain his opinion that the fossils in the rocks had been purposely placed there by the devil, in order to deceive, mislead and perplex mankind. On the other hand, an opinion of a contrary tendency was promulgated in the latter half of the previous century by a Swiss naturalist, Bertrand, who suggested that the fossil plants and animals had been placed there directly by the Creator, with the design of displaying thereby the harmony of His work, and the agreement of the productions of the sea with those of the land.

the fossiliferous formations of the earth's crust within the space of one hundred and fifty days during which "the waters prevailed upon the earth, and all the high hills that were under the whole heaven were covered." It was enough for them to obtain warrant from Scripture that, since the creation of animal life, the dry land had been submerged, and to adduce evidence from the rocks which they could claim as striking corroboration of the truth of the biblical story. Hence the "diluvialists," or those who claimed the Deluge as a leading geological event in the history of the earth, formed for many years a powerful body of controversialists, who owed their influence and popularity more to the impression that they were the champions of orthodoxy than to the convincing nature of their reasoning.

There could not, however, fail to be some observers who, after making themselves acquainted with the fossiliferous strata, found it impossible to believe that such piles of rock, crowded with a succession of organic remains, could have been the work of a transient inundation such as Noah's Flood confessedly was. Some of these men, struck with the rapidity with which detrital materials can be accumulated on the surface of the earth by volcanic outbursts, imagined that the stratified rocks might have been formed by the operation of active volcanoes. The volcanic eruptions of Italy and the Aegean Sea had greatly impressed the minds of Italian writers, who felt that if, as in the case of Monte Nuovo on the shore of the bay of Naples in year 1538, a hill, nearly 500 feet high, could be piled up in two days around a volcanic vent, it was at least conceivable that the whole of the fossiliferous formations might have been deposited by the same agency during the last 6000 years. So vague and inaccurate was the knowledge of rocks at that time, that those who started this notion seem to have had no suspicion of how entirely different in character and origin the ordinary fossiliferous formations of the earth's crust are from volcanic productions. Several generations had still to pass, and detailed observations on stratified rocks had to be laboriously made in many countries, before the truth could be finally established that the fossiliferous formations, many thousand feet in thickness, contain a long record of geographical changes on the face of the globe, and of a marvellous succession of organic types which required a vast series of ages for their evolution.

During the sixteenth, seventeenth and a great part of the eighteenth century, the controversy over organic remains and the part played by the Flood, while keeping alive an interest in the subject, undoubtedly hindered the advance of rational conceptions of the fundamental facts of geological history. It was singularly unfortunate for the progress of this branch of science that it should have aroused such ecclesiastical antagonism. For the true modern spirit of observation and experiment had long been abroad and at work in other branches of scientific inquiry wherein the Church saw no danger, and where churchmen were often among the foremost leaders. The necessity for a close scrutiny of Nature, as the basis of sound deduction, had for generations been recognised by some of the more thoughtful minds before it was developed into a system by Bacon. Even as far back as the latter half of the sixteenth century, the method of practical research, as opposed to mere book-knowledge and theory, had been advocated even for the investigation of the rocky part of the earth. It was proclaimed, in no uncertain voice, by the learned and versatile Dane, Peter Severinus, who counselled his readers thus : " Go, my sons, sell your lands, your houses, your garments and your jewelry; burn up your books. On the other hand, buy yourselves stout shoes, get away to the mountains, search the valleys, the deserts, the shores of the sea, and the deepest recesses of the earth ; mark well the distinctions between animals, the differences among plants, the various kinds of minerals, the properties and mode of origin of everything that exists. Be not ashamed to learn by heart the astronomy and terrestrial philosophy of the peasantry. Lastly, purchase coals, build furnaces, watch and experiment without wearying. In this way, and no other, will you arrive at a knowledge of things and of their properties." [1] The modern spirit of investigation in natural science could not be more clearly or cogently enforced than it was by this professor of literature and poetry, of meteorology and of medicine, in the year 1571.[2]

[1] Petrus Severinus, *Idea Medecinae Philosophicae*, 1571, p. 73, cap. vii. De principiis corporum (cited by D'Aubuisson).

[2] It is curious to find a parallel passage to this extract written a hundred years later by Robert Hooke. He declared that, in spite of all the knowledge that had been acquired respecting the

A brief survey of the progress of inquiry in Italy will supply the best illustration of the slow advance which was made in the demolition of long established prejudice, and in paving the way for the ultimate establishment of a philosophical conception of the past history of the earth. One of the earliest observers whose opinions have been recorded was the illustrious painter, architect, sculptor, and engineer Leonardo da Vinci (1452-1519). His attention having been aroused by the abundantly fossiliferous nature of some of the rocks in northern Italy, in which canals were cut, he concluded that the shells contained in these rocks had once been living on the sea-floor, and had been buried in the silt washed off the neighbouring land. He ridiculed the notion that they could have been produced by the influence of the stars, and he asked where such an influence could be shown to be at work now. But he pointed out that besides the shells, there were at various heights, terraces of gravel composed of materials that

world we inhabit, an adequate natural history of the earth could hardly be prepared until "after some ages past in making collections of materials for so great a building, and the employing a vast number of hands in making this preparation." He instanced the various kinds of observers required and the methods and instruments to be employed by them, "as by fire, by frost, by menstruums, by mixtures, by digestions, putrefactions, fermentations, and petrifactions, by grindings, brusings, weighings and measuring, pressing and condensing, dilating and expanding, dissecting, separating and dividing, sifting and streining; by viewing with glasses and microscopes, smelling, tasting, feeling, and various other ways of torturing and wracking of natural bodies, to find out the truth or the real effect, as it is in its constitution and state of being." "Discourse of Earthquakes," *Posthumous Works*, p. 279.

evidently been rounded and accumulated by
ing water.

he discussion received a fresh impetus from the
idance and variety of the organic remains in the
ks of stone brought for the repair of the Citadel
an Felice at Verona, in the year 1517. In the
st of the keen discussion that arose over these
ls, the learned men of the country were con-
:d, including Fracastoro (1483-1553) who after
g Professor of Philosophy at Padua had returned
his native city, Verona, to practice there as a
sician. When various theories had been pro-
nded, he announced his own opinion that the
ls could never have been left by the Mosaic
ge, which he maintained had only been a tem-
iry inundation, caused by heavy rains, and would
: scattered the shells over the surface of the
ind, instead of burying them deep within the
:a that form the mountains whence the stones
been quarried. He showed the absurdity of
buting such organised forms to any imaginary
tic force, and insisted that the fossils were
oubtedly at one time animals that lived and
tiplied where their remains are now found, and
efore that the mountains have been successively
fted above the sea.[1]

ardano (1552) pointed to fossil shells as certain

:. Brocchi, *Conchologia Fossile Subapennina,* Vol. i., " Discorso sui
-essi dello studio della Conchologia Fossile in Italia," p. v. This
contains a valuable summary of the progress of the science of
shells in Italy from the year 1300 down to 1810. The work
·o quarto volumes was published in 1814.

evidence that the sea once covered the sites of the hills. His contemporary, Mattioli, on the other hand, supported the old figment of the *materia pinguis*, though admitting that porous bodies, such as the bones and shells so abundant in Italy, might be turned into stone by being permeated by a petrifying juice. He is said to have been the first writer who published a reference to the fossil fishes of Monte Bolca. The skilful anatomist Falloppio (1557), when he met with bones of elephants, teeth of sharks, shells and other fossils, refused to admit them to be anything but earthy concretions, because he deemed that to be a simpler solution of the problem than to suppose that the waters of the Deluge could have reached as far as Italy. Aristotle had decided against any universal flood, and the authority of this philosopher was then about as potent as that of Holy Writ. So much did Falloppio lie under the influence of this prejudice, that he thought it not unlikely that the potsherds of Monte Testaceo at Rome were in like manner natural productions of the earth.

An important mineral collection, containing many fossil shells, which had been gathered together in the Vatican by Pope Sixtus V., was described and excellently figured by Mercati (1574) who, however, with all these well preserved organisms under his eyes, denied their true organic nature, and came to the conclusion that they were mere stones that had assumed their present shapes under the influence of the celestial bodies. It is worthy of notice that another collection of natural history objects which, in the latter half of the same century had been formed at Verona, was described by Olivi (1584) who regarded the fossil organisms as mere sports of Nature. Cesalpino (1566) who had distinguished himself as a botanist, turned in his later years to mineral studies, and wrote a volume *De Metallicis*, which may still be usefully consulted for information on the stones and ores of Italy.   He recalled attention to the true doctrine regarding fossil shells, which he looked upon as organisms that had been left by the retiring sea, and had been turned into stone by the petrifying influence of the surrounding rock.   Majoli suggested that fossil shells on the land had been ejected from the sea-floor by submarine volcanic explosions.

In the crowd of Italian writers who took part in this long controversy, by far the most illustrious was Nicolas Steno (1631-1687).   Born in Copenhagen, he studied medicine and took his degree there, afterwards passing to Leyden and then to Paris, where he remained two years, attaining great distinction by his discoveries in human anatomy.   He next travelled through Austria and Hungary, and eventually settled in Florence where, at the age of thirty-six, he was appointed physician to the Grand Duke Ferdinand II.   Not long thereafter, reflecting on the arguments which had been put before him by Bossuet in Paris, he abjured the Lutheran protestantism in which he had grown up, and became a member of the church of Rome.   His European reputation led to repeated invitations being sent to him from King Christian V. of Denmark to accept the Chair of Anatomy in Copenhagen.   To these solicitations he at last yielded, but although he had full authority to exercise the rites of Roman Catholicism, he now encountered so many unpleasant-nesses in the Protestant community of his native city that he finally quitted his fatherland, and returned to Florence, where he was entrusted with the education of the son of the Grand Duke Cosmo III. Gradually becoming entirely devoted to a religious life, he took orders and in 1677 was named Bishop of Heliopolis and Vicar Apostolic in the north of Europe. He thereafter employed his leisure in composing a series of theological works. But it is upon the value of his anatomical and geological writings that his fame mainly rests. In 1667, soon after first settling in Florence, he published the anatomy of the head of a dog-fish and discussed the question whether the "glossopetrae," or sharks' teeth, found in the rocks, belonged to such fishes, or were mere mineral concretions, produced by some process within the stone in which they lie. Though he inclined to believe them to be truly of organic origin, his statements were made with so much timid reservation as to show how cautious even the acutest intellects were constrained to be in touching on any subject likely to rouse the orthodox prejudices of the age. Two years afterwards, however, having meanwhile enlarged his acquaintance with the rocks and fossils of Northern Italy, he proclaimed with frank boldness his conviction that the fossils were once living things, and that they and the strata con-taining them revealed a record of part of the history of the earth.

In 1669 there appeared in Florence his treatise

De Solido intra solidum naturaliter contento, which must be regarded as one of the landmarks in the history of geological investigation. It was meant to be introductory to a fuller work on the same subject, but this expansion was never written. The following digest of the contents of the treatise will show how far Steno had advanced beyond any of his predecessors or contemporaries, and how modern and familiar some of his original views now appear.

The strata of the earth are such as would be laid down in the form of sediment from turbid water. The objects enclosed in them, which in every respect resemble plants and animals, were produced exactly in the same way as living plants and animals are produced now. Where any bed encloses either fragments of another, and therefore older, bed, or the remains of plants or animals, it cannot be as old as the time of the Creation. If any marine production is found in any of these strata, it proves that at one time the sea has been present there ; while, if the enclosed remains are those terrestrial plants or animals, we may suspect the sediment to have been laid down on land by some river or torrent.

Similarity of composition in a series of strata proves that the fluid from which the sediment was deposited continued to be unaffected by other fluids coming from other directions at different times : on the other hand, a diversity in the character of the strata points either to a commingling of different kinds of fluids, bearing divers sediments, and caused perhaps by violent winds and rains, or to a diversity in the composition of the sediment, of which the heavier materials would first sink to the bottom. The presence of coals, ashes, pumice, bitumen or burnt substances shows the former neighbourhood of some subterranean fire.

Steno established by direct observation some important axioms in stratigraphy. Every stratum, he said, has been laid down upon a solid subjacent surface. The lowermost strata must have become firm before the uppermost were deposited. A stratum must originally have terminated laterally against a solid body, or else must have extended over the whole earth, so that when the truncated ends or edges of strata are exposed, we must either seek for evidence of their former prolongation, or for the solid surface against which they ended and which kept their materials from slipping down.[1] As each bed at the time of its formation was covered only with fluid, when the lowest member of a series was laid down none of those above it had yet been deposited.

The bottom of a series of strata necessarily conforms to the irregularities of the surface on which it has been deposited, but the upper surface, where the rocks are in their original position, is parallel to the horizon or nearly so. Hence all strata save the lowermost lie between two plains approximately parallel with the horizon. We must, therefore, conclude that strata which are now vertical or inclined to the horizon were originally nearly or quite horizontal.

That the edges or sides of the strata are laid bare

---

[1] Steno had not realised the really lenticular character of all sedimentary strata. But his conclusion that the truncated ends of strata on a cliff-face point to the former continuation of the strata beyond their present termination, is now a commonplace in geology.

in so many places, is to be ascribed to the operation of running water which dissolves and transports earthy substances to lower levels, and also to the action of fire in dissipating solid bodies, and ejecting them above ground. Thus precipices and channels are produced on the surface of the earth, and caverns and tunnels underneath. The strata are sometimes disrupted by the sudden rise of subterranean exhalations ; at other times they are broken up by the falling in of the roofs of cavernous spaces inside the earth. Hence they are thrown into a great variety of different positions, being sometimes vertical, more often inclined at various angles, occasionally even bent into arches.

This alteration in the original position of strata is the real cause of the inequalities of the earth's surface, such as mountains and plains. Some mountains have also been produced by the outburst of fires from inside the earth, whereby ashes and stones, together with sulphur and bituminous substances, have been cast forth. It is easy to perceive that all our mountains have not been in existence since the beginning of things.

Steno then proceeds to show that by the disruption of the strata, outlets have been provided for the escape of materials from inside the earth. Chief among these are the springs of water that issue from the hills. The cracks, fissures and cavities of the strata have served as receptacles for most minerals, whether introduced by vapours or otherwise. The question of the origin of rock-crystal gives the author occasion to discourse on the crystallography of this mineral, and on the conditions in which crystalline substances and ores have been produced within the earth.

Among the solids naturally enclosed within other solids, Steno includes, as specially deserving of consideration, fossil shells. His anatomical experience enables him to declare with confidence that even if no living marine shells had ever been seen, the internal structure of the fossils demonstrates that they once formed parts of living animals. He shows that the fossils vary in character according to the extent to which they have been petrified, some still retaining their original composition and internal structures, others having become entirely crystalline, as in those enclosed in marble. He points out further that over and above the predominant testaceous fossils, remains of many other marine animals have been preserved in the strata, such as teeth and vertebrae of dog-fishes, and all kinds of fish-skeletons, while other strata have furnished the skulls, horns, teeth and bones of land animals.[1] Against those who found an insuperable difficulty in granting the length of time required for all the vicissitudes indicated by the strata and their fossils, Steno argues that many of the organic remains found in the rocks must be as old as the general Deluge, and he proceeds to present a summary of what he conceives to have

[1] It is curious to observe that Steno, while he recognised that teeth and bones exhumed from the Agro Aretino were those of elephants, did not realise that they too must be regarded as of prehistoric age. He supposed them to be relics of the African elephants brought into Italy by Hannibal. Brocchi has pointed out that after the battle of the Trebbia the thirty-seven elephants which the Carthaginian general had by the side of the Rhone were reduced to one single animal. *Op. cit.* p. xv.

been the geological history of Tuscany. In this summary he illustrates the structure of the country by a series of diagrams which show how clearly he had grasped some of the fundamental principles of stratigraphy. He recognises evidence of six distinct chronological phases, and is inclined to believe that the same sequence will be found all over the earth. In the first phase, the region was entirely submerged under the sea, from which were deposited the strata containing no remains of plant or animal life. In the second phase, the land appeared as a dry plain, raised out of the sea. In the third, the face of the earth was broken up into mountains, crags and hills. In the fourth, the land was once more submerged, perhaps owing to a change in the centre of the earth's gravity. In the fifth, the land reappeared and displayed wide plains, formed apparently from the sediments carried off from the land by the large rivers and by the innumerable torrents which every day are extending the shores and leaving new lands to be occupied by fresh inhabitants. In the sixth and last phase, the elevated plains were eroded by running water and partly also by the co-operation of subterranean fire, so as to be altered into channels, valleys and precipices.

Steno's treatise stands out far above all the writings of his own or of previous generations in respect to the minuteness and accuracy of his observations of Nature and the originality and truth of most of the deductions which he drew from them. He was the first clearly to perceive that the strata of the earth's crust contain the records of a chronological sequence of events, and that the history of the earth must be deciphered from them.

He laid down for the first time some of the fundamental principles of stratigraphy.   He recognised the
predominant influence of running water in carving out
the inequalities on the surface of the land.   It is
true that he had no clearer notions than had obtained
for so many centuries regarding the true nature of
volcanic action, which he still regarded as due to the
subterranean combustion of carbonaceous substances.
He was hampered too by the prevailing theological
doctrine that the earth could not be more than some
6000 years old, and that the fossiliferous strata had
been mainly deposited during or since Noah's Deluge.
But his name must be enrolled high in the list of
those who by careful observation and deduction helped
to lay the foundations of modern geology.

Another illustrious observer in the geological domain
appeared in Italy when Steno, in his twenty-fifth year,
was rapidly rising into fame as an anatomist.   Antonio
Vallisneri (1661-1730) became professor of medicine
in Padua.   In the course of his journeys he had
opportunities of seeing much of the geology of his
native country and of forming a clearer conception
of the fossiliferous formations of the great central
mountain-chain than anyone had done before him.
He looked upon the shells in the rocks as remains
of mollusks that once undoubtedly lived in the sea.
In criticising the cosmological hypothesis of Woodward (to be afterwards alluded to), he showed how the
Italian marine formations extend not only throughout
the peninsula but over a large part of Europe, and he
inferred that there was a time when the sea covered
the whole surface of the globe.   He believed that it

must have remained in that position for a long period, and that its effects were altogether distinct from those of the temporary Deluge of Noah. He wrote on the origin of springs, maintaining that they do not come from the sea, through subterranean passages in which they lose the saline constituents of sea-water—a belief that had survived from antiquity and was still defended as resting on scriptural evidence. He connected springs with the structure of the rocks through which they rise.[1]

To one other notable Italian writer, who appeared in the first half of the eighteenth century, reference may here be made. Anton-Lazzaro Moro (1687-1740) wrote a treatise *De' Crostacei e degli altri marini Corpi che si truovano su' Monti* (Venice, 1740). The grotesque speculations of Burnet and Woodward, which will be more particularly referred to on a later page, had already appeared in England and had found their way into the Continent. A large part of Moro's work is devoted to a destructive criticism of the cosmogonies of these authors. He then proceeds to discuss the possibility of explaining the position of fossil shells in the mountains by reference to the Noachian Deluge, and he dismisses this supposition as untenable. He next inquires in what manner the phenomenon can be explained from actual observations of natural processes. After giving an account of the uprise of a new volcanic island in the Greek Archipelago in the year 1707, of the appearance of Monte Nuovo near Naples in 1538, and of the

---

[1] Vallisneri's treatise *Dei Corpi marini che sui monti si trovano* was published at Venice in 1721, when its author was sixty years of age.

recorded eruptions of Vesuvius and Etna, and starting
with the proposition that the fossil shells are really
productions of the sea, he proceeds to unfold his
theory that the position of these shells, and the origin
of the rocks that enclose them, are to be assigned to
the operation of volcanic action.

In the beginning, he says, the globe was completely
covered with water, which was then fresh and perhaps
not more than 175 perches in depth. No prominences
diversified the smooth stony surface of the globe
which underlay the water. On the third day of
creation, however, when it pleased the Almighty to
reveal the solid earth, vast subterranean fires were
kindled, whereby the surface of stone was broken up,
and huge masses of it began to appear above the
water, so as to form the land and mountains. These
disrupted masses, while rising or after they had risen,
and in some cases even before they appeared above
the water, were rent open by the violence of the
subterranean fires, and they discharged from their
orifices vast quantities of material, such as earth, sand,
clay, stones both solid and liquid, metals, sulphur,
salts, bitumen and every kind of mineral substance.
Part of this material flowed in river-like streams
down the sides of the mountains into the water
below, part fell in showers from the air into which
the ejected detritus had been hurled by the impetuosity
of the fire. The saline and bituminous ingredients
now began to give to the water the salt and bitter
taste which the sea has retained ever since, while the
other insoluble substances formed a new bottom above
the original stony surface.

As the mountains increased in number by the outburst of new vents and continued to cast forth loose materials, they gradually piled up on the sea-floor many various strata which, especially near the eruptive centres, eventually rose above the surface of the water. The sea grew deeper or its surface rose higher, the more its area was diminished. Fires also afterwards burst out from below the submarine strata, and continued to eject fresh materials which formed new strata that extended beyond those of earlier date. New islands were formed, or were added to older islands or to the continents.

As yet no plants or animals existed. But while the water continued to grow more saline, plants began at last to appear both in the sea and on land. Animals too entered upon the scene, first in the sea, living in the soft sand and among the debris cast out by the mountains, and seldom wandering far from their native places. The dry land became covered with verdure and gave birth to terrestrial animals, finally followed by the advent of man, who then took his place as an inhabitant of this first and most ancient land-surface.

In course of time, the same sequence of events continuing, new mountains emerged from the bosom of the earth, and like their predecessors vomited forth fresh materials which were once more spread out over the floor of the sea and the surface of the land. The strata that were thus deposited in the sea would contain marine productions, while those formed on the land would preserve terrestrial remains, including articles in metal, marble or carved wood as relics of a human population. Some of these land-surfaces, remaining long exposed to the open-air, were covered with new strata, which when they differed in composition from those buried below them, would produce plants and animals distinct from any of those which had previously existed on the same sites. And since the newer strata were not all laid down universally and at the same time, but successively during the course of centuries and at different seasons of the year, seeds and fruits in mature and immature condition would be entombed, as may be illustrated by many examples that have actually been obtained from excavations in which, at different levels, old soils represent inhabited and cultivated surfaces of land.

Moro had to take care that his cosmogony did not contradict but only supplemented the orthodox reading of the first Chapter of the Book of Genesis. That he succeeded in this aim is indicated by the imprimatur at the end of his treatise, wherein the reformers of studies testify that the book contains nothing contrary to the Holy Catholic Faith, nor anything adverse to Princes or to morals. Though he declined to adopt the popular notion that the stratified rocks had been formed during Noah's Flood, he still felt bound to account for their deposition within the orthodox limits of time. Public attention had been called to the rapid accumulation of materials around active volcanic vents, and Moro, availing himself of the original suggestion of Majoli, boldly claimed that all the stratified rocks which form the mountains consist of materials successively erupted by volcanoes. He does not seem to have ever studied the nature of true volcanic products, nor to have been familiar with the characteristic features of the limestones and other calcareous strata in which so large a proportion of fossil organic remains is preserved. He added little to the more luminous conceptions of Steno and Vallisneri. But his influence was not inconsiderable in rousing interest in the themes of which he treated. Nine years after his book appeared, the Carmelite friar Generelli, published an exposition of Moro's views, which he placed in a clearer light than his master had done.

The progress of geological inquiry in Europe during the seventeenth century was marked by a characteristic feature—the development of a series of cosmogonical systems, in which the only common basis of speculation was the effort to account for the origin of our globe and of our universe, in harmony with the teaching of the Church. Science had not advanced far enough to afford any firm basis for speculations of this nature, and consequently the lack of data was in too many cases supplied by wholly imaginary pictures of the history of creation. The systems of cosmogony thus framed, though some of them attained considerable fame in their day, obstructed the progress of inquiry, inasmuch as they diverted attention from the observation of Nature into barren controversy about speculations. In vain did those who had mastered some of the elementary truths about the crust of the earth, oppose and even ridicule these fanciful systems. The cosmogonists were not disconcerted when phenomena were appealed to that contradicted their theories, for they usually never

E

saw such phenomena, and when they did, they easily explained them away. Some of these writers were divines, yet even when they were laymen they felt themselves, down to the middle of the eighteenth century, bound to suit their speculations to the received interpretation of the books of Moses. Looking back from our present vantage ground, it is difficult to realise that even the little which had been ascertained about the structure of the earth was not sufficient to prevent some, at least, of the monstrous doctrines of these theorists from being promulgated. It was a long time before men came to understand that any true theory of the earth must rest upon evidence furnished by the globe itself, and that no such theory could properly be framed until a large body of evidence had been gathered together.

Nowhere did speculation run so completely riot as in England with regard to theories of the origin and structure of our globe. This craze reached its height during the latter part of the seventeenth century. In 1681 Thomas Burnet published in Latin his *Sacred Theory of the Earth*. This work, republished in English, and favoured with the patronage of Charles II., enjoyed a wide popularity and made some impression even on the Continent. It discoursed of the original structure of our planet, and of the changes which it was destined to undergo until " the consummation of all things." As its title denotes, the book was meant to support orthodox religion. With this view, the Deluge was taken as one of the great events in the history of the planet. Previous to that time, it was asserted, there had been perpetual spring upon the earth, but the wickedness of mankind led to a cata-strophe in which the sun's rays split open the crust of the earth, and allowed the central abyss of waters to burst forth and overwhelm the inhabited lands.

William Whiston in his *New Theory of the Earth* (1696) propounded almost more extravagant specula-tions. He supposed that at the time of the Creation the earth did not rotate on its axis, but that after the Fall of Man it began to do so. When the years had passed until the time of Noah, a comet on 18th November B.C. 2349 sent its tail over the equator, and caused a gigantic downpour of rain, while at the same time the internal abyss of waters broke forth and inundated the land. It was from the "chaotic sediment of the flood" that the various stratified formations of the earth's crust were deposited.

Another English writer who attributed similar important effects to the Deluge was John Woodward, familiarly remembered by the bequest of his collection of specimens to the University of Cambridge, and by the Professorship of Geology there which perpetuates his name. He had an intimate acquaintance with the stratified formations of a large part of England and with their characteristic fossils. While firmly convinced that these fossils were really the remains of once living plants and animals, he could not free himself from the incubus of the prevailing theological prejudice. In his *Essay towards a Natural History of the Earth* (1695) he ranged himself with those who maintained that the shells in the rocks were relics of Noah's Flood. He held a common belief of his day that the interior of the earth was once full of water, which at the time of that calamity, when the fountains of the great deep were broken up, burst forth and swept over the face of the globe. The disrupted and disintegrated crust was mingled with the diluvial waters, from which the sediments ultimately settled down on the bottom in the order of their gravity. By a curious perversity of judgment, Woodward persuaded himself that the fossils had followed the same rule and that the heaviest were found in the lowest strata, the lightest in the uppermost—a statement afterwards sharply criticised by Ray.

Woodward's most important contribution to science is his catalogue of the fossils which in the course of long years he had collected in England, and which now form an interesting portion of the Sedgwick Museum at Cambridge. It is entitled "An attempt towards a Natural History of the Fossils of England etc., or a Catalogue of English Fossils" in the collection of J. Woodward M.D.   2 vols 1728-29.

Of a totally different stamp from the cosmogonists above mentioned was the mathematician and natural philosopher Robert Hooke (1635-1703), one of the most brilliant, ingenious, and versatile intellects of the seventeenth century. Among the many subjects to which he directed his attention and on which his remarkable powers of acute observation and sagacious reflection enabled him to cast light, some of the more important problems of geology must be numbered. As "Curator of Experiments" to the Royal Society, and as one of the most active members of that body, he had frequent opportunities of discoursing on the topics which engaged his thoughts.   From time to time he lectured on what would now be called physical geography and geology. Such lectures as remained in manuscript after his death were collected and published in a folio volume of posthumous works (London, 1705). The largest section of this book consists of "Lectures and Discourses of Earthquakes and Subterraneous Eruptions, explicating the Causes of the Rugged and Uneven Face of the Earth; and what Reasons may be given for the frequent finding of Shells and other Sea and Land Petrified Substances scattered over the whole Terrestrial Superficies."[1]

Beginning with an account of "figured stones" or organic remains imbedded in rocks, illustrated with well-drawn figures of fossils, Hooke discusses the difficulties met with in explaining the nature and origin of these objects, and proves in a series of propositions that the fossils are either the organisms themselves turned into stone, or the impressions left by them;[2] that a great part of the surface of the earth has been transformed since the Creation, sea being turned into

---

[1] Though the volume did not appear until after the author's death, the first discourse seems to have been given in 1668.

[2] The truly organic nature of the fossils is the subject of a careful demonstration by Hooke, in the course of which he remarks "that it is contrary to all the other acts of Nature, that does nothing in vain, but always aims at an end, to make two bodies exactly of the same substance and figure, and one of them to be wholly useless, or at least without any design that we can with any plausibility imagine." The fossils "if they were not the shells of fishes, will be nothing but the sportings of Nature, as some do finely fancy, or the effects of Nature idely mocking herself, which seems contrary to her gravity." *Posthumous Works*, p. 318.

land, land into sea, mountains into plains and plains
into mountains ; that most places where fossil plants
or animals have been found have lain under water,
" either by the departing of the water to another part
or side of the earth, by the alteration of the centre of
gravity of the whole bulk, which is not impossible ;[1]
or rather by the eruption of some kind of subterraneous
fires, or earthquakes whereby great quantities of earth
have then been raised above the former level of those
parts " ; that not improbably the tops of the highest
mountains in the world have been under water, these
elevations of the land having most probably been
the effects of some very great earthquake ; that the
greatest part of the inequalities of the earth's surface
may have been caused by " the subversion and
tumbling thereof by some preceding earthquakes " ;
that " there have been many other species of creatures
in former ages, of which we can find none at present ;
and that 'tis not unlikely also but that there may be

---

[1] The possible change of the earth's centre of gravity is fully
discussed by Hooke in several discourses. A passage in which the
idea is expressed gives a vivid picture of the philosopher's prescient
outlook in terrestrial physics. He conceives that a very great earthquake (using that word for any kind of displacement of the
terrestrial crust) might not impossibly alter the centre of gravity
and also the axis of rotation. He thinks that the diurnal rotation
and annual revolution of the globe may once have been made in
a much shorter time than now, so that a day and a year at the
beginning of the world would not have been so long as now
when these motions have become slower. He further suggests
that " the fluid medium in which the earth moves, may after a
thousand revolutions, a little retard and slaken that motion, and
if so, then a longer space of time will pass while it makes its
revolution now than it did at first." *Op. cit.* p. 322.

diverse new kinds now, which have not been from the beginning."

With regard to the inequalities of the earth's surface, Hooke enters fully into the effects of the earthquakes by which he thinks they have been produced. Some earthquakes raise the earth's surface, either by upheaval or by piling up "a great access of new earth"; others depress the surface : those of a third type disrupt and subvert parts of the earth; while by a fourth class liquefactions, vitrifications, calcinations, sublimations and other effects are produced. He shows how universal is this active principle of terrestrial change, no country in the whole world having escaped being shaken sometime or other by earthquakes.

Having demonstrated from organic remains that the dry land must have lain for some time under water, Hooke argues that this water could not have been the Flood of Noah, which did not continue long enough "for the production and perfection of so many and so great and full-grown shells ; besides, the quantity and thickness of the beds of sand with which they are many times found mixed, do argue that there must needs be a much longer time of the sea's residence above the same, than so short a space can afford."[1] The large size of some of the shells as well as their resemblance in form to some of those found in tropical seas leads him to ask whether it is impossible that the South of England, where these shells are found, may for some ages past have lain within the Torrid Zone. Thus fossil organic remains

[1] p. 341.

were in Hooke's eyes not mere curiosities, but valuable records of the past history of the earth. " I do humbly conceive," he remarks, " (tho' some possibly may think there is too much notice taken of such a trivial thing as a rotten shell, yet) that men do generally too much slight and pass over without regard these records of antiquity which Nature have left as monuments and hieroglyphick characters of preceding transactions in the like duration or transactions of the body of the Earth, which are infinitely more evident and certain tokens than anything of antiquity that can be fetched out of coins or medals, or any other way yet known, since the best of those ways may be counterfeited or made by art and design, as may also books, manuscripts and inscriptions, as all the learned are now sufficiently satisfied, has often been actually practised ; but those characters [fossil shells] are not to be counterfeited by all the craft in the world, nor can they be doubted to be, what they appear, by any one that will impartially examine the true appearances of them : And tho' it must be granted that it is very difficult to read them and to raise a *chronology* out of them, and to state the intervalls of the times, wherein such or such catastrophies and mutations have happened ; yet 'tis not impossible, but that much may be done even in that part of information also."[1]

Hooke does not appear to have formed any very clear ideas either as to the causes of earthquakes or the nature of volcanic action. He connects the two classes of phenomena together, and in various places

[1] p. 411.

alludes to them as effects of "the general congregation of sulphureous, subterraneous vapours." He thinks that the observed greater frequency of earthquakes and volcanoes on islands and sea-coasts may possibly be due to "the saline quality of the sea-water which may conduce to the producing of the subterraneous fermentation with the sulphureous minerals there placed." "These fermentations subjacent to the sea, being brought to a head of ripeness, may take fire, and so have force enough to raise a sufficient quantity of the earth above it to make its way through the sea, and there make itself a vent." "The foment or materials that serve to produce and effect conflagrations, eruptions or earthquakes, I conceive to be somewhat analogous to the materials of gunpouder."[1] This philosopher had therefore advanced no further, in regard to the hypogene agents in geology, than the writers of antiquity and of the middle ages.

How far the ideas imposed by the prevailing theological beliefs of the period could influence even a man of eminent scientific ability is perhaps most fully illustrated in the case of John Ray (1627-1705), the ablest botanist and zoologist of his day, to whom science has been indebted for some masterly contributions to its progress. With his wide sympathies for Nature, he could hardly avoid entering the geological field, and as he was a loyal and devoted member of the Church of England, he could scarcely escape from carrying with him more or less of the ecclesiastical prejudices of his time. Where these prejudices were not involved he could see things as they are, and draw

[1] pp. 421, 424.

the natural inferences to which they lead. Thus he
entered fully and sagaciously into the theory of
springs, quoting his own experience at his country
home, and showing conclusively, in opposition to
Hooke, that it is not by dews condensed on the
mountains but by the water supplied by rain that
springs are fed. He watched, too, the effects of
running water, especially the manifest action of "rains
continually washing down and carrying away earth
from the mountains," and the destruction of the
shores by the perpetual working of the sea, and he
believed that in the end, by the combination of these
processes, the whole dry land might possibly be reduced below the sea-level.[1]

When Ray came to discuss "formed stones," or
"sea-shells and other marine bodies found at great
distances from the shores," he was obviously no longer
free to do so untrammelled as to what conclusions
he might draw from them. He caustically criticises
Woodward's diluvial theory, remarking that he suspected that author to have invented part of his theory
to solve supposed facts which are not generally true.
But though he had "spent many thoughts" on this
subject, he confesses that he could not fully satisfy
himself as to the nature and real origin of the
"formed stones." He balances the arguments for
and against their truly organic origin, seeming at one
moment to agree with those who regarded them as

---

[1] *Miscellaneous Discourses concerning the Dissolution and Changes of the
World*, by John Ray, Fellow of the Royal Society, London, 1692,
pp. 44-56, and *Three Physico-Theological Discourses*, 4th Edit., 1721,
pp. 89-114, 245.

"originally formed in the places where they are now found by a spermatic principle," and yet unable to resist the evidence that "these bodies owe their original to the sea, and were sometimes the shells or bones of fishes."

As regards hypogene phenomena Ray made no advance. Thus he says : "That the cause of earthquakes is the same with that of thunder, I doubt not, and most learned men are agreed ; that is, exhalations or steams set on fire, the one in the clouds, the other in the caverns of the earth."[1] Volcanoes are regarded by him as connected with earthquakes and due to the heating of "steams or damps" within subterranean caverns "by a colluctation of parts," whereby combustible materials in the hollows of the mountains are set on fire and the metals and minerals are melted down, while if water enters these caverns "it mightily increaseth the raging of the mountain, for the fire by the help thereof throws up earth and stones, and whatever it meets with."[2] Yet Ray, while he "utterly disallowed and rejected" Descartes' theory of the origin of the earth, was not unwilling to admit the existence of a central fire, more especially as it would presumably support the references to Hell in the Bible. But he does not appear to have ever thought of connecting this possible central fire with the operations of active volcanoes.

That Ray, in spite of his instinct as a naturalist and keen observer, should have been shaken in his opinion that the fossils in the rocks are the remains of once living things, can hardly surprise us when we

---

[1] *Three Physico-Theological Discourses*, p. 258. [2] p. 268.

remember that the two men who in all England had
the most extensive acquaintance with fossils refused
to admit them to be of organic origin.   Martin
Lister (1638-1712), an active and able fellow of the
Royal Society, published a remarkable history of all
the shells then known, with accurate plates, which
included not only the living species but many fossil
forms placed with them for comparison. Yet strange
to say, he stoutly refused to believe that the fossils
had ever belonged to living creatures.   " For our
English inland quarries," he said, " I am apt to think
there is no such matter as petrifying of shells in
the business ; but that these cockle-like stones are
everywhere as they are at present, *lapides sui generis,*
and never were any part of an animal," that they
" have no parts of a different texture from the rock
or quarry whence they are taken, that is, that there
is no such thing as *shell* in these resemblances of
shells."   He admitted that some of the fossils are
like *Murices*, or *Tellinae* or *Turbines*, etc., yet he had
never met with any one of them on any English
sea-shore or fresh-water ; whence he concluded "that
they were not cast in any animal-mold, whose species
or race is yet to be found in being at this day."
Having made up his mind with the evidence fully
before him, it was only natural that, as Woodward
tells us, " he bravely continued to the last firm and
unshaken in his opinions."

   Lister made the ingenious suggestion that volcanic
eruptions may be due to the subterranean decomposition of iron-pyrites. Even among those who from

---

[1] *Phil. Trans.* vol. v. (1671), p. 2282.

time immemorial had regarded volcanic action as arising from the combustion of inflammable materials in the crust of the earth, much difficulty and divergence of opinion existed respecting the active cause that set these materials on fire. Lister's suggestion had the merit of being a *vera causa*, from which undoubtedly the spontaneous combustion of carbonaceous strata has often arisen.

To geologists perhaps not the least memorable of Lister's contributions to the progress of science was a proposal made by him for the first time for the construction of what we now call geological maps. This subject will be more particularly referred to in Chapter XIV.

Robert Plot in his *Natural History of Oxfordshire* (1677) described Nature's "extravagancies and defects, occasioned either by the exuberance of matter or obstinacy of impediments, as in monsters; and then lastly as she is restrained, forced, fashioned or determined by artificial operations." Though he gave a map and sixteen beautifully engraved plates which included representations of fossils, he stated seven reasons for rejecting the idea that the fossils " owed their form and figure to the shells of the fishes they represent " and for concluding that these objects or " formed stones " must be regarded as " *lapides sui generis*, naturally produced by some extraordinary plastic virtue, latent in the earth, or quarries where they are found." [1]

With these writers may here be included the Celtic scholar and antiquary, Edward Lhuyd (1660-1709) who

[1] *Op. cit.* 2nd Edit. (1705), p. 112.

published a Latin treatise in which he gave excellent
plates of a thousand fossils preserved in the Ash-
molean Museum, Oxford. He was a valued correspondent of Ray, who quotes him as suggesting that
the fossils enclosed within rocks might possibly be
" partly owing to fish-spawn received into the chinks
of the earth in the water of . the Deluge," and as
speculating " whether the exhalations which are raised
out of the sea, and falling down in the rains, fogs,
etc., do water the earth, to the depth here required,
may not from the *seminium* or spawn of marine
animals, be so far impregnated with, as to the naked
eye invisible, *animalcula* (and also with separate or
distinct parts of them), as to produce these Marine
Bodies, which have so much excited our admiration,
and indeed baffled our reasoning, throughout the
globe of the earth."[1]

[1] Ray, *Three Physico-Theological Discourses* (1721) p. 190. In the
long letter from which these sentences are taken Lhuyd brings
forward a number of shrewd arguments against ascribing fossil
shells and plants to Noah's Flood.

CHAPTER III

FROM the middle of the seventeenth to the middle of the eighteenth century there appeared at intervals on the Continent a series of cosmogonists of a very different stamp from those alluded to in the last chapter. They were men who took a broad view of the world and endeavoured to trace its origin and progress in the light of what was then known of the laws of Nature. The earliest of these illustrious writers was the distinguished philosopher Descartes (1596-1650) who, in his *Philosophiae Principia*, published in 1644, gave an exposition of what he conceived to have been the origin and history of our globe. He supposed the various planetary bodies to have been originally glowing masses like our sun. The earth in his view consists of three distinct regions. In its centre lies a nucleus consisting of incandescent self-luminous matter, like that of the sun. The middle zone is composed of an opaque solid substance which was at first very liquid. The outer region, comprising all the materials of which we have actual cognisance, consists of the debris of the clouds or spots which, like those of the sun, gathered on the surface of the globe while still an intensely hot body.   These spots were no doubt again and again melted down as they formed, until the whole globe had cooled sufficiently to allow them to aggregate into a solid external crust.   The outer region of the planet, as the earth drew towards the sun, separated into different portions that arranged themselves one above another, according to their relative densities, the atmosphere being uppermost, then the water, while below these the more solid matter took the form of an outer layer of stone, clay, sand and mud, and an inner more solid and heavy layer whence all the metals come.   Descartes supposed that the heat and light of the sun could penetrate into the innermost parts of the earth and there, during day and summer, in the early stages of the planet's history, exerted so potent an influence as to lead to the rupture of the outer crust, of which some projecting portions rose above the waters and formed land.

This philosopher further suggested that certain exhalations from the inner parts of the earth turn into oil, but when they are in a state of violent motion and in that condition enter cavities or fissures which pre-viously contained air, they pass into a heavy thick smoke, like that of a newly extinguished candle. When a spark of fire is excited in these places the whole of the smoke bursts into flame, and becoming suddenly rarefied presses with great violence against its con-taining walls, especially when it includes a quantity of volatile salts and spirits.   Hence arise earthquakes. It sometimes happens also that the flame which causes earthquakes breaks open the top of a mountain and issues thence in great volume, hurling forth much earth mingled with sulphur or bitumen. These mountains may continue to burn for a long time, until all the sulphur or bitumen is consumed. Descartes thought that the subterranean fires might be kindled by the spirits inflaming the exhalations, or by the fall of masses of rock and the consequent sparks produced by their friction or percussion.

Still more memorable than the cosmological speculations of Descartes were those of the philosopher Leibnitz (1646-1716), whose capacious mind embraced every department of human knowledge, and whose acute and original genius threw new light into each. Among the subjects that engaged his thoughts was the problem of the origin and early history of our globe, regarding which he propounded views that have been accepted by the physicists of our own day. A summary of these opinions was first promulgated by him in a communication to the *Acta Eruditorum* of Leipzig, published in 1693, but the fuller statement contained in his remarkable treatise, the *Protogaea*, did not appear till 1749, thirty-three years after his death. Like Descartes, he believed that our planet was once a smooth incandescent molten globe, which has ever since been cooling, contracting and becoming rugose on the surface. When the temperature of the outer parts had sufficiently fallen, a glassy and slaggy crust began to form on the outside, portions of which he supposed to be recognisable in the primitive crystalline rocks, such as granite and gneiss. Out of the vaporous atmosphere, as the whole planet cooled, the water

condensed into liquid form and made the ocean, which
by washing the debris of the crust, dissolved out the
soluble ingredients and became salt.   As the thickness
of the crust increased, its solidification was accompanied
by the formation of immense cavities containing air
or water, the roofs of which, when they sank down,
would form valleys, while the other more solid parts
would rest like columns and give rise to mountains.
By the disruption of the crust, whether owing to its
weight or to gaseous explosions, vast inundations would
be produced which rushing over the face of the globe
would sweep a great amount of sediment together
and allow of the accumulation of sedimentary formations.   Thus the face of the earth would be often
renovated until, as the various disturbing forces quieted
down and become more equable in their action, a
more stable condition of things (*consistentior rerum
status*) arose.   In these reactions Leibnitz clearly recognised the working of the two great classes of
geological causes, in the first place the internal
heated nucleus whence igneous rocks proceed, and in
the second place, the superficial waters whereby hollows
are eroded on the earth's surface and sedimentary rocks
are formed.

As if he considered their obvious connection with
the internal fire a sufficient explanation of their occurrence, Leibnitz passes briefly over the subject of
earthquakes and volcanoes.   Yet he seems still to
entertain the old notion that actual combustion takes
place as part of these subterranean disturbances, for
in alluding to the underground fires that feed volcanoes, he mentions the deposits of stone-coal and

sulphurous materials, native sulphur, and springs of naphtha, and remarks "it is not unreasonable to believe that since the Deluge there have been partial fires, the date of which is not known, but which occurred at a time when combustible substances were more plentifully distributed in the thickness of the earth than they are now."

A considerable part of the *Protogaea* is devoted to a discussion of the evidence from organic remains enclosed in the sedimentary formations. In showing how perfectly and in what minute detail the structure of fishes and other organisms is reproduced in these fossils, Leibnitz ridicules the absurdity of calling them "sports of Nature," and points out how much more willingly we should admit the operation of an obvious and regular cause than a mere game of chance or other fanciful suggestion, under which the conceited ignorance of the learned had taken shelter. He insists on discriminating between the polygonal forms of crystals and the shapes of fossils, which had all been classed as arising from the same plastic force, and he complains of the facile credulity which could bring men not only to confound these utterly distinct things, but to believe that Nature could have manufactured within the rocks historical and mythological pictures, such as Apollo and the Muses in veins of agate, the pope and Luther in the stone of Eisleben, and sun, moon and stars in marble.

Leibnitz takes note of the astonishment expressed by some writers that for many of the "figured stones" no analogies had been discovered in the living world of to-day, or at least in the regions where these objects are found. He asks in reply whether any one had yet explored the depths of the ocean, or how many animals, hitherto unknown, remained still to be discovered in the New World. " Is it not to be presumed," he enquires, " that in the great changes which the earth has undergone a great many animal forms have been transformed ? " After describing a number of instances in which a succession of strata has been ascertained to contain different platforms of organic remains, pointing to advances and retreats of the sea, he concludes his treatise with these words : " Thus Nature fills for us the place of history ; while on the other hand, our history pays back to Nature this service, that it takes care that her illustrious works, so far as. we have been able to perceive them, shall not remain unknown to our posterity." [1]

We have now to notice the work of a writer of an utterly different type from the two philosophers just spoken of. Though hardly deserving to be regarded as a man of science, Benoit de Maillet (1656-1738), French diplomatist and traveller, was a keen and shrewd observer of Nature, and his speculations were not without their influence on the progress of geology. In the course of his long life he saw much of the countries bordering both sides of the Mediterranean basin, and gathered together stores of information regarding the physical aspect and historical changes in the surface of these countries. Being led to speculate on the probable origin and future fate of this globe and its inhabitants, he arrived at conclusions which were at least conspicuously unorthodox.

[1] *Protogaea*, p. 86.

In committing them to paper he ingeniously contrived to put them into the mouth of an Indian philosopher, but even with this precaution he did not venture to publish them, and his treatise only saw the light at Amsterdam in 1748, ten years after his death. It bore the title of *Telliamed* [his own name spelt backwards] *ou Entretiens d'un Philosophe Indien avec un Missionaire Français.*

The main purport of the book is to demonstrate that this globe was once completely surrounded with water, which has been gradually disappearing and will continue to diminish, until the planet is desiccated and is finally burnt up by the outbreak of volcanic forces from within. We cannot doubt, so the author believed, that this globe is the work of the sea and has been formed in its bosom, in the same way that similar formations are even now deposited in its waters. All mountains consist of sand, mud or other sedimentary materials, and have been formed by the sea. The oldest and highest are composed of a simple and uniform substance, in which few or no traces of animal life have been preserved. As the sea, in its subsidence, laid bare the summits of these earliest mountains, the waves beat on their sides, and the materials of new mountains were thus obtained, in which organic remains became increasingly abundant. That the various sediments should be arranged one above another in successive strata, is shown to be what might be expected from the action of the sea along its coasts and over its bottom at the present time. Emphasis is laid on the prodigious abundance of marine fossils from below sea-level up to the mountain tops as proof of the former submergence of the land and of the mode in which the rocks of the land have been formed.   The author sagaciously calls attention to the fact that, instead of being indiscriminately huddled together in the strata, the fossils are found to lie on the planes of stratification, just as the shells and other organisms of the present sea are strewn over the surface of the sea-floor.

Telliamed, the Indian Philosopher, ridicules the notion that these universal marine formations could have been laid down by Noah's Flood, which he affirms was a local and transient inundation.   He asserts that the valleys and other hollows of the earth's surface have been scooped out by marine currents during the sinking of the sea, leaving the mountainous ridges standing up between them.   The diminution of the water is regarded by him as due to evaporation, whereby the vapour is carried through space to the extremity of the vortex wherein the dust and the particles of water are once more condensed upon other globes.

Methods are described for measuring the rate of the lowering of the sea-level, and as the result of observation it is estimated that the diminution amounts to as much as three or four inches in a century, or about three feet in a thousand years.   A time will come when the Black and Mediterranean seas will be isolated into lakes, like the Caspian, and when the Atlantic will be laid dry, save perhaps some restricted remnant in its deeper part, while the rivers of the Old and New World will mingle their waters together.

Volcanoes, in the cosmogony of Telliamed, are due to the combustion of the oils and fats of the various animals entombed in the sediments of which the mountains have been formed. These volcanoes, by communicating with each other, will ultimately extinguish all life, and finally lead to the total conflagration of our globe, which will then become a true sun, until having consumed all the combustible material that maintained this prodigious heat, it will once more cool down and become opaque.

But the most curious speculations of Telliamed are those in which he discusses the problem of the origin of the various races of animal life. He supposes the plants and animals of the land to have been derived from those of the sea. But the data which he advances in support of his notions of evolution seem to us now almost childishly absurd. He speaks of rose-trees which had their blooms quite red when they were taken out of the sea. He affirms that there exist on land no walking, flying, or creeping creatures which have not their analogues in the sea, and that their transference from one region to the other is not only probable but can be proved by a vast number of actual examples. He illustrates what he conceives to be the natural course of transformation by picturing flying fishes which somehow should fall among reeds or rushes and be unable to resume their flight. Their exertions would increase their aptitude to use their wings, but the dry air would split these membranes and raise up the scales of their bodies into a kind of down, the little fins under their belly, which once helped them to swim, would now become feet which would enable them to walk on the land. Then follows an account of seals, sea-dogs, and the origin of man, wherein the author states that he will scrupulously reject everything which might be regarded as fanciful, and that he will confine himself to well-attested and recent facts. He then gravely recites a number of tales of mermen and mermaids, of savage dumb men, like apes, of men with tails, of giants and dwarfs, and he comes to the conclusion that as all the species of mermen are still unknown, it is not yet possible to trace from which of them the various races of mankind have been derived. He sees no difficulty in the transition of men from the water to the air, and thinks that this passage is easiest in polar regions, where probably the transformation of mermen into ordinary men is always most common.

The last and not the least eminent of the cosmogonists who may be cited in this retrospect is the illustrious naturalist G. L. Leclerc de Buffon (1707-1788)—one of the great pioneers in science who figure so conspicuously in the history of France. At first he interested himself in physics and mathematics, but gradually widened his outlook, and conceived broad and profound ideas regarding the whole realm of Nature. Endowed with a spirit of bold generalisation, and gifted with a style of singular clearness and eloquence, he was peculiarly fitted to fascinate his countrymen, and to exercise a powerful influence on the scientific progress of his age. He is the central figure in a striking group of writers and observers who placed France in the very front of the onward march of science, and who laid some of the foundation-stones of modern geology.

The introductory portion of Buffon's voluminous *Natural History* was devoted to a Theory of the Earth. Though written in 1744, it was not published until 1749. The author had meditated long and deeply on the meaning of the fossil shells found so abundantly among the rocks of the earth's crust, and had recognised that, as they demonstrate the condition of the globe not to have been always what it is now, any true theory of the earth must trace the history of the planet back to a time before the present condition was established. Like Descartes and Leibnitz, he saw that this history must be intimately linked with that of the solar system, of which it formed a part. He thought that the various planets were originally portions of the mass of the sun, from which they were detached by the shock of a comet, whereby the impulse of rotation and of revolution in the same general plane was communicated to them. In composition, therefore, they are similar to their parent sun, only differing from that body in temperature. He inferred that at first they were intensely hot and self-luminous, but gradually became dark as they cooled, the central sun still remaining in a state of incandescence.

Though the hypothesis of a cometary shock is not now entertained, it is impossible to refuse our admiration to the sagacity of a man who tried to solve the problem of planetary evolution by the application of the laws of mechanics. The geological portion of his theory, however, was loaded with several crude con-

ceptions. The enormous numbers and wide diffusion
of fossil shells, which had so vividly impressed his
imagination, proved to him that the land must have
lain long under the sea. But he had no idea of any
general cause that leads to elevation of the sea-bottom
into land. He was thus constrained to resort to his
imagination for a solution of the problem. Burnet
had supposed the original ocean to be contained within
the earth, and that it only escaped at the time of
the Flood, when, by the heat of the sun, the crust
of the globe had cracked, and thus allowed the pent-
up waters to rush out. Buffon's theory was hardly
less fanciful. But he reversed the order of events.
He inferred from the abundance of fossil shells that
there had once been a universal ocean, and that by
the giving way of the crust, a portion of the waters
was engulfed into caverns in the interior, so as to
expose what are now mountains and dry land.

For some thirty years after the publication of his
Theory, Buffon continued to work industriously in all
departments of natural history. At last, in 1778,
having long meditated on the problem of the origin
of the earth, he published his famous *Époques de la
Nature*. In this work he arranged the history of the
globe in six epochs—intervals of time of which the
limits, though indeterminate, seemed to him none the
less real. He tried indeed to form some idea of their
duration on the basis of a series of ingenious experiments with globes of cast-iron of different sizes, and
though the method on which he proceeded could not
give him reliable results, and his estimates have accordingly no scientific value, they possess the highest

historical interest, first as the earliest recorded attempt to compute the probable age of the earth and of the planets from physical observations, and secondly as an epoch-making departure from the old and orthodox notion that our globe came into existence only some six thousand years ago. In discussing the Biblical narrative of the Creation, Buffon boldly asks what we can possibly understand by the six days, if not six periods of time or intervals of duration. Though referred to in the Book of Genesis as days, for want of another term, they can have no relation to our actual days, seeing that no fewer than three of them had passed away before the sun was fixed in the firmament. "The sense of the narrative seems to require that the duration of each 'day' must have been long, so that we may enlarge it to as great an extent as the truths of physics may demand."[1]

The First Epoch embraced the primeval time when the earth, newly torn from the sun, existed still as a molten mass which, under the influence of rotation, assumed its oblate spheroidal form. The transition from fluidity to solidity, and from luminosity to opacity was brought about entirely by cooling, which commenced at the outer surface. A crust was thus formed, outside of which the substances still in a vaporous condition, such as air and water, remained as a hot æriform envelope, while the interior still continued liquid. The period of incandescence before the globe consolidated to the centre was computed by Buffon to have amounted to 2936 years while the period during which the surface remained too hot to be

---

[1] *Histoire Naturelle*, tome III. p. 104.

touched, and therefore unfit for living beings, comprised about 35,000 years.

The Second Epoch was characterized by the consolidation of the molten globe, and the appearance of hollows and ridges, gaps and swellings, over its surface, and cavernous spaces in its interior, such as may be seen in a globe of fused metal after it has cooled. These inequalities in the crust of granite, gneiss and other ancient crystalline rocks, gave rise to the earliest or primitive mountains and valleys of the higher portions of the land. During the process of consolidation, cracks arose in which metalliferous veins were formed by sublimation or fusion. Up to the end of this period, the globe remained intensely hot and its water still existed only among the vapours of the atmosphere.

The Third Epoch, which began about 35,000 years after the birth of the earth, included the time when the waters were condensed so as to descend and remain on the sufficiently cooled surface of the globe. So vast was the sea at first that its surface stood from 9000 to 12,000 feet higher than it does now, as was supposed to be indicated by the heights at which marine organisms are found in the rocks of the mountains. The waters were at first boiling, and as they cooled, animal life was introduced into them. This life must have been in many ways different from that of our present seas. The oldest species, which are nowhere now to be found alive, flourished during the first ten or fifteen thousand years after the seas had been gathered together. If a collection of fossils were made from the highest parts of the mountains, Buffon thought that it might be possible to decide as to the relative antiquity of species. Nature was then, as it seemed to him, in her first vigour, and fashioned larger types of life than now survive. When the earliest condensation of water took place upon the still warm surface of the globe, great corrosion of that surface was effected. The decomposed rocks gave rise to much clay, which was washed off into the sea, there to form the various argillaceous sediments now to be seen on the land. As life increased in the sea, the calcareous fossiliferous formations were deposited which constitute so much of the existing land. Buffon supposed that the sea in which all the fossiliferous strata were accumulated must have covered the land for at least 20,000 years. The parts of the earth's surface that rise into land were now covered with dense forests.

The Fourth Epoch witnessed the emergence of the lower part of the land, owing to the sinking of the waters through cracks into cavities in the interior of the globe. Buffon estimated that 20,000 years were required for the lowering of the sea from its original to its present level. Profoundly as he had meditated on the structure of the earth, he had during thirty years made no advance in his views of the origin of the dry land, nor had he obtained any more light on volcanic phenomena than his predecessors had possessed. He estimated that a hundredth or a two-hundredth part of the surface of the earth was covered with dense vegetation, and that vast quantities of this vegetation were swept down into the lower places of the earth's surface and into the fissures of the rocks. He supposed that meeting there with the substances sublimed by the great internal heat these carbonaceous accumulations would form the first provision of aliment for the volcanoes which were now to make their appearance. Volcanic energy, in his view, arises from " the effervescence of the pyritous and combustible stones," combined with the effective co-operation of subterranean electricity, which he believed to be likewise a powerful agent in the production of earthquakes. Volcanoes, however, can only become active by " the conflict of a great mass of water with a great body of fire." Hence they are always near the sea. Buffon computed that the first volcanoes did not arise until some 50,000 years of the earth's history had elapsed, by which time a sufficient quantity of combustible materials had been accumulated to furnish them with fuel, and he drew a graphic picture of the frightful condition of our planet when its surface was at once ravaged by fire and devastated by debacles of water. Only after the cessation of such turmoil could terrestrial animals come into being. During this period the retreating waters of the ocean gave birth to powerful currents, whereby hollows were scoured out of the still comparatively soft sedimentary strata, and thus were originated the valleys of the land which have subsequently been widened and deepened by subaerial denudation.

The Fifth Epoch was marked by a calmer time which witnessed the advent of huge pachyderms— elephants, rhinoceroses, and hippopotamuses—in the northern regions, where at that time a warm climate stretched continuously from Asia and Europe into America. This introduction of terrestrial animal life is placed by Buffon 55,000 or 60,000 years after the beginning of the world, or about 15,000 years before our own time.

The Sixth Epoch was marked by the separation of the two continents of the Old and New Worlds, which, as was inferred from the presence in each of them of what were supposed to be the same fossil mammals, were believed to have been originally united. Buffon placed this event 10,000 years before his time. The same period also saw the submergence that isolated Greenland from Europe, Canada and Newfoundland from Spain, and gave rise to so many insular tracts in the north Atlantic. The history of other late topographical features of the earth's surface, such as the Mediterranean, the Bosphorus, and the Black Sea, is next sketched, and is connected with the occurrence of successive deluges and ruptures of land-barriers.

Buffon added a seventh epoch, in which he traced the commanding influence of man in modifying the surface of the earth.

Recognising the powerful agency of rivers and the sea in washing away the materials of the land, he believed that by this action the whole of the existing continents will finally be reduced and covered by the ocean; and he conceived that by the same series of changes new lands will ultimately be formed. He foresaw, however, the final extinction of our globe as a habitation for sentient beings, but not after the manner of the orthodox creed that the heavens and the earth are at last to melt with fervent heat. Buffon recognised proofs of the gradual refrigeration of our planet and he estimated that this process would continue for yet 93,000 years by which time the globe would have become colder than ice. Then this beautiful Nature, which with its tribes of plants and animals, will have existed for 132,000 years, will perish.

In breadth and grandeur of conception Buffon far surpassed the earlier writers who had promulgated theories of the earth. The rare literary skill with which, in his masterpiece, the *Époques*, he presented his views, enabled him to exercise a powerful influence on his contemporaries, to direct their attention to the deeply interesting problems of which he wrote, and to give to natural science a far wider popularity than it had before enjoyed. If looking back from our present knowledge, we may be inclined to regard his eloquent pages rather in the light of a pictorial vision of what his brilliant imagination bodied forth as the origin of things, than a sober attempt to work out a theory on a basis of widely collected, carefully sifted and systematically co-ordinated facts, we must remember that science had not yet advanced far enough to provide such a basis. It was his great merit to have pointed out that the history of our earth is a long chronological record, the memorials of which are to be read in the frame-work of the globe itself, and to have himself applied the historical method to its interpretation. Nor were his services less conspicuous in breaking down the theological barrier which, after so many centuries, still blocked the way towards a free and unfettered study of the crust of the earth. So powerful in his time did the ecclesiastical authorities

continue to be, that we are told how, though the
Époques was a work on the preparation of which he
had spent much time and thought and which he longed
to publish, he had cautiously to feel his way and pay
court to some of the doctors of the Sorbonne, and how
it was only after having secured, if not the votes, at
least the silence of the majority of a corporation which
tyrannised over thought, that he ventured to send his
treatise to the printer. His friends, however, remained
anxious on his account, until whether because religious
intolerance was growing less with the advance of
science, or because the clerical powers were satisfied
with professions of faith and protestations of belief
on the part of the author, the work was allowed to
pass peaceably on its way to popularity. Although
this treatise shows that the long interval of thirty years
after the appearance of the *Théorie* had given greater
freedom and had still further enlarged his views of
nature, he was evidently unaware of much that had
been observed and described during that interval by
his own countrymen and in other parts of Europe.
In particular he does not seem to have been acquainted
with the progress that had been made in evolving a
stratigraphical succession among the fossiliferous formations in Germany, Italy, and England. One would
hardly suppose from his chapters that so much information had now been amassed regarding fossil organic
remains.

The prolonged controversy over the nature and
origin of the " figured stones " had this good result
that it not only drew general attention to these objects,
but developed a passion for collecting them, and thus

led to the formation of numerous cabinets or museums
wherein they found a conspicuous place among other
illustrations of natural history. They were likewise
made the subject of description in an increasing number of treatises, and of delineation on engraved plates,
although the question was still hotly disputed whether
these objects should be considered as mere sports of
Nature or as relics of once living things and memorials
of the Deluge. Reference was made in the last chapter
to one or two of the oldest of these collections of
fossils, and to the earlier illustrated works in some of
which the fossils were treated as mere " figured stones."
After the appearance of the volumes by Lister and
others in England, Switzerland became the birthplace
of a number of treatises on the subject written, some
in Latin and others in German. One of the earliest
of these, the *Historia Lapidum Figuratorum Helvetiae*
of K. N. Lang was published in 1708 at Venice, and
contained a crude classification of these objects, in
which minerals, concretions and fossil remains of
animals and plants were all included. This author,
though he recognised the resemblance of some of the
fossil shells to species now living, believed that their
germs were transported as fine dust from the ocean and
germinated among the rocks.

More important were the treatises of J. J. Scheuchzer (1672-1733) of Zurich. In the year 1702 this
writer published a work with the title *Specimen Litho-
graphiæ Helveticae curiosæ*, in which he described
" figured stones " as sports of Nature. But having
afterwards procured a copy of Woodward's *Essay*,
which he translated into Latin, he adopted the opinion

that these stones are relics of the Deluge, and upheld this view in his subsequent writings. He was a most active observer and prolific author. His *Natur-Historie des Schweizerlandes* is a remarkable dissertation, in which the climate, topography, hydrology (including glaciers), meteorology and mineralogy of the country are well described. There is a section devoted to " Relics of the Deluge found in Switzerland," wherein are described a number of fossil plants and shells, concluding with a paragraph on " Men." At that time he confesses that so rare were human remains in the fossil state that none had yet turned up in his own country, unless he might include the gigantic bones found in Canton Lucerne, though he hopes that some will be found at such time as God may please. This hope he thought was at last realised towards the end of his life by the discovery at Oeningen of a skeleton which he had no doubt was a relic of " one of the infamous men who brought about the calamity of the Flood." He took some pains to let the world know of this important discovery. Thus in a Latin letter to Sir Hans Sloane, to be communicated to the Royal Society of London, into which body Scheuchzer had been elected, he gave a brief description of the specimen, and estimated the stature of the fossil man to have been about the same as his own, or $58\frac{1}{2}$ Paris inches. A fuller account formed the subject of his famous tract, *Homo Diluvii Testis* (1726). This celebrated specimen, afterwards shown by Cuvier to be not a human skeleton, but that of a large salamander, is now preserved in the Teyler Museum at Haarlem.

Scheuchzer wrote a useful catalogue of the names

which up to his time had been given to the "figured stones" (*Sciagraphia Lithologica Curiosa ; seu Lapidum Figuratorum Nomenclator*), and gave references to some of the published descriptions of them. He was likewise the author of a *Herbarium Diluvianum*, containing a series of fourteen good plates of fossil plants, together with some corals and other plant-like organisms. As a further indication of his connection with England and the Royal Society, it may be mentioned that the first of these plates is inscribed to the Archbishop of Canterbury, and the second to Sir Isaac Newton.

To one further treatise of the Zurich professor reference may here be made for the quaint humour which runs through it. It is a thin small quarto in Latin, with the title *Piscium Querelæ et Vindiciæ*, 1708. The fossil fishes are represented as assembled in council to protest against their treatment by the descendants of the wicked men that brought on the Flood by which these very fishes had been entombed. They discourse of "the irrefragable witness of the universal Deluge which by the care of Providence their dumb race places before unbelievers for the conviction of the most daring atheists." Specimens of their fossil brethren are appealed to—pike, trout, eel, perch, shark—and their well-preserved minute structure of teeth, bones, scales and fins is pointed to as a triumphant demonstration that such perfect anatomical detail could be fabricated by no inorganic process within the rocks, as had been maliciously affirmed.

It was from Nuremburg that the most important work on fossils was issued during this period. Among the natives of that quaint old town, George Wolfgang Knorr (1705-1761), who followed the occupation of an engraver, developed such an enthusiasm for natural history objects that he specially devoted himself to the preparation of finely-engraved plates, for the illustration of works on botany and conchology, as well as on art.   In the end, he began to collect fossils, and to prepare engravings of them and of other specimens contained in some of the cabinets which were now becoming numerous all over Europe.   It was his intention to publish a treatise on the subject fully illustrated by himself.   He had completed the first volume, but died before any further portion of the work was ready.   It is hardly possible to exaggerate the beauty and fidelity of the representations of the fossils in his plates.   No such illustrations had ever before appeared, and they have hardly been surpassed since.   By delicate lines on the copper plates the most minute intricacies of structure are reproduced, and by thin washes of colour the tints of the original specimens are represented.   His renderings of dendritic markings, landscape-marble, fossil plants, crustacea, crinoids, fishes and other fossils are admirable examples of the union of artistic workmanship with scientific accuracy.   Fortunately for Knorr's reputation and the progress of science, another enthusiast was ready to take up the work where the Nuremburg artist had left it.   J. E. I. Walch (1725-1778) who held the appointment of Professor of Eloquence and Poetry in the University of Jena, was also a collector and student of minerals, rocks and fossils, and in 1762 published an excellent little volume, *Das Steinreich*,

which gives a rough classification of rocks according
to their structure, such as Granular, Lamellar, and
Filamentous. He was prevailed upon by Knorr's
executors to undertake the continuation and publication of the work of the deceased artist. As a large
amount of the materials for the plates had already
been arranged by Knorr, the hands of the continu-
ator were rather tied in regard to the treatment of
the subject. But Walch with remarkable industry and
perseverance pursued his task until four folio volumes
of text and nearly 300 plates had been completed and
published under the title of *Lapides Diluvii Universalis
Testes—Sammlung von Merckwurdigkeiten der Natur zum
Beweis einer allgemeinen Sündfluth.* The fourth and
last volume containing Systematic Tables and an
Alphabetical Index, affording a guide to the contents
of the whole work, was published in 1778. In spite
of the diluvial creed of the authors, this fine publication marks a notable advance in the palaeontological
department of geology. It presents an instructive
and detailed statement of all that was known on the
subject at the time, with abundant references to the
writings of previous authors.

The craze for collecting " figured stones " and other
mineral curiosities, together with the ignorant credulity
of many of the collectors, led to the occasional per-
petration of practical jokes. One of the most famous
instances of this tendency was that of the tricks played
off upon the learned Würtzburg Professor, J. B.
Beringer, who, having with great enthusiasm and with
the help of his students made a collection of fossils
from the Triassic strata of his neighbourhood, published

in 1726 an illustrated work upon his discoveries. Among the objects depicted by him were figures of celestial bodies, and other remarkable things which he unsuspectingly regarded as of equal significance. When, however, his youthful companions went so far as to manufacture still more grotesque "figured stones," and dropped them in the quarries into which they led him that he might himself discover them; and more especially when, at last, besides Hebrew letters, he found his own name inscribed on the stone, the truth dawned on him that he had been hoaxed. He did his best to buy up the edition of his work in which so many of the tricks had been unsuspectingly figured and described. But some copies still survive, and examples of the manufactured fossils are preserved in the museums of Wûrtzburg and Munich.

CHAPTER IV

Wʜɪʟᴇ in England, Switzerland, Italy, and Germany the study of fossils was making progress in spite of the controversies to which the subject gave rise, in France for a time less advance could be perceived.   It is true that as far back as 1580 the celebrated ceramic artist Bernard Palissy had published some important observations on the petrifaction of wood, as well as on shells and fishes in the rocks, and had called attention to these objects in proof of the former presence of the sea or of lakes, where such organic remains are now found.   But it was not until the early part of the eighteenth century that France produced a man worthy to stand in the front rank of the early founders of geology and of whose career some detailed notice may here be given.   While Buffon was indulging in his brilliant speculations as to the origin and history of the earth there lived in Paris at the same time a student of Nature, belonging to a totally different type, who, shunning any approach to theory, dedicated himself with the enthusiasm of a true naturalist to the patient observation and accumulation of facts regarding the rocks of the earth's crust, and to whom modern geology owes a deep debt of gratitude, that has never yet been adequately paid. This man, Jean Étienne Guettard (1715-1786), was born in the year 1715 at the little town of Étampes, about thirty miles S.W. from Paris.[1] As the grandson of an apothecary there, he was destined to succeed to the business of compounding and selling drugs. Before he left home for his professional education, he had already developed a passion for natural history pursuits. When still a mere child, he used to accompany his grandfather in his walks, and his greatest happiness was found in collecting plants, asking their names and learning to recognize them, and to distinguish their different parts. Every nook and corner around Étampes became familiar to him, and in later years he loved to revisit, with the eye of a trained naturalist, the scenes which had fascinated his boyhood. In his writings he loses no opportunity of citing his native place for some botanical or geological illustration. Thus, at the very beginning of a long and suggestive memoir on the degradation of mountains, to which further reference will be made in the sequel, his thoughts revert to the haunts of his infancy, and the first illustration he cites of the processes of decay which are discussed in that paper is taken from a picturesque rock overlooking the valley of the Juine, under the shade of which he used to play with his companions.[2]

[1] For the biographical facts here given I am indebted to the *Éloge* of Guettard by Condorcet (*Œuvres*, edit. 1847, vol. iii. p. 220) and to the personal references which I have met with in Guettard's writings.

[2] *Mémoires sur différentes parties des Sciences et des Arts*, tome iii. p. 210 (1770).

Having gained the favourable notice of the famous brothers Jussieu, who gave renown to the botanical department of the Jardin des Plantes, he was allowed by his grandfather to choose a career that would afford scope for his ardour in science. Accordingly he became a doctor in medicine. Eventually he was attached to the suite of the Duke of Orleans, whom he accompanied in his travels, and of whose extensive natural history collections he became custodian. On the Duke's death he enjoyed from his son and successor a modest pension ·and a small lodging in the Palais Royal at Paris.

It was to botany that his earlier years of unwearied industry were mainly given. In the course of his botanical wanderings over France and other countries, he observed how frequently the distribution of plants is dependent upon the occurrence of certain minerals and rocks. He was led to trace this dependence from one district to another, and thus became more and more interested in what was then termed "mineralogy," until this subject engrossed by far the largest share of his thoughts and labours.

But Guettard was more than merely a mineralogist. Although the words "geology" and "geologist" did not come into use for half a century later, his writings show him to have been a geologist in the fullest sense of the word. He confined himself, however, to the duty of assiduous observation, and shunned the temptation to speculate. He studied rocks as well as minerals, and traced their distribution over the surface of Europe. He observed the action of the forces by which the surface of the land is modified, and he produced some memoirs of the deepest interest in physiography. His training in natural history enabled him to recognize and describe the organisms which he found in the rocks, and he thus became one of the founders of palæontological geology. He produced about 200 papers on a wide range of subjects in science, and published some half-dozen quarto volumes of his observations, together with many excellent plates.

It is astonishing that this man, who in his day was one of the most distinguished members of the Academy of Sciences of Paris, and who undoubtedly is entitled to rank among the few great pioneers of modern geology, should have fallen into complete oblivion in English geological literature. I shall have occasion to show that the process of ignoring him began even in his lifetime, and that, though free from the petty vanities of authorship, he was compelled in the end to defend his claim to discoveries that he had made. After his death he was the subject of a kindly and appreciative *éloge* by his friend Condorcet, the perpetual Secretary of the Academy.[1] His work was noticed at length in the great *Encyclopédie Méthodique* of Diderot and D'Alembert, published thirteen years after he was laid in the grave.[2] Cuvier

---

[1] *Œuvres de Condorcet*, vol. iii. p. 220.

[2] *Géographie Physique* by Desmarest, forming vol. i. of the *Encyclopédie*, and published An III (1794). The article on Guettard (by Desmarest) gives a critical review of his work, especially of those parts of it which bear on physical geography. The large number and value of his observations on fossil organisms is admitted. But his method of constructing mineralogical maps is severely

in his *éloge* of Desmarest gave to Guettard the credit of one of his discoveries.[1] But his work seems to have been in large measure lost sight of until in 1862,[2] and again in 1866,[3] the Comte d'Archiac dwelt at some length on his services to the progress of geology. More recently Guettard's labours have been the theme of sympathetic comment from Ch. Sainte-Claire Deville[4] and Aimé de Soland.[5]

In the geological literature of the English-speaking countries, however, we shall search in vain for any adequate recognition of the place of this early master of the science. The famous classic, Conybeare and Phillips' *Outlines of the Geology of England and Wales*, contains a reference to the French observer as the

handled, and his claim to the discovery of the extinct volcanoes of Auvergne is contemptuously rejected. The whole tone of the article is somewhat ungenerous. The imperfections of Guettard's work are fully set forth, but little is said of its merits.

[1] Cuvier's *Éloges Historiques*, vol. ii. p. 354 (1819).

[2] A. d'Archiac, *Cours de Paléontologie Stratigraphique*, pp. 284-304, 1862.

[3] A. d'Archiac, *Géologie et Paléontologie*, 1ʳᵉ partie, pp. 112-118 (1866). The account of Guettard in this work is little more than a condensation of the narrative in the author's previous *Cours*. Even after these appreciative references Lecoq in his *Époques Géologiques de l'Auvergne* omits Guettard's name from the list of those he specially cites, and when he has occasion to mention him, does so in a very grudging spirit. See his Introduction, p. xiii. and vol. iii. p. 155.

[4] *Coup d'œil historique sur la Géologie*, pp. 311-314 (1878).

[5] "Étude sur Guettard," *Annales de la Société Linnéenne de Main-et-Loire*, 13ᵐᵉ, 14ᵐᵉ, et 15ᵐᵉ années, pp. 32-88 (1871, 1872, 1873). This appreciative essay contains a list of Guettard's publications.

first man who constructed geological maps. Scrope[1] and Daubeny[2] cite him for his observations in Auvergne. But Lyell in his well-known summary of the progress of geology does not even mention his name.

It is difficult to account for this neglect. Possibly it may be partly attributable to the cumbrous and diffuse style in which Guettard wrote,[3] and to the enormous bulk of his writings. When a man contributes scores of voluminous papers to the transactions of a learned academy ; when he publishes, besides, an armful of bulky and closely printed quartos, and when these literary labours are put before the world in by no means an attractive form, perhaps a large share of the blame may be laid to his own door. Guettard may be said to have buried his reputation under the weight of material which he left to support it.

I cannot pretend to have read through the whole of these ponderous volumes. The leisure of a hard-worked official does not suffice for such a task. But I have perused those memoirs which seemed to me to give the best idea of Guettard's labours, and of the value of his solid contributions to science. And I shall now proceed to give the results of my reading. No one can glance over the kindly *éloge* by Condorcet

---

[1] *Geology and Extinct Volcanoes of Central France*, p. 30, 2nd edition, 1858.

[2] *Description of Active and Extinct Volcanoes*, p. 729, 2nd edition (1848).

[3] Of this defect no one was more sensible than the author himself. See his *Mémoires sur différentes parties des Sciences et des Arts*, tome v. p. 421.

without a feeling of respect and sympathy for the man who, under many discouragements, and with but slender means, succeeded in achieving so much in such a wide circle of acquirement. And there is thus no little satisfaction in resuscitating among English and American geologists the memory of a man in whom I trust that they will recognise one of the founders of their science, deserving a place not inferior to that of some whom they have long held in honour.

And first with regard to Guettard's labours in the domain of geographical geology, or the distribution of rocks and minerals over the surface of the earth. I have referred to the manner in which he was gradually drawn into this subject by his botanical excursions. As the result of his researches, he communicated in 1746 to the Academy of Sciences in Paris a memoir on the distribution of minerals and rocks.[1] Having been much impressed by the almost entire absence of certain mineral substances in some places, though they were abundant enough in others, he was led to suspect that these substances are really disposed with much more regularity than had been previously imagined. He surmised that, instead of being dispersed at random, they were grouped in bands which have a character- istic assemblage of minerals and a determinate trend, so that when once the breadth and direction of one of these bands is known, it will be possible, even where the band passes into an unknown country, to tell beforehand what minerals and rocks should be found along its course.

[1] *Mém. Acad. Roy. France,* vol. for 1751.

The first sentences of his remarkable *Mémoire et Carte Minéralogique* are well worth quoting. "If nothing," he remarks, "can contribute more towards the formation of a physical and general theory of the earth than the multiplication of observations among the different kinds of rocks and the fossils which they contain, assuredly nothing can make us more sensible of the utility of such a research than to bring together into one view those various observations by the construction of mineralogical maps. I have travelled with the view of gaining instruction on the first of these two points, and following the recommendation of the Academy, which wished to have my work expressed on a map, I have prepared such a map, which contains a summary of all my observations."

The idea of depicting the distribution of the mineral products of a country upon a map was not original with Guettard or the Academy of Sciences. It will be pointed out in a subsequent chapter that, as far back as the later years of the previous century, a scheme of this kind was submitted to the Royal Society of London by Martin Lister.[1] There is no evidence, however, that this scheme was known to Guettard, who, though he obtained a large amount of information about English mineral products, probably derived it all from French translations of English works. He does not appear to have read English. Guettard inferred, from his observations over the centre and north of France, that the several bands of rocks and minerals which he had detected were disposed round Paris as

---

[1] The early history of geological map-making is briefly outlined in chapter xiv. of the present volume.

a centre. The area in the middle, irregularly oval in
shape, comprised the districts of sand and gravel,
whence he named it the Sandy band. It was there
that the sandstones, millstones, hard building stones,
limestones, and gun-flints were met with. The second
or Marly band, exactly surrounding the first, consisted
of little else than hardened marls, with occasional
shells and other fossil bodies. The third band, called
the "Schitose" [Schistose] or metalliferous, encircled
the second, and was distinguished by including all the
mines of the different minerals, as well as the pits and
quarries for bitumen, slate, sulphur, marble, granite,
fossil wood, coal, etc.

Having convinced himself that these conclusions
could be sustained by an appeal to the distribution of
the minerals in the northern half of France, he proceeded to put upon a map the information he had
collected. Using chemical and other symbols, he
placed a sign at each locality where a particular mineral substance was known to exist. Moreover, employing a variety of engraved shading, he showed in a
general way the position and limits of the great Paris
basin. The marly band surrounding the central tract
of sandy Tertiary strata was represented as sweeping
inland from the coast between Boulogne and Dieppe,
through Picardy and the east of France to the Bour-
bonnais, where, turning westward, it reached Poitou,
and then struck northward to the coast west of the
mouth of the Seine. Though erroneously grouping
Secondary sometimes with Palæozoic, sometimes with
Tertiary strata, and not accurately coinciding with the
modern divisions of the stratigraphical series, the map

nevertheless roughly expresses the broad distribution of the formations.

Having put his data on the map of France, he came to see that his three bands were abruptly truncated by the English Channel and Strait of Dover. Carrying out the principles he had established, he conjectured that these bands would be found to pass under the sea and to re-emerge on the shores of England. To test the truth of this hypothesis, he ransacked the French versions of two once famous English books—Joshua Childrey's *Britannia Baconica*,[1] and Gerard Boate's *Ireland's Naturall Historie*.[2] He found much in these volumes to confirm his surmise. Availing himself of

[1] " *Britannia Baconica*, or the natural rarities of England, Scotland and Wales, according as they are to be found in every shire, historically related according to the precepts of the Lord Bacon." London, 1660. A French translation was published in 1662 and 1667.

[2] " *Ireland's Naturall Historie*, Being a true and ample description of its situation, greatness, shape and nature ; of its hills, woods, heaths, bogs ; of its fruitful parts and profitable grounds, with the severall ways of manuring and improving the same ; with its heads or promontories, harbours, roades, and bayes ; of its springs and fountains, brookes, rivers, loghs ; of its metalls, minerals, freestone, marble, seacoal, turf and other things that are taken out of the ground. And lastly of the nature and temperature of its air and season, and what diseases it is free from or subject unto ; Conducing to the advancement of navigation, husbandry and other profitable arts and professions. Written by Gerard Boate, late Doctor of Physick to the State in Ireland, and now published by Samuel Hartlib, Esq., for the common good of Ireland, and more especially for the benefit of the Adventurers and Planters there." It was published in London in 1652, and was dedicated to Oliver Cromwell. A French version, under the title of *Histoire Naturelle d'Irelande*, was published at Paris in 1666 (*Dict. Nat. Biog., sub voc.* Boate).

H

the information afforded by them, he affixed to the map of England the same system of symbols which he had used on that of France, and roughly indicated the limits of his bands across the south-eastern English counties. This portion of his work, however, being founded on second-hand knowledge, is more vague and inaccurate than that which was based on his personal observations in France.

As an example of the painstaking earnestness with which Guettard made his geological notes, it may be mentioned that among the symbols he employed on his map there was one for shells or marine fossil bodies, and that this sign is plentifully sprinkled over the map. His reading enabled him also to insert the symbol on many parts of the map of England, all the way from the Wash to Sussex. On the map of France, he was able to introduce an additional sign denoting that the shells were not in mere loose deposits, but formed part of solid stone. In a second map, on a smaller scale, accompanying the same memoir, and embracing the whole of Western Europe from the north of Iceland to the Pyrenees and the Mediterranean, Guettard marked by his system of notation the localities where various metals, minerals and rocks were known to exist. In this way he brought into one view a large amount of information regarding the geographical distribution of the substances which he selected for illustration.

This memoir, with its maps, seems to have gratified the Academy of Sciences, for not merely was it inserted in the volume of Transactions for the year, but in the Journal or annual summary of the more important work of the Academy, it occupies a conspicuous place. The official record announced that a new application of geography had been inaugurated by the author, who, neglecting the political limits traced on maps, sought to group the different regions of the earth according to the nature of the substances that lie beneath the surface. " The work of M. Guettard," it is further remarked, " opens up a new field for geographers and naturalists, and forms, so to speak, a link between two sciences which have hitherto been regarded as entirely independent of each other." [1]

I have dwelt at some length on this early work of Guettard because of its importance in the history of geological cartography. These maps, so far as I know, were the first ever constructed to express the superficial distribution of minerals and rocks. The gifted Frenchman who produced them is thus the father of all the national Geological Surveys which have been instituted by the various civilised nations of the Old and the New Worlds.

This effort in mineralogical map-making was merely the beginning of Guettard's labours in this department of investigation. " If you will only let me have a proper map of France," he used to say, " I will undertake to show on it the mineral formations underneath." When Cassini's map appeared, it enabled him to put his design into execution. After incredible exertions, during which he had the illustrious chemist Lavoisier[2] as an assistant, he completed

---

[1] *Mém. Acad. Roy. Sciences*, 1751 ; *Journal*, p. 105.

[2] See on the subject of Lavoisier's co-operation, D'Archiac's *Paléontologie Stratigraphique*, p. 290, and *postea*, p. 343.

the mineralogical survey of no fewer than sixteen sheets of the map. These labours involved journeys so frequent and prolonged that it was estimated that he had travelled over some 1600 leagues of French soil. At last, finding the work beyond his strength, he left it to his successor Monnet, by whom the sixteen maps and a large folio of explanatory text were eventually published.[1]

It must be acknowledged, however, that Guettard does not seem to have had any clear ideas of the sequence of formations and of geological structure ; at least there is no sign of any acquaintance with these in his maps or memoir. His work, therefore, excellent as it was for the time, contained little in common with the admirable detailed geological maps of the present day, which not only depict the geographical distribution of the various rocks, but express also their relations to each other in point of structure and relative age, and their connection with the existing topography of the ground.

In the course of his journeys, Guettard amassed a far larger amount of detailed information than could be put upon his maps. From time to time he embodied it in voluminous essays upon different regions. The longest and most important of these is one in three parts on the mineralogy of the neighbourhood of Paris, in which, besides giving an account of the distribution of the minerals and rocks, he pays special attention to the organic remains of that interesting tract of country, and figures a large number of shells from

[1] *Atlas et Description Minéralogiques de la France, entrepris par ordre du Roi par MM. Guettard et Monnet,* 1780.

what are now known as the Secondary and Tertiary formations.

His natural history predilections led him to take a keen interest in the fossils which he himself collected, or which were sent up to Paris from the country for his examination. He devoted many long and elaborate memoirs to their description, and figured some hundreds of them. I may mention, as of particular interest in palæontological investigation, that Guettard was the first to recognise trilobites in the Silurian slates of Angers. In some specimens which had been sent up to the Academy from the quarries of that district, he observed numerous impressions of organic remains, which he referred to sea-weeds and crustacea. The latter he sagaciously compared to modern crabs and prawns. They are well-marked trilobites, and his figures of them are so excellent that the genera, and even in some cases the species, can easily be made out. His representation of the large *Illænus* of these Lower Silurian slates is specially good. His memoir, read before the Academy in 1757, and published in 1762,[1] is thus a landmark in geological literature, for it appeared eighty years before Murchison's *Silurian System* made known the sequence and abundant organic remains of the Silurian rocks of Wales.

Guettard's labours in palæontology ranged over a wide field. We find him at one time immersed in all

[1] " Sur les Ardoisières d'Angers," *Trans. Acad. Roy. Sciences*, 1762, p. 52. The Dudley trilobite of the Upper Silurian limestone of England had been figured and described by Lhuyd in his *Lithophylacii Britannici Iconographia* (1699), Epist. i. p. 96 and Pl. xxii.; a figure of it was subsequently given in *Phil. Trans.* 1754, Pl. xi. Fig. 2.

the details of fossil sponges and corals. At another, he is busy with the mollusca of the Secondary and Tertiary rocks. Fossil fishes, carnivora, pachyderms, cetacea—all interest him, and find in him an enthusiastic and faithful chronicler. His descriptions are not of the minutely systematic and technical order which has prevailed since the time of Linnæus. Yet some of his generic names have passed into the language of modern palæontology, and one of the genera of Chalk sponges which he described has been named after him, *Guettardia*. He had within him the spirit of the true naturalist, more intent on understanding the nature and affinities of organic forms than on adding new names to the scientific vocabulary. His descriptions and excellent drawings entitle him to rank as the first great leader of the palæontological school of France.

As far back as the year 1751, when he was thirty-six years old, he presented to the Academy a memoir on certain little-known fossil bodies, in which he struck, as it were, the keynote of his future life in regard to the organic remains enclosed within the stony records of former ages. Like a man entering a vast charnel-house, he sees on every side proofs of dead organisms. Others had observed these proofs before him, and had recognized their meaning, and he alludes to the labours of his predecessors. He especially singles out Palissy, who, as already remarked, was the first in France, some two hundred years before, to embrace fossil shells in his view of Nature, to maintain that they are the productions of the sea, not of the earth, as had been supposed, and to demonstrate from them that France once lay beneath the sea, which had left behind it such vast quantities of the remains of the creatures that peopled its waters.

In Normandy, whence many of Guettard's early collections came, and where the people of the country looked upon certain fossil bodies as forms of fruit—pears and apples that had fallen from the trees and taken a solid form within the earth—he tells how half-witted he seemed to them when he expressed a doubt regarding what they believed to be an obvious truth. He recognised the animal nature of the organisms, and asserted that the so-called peaches, apples and pears all belonged to the class of corals, though many of them are now known to be sponges.

Of all his numerous and voluminous essays on palæontological subjects, perhaps that which most signally displays Guettard's modern and philosophical habit of mind in dealing with fossil organisms is a long paper in three parts, which appeared in 1765 under the title, " On the Accidents that have befallen Fossil Shells compared with those which are found to happen to Shells now living in the Sea." [1] The controversy about " figured stones " had not yet died out, and there were still not a few observers who continued to believe that the apparent shells found in the rocks of the land never really belonged to living creatures, but were parts of the original structure of the earth. It is difficult, perhaps, to imagine ourselves in the position of naturalists who even as late as the middle of the eighteenth century, could still honestly persuade themselves that the organic remains of fossiliferous

[1] *Trans. Acad. Roy. Sciences* (1765), pp. 189, 329, 399.

formations are entirely deceptive and never formed part of living plants or animals. Yet unless we make the effort to realise the attitude of men's minds in those days, we cannot rightly appreciate the acumen and sagacity of the arguments with which Guettard assailed these opinions. In much detail, and with many admirable illustrations drawn from his personal observations all over France, he demonstrated that fossil shells often have attached to them other shells, and likewise barnacles and serpulæ; that many of them have been bored into by other organisms, and that in innumerable instances they are found in a fragmentary and worn condition. In all these respects the beds of fossil shells on the land are shown to present the closest possible analogy to the floor of the present sea, so that it becomes impossible to doubt that the accidents which have affected the fossil organisms arose from precisely the same causes as those of exactly the same nature that still befall their successors on the existing ocean bottom.

Of course nowadays such reasoning appears to us so obvious as to involve no great credit to the writer who elaborated it. But we must remember the state of natural knowledge one hundred and forty years ago. As an example of the method of explaining and illustrating the former condition of the earth's surface by what can be seen to happen now, Guettard's memoir is unquestionably one of the most illustrious in the literature of geology, opening up, as it did, a new field in the investigation of the history of our globe, and unfolding the method by which this field must be cultivated.

On what is now known as Physiographical Geology, or the discussion of the existing topography of the land, this same illustrious Frenchman left the impress of his mind.   I will cite only one of his contributions to this subject—a memoir " On the Degradation of Mountains effected in our Time by heavy Rains, Rivers and the Sea."[1]   This work, which occupies about 200 quarto pages, deals with the efficacy of moving water in altering the face of the land.   At the very beginning of it, he starts with a reminiscence from the scenes of his infancy, and weaves it into the story he has to tell of the ceaseless degradation of the terrestrial surface.   He remembers a picturesque crag of the Fontainebleau sandstone which, perched above the slopes of a little valley, had been worn by the weather into a rudely-formed female figure holding an infant, and had been named by the peasantry the Rock of the Good Virgin.   That crag, under which he used to play with his schoolmates, had in the interval of less than half a century gradually crumbled away, and had been washed down to the foot of the declivity.   In the same neighbourhood he had noticed at successive visits that prominent rocks had made their appearance which were not previously visible.   They seemed, as it were, to start out of the ground, yet he knew that they arose simply from the removal of the material that once covered them. In like manner, ravines of some depth were in the course of a few years cut out of ground where there had before been no trace of them.   In these

[1] See vol. iii. of his *Mémoires sur différentes parties des Sciences et des Arts*, pp. 209-403.

striking examples of the general disintegration, he sees only the continual operation of "gentle rains and heavy downpours."[1]

From illustrations supplied by his own earliest observation, he passes on to others drawn either from his personal researches or his reading, and exemplifying the potent influence of heavy rains and flooded streams. Not only are the solid rocks mouldering down and strewing the slopes below with their debris, but the sides of the hills are gashed by torrents, and narrow defiles are cut in them, like the Devil's Gap in Normandy.[2] He combats the notion that land-slips, such as had occurred at Issoire in Auvergne in the year 1733, were caused by internal fires or subterranean winds, and agrees with a previous writer in regarding them as the result of the penetration of water from the surface into the interior of the hill. He thus recognises the efficacy of subterranean as well as superficial water, in changing the face of a country.

He believes the sea to be the most potent destroyer of the land, and as an instance of its power he was accustomed to regard the chalk cliffs of the north-west of France as the relics of a great chain of hills, of which the greater part had been swept away by the sea.[3] He shows, further, that while the hills are worn down by the waves, by the rains, and by the inundations to which the rains give rise, the materials removed from them are not destroyed, but are deposited either on the land or along the shores of the

---

[1] "Des pluies et des averses," *Op. cit.* p. 210.
[2] P. 214.   [3] Pp. 220, 222.

sea.[1] He further points out that the detritus of separate river-basins may greatly differ, and that materials may be carried into districts where the rocks are entirely distinct from those in the areas whence the transport has taken place. He refers to the practical value of this observation in questions regarding the source of minerals, ores and useful stones.[2]

He is thus led to give, from his wide knowledge of France, a sketch of the character of the rocks in the different river-basins of the country, and the nature of the materials which the rivers have in each case to transport. He passes in review all the large streams that enter the Atlantic from the Rhine to the shores of Gascony, and considers, likewise, the Rhone with its tributaries on the Mediterranean side of the watershed.[3] He infers that all the debris derived from the waste of the land is not carried to the sea, but that a great deal of it is deposited along the borders of the streams, and that though it may be removed thence, this removal must require many ages to accomplish. He thinks that the levels of the valleys are at present being raised owing to the deposit of detritus in them.[4] The plains watered by the rivers are one vast sheet of gravel, the streams having changed their courses again and again, so as to flow in turn over every part of these alluvial tracts. The thickness of detritus brought down by the rivers gradually increases towards their mouths. Near their sources, on the other hand, any sediment which is deposited is in a manner superficial, and is

[1] P. 222.   [2] P. 223.
[3] P. 225-324.   [4] P. 326.

liable to continued removal and transportation farther down.

The fragmentary material that is accumulated along the margin of the sea is, in Guettard's view, derived either from what is borne down by rivers, or from what is made by the sea itself, the whole being ground into powder by the long-continued beating of the waves. The sea not only acts on its shores, but on submerged rocks, and the detritus thus produced is mingled with the triturated remains of corals, shells, fish-bones and marine plants.[1]

Comparatively little information had been gathered in Guettard's time as to the condition of the sea-bottom. There is thus a peculiar interest in noting the ideas which he expresses on this subject. He thinks that, besides what is laid down upon the shore, another portion of the detritus is borne away seawards, and gradually settles down on the sea-floor. As the nature of the part so transported must depend on that of the material on the shore, he is led to enter upon a minute examination of the mineral constitution of the coast-lines of France, both on the Atlantic and Mediterranean margins of the country.[2]

He recognises that soluble substances may be carried for great distances from the land, and may remain dissolved in the sea-water for a very long time. He even conjectures that it is possibly these substances that impart its salinity to sea-water.[3]

From all the soundings available in his day, he concludes that the bottom of the sea is, throughout

[1] P. 328.   [2] P. 328.   [3] P. 360.

its whole extent, covered mostly with sand, which is probably not derived from the detritus of rivers.[1] He observes, regarding this widely-diffused deposit, that it might be thought to be due to the grinding down of submarine rocks by the sea itself. But he contends that "how violent soever may be the movements of the sea, they can have but little effect, save on those rocks which emerge above the level of the water, the greatest storms being little felt except on the surface, and for a short way below it." In this sagacious and generally accurate inference, however, he was long before anticipated by Boyle.

Considering, further, the problem presented by the general diffusion of sand over the bed of the sea, he thinks that the erosive influence of the ocean cannot be enough to account for this deposit, which is spread over so vast an area. He concludes, therefore, that the sand must date back to the remote ages of the destruction of the mountains. The submarine rocks met with in sounding are, he thinks, unquestionably the remains of mountains formerly destroyed, and the detached boulders similarly discovered are no doubt the result of the destruction of these rocks, though in some cases they may have been derived from neighbouring islands where such exist.[2]

No argument against this view of the high antiquity of the sandy sediment on the sea-floor can, he believes, be drawn from the presence of shells, either singly or in numbers, in this sand. These he regards as obviously the relics of molluscs of the present time, those of former ages having been long ago destroyed.[3]

[1] P. 401.   [2] Pp. 401, 402.   [3] P. 402.

He remarks, in conclusion, that " it follows, from all the observations here recited, that the deposits laid down by the sea along its shores are sandy and loamy ; that these deposits do not extend far out to sea ; that, consequently, the elevation of new mountains in the sea by the deposition of sediment is a process very difficult to conceive ; that the transport of the sediment as far as the equator is not less improbable ; and that still more difficult to accept is the suggestion that the sediment from our continent is carried into the seas of the New World.   In short, we are still very little advanced towards the theory of the earth as it now exists.   All the systems which have been devised in this subject are full of difficulties which appear to me to be insoluble."   He proposes, finally, to return, should the occasion present itself, to these questions, which are " all the more interesting the more difficult they are to elucidate." [1]

It cannot be claimed that such enlightened views regarding the subaerial degradation of the land were now for the first time proclaimed to the world. Guettard had been to some extent preceded by other writers.   Thus the English naturalist Ray, some ninety years before, had pointed out how in course of time the whole dry land might be washed into the sea (*ante*, p. 74).   Generelli, too, in his defence of Lazzaro Moro, twenty years before the appearance of Guettard's volume, had dwelt on the evidence of the constant degradation of the mountains by running water, as an argument for the existence of some other natural cause, whereby, from time to time, land was

[1] Pp. 402, 403.

upraised to compensate for the universal waste. It must be admitted, however, that no one had elaborated the subject so fully until it was taken up by the French observer, and that he was the first to discuss the whole phenomena of denudation, apart altogether from theory, as a great domain for accurate and prolonged observation.

I have reserved for mention in the last place the discovery for which chiefly Guettard's name has received such mention as has been accorded to it in English scientific literature. He was the first to ascertain the existence of a group of old volcanoes in the heart of France. This contribution to the geology of the time may seem in itself of comparatively small moment, but it proved to be another important onward step made by the same indefatigable and clear-sighted naturalist, and laid the foundations of another department of the natural history of the earth. It became also the starting-point of one of the great scientific controversies of the latter half of the eighteenth and the first decades of the nineteenth century. There is thus a peculiar interest in watching how the discovery was made and worked out by the original observer.

The story goes back to the early months of 1752, for on the 10th of May of that year Guettard read to the Academy a " Memoir on Certain Mountains in France which have once been Volcanoes." [1] He tells how he had undertaken further journeys for the purpose of obtaining additional information towards the correction and amplification of his map of France,

[1] *Mém. Acad. Roy. Sciences*, vol. for 1756, p. 27.

showing the distribution of his " bands " with their
characteristic minerals. He was accompanied by his
former schoolfellow and then his valued friend, Malesherbes. On reaching Moulins on the Allier, he was
struck by the nature of the black stone employed
for mile-posts, and felt certain that it must be of
volcanic origin. On inquiring whence the material
came, and learning that it was from Volvic, " Volvic ! "
he exclaimed, " Volcani Vicus ! " and at once determined to make without delay for this probably volcanic
centre.[1] His excitement in the chase after an unknown
volcano seems to have increased with every step of
the journey, as more and more of the dark stone
appeared in the buildings by the roadside. At Riom
he found the town almost entirely built of the material,
which he felt sure he had now run nearly to earth.
Learning that the quarries were still some two leagues
distant, he pushed on to them, and great was his
delight to find all his suspicions amply confirmed.
He recognised the rock as a solidified current of lava
which had flowed down from the high granitic ridge
for some five miles into the plain below, and he found

[1] Twenty-eight years after this discovery Guettard found himself
forced to defend his claim to be the discoverer of the old volcanoes
of Central France, and to ask his friend Malesherbes for his testimony to the justice of that claim. Malesherbes accordingly wrote
him a letter giving an account of their journey to Auvergne, which
Guettard printed in the preface to his treatise, in two volumes, on
the mineralogy of Dauphiné. It is curious that, with the statements
of the two travellers long before in print, Scrope should have
published a totally inaccurate version of the journey in the first
edition of his *Volcanoes of Central France*, and should have repeated
it in the second edition.

the actual cone and crater from which the molten flood had issued.

We can follow the enthusiastic explorer with warm sympathy as he eagerly and joyously sees at each onward step some fresh evidence of the true volcanic nature of the rocks around him. Though he had never beheld a volcano, he was familiar with their outlines, from the available engravings of the time. Ascending a hill beyond the quarries, he perceives its conical form to be that of a typical volcano.[1] As he climbs the rough slopes, he identifies the crumbling debris of black and red pumice, together with the blocks of rugged spongy slags and scoriae, as manifestly the products of a once active volcanic vent. When he reached the truncated summit of the hill, what must have been his delight to behold below him the smooth-sloped hollow of the crater, not now belching forth hot vapours and ashes, but silent and carpeted with grass ! For centuries the shepherds had pastured their flocks on these slopes, and the quarrymen had been busy cutting and sending off the lava for roads and buildings, but no one had ever suspected that this quiet and lonely spot retained such striking monuments of subterranean commotion.

Descending to the great lava-stream, Guettard scrutinized its structure as laid open in the quarries, and at once noticed how different in character it was from any other rock he had ever seen in France. He observed

[1] Desmarest affirms that it was not the Puy de la Nugère, the source of the Volvic lava, which Guettard ascended, but the Puy de la Bannière, and that the former hill was unknown to him. *Encyclopédie Méthodique, Géographie Physique,* vol. i. p. 187.

it to be divided into sheets inclined with the general
slope of the ground, but separated from each other
by layers of clay, earth or sand, as in the case of sedimentary formations, yet solid, and breaking easily in
any direction, so as to lend itself readily to the arts
of the stone-mason.

Travelling southward along the base of the picturesque ridge of the Puys, Guettard and Malesherbes
reached Clermont, where they procured the services
of an intelligent apothecary, who had some knowledge
of the topography of the hills. They climbed the
steep slopes of the Puy de Dôme—a hill made famous
by Pascal. Everywhere they noticed volcanic debris
partially concealed under vegetation. If the view from
the first volcano above Volvic delighted the travellers,
we can imagine their amazement and pleasure when
the marvellous panorama around the highest craterless
summit spread itself like a map around them. As
their eyes ranged over that array of old volcanoes, so
perfect in form that it is difficult to believe them to
have been silent ever since the beginning of human
history, they could mark the cones rising one behind
the other in long procession on the granite ridge,
each bearing its cup-shaped crater atop.

In descending from the mountain they came upon
another crater, probably that of the Petit Puy de
Dôme, a singularly perfect example of the type, some
300 feet deep, and the same in diameter of rim, with
such regular and smooth slopes that it has been named
by the shepherds the Hen's Nest. Everywhere they
encountered quantities of pumice, which so entirely
convinced Guettard of the true volcanic nature of the

district, that he found it unnecessary for his immediate purpose to examine the rest of the puys. Their Clermont guide, though he had previously wandered over the hills, had never suspected their volcanic origin; but he seems to have learnt his lesson promptly, for he soon afterwards, at Guettard's request, sent some details, and wrote about eruptions and explosions as if he had been long familiar with their effects.

Not only did Guettard detect some sixteen or seventeen cones, but he observed that their craters looked in different directions, and he thought that they probably belonged to different periods of eruption. The travellers pushed on to the great volcanic centre of Mont Dore. But Guettard was there less successful. He was unaware of the influence of long-continued denudation in altering the external forms of volcanic hills, and was disposed to regard his ill success as probably due to the mantle of vegetation by which so much of the ground was concealed.

The journey in Auvergne was too brief and hurried to admit of any single point being fully worked out. But Guettard believed that he had amassed material enough to prove the main question which interested him—that there had formerly been a series of active volcanoes in the heart of France. So he prepared an account of his observations, and read it to the Academy of Sciences on 10th May, 1752.

This early memoir on the extinct volcanoes of Europe must not be tried by the standard which has now been attained in the elucidation of volcanic rocks and the phenomena of ancient eruptions. We should be unjust if we judged it by the fuller knowledge

obtained of the same region of France by the more
detailed examination of other observers even in Guettard's lifetime. Desmarest, whose splendid achievements will be referred to in the next chapter, was
conspicuously guilty of this injustice. He would never
allow Guettard credit for his work in Auvergne, finding fault with it because it was imperfect and inaccurate.
He wished that, before writing on the subject at all,
his predecessor had studied the ground more carefully
and in greater detail, and had attended to the different
conditions and dates of the eruptions. "Can we
regard as a true discovery," he asks, "the simple
recognition of the products of volcanic action, when
the facts are presented with so little order and so
much confusion? Such a discovery implies a reasoned
analysis of all the operations of fire, of which the
results have been studied, so as to reveal the ancient
conditions of all the volcanic regions. Without this
it is impossible to dignify the recognition of a few
stones with the name of a discovery that will advance
the progress of the natural history of the earth." [1]
Could any judgment be more unfair? As if no
discovery is entitled to the name, unless it has
been elaborated in the fullest detail and followed to
its remotest consequences! When one of Guettard's
countrymen and contemporaries could write thus of
his claims to recognition, it is not surprising that for
the best part of a century his name should have
almost entirely passed out of mind.

That Guettard preceded every one else in the
recognition of the old volcanoes of Auvergne, and

[1] *Géographie Physique*, Art. "Guettard."

that he thus became the originator of the Vulcanist party in the famous warfare at the end of last century, in no way diminishes the claim of Desmarest to occupy the foremost place among the Vulcanists, and to be ranked as the real founder of volcanic geology. I shall have occasion to dwell at some length on Desmarest's work, which for accuracy and breadth has never been surpassed.

Guettard, having never seen a volcano, was guided in his observations and inferences by what he had read of volcanic countries, and what he had learnt about lavas by familiarity with specimens of these rocks brought from Vesuvius and other modern volcanoes. He noted the close resemblance between the rocks of Auvergne and the Italian lavas, not only in appearance, density and other characters, but in their position on the ground, the specimens which he had gathered from the bottom, sides and crests of the puys having each their own distinctive peculiarities, as in existing volcanoes. He compared the curved lines on some of the rocks of Mont Dore and the Puy de Dôme with the ropy crusts of certain Vesuvian lavas.

When this distinguished man stepped from the observation of fact into the region of theory, he at once fell into error, but the error was one which, as we have seen, had passed current as obvious truth for more than 2000 years. "For the production of volcanoes," he remarks, "it is enough that there should be within these mountains substances that can burn, such as petroleum, coal or bitumen, and that from some cause these materials should take fire. Thereupon the mountain will become a furnace, and the fire, raging furiously within, will be able to melt and vitrify the most intractable substances." [1] He finds evidence in Auvergne of this presumed connection between the combustion of carbonaceous substances and volcanic eruptions, and he cites in illustration the Puy de Crouel and Puy de la Poix, near Clermont, where the black bituminous material can actually be seen at the surface. Summing up his observations he concludes thus: "I do not believe that the reality of our volcanoes will now be called in question, save perhaps from anxiety for the safety of the districts around them. For myself, confident as to the first point, I confess that I share in the anxiety regarding the second. Hot springs have generally been regarded as due to some kind of concealed volcanoes. Those of Mont Dore rise at the very foot of the mountains; those of Clermont are only some two leagues from the chain of the Puys. It may very well be that their high temperature is kept up by the same internal fires which formerly had a communication with these extinct volcanoes, or might now easily establish one should they increase in activity." [2]

His fears for the safety of the Auvernois were by no means shared by the people themselves, for they refused to believe that the Puys, which they had known from infancy as quiet, well-behaved hills, had ever been anything else, and they looked upon the

[1] *Trans. Roy. Acad. Sciences* for 1756, p. 52. This adoption of the time-honoured belief is severely criticised by Desmarest, but the same belief was subsequently accepted by Werner, and became a prominent item in the Wernerian creed.

[2] *Op. cit.* p. 53.

learned doctor's descriptions of the former eruptions as mere speculation of his own manufacture.

In taking leave of Guettard's scientific labours, I must refer to one further essay of his, on account of its connection with his work among the old volcanoes of Auvergne. Eighteen years after his memoir on these hills had been read to the Academy, he published a paper "On the Basalt of the Ancients and the Moderns."[1] The furious war over the origin of basalt, of which I shall give some account in a later chapter, had not yet definitely begun. Various writers had maintained that this rock is of volcanic origin, and we might have supposed that Guettard's experience in Auvergne would have led him to adopt this correct opinion. So far from doing so, however, he entered into an elaborate discussion to show that basalt could not be a volcanic rock. He admitted that it is found among volcanic masses, but he accounted for its presence there by supposing that in some cases it was already in that position before the eruptions, in others that it had been laid down upon the lavas after they had consolidated. "If a columnar basalt can be produced by a volcano," he asks, "why do we not find it among the recent eruptions of Vesuvius and other active volcanoes?" After reviewing all that had then been written on the subject, he concludes that "basalt is a species of vitrifiable rock, formed by crystallization in an aqueous fluid, and that there is no reason to regard it as due to igneous fusion."[2]

[1] *Mémoires sur différentes parties des Sciences et des Arts*, tome ii. p. 226 (1770).

[2] *Op. cit.* p. 268.

We may gather how little was then known of the characters of modern lavas when Guettard was ignorant of the occurrence of columnar structure among them.[1] He was as hopelessly wrong in regard to the origin of basalt, as he was with respect to the nature of volcanic action. How this error originated will appear in an examination of the controversy to which basalt gave rise. But the most interesting feature in the passage just cited from Guettard is not his mistake about basalt, but his clear enunciation of his belief in its deposition from aqueous solution, for he thus forestalled Werner in one of the most keenly disputed parts of his geognosy.

I know nothing more whimsical in the history of geology than that the same man should be the parent of two diametrically opposite schools. Guettard's observations in Auvergne practically started the Vulcanist camp, and his promulgated tenets regarding basalt became one of the watchwords of the Neptunists.

The notable Frenchman, of whose work I have now attempted to give an outline, must have been a singular figure as he moved about among his contemporaries. Endowed with a healthy constitution, he had strengthened it by travel, and by a hard and sober life. At last he became liable to attacks of a heavy lethargic sleep, during one of which his foot was burnt. The long and painful healing of the wound he bore with stoical patience, though often convinced of the uselessness of the remedies applied. "I see

[1] We shall find that this ignorance continued for many years after Guettard's time, and was characteristic of the Wernerian school.

quite well," he would say, "that they want to ward off the stroke; but they will not succeed." The idea of the kind of death that would terminate his life never left his mind, but did not in the least affect his cheerfulness. He continued to come assiduously to the meetings of the Academy of Sciences alone and on foot, taking only the precaution to carry in his pocket his full address, that in case of anything happening to him, he might be taken home. By degrees he declined to dine with his friends, and then went seldom to see them, quietly assigning as his excuse the fear of troubling them with the sight of his death. He passed away at last on the 7th of January 1786 at the age of seventy-one years.

The kindly *éloge* of Condorcet enables us to form some idea of the character and peculiarities of the man. From his childhood onwards he was eminently religious. His nature was thoroughly frank and honest, simple and unambitious. Scrupulously exact in his own dealings with fact, he hated everything savouring in the least of insincerity and subterfuge. His transparent sincerity gained him friends everywhere; yet he was readily irritated, and had a certain brusqueness of manner, which perhaps detracted from the charm of his character and led to his being sometimes much misunderstood. One of his acquaintances once thanked him for having given a vote in his favour. "You owe me nothing for that," was Guettard's abrupt reply. "If I had not believed that it was right to give it to you, you should not have had it; for I don't like you." Condorcet tells how, when they met at the Academy on the occasion of the delivery of the customary *éloges* of deceased members, Guettard, who looked on all these things as unveracious statements, would say to the perpetual Secretary, " You are going to tell a lot of lies. When it comes to my turn I want only the truth told about me." Condorcet, in sketching the defects as well as the excellences of his friend's character, remarks that in fulfilling his wishes in the strictest sense, he is rendering to Guettard the homage that he himself would most have desired. So little did he try to seem better than he was, that his defects might be most prominent to those who merely casually met him, while his sterling qualities were known only to his friends. " Those who knew Guettard merely by some brusque answer or other indication of bad temper," his biographer remarks, " would be surprised to learn that this man, so severe in appearance, so hard to please, forced by the circumstances of his position to live alone, had actually adopted the large family of a woman who had been his servant, brought up the children and watched over the smallest details of their education ; that he could never see any one in distress without not only coming to his help, but even weeping with him. He bore the same sensibility towards animals also, and expressly forbade that any living creature should be killed for him or at his house. He was a man who, losing control of his words when in bad humour, had quarrelled more than once with each of his friends, yet had always ended by loving them and being loved more than ever by them ; who had hurt most of his associates in his disputes with them, but yet had preserved the friendship of several of them, and had never diminished in any one of them the esteem which it was impossible to refuse to his character and his virtues." [1]

Guettard's position in the history of science is that of an indefatigable and accurate observer who, gifted with a keen eye, well-trained powers of investigation, and much originality of mind, opened up new paths in a number of fields which have since been fruitfully cultivated, but who rigidly abstained from theory or speculation. In geology, he deserves to be specially remembered as the first to construct, however imperfectly, geological maps, the first to make known the existence of extinct volcanoes in Central France, and one of the first to see the value of organic remains as geological monuments, and to prepare detailed descriptions and figures of them. To him also are due some of the earliest luminous suggestions on the denudation of the land by the atmospheric and marine agents. "By his minute and laborious researches he did more to advance the true theory of the earth (on which, however, he never allowed himself to hazard a single conjecture) than the philosophers who have racked their brains to devise those brilliant hypotheses, the phantoms of a moment, which the light of truth soon remands into eternal oblivion." [2]

. [1] Condorcet's *Éloge*, pp. 238, 240.   [2] Condorcet, *op. cit.*

CHAPTER V

The leading position acquired by France in the investigation of the history of the earth, through the labours of such men as Descartes, Buffon and Guettard, was well maintained in the later decades of the eighteenth century. Geology indeed as a distinct science did not yet exist. The study of rocks and their contents was known as mineralogy, which as a pursuit, often of economic value, had been in vogue for centuries. The idea that beyond the mere variety of its mineral contents, the crust of the earth contained a record of the earth's evolution, for many ages before the advent of man, only very slowly took definite shape. Buffon partly realized it; Guettard had a fuller perception of its nature, though he failed to observe proofs of a long succession of changes earlier than the present condition of the surface.

One of the most valuable parts of Guettard's work was his recognition of the existence of volcanic rocks in regions far removed from any active volcano. We have seen that he was led to this important deduction by a train of observation and inference, and that although he never worked out the subject in detail, the credit of the first discovery, denied to him in his lifetime and after it, must in common fairness be assigned to him.

Central France was the region that furnished Guettard with his proofs of extinct volcanoes. It was the same region that afterwards supplied fuel to the controversy over the origin of basalt which raged with fury for so many years, and it was from this region also that the proofs were obtained which more than any others brought that controversy to an end. The story of this old battle is full of interest and instruction. We learn from it how the advance of truth may be impeded by personal authority; how, under guise of the most rigorous induction from fact, the most perverse theories may be supported; how, under the influence of theoretical preconceptions, the obvious meaning and relations of phenomena may be lost sight of, and how, even in the realm of science, dry questions of interpretation may become the source of cruel misrepresentation and personal animosity.

To understand the history of this controversy, we must trace the career of another illustrious Frenchman who, with less opportunity for scientific work than Guettard, less ample qualifications in all departments of natural science, and less promptitude in putting the results of his observations into tangible form, has nevertheless gained for himself an honoured place among the founders of modern geology.

Nicholas Desmarest (1725-1815) was born in humble circumstances at Soulaines, a little town in France between Bar-sur-Aube and Brienne, on 16th September

1725.[1] He was thus exactly ten years younger than Guettard. So pinched were the conditions of his youth that he could hardly read even when fifteen years old. From that time, on the death of his father, better prospects dawned upon him. The parish priest urged his guardian to have him educated, as far as the slender means left for his sustenance would allow. He was accordingly sent to the college of the Oratorians of Troyes; but the pittance available for his benefit was exhausted by the first few terms of his stay there. He had, however, made such marked progress that his teachers, interested in his career, were glad to continue gratuitously the instruction for which he could no longer pay. At the end of his time with them, they passed him on to their brethren in Paris.

Having made some advance, especially in geometry and physics, he was able to support himself by private teaching and other labours which, however, barely provided the necessaries of life. After some ten years of this drudgery, the studies which had been his occupation and solace, came at last to be the means of opening up a new and noble career to him.

The appearance of Buffon's *Theory of the Earth*, in 1749, had had a powerful influence in France in directing attention to the revolutions through which our globe has passed. Among the results of this influence, a society which had been founded at Amiens by the Duc de Chaulnes, proposed in 1752 a prize

---

[1] The biographical details of the following sketch are taken from the well-known eloquent *Éloge* of Desmarest by Cuvier, *Recueil des Éloges Historiques*, edit. 1819, vol. ii. p. 339.

for an essay on the question whether England and France had ever been joined together. The subject caught Desmarest's fancy, he made some investigations, sent in an essay and carried off the prize.

Cuvier, in his *Éloge*, remarks on the strong contrast between the way in which Desmarest approached his task and that in which Buffon, who had aroused public attention to these subjects, was accustomed to deal with them. The young aspirant to fame, then twenty-eight years of age, allowed himself no hypothesis or theory. He would not travel beyond the positive facts and the inferences that might be legitimately deduced from them. Dealing with the correspondence between the material forming the opposite cliffs of the two countries (which had already been pointed out by Guettard), and with the form of the bottom of the shallow strait, he passed on to consider the former prevalence in England of many noxious wild animals, which could not have swum across the sea, and which man would certainly have taken care not to introduce. From a review of all the considerations which the subject presented, he drew the inference that a neck of land must once have connected England and France, and that this isthmus was eventually cut through by the strong currents of the North Sea.

This essay, so different in tone from the imaginative discourses of Buffon, attracted the attention of D'Alembert, and led him to seek the acquaintance of its author. The friendship of this great man was itself a fortune, for it meant an introduction into the most learned, intelligent, and influential society of the day.

Desmarest was soon actively employed in tasks for which his knowledge and capacity were found to fit him, and thenceforth his struggle with poverty came to an end. Among those who befriended him, the young Duc de la Rochefoucault was especially helpful, taking him on his travels and enabling him to see much of France and Italy.

Shortly after the middle of the eighteenth century, the Governments of Europe, wearied with ruinous and profitless wars, began to turn their attention towards the improvement of the industries of their peoples. The French Government especially distinguished itself for the enlightened views which it took in this new line of national activity. It sought to spread throughout the kingdom a knowledge of the best processes of manufacture, and to introduce whatever was found to be superior in the methods of foreign countries. Desmarest was employed on this mission from 1757 onwards. At one time he would be sent to investigate the cloth-making processes of the country: at another to study the various methods adopted in different districts in the manufacture of cheese. Besides being deputed to examine into the condition of the industries of different provinces of France, he undertook two journeys to Holland to study the paper-making system of that country. He prepared elaborate reports of the results of his investigations, which were published in the *Mémoires* of the Academie des Sciences, or in the *Encyclopédie Méthodique*. At last in 1788 he was named by the King Inspector-General and Director of the Manufactures of France.

He continued to hold this office until the time of the Revolution, when his political friends—Trudaine, Malesherbes, La Rochefoucault, and others—perished on the scaffold or by the knife of the assassin. He himself was thrown into prison, and only by a miracle escaped the slaughter of the 2nd September. After the troubles were over, he was once more called to assist the Government of the day with his experience and judgment in all matters connected with the industrial development of the country. It may be said of Desmarest that "for three quarters of a century it was under his eyes, and very often under his influence, that French industry attained so great a development."

Such was his main business in life, and the manner in which he performed it would of itself entitle him to the grateful recollection of his fellow-countrymen. But these occupations did not wholly engross his time or his thoughts. Having early imbibed a taste for scientific investigation, he continued to interest himself in questions that afforded him occupation and solace, even when his fortunes were at the lowest ebb.

"Resuming the rustic habits of his boyhood," says his biographer, "he made his journeys on foot, with a little cheese as all his sustenance. No path seemed impracticable to him, no rock inaccessible. He never sought the country mansions, he did not even halt at the inns. To pass the night on the hard ground in some herdsman's hut, was to him only an amusement. He would talk with quarry-men and miners, with blacksmiths and masons, more

readily than with men of science. It was thus that
he gained that detailed personal acquaintance with
the surface of France with which he enriched his
writings."

During these journeyings, he was led into Auvergne
in the year 1763, where, eleven years after Guettard's
description had been presented to the Academy, he
found himself in the same tract of Central France,
wandering over the same lava-fields, from Volvic to
the heights of Mont Dore.   Among the many puzzles
reported by the mineralogists of his day, none seems
to have excited his interest more than that presented
by the black columnar stone which was found in
various parts of Europe, and for which Agricola,
writing in the middle of the sixteenth century, had
revived Pliny's old name of "basalt."   The wonderful symmetry, combined with the infinite variety of
the pillars, the vast size to which they reached, the
colossal cliffs along which they were ranged in
admirable regularity, had vividly aroused the curiosity
of those who concerned themselves with the nature
and origin of minerals and rocks.   Desmarest had
read all that he could find about this mysterious
stone.   He cast longing eyes towards the foreign
countries where it was developed.   In particular, he
pictured to himself the marvels of the Giant's Causeway of the north of Ireland, as one of the most
remarkable natural monuments of the world, where
Nature had traced her operations with a bold hand,
but had left the explanation of them still concealed
from mortal ken.   How fain would he have directed
his steps to that distant shore.   Little did he dream

that the solution of the problems presented by basalt was not to be sought in Ireland, but in the heart of his own country, and that it was reserved for him to find.

Before referring to the steps in Desmarest's progress towards the discovery of the origin of basalt, let me briefly sketch what was known on the subject at the time when he began his researches. Agricola had mentioned that this dark prismatic stone was to be seen in different parts of Germany, and in particular that it formed the eminence on which the old castle of Stolpen in Saxony had been built.[1] It was afterwards found to be abundantly distributed, not only in Saxony, but in Silesia, in Cassel, and in the valley of the Rhine above Cologne.[2] In these places it is generally to be seen in detached eminences, frequently capping hills, and presenting its vertical columns in rows along its edges. There is nothing about it which in those days was likely to suggest a volcanic origin. The exposures of it in Germany usually belong to an older geological period than the comparatively recent lava-streams of Auvergne, and in the course of time the cones and craters and scoriae, that no doubt originally marked these sites, have gradually disappeared.

The Giant's Causeway, too, though it displays on a far more colossal scale the characteristic structure and scenery of basalt, is equally silent in regard to

---

[1] *De Natura Fossilium*, lib. vii. p. 315. Folio, Basel, 1546.

[2] Various authors who had noticed the occurrence of basalt before the publication of his memoir are cited by Desmarest. *Mém. Acad. Roy. Sciences*, vol. for 1774, p. 726 *et seq.*

its origin. The marvels of this part of the coast of Ireland had frequently been brought to the notice of the learned, from the latter part of the seventeenth century onward.[1] But here as elsewhere, it was rather the symmetrical structure of the rock than the mode of its formation that engaged the attention of the older observers. Even as far back as the year 1756, one of these writers pointed out the remarkable resemblance of certain rocks in Nassau and in the district of Trèves and Cologne to the Giant's Causeway, which by that time had . become famous.[2]

The Western Islands of Scotland, which far surpass the Irish coast in the extent and magnificence of their basalt cliffs, were still unknown to the scientific world. The first report about their wonders seems to have reached London in the spring of 1761, when the Bishop of Ossory sent to the Royal Society a letter he had received from E. Mendez da Costa telling him that "in Cana Island to the southward of Skye and near the island of Rum the rocks rise into polygon pillars . . . jointed exactly like those of the Giant's Causeway."[3] But it was reserved for Sir Joseph Banks to give the first detailed account of the cliffs of Staffa and Fingal's Cave, which from that time shared with the Giant's Causeway in the

---

[1] See Sir R. B., *Phil. Trans.* xvii. (1693) p. 708 ; S. Foley, xviii. (1694) p. 170, with a map and bird's-eye view. T. Molyneux, *Ibid.* p. 181 and xix. (1698) p. 209, with drawings of the columns. R. Pocock, xlv. (1748) p. 124, and xlviii. part i. (1754), with further figures illustrating the jointing of the columns.

[2] A. Trembly, *Phil. Trans.* xlix. (1756) p. 581.

[3] *Phil. Trans.* lii. (1761) p. 163.

renown that drew a yearly increasing number of travellers to these distant shores.[1]

Much had thus been learnt as to the diffusion of basalt in Europe, and many excellent drawings had been published of the remarkable prismatic structure of this rock. But no serious attempt seems to have been made to grapple with the problem of its origin. Some absurd notions had indeed been entertained on this subject. The long regular pillars of basalt, it was gravely suggested, were jointed bamboos of a former period, which had somehow been converted into stone. The similarity of the prisms to those of certain minerals led some mineralogists to regard basalt as a kind of schorl, which had taken its geometrical forms in the process of crystallization. Romé de Lisle is even said to have maintained that each basalt prism ought to have a pyramidal termination, like the schorls and other small crystals of the same nature.[2]

Guettard, as we have seen, drew a distinction between basalt and lava, and this opinion was general in his time. The basalts of Central and Western Europe were usually found on hill tops, and displayed no cones or craters, or other familiar sign of volcanic action. On the contrary, they were not infrequently found to lie upon, and even to alternate

[1] See Pennant's *Tour in Scotland*, 1772, where Banks' narrative is inserted with a number of excellent engravings of the more remarkable features in Staffa.

[2] In the second edition of his *Crystallographie* (1783) he clearly distinguishes between crystallization and basaltic structure. The latter he regards as due to desiccation or cooling, tome i. p. 439.

with, undoubted sedimentary strata. They were, therefore, not unnaturally grouped with these strata, and the whole association of rocks was looked upon as having had one common aqueous origin. It was also a prevalent idea that a rock which had been molten must retain obvious traces of that condition in a glassy structure. There was no such conspicuous vitreous element in basalt, so that this rock, it was assumed, could never have been volcanic.[1] As Desmarest afterwards contended, those who made such objections could have but little knowledge of volcanic products.

We may now proceed to trace how the patient and sagacious Inspector of French industries made his memorable contribution to geological theory. It was while traversing a part of Auvergne in the year 1763 that he detected for the first time columnar rocks in association with the remains of former volcanoes. On the way from Clermont to the Puy de Dôme, climbing the steep slope that leads up to the plateau of Prudelle, with its isolated outlier of a lava-stream that flowed long before the valley below it had been excavated, he came upon some loose columns of a dark compact stone which had fallen from the edge of the overlying sheet of lava. He found similar columns standing vertically all along the mural front of the lava, and observed that they were planted on a bed of scoriæ and burnt soil, beneath which lay the old granite that forms the foundation rock of the region. He noticed still

[1] See for instance Wallerius' *Mineralogia* (1773), i. p. 336, replied to by Desmarest, *Mém. Acad. Roy. Sciences* (1774), p. 753.

more perfect prisms a little further on, belonging
to the same thin cake of dark stone that covered
the plain which leads up to the foot of the great
central puy.

Every year geological pilgrims now make their
way to Auvergne, and wander over its marvellous
display of cones, craters and lava-rivers. Each one
of them climbs to the plateau of Prudelle, and from
its level surface gazes in admiration across the vast
fertile plain of the Limagne on the one side, and
up to the chain of the puys on the other. Yet
how few of them connect that scene with one of
the great triumphs of their science, or know that
it was there that Desmarest began the observations
which directly led to the fierce contest over the origin
of basalt !

That cautious observer tells us that amidst the
infinite variety of objects around him, he drew no
inference from this first occurrence of columns, but
that his attention was aroused. He was kept no
long time in suspense on the subject. "On the
way back from the Puy de Dôme," he tells us, "I
followed the thin sheet of black stone and recognised
in it the characters of a compact lava. Considering
further the thinness of this crust of rock, with its
underlying bed of scoriæ, and the way in which it
extended from the base of hills that were obviously
once volcanoes, and spread out over the granite, I
saw in it a true lava-stream which had issued from
one of the neighbouring volcanoes. With this idea
in my mind, I traced out the limits of the lava,
and found again everywhere in its thickness the

faces and angles of the columns, and on the top their cross-section, quite distinct from each other. I was thus led to believe that prismatic basalt belonged to the class of volcanic products, and that its constant and regular form was the result of its ancient state of fusion. I only thought then of multiplying my observations, with the view of establishing the true nature of the phenomenon, and its conformity with what is to be found in Antrim— a conformity which would involve other points of resemblance."

He narrates the course of his discoveries as he journeyed into the Mont Dore, detecting in many places fresh confirmation of the conclusion he had formed. But not only did he convince himself that the prismatic basalts of Auvergne were old lava-streams, he carried his induction much further and felt assured that the Irish basalts must also have had a volcanic origin. "I could not doubt," he says, "after these varied and repeated observations, that the groups of prismatic columns in Auvergne belonged to the same conformation as those of Antrim, and that the constant and regular form of the columns must have resulted from the same cause in both regions. What convinced me of the truth of this opinion was the examination of the material constituting the Auvergne columns with that from the Giant's Causeway, which I found to agree in texture, colour and hardness, and further, the sight of two engravings of the Irish locality which at once recalled the scenery of parts of Mont Dore. I draw, from this recognised resemblance and the facts that establish it, a deduction which appears to be justified by the strength of the analogy—namely, that in the Giant's Causeway, and in all the prismatic masses which present themselves along the cliffs of the Irish coast, in short even among the truncated summits of the interior, we see the operations of one or more volcanoes which are extinct, like those of Auvergne. Further, I am fully persuaded that in general these groups of polygonal columns are an infallible proof of an old volcano, wherever the stone composing them has a compact texture, spangled with brilliant points, and a black or grey tint."

Here, then, was a bold advance in theoretical as well as observational geology. Not only was the discovery of Guettard confirmed, that there had once been active volcanoes in the heart of France, but materials were obtained for explaining the origin of certain enigmatical rocks which, though they had been found over a large part of Europe, had hitherto remained a puzzle to mineralogists. This explanation, if it were confirmed, would show how widely volcanic action prevailed over countries wherein no sign of an eruption has been witnessed since the earliest ages of human history.

Desmarest was in no hurry to publish his discovery. Unlike some modern geologists, who rush in hot haste into print, and overload the literature of the science with narratives of rapid and imperfect observations, he kept his material beside him, revolving the subject in his mind, and seeking all the information that he could bring to bear upon it. He tells us that

in the year following his journey in Auvergne, he spent
the winter in Paris, and while there, laid before the
Intendant of Auvergne the desirability of having the
volcanic region mapped. His proposition was accepted,
and Pasumot, one of the state surveyors, was entrusted
with the task of making a topographical map of the
region from Volvic to beyond Mont Dore.   The
whole of the summer of 1764 was taken up with
this work. Desmarest accompanied the geographer,
who himself had a large acquaintance with the mineralogy of his day.   The final result was the production
of a map which far surpassed anything of the kind
that had before been attempted, in the accuracy,
variety, and clearness of its delineations of volcanic
phenomena.

   At last, in the summer of 1765, after two years
of reflection, Desmarest communicated to the Academy
of Sciences at Paris the results at which he had arrived.
But even then he showed his earnest desire for the
utmost accuracy and fulness attainable. He kept back
his paper from publication. Next year he returned
to Auvergne, after a prolonged journey through the
volcanic regions of Italy, from the Vicentin and Padua
southwards to Naples and Vesuvius. In 1769 he
once more revisited the volcanoes of Central France,
extending his excursions into the Cantal.   In the early
part of the summer of 1771 he again brought before
the Academy the results of his researches on the origin
and nature of basalt, embodying in his Memoir the
mass of material which his extended travel and mature
reflection had enabled him to bring together.   But
it was not until three years later, viz., in 1774, that

his long-delayed essay at last appeared in the annual volume of the *Memoirs of the Academy*. Life was more placid in those times than it has since become. The feverish haste to be famous, and the frantic struggle for priority, which are now unhappily so rampant, were but little known in Desmarest's days. He kept his work eleven years beside him, enriching it continually with fresh observations drawn from extended journeys, and thus making his conclusions rest on an ever-widening basis of accurately determined fact.

The Memoir, as finally published, was divided into three parts, two of which appeared together, the third not until three years later. In the first part, the author narrated his observations in Auvergne and other districts, bearing on the nature of basalt. It would take too much space here to follow him through his survey of the regions where he found the evidence which he brought forward. Let me refer merely to the concluding pages, in which he states his opinion as to the origin of the columnar rock which he had tracked with such diligence from district to district. His account, he remarks, would be incomplete if he did not indicate at the same time the materials which have been melted by the fire in order to produce basalt. He had collected a series of specimens of granite which he believed to represent these materials. They had undergone different degrees of alteration, some showing still their spar, quartz or other minerals, while others had partly undergone complete fusion. He had convinced himself that various other volcanic rocks besides basalt had resulted from the fusion of granite, the base of which may have been completely melted, while the quartz of the original rock remained unchanged. He was not aware that the difference of chemical composition demonstrates that the melting of granite could never have produced basalt.

These ideas, which we now know to be erroneous, might readily occur to the early observers. It is undoubtedly true that pieces of more or less completely melted granite are to be found among the ejections of old volcanoes, and the inference would not unnaturally suggest itself that if our artificial fires, kindled by the combustion of carbonaceous substances, are sufficient to melt rocks, the far more gigantic conflagrations of such combustible materials, caused by natural processes in the bowels of the earth, when concentrated at one point underneath a volcano, may fuse the surrounding and overlying rocks, and expel streams of molten material. We shall find that Werner adopted this antiquated opinion, and that through him it became predominant over Europe, even after more enlightened conceptions of the subject had been announced. Desmarest does not, indeed, seem to have had at this time, if ever, any very definite conception of the origin of the high temperature within volcanic reservoirs. Nor had chemistry yet afforded much assistance in ascertaining the resemblances and differences among rocks and minerals. His mistakes were thus a faithful reflex of the limited knowledge of the period in which he wrote.

In the second part of his Memoir, Desmarest gives a historical narrative of all that had been written before his time on the subject of basalt. The most interesting and important passages in this retrospect are the com-

ments of the author on the writings which he summarises, and the additions which he is thereby enabled
to make to the observations already given by him.
He confesses that, had he begun his investigations
among such isolated patches of basalt as those capping
the hills in Cassel and Saxony, he would never have
been able to affirm that basalt is only a lava. But he
had encountered such perfect demonstration of the
volcanic nature of the rock, tracing it with its fresh
scoriæ up to the very craters whence it flowed, that
he could not allow this clear evidence to be invalidated,
or even weakened, by cases where the volcanic origin
had been more or less obscured.

It is at this point in his investigation that the genius
of Desmarest shines with a brilliance far above that of
any of his Continental contemporaries who concerned
themselves with geological problems. Guettard had
clearly indicated the volcanic origin of the puys of
Auvergne, and no great acumen was needed to follow
up the clue which he had thus given. But to trace a
pathway through the maze of lavas of many different
ages, to unite and connect them all in one method of
interpretation, and thus to remove the endless difficulties and harmonise the many apparent contradictions
which beset the investigation, was a task which called
forth the highest powers of observation and induction.
Among the many claims of France to the respect and
gratitude of all students of geology, there is assuredly
none that ought to be more frankly recognised than
that, in her wide and fair domain, she possessed a
region where the phenomena were displayed in un-
rivalled perfection, and that in Desmarest she could

claim a son gifted with the skill, patience, imagination, and originality that qualified him so admirably for the laborious task which he undertook. His achievements form one of the most notable landmarks in the early history of geology.

Desmarest, wandering over the volcanic districts of Central France, had been profoundly impressed, as every traveller must be, by the extraordinary varieties in the condition of the various lava-currents. Some of these sheets of rock retain still the dark, verdureless, rugged surfaces which they assumed ages ago when their molten floods stiffened into stone. Others have lost their covering of scoriæ, and are seen clinging to the sides of valleys, in positions which seem impossible for any lava-current to have taken. Others are perched in solitary outlying sheets on the tops of plateaux, with no cone near them, nor any obvious source from which they could have flowed.

Pondering on these apparently contradictory phenomena, Desmarest, with the inspiration of true genius, seized on the fruitful principle that would alone explain them. He saw that the varying conditions of the several lavas were due to the ceaseless influence of atmospheric denudation. He convinced himself that the detached outliers of basalt, capping the ridges and plateaux are really remnants of once continuous sheets of lava, and that their isolation, together with the removal of their original covering of scoriæ and slags, is to be ascribed to the operations of rain and melted snow. The depth of the valleys cut through these lava-platforms was found by him to be commensurate with the antiquity of the lavas, and with the size of the streams that flowed between the severed escarpments.

He ascertained that, in proportion to their antiquity, the lava-streams had lost, one after another, the usual outward features of the younger sheets. The superficial scoriæ had disappeared, and the craters were worn away, until only scattered outliers of compact dark rock remained. Yet between this extreme and that of the most recent eruptions, where the lavas, in unbroken, rugged, cavernous sheets, extend from their craters down into the present valleys, where they have driven aside the running streams, every intermediate stage could be found.

Thus the doctrine of the origin of valleys by the erosive action of the streams which flow in them, though it has been credited to various writers,[1] was first clearly taught from actual concrete examples by

[1] Thus by Lyell and Murchison it was ascribed to H. B. de Saussure, Playfair, and Montlosier, *Edin. New Phil. Journ.* vol. vii. (1829), p. 15. In England it has been more commonly assigned to Hutton and Playfair, and to Scrope. The ascription of the doctrine to Montlosier was singularly unfortunate. That writer states that it had been the labour of his life (he was 34 years of age at the time he wrote) to study the valley system of Auvergne, and that he was on the point of publishing his opinion that the valleys have been carved out by the streams which still flow in them, when he discovered that De Saussure had already published the same conclusion. De Saussure's second volume from which Montlosier quotes was published in 1786. But Desmarest's memoir, in which the subaerial origin of the Auvergne valleys was proclaimed, had appeared some twelve years earlier. Montlosier was acquainted with that Memoir, for he cites it more than once. The doctrine of the carving out of valleys by atmospheric denudation became a prominent part of Hutton's theory of the earth. See also *ante*, p. 121, for Guettard's views.

Desmarest.   The first attempt to trace back the history
of a landscape, to show its successive phases, and to
connect them all with the continuous operation of the
same causes which are still producing like effects, was
made by this illustrious native of France.

So satisfied was Desmarest with the proofs furnished
by Auvergne regarding the volcanic origin of basalt,
that he coined the term " basalt-lava," with an apology
to the mineralogists, and remarked that when once
the characters of this rock have been appreciated, it
may be recognised everywhere, in spite of the most
stupendous degradation.   Casting his eye over the
map of Europe, and noting the localities from which
the occurrence of basalt had been reported, he saw
two great regions of ancient volcanic activity in the
heart of the continent.   One of these lay to the east,
along the confines of Saxony and Bohemia into Silesia,
from Freiberg to Lignitz ; the other stretched from
the Rhine above Cologne, through Nassau, Hesse-
Darmstadt, and Cassel.

The map which has been already referred to as
accompanying this remarkable memoir, depicts with
great clearness the grouping of the volcanoes over a
large part of Auvergne.   It represents them by distinct
kinds of engraving, so as to show four classes differing
from each other in age and other characters.   The
first of these classes includes the younger lava-streams,
not yet cut through by running water, and still connected with their parent cones.   The second embraces
those lavas which bear decomposed earthy materials
on their surface, and from which their original craters
have disappeared.   In the third class are ranged those

lavas which have been reduced to detached outliers separated by valleys; while in the fourth, some isolated masses are placed which Desmarest thought had been " melted in place," or erupted where they now appear.

The third part of the memoir, though read with the second part in 1771, was not published until 1777. In this essay the author discussed the basalt of the ancients, and the natural history of the various kinds of stones to which at different times the term basalt had been applied.

It is interesting to follow the slow elaboration of his views through his successive memoirs. We must remember that, during those busy years, his time and thoughts were chiefly taken up with the inquiries into industrial development which the Government of the day had entrusted to him, and which necessitated frequent and prolonged journeys, not only in France, but in other countries of Europe. Being convinced that the great questions in physical geography which specially occupied his attention could best be studied in Auvergne, he returned to that region at every available opportunity, revisiting again and again localities already familiar to him, and testing his deductions by fresh appeals to nature. Four years after his great monograph on the origin of basalt had been read to the Academy of Sciences, he presented another essay, developing still further the ideas of denudation and successive eruptive periods which had been briefly sketched in his first communication. The scope of this new effort may be judged of from its full title: " On the Determination of Three Epochs of Nature from the Products of Volcanoes, and on the Use that

may be made of these Epochs in the Study of Volcanoes." This essay was laid before the Academy
in the year 1775. An extract from it appeared after
the lapse of four years,[1] but the full paper was not
published until the year 1806[2]—no less than thirty-one
years after its original preparation. During this long
interval the controversy about the origin of basalt
had extended over most of the countries of Europe,
and had involved the very subjects of which Desmarest
treated. He himself, keenly as the matters in dispute
interested him, took no part in the warfare. In his
memoir he ignores the combatants and their strife,
but quietly repeats and strengthens statements which
he had published a generation before, and which, had
they been properly considered and verified, would have
prevented any controversy from ever arising. This
dispute will further occupy our attention in later
pages of this volume. In the meantime let us consider
the character of Desmarest's long-delayed contribution
to the literature and theory of geology.

The progress of his investigations had led him to
perceive the necessity of correlating the various phenomena connected with ancient volcanoes, and especially
with reference to the questions of their relative age and
of the alterations they have undergone from exposure
to the elements. The facts known to him suggested
an arrangement of them into three groups or epochs,
which were not meant to imply definite periods of
time or precise dates, but would express the idea of

---

[1] *Journal de Physique,* tome xiii. (1779), p. 115.

[2] *Mém. de l'Instit. des Sciences Math. et Phys.* tome vi. (1806), p. 219.
It was read again on 1st Prairial, An XII (20th May, 1804).

a recognisable succession of events. His researches
had assured him that the volcanic history of Auvergne
" formed a whole, which, though incomplete, showed
that Nature had followed the same order of procedure
in the most remote ages as in the most recent times."

In co-ordinating the appearances presented by the
different volcanic masses, he began with the consideration of what were obviously the youngest, on the
principle that the last operations of Nature are simpler,
and have undergone less modification from the influences which are continually changing the face of
the land. He perceived that volcanoes are only temporary accidents in the midst of the ordinary and
normal operations of nature, that the materials erupted
by volcanoes, at various intervals from a remote
antiquity, must have suffered from the universal
degradation, and that the extent of their waste would
be proportionate to the length of time during which
the loss had been continued. The latest lavas must
unquestionably present most nearly the primitive forms
of volcanic masses, and should thus serve as a standard
for comparison, to be kept before the eyes of every
observer who would judge correctly of the extent and
progress of the alteration that is to be seen in other
regions.

The first of his three periods includes the products
of still active and recently extinct volcanoes. These
are distinguished by the association of crater-bearing
cones of cinders and scoriæ, with streams of rugged
lava, which can be followed from the cones into the
surrounding country over which they have flowed.
The most modern lava-streams are not cut through

by valleys, but form continuous sheets. Yet within
the limits of this first epoch proofs of alteration manifest themselves. The loose scoriæ and cinders are
washed down to lower levels, the cones are attacked
and the lavas begin to be trenched. As these changes
advance, the flow of running water gradually cuts
through the sheets of lava, and forms valleys across
them. The epoch embraced all the ages required
for this erosion, and during its continuance repeated
outflows of lava took place. Each of these currents
of melted rock would seek the lowest levels, and would
thus mark the valley-bottom of its time, in the long
process of excavation.

In the records of the second epoch, the scoriæ and
ashes have been swept away, the cones have entirely
disappeared, and the streams of lava have been cut
into separate patches by the erosion of the valleys,
above which they are now left perched as high plains
or plateaux. Notwithstanding the stupendous results
thus achieved, Desmarest seeks no vast terrestrial disturbance to account for them. He finds their explanation in the working of the very same meteoric agents
which are still carrying on the same process of degradation. The cellular parts of the lavas, under the
influence of the weather, crumble down into mere
loose earth, which is easily washed away by rain and
melted snow, leaving only the harder and more
resisting core of more solid rock. In like manner,
the loose materials of the cones are removed, until
perhaps only masses of lava remain behind that may
have solidified at their bottoms. By this series of
operations an entire transformation is wrought on the

face of the country. Lavas which originally covered the floors of valleys, as the ground around them is lowered, are at last turned into high tablelands, and are still further cut through and separated into detached portions, according to the multiplication and deepening of the ravines and valleys by which they are traversed. To realise the ancient continuity of these venerable lava-sheets, we must in imagination fill up the valleys, and thus restore the slope or plain over which the molten rock originally flowed.

As all the scoriæ and craters are gone, the only way of detecting an eruptive centre in the volcanic products of this epoch is to find the point of common origin for several streams, such points being often marked by large isolated patches of lava (culots).

Desmarest arrives at the important conclusion that the lavas of his second epoch were erupted before the excavation of the present valleys out of the original plain over which the streams of basalt were poured. The volcanic events of which they are the memorials must thus go back to a remote antiquity, for the erosion of valleys is obviously an exceedingly slow process. But these lavas are evidently much younger than the horizontal sedimentary strata and the granite which these strata overlie, both of these groups of rock being also trenched by the valleys.

The third and most ancient epoch is denoted by a series of lavas, which, instead of overlying the sedimentary strata, underlie them or are interstratified with them. These sediments are now recognized as the deposits of one of the old Tertiary lakes of Europe. Their layers are full of land-plants, land and fresh-

water shells, and remains of terrestrial mammals.   But
to Desmarest they were proofs of the former presence
of the sea over the heart of France.   He inferred that
the pebbles of various lavas which he found among
these strata denoted former volcanic eruptions, before
the accumulation of the marine deposits.   But he
noticed also indications of the discharge of lava
during the sojourn of the sea over this region.   He
believed that his third epoch must have lasted some
considerable time, so as to permit the deposition of
600 or 900 feet of horizontal sediments above the
lowest lavas.[1]

He remarks that from ignorance of this method of
following the sequence of eruptions and the effects
of continuous waste, naturalists had failed to detect
the existence of lavas of the second and third epochs
in districts where eruptions of the first epoch were
no longer to be recognized.   These observers, he
contended, had misread the evidence of nature,
referring what were undoubtedly volcanic rocks to
deposition from water, to schists, and to *pierre de
corne*, and on the other hand mistaking for volcanic
craters what were only hollows dug out by running
water in the lavas of the second, or even of the first
epoch.

[1] In the article "Auvergne" in his *Géographie Physique*, p. 882
(published in 1803), he briefly summarises his three epochs thus—"I
have distinguished three kinds of volcanoes in Auvergne, first, ancient
volcanoes; second, modern volcanoes; and third, submarine volcanoes." Probably most of the lavas of his third epoch are rather
of the nature of intrusive sills.   The subject of ancient volcanic
rocks interstratified among sedimentary deposits is discussed in
chapter viii.

The sagacity of these generalisations has been amply sustained by the reseaches of later times. Alike in volcanic geology and in the doctrines of denudation, the labours of Desmarest marked the rise of a new era in the investigation of the past history of the earth. They showed how patient detailed research could solve some of the most transcendently interesting problems in geology, and how the minute and philosophical investigation of one small area of the globe could furnish principles of universal application.

In one respect, perhaps, this far-seeing observer seems to have been almost afraid to push his views of denudation to their logical conclusion. There occur in Central France many flat, isolated areas of basalt, capping detached hills and fragments of plateaux, not apparently connected with any visible lava-current or centre of eruption. The origin of these patches (called by him "culots"), was explained by supposing them to mark the positions of volcanic vents up which the melted material had risen without flowing out, and where it had solidified within the crater, being retained by the encircling wall of scoriæ and cinders. The removal of the surrounding loose material would, he thought, leave the lava as a cake with steep scarped sides crowning the slopes below. Possibly some of his culots originated in the way supposed, but there can be little doubt that most of them are remnants of lava-streams reduced to almost the last stage by the progress of denudation.

From the long intervals which he allowed to elapse between the presentation of his papers to the Academy and their final publication, it might be supposed that

Desmarest was probably of a procrastinating, possibly even of an indolent, temperament. Yet, when we consider the amount of work, official and scientific, which he accomplished, we must acquit him of such an imputation.   His voluminous reports on the various industries of France show how actively and zealously he laboured in his official harness.   But perhaps the best proof of his indefatigable industry was his colossal *Géographie Physique*, which he undertook as part of the famous *Encyclopédie Méthodique* founded by Diderot and D'Alembert.   The exhaustive treatment of his subject may be inferred from the fact that after devoting to it four massive quarto volumes of from 700 to 900 pages each, he had only got to the letter N when death closed his labours.

The first volume of this great work is in many respects the most interesting.   The author in his preface tells how he means to exclude from his task all discussion of theories of the earth, for, as he frankly confesses, he had long looked upon these theories as utterly opposed to the principles of Physical Geography.   But on second thoughts, as unfortunately such theories really existed, having much the same relation to Physical Geography that fable bears to history, he had resolved to give a summary of the subject, thus conforming to the practice of some writers who begin their histories with a brief mention of the heroic times.[1]   Accordingly he devotes the first volume to notices of the more important authors who had treated of his subject, excluding those who were still alive.   He made, however, exceptions to

---

[1] *Géographie Physique*, vol. i. (1794), preface.

this exclusion in favour of Pallas and Hutton. Though he undertook to present merely an impartial summary of the opinions of other writers, it is instructive to have these summaries from the hand of a man like Desmarest, who was contemporary with many of those of whom he discourses. The interspersed comment and criticism in his notices are specially valuable.

The other three volumes were devoted to descriptions of places, districts, and countries, and to articles or subjects in Physical Geography—a branch of knowledge which Desmarest regarded as embracing two equally important and closely related subjects—the interior structure of the globe and its external form. Geology was not yet admitted to a formal place among the sciences, but geological questions occupy a prominent place in the massive quartos of the *Encyclopédie Méthodique*.[1]

The delays that attended the publication of Desmarest's important and original observations and deductions respecting the volcanic geology of Auvergne reached their climax in the case of his detailed map of that region. We have seen that at his instigation a topographical survey of Auvergne on a large scale was begun as far back as 1764, and that reductions of this map accompanied his Memoirs presented to the

[1] Vol. i. of the *Géographie Physique* appeared in An III (1794); vol. ii. in 1803 ; vol. iii. in 1809, and vol. iv. in 1811. Among the geological articles of interest in these volumes reference may be made to those on Antrim, Auvergne, Basalte, Chaussée des Géans, and Courans. Vol. v., left unfinished by Desmarest, was continued by Bory de St. Vincent, Doin, Ferry, and Huot, and was not published until 1828.

Academy of Sciences.   The map itself, however, with
all its elaborate detail, bearing on the history of the
volcanoes of Central France, still remained in his
hands.   Year after year he sought to bring it nearer
to his ideal of perfection.   Every part of the region
had been scrupulously examined by him, every puy
was set down, every crater was carefully drawn, every
current of lava was traced out from its source to its
termination, every detached area of basalt was faith-
fully represented.   By a system of hachures and signs
the modern and ancient lavas were discriminated.   But
he still kept the work back, and when he died it
remained unpublished.

Of all his contributions to the progress of geology,
this map must be considered the most memorable.
It was the compendium of all his toil in Auvergne,
and showed, as in a model, the structure of the country
which he had so patiently and successfully elucidated.
The reduced map published in his first Memoir and
the portions of the map issued with his second Memoir,
were all that he allowed to appear in his lifetime,
but they failed to impress the minds of his contemporaries, as the entire map would have done, with
its complete and clear delineation of the whole district.
Labouring after a perfection which he could not attain,
he not only lost the credit which the map would
have brought him in his lifetime, but he retarded
the progress of the sound views which he himself
held and wished to see prevail.   Had this truly admirable map been published by him, together with a
general description of the volcanoes depicted on it, his
name would have been placed at once and by universal

assent at the head of the geologists of his day, and the miserable controversy about the nature of basalt would either never have arisen, or could have been speedily set at rest. Cuvier tells us that Desmarest himself was fully conscious of the desirability of publishing the map, but his life slipped away as he still aimed at further improvement of it. Yet he could not bear that other observers should enter his volcanic region and describe its features. It used to be said that he seemed to look on Auvergne as his own property, and certainly he was the legitimate owner of many of the observations made there after him.

Cuvier, who knew him well and who had watched with interest his declining years, gives us a vivid picture of Desmarest. The illustrious geologist was little fitted to push his way in a society where the most successful art was that of self-advertisement. He took no more pains about his private interest than he did about his rights in regard to scientific discovery, importuning neither the dispensers of fortune nor those of fame. With his crust and his cheese, he said, he needed no Government help to visit the manufactories or the mountains. In short, in studying all the processes of art, all the forces of nature, he had entirely neglected those arts that sway the world, because nothing which agitates the world could move him. Even works of wit and imagination remained unknown to him, because they did not lie within the range of his studies. His friends used jocularly to affirm that he would have broken the most beautiful statue in order to ascertain the nature of an antique stone, and this character was so widely given to him

that at Rome the keepers of the museums felt some
alarm in admitting him.   In society, too, things, whatever they might be, affected him on one side only.
For instance, when an Englishman was recounting
at the house of the Duchesse d'Anville the then recent
thrilling incident in Cook's first voyage, when his
vessel, pierced by a point of rock, was only saved
from sinking by the stone breaking off and remaining
fixed in the hole, every one present expressed in his
own way the interest he felt in the story.   Desmarest,
however, quietly inquired whether the rock was basaltic
or calcareous.

A character so little affected by external things
was naturally immovable in regard to relations and
habits.   From the earliest days when he began to
be known, he had been engaged to pass his Sundays
at Auteuil with a friend.   Ever afterwards he would
appear there on the usual day, even when his friend
was dead, and when age no longer allowed him to
enjoy the country ; and as he had from the first
gone on foot, he always went there on foot until he
was eighty-five years old.   All that his family could
then prevail upon him to do was to take a carriage.

Nor was he less constant in more trivial affairs.
Never did he dine or go to bed later one day than
another.   Nobody remembered ever to have seen him
change the cut of his clothes, and down to his last
days his wig and his coat recalled the fashions in
vogue under the Cardinal de Fleury.

After recalling his kindliness and helpfulness to
poor inventors, for whom he ever evinced the heartiest
sympathy, his biographer concludes in eloquent words,

with which I may fitly close this sketch of Desmarest's career. "The Academy of Sciences saw in him, as it were, the monument of a bygone age, one of those old philosophers, now too few, who occupied only with science, did not waste themselves in the ambitions of the world, nor in rambling through too wide a range of study, men more envied than imitated, who have supplied us with that succession of octogenarians and nonagenarians, of which our history is full. Living like these worthies, Desmarest fulfilled a similar career, and reached, without infirmities or any grave malady, the age of ninety years. He died on the 20th September 1815.

"During his protracted lifetime, he saw the Academy twice renewed. Among so large a number of colleagues he doubtless recognised that there were many who equalled or even surpassed him in enlightenment or in mental power, but he had the happiness to be assured that his name would last as long as that of any one among them."

For the sake of continuity in the narrative, I have traced the labours of Desmarest from their beginning to their close without adverting to those of his contemporaries. His views regarding the volcanic origin of Basalt were adopted by a number of good observers, among whom reference may be made to Raspe,[1]

[1] R. E. Raspe (1737-1794) had a singularly eventful life. Born in Hanover of poor parents, he obtained his education at the Universities of Göttingen and Leipzig, and obtained an appointment at the latter, where he translated the philosophical works of Leibnitz. After various changes of occupation, he became keeper of the collection of antique gems and medals, and began to study geological subjects. In 1769 he communicated to the Royal Society of London a paper

Fortis,[1] Dolomieu,[2] Faujas de St. Fond, Montlosier, and Breislak.[3]   But a still more numerous and more

on the former existence of mammoths in the northern regions, and was afterwards elected an honorary Fellow of the Society. His industry and the wide range of subjects on which he employed his facile pen were truly remarkable.   In 1775, after being sent to Italy to collect antiquities and other objects for the Landgrave of Hesse, he was accused of peculation, and was arrested.   He succeeded, however, in escaping to England and spent there the remainder of his life.   He spoke and wrote English well, and among the works which he published in this country was an interesting little volume entitled *An Account of some German Volcanoes and their Productions* (1776). Turning his knowledge of minerals to account, he obtained a precarious, and apparently not always honest, livelihood as a mining prospector.   He is understood to have been the prototype of Dousterswivel in Scott's novel *The Antiquary*.   But his chief title to fame must be admitted to be his authorship of the original *Baron Munchausen's Travels*.   He had finally to escape to a remote part of Ireland, and died at Muckross in 1794.

[1] J. B. A. Fortis (1741-1803) was born at Padua and was educated for the church in the order of St. Augustine, but was eventually allowed to spend his time in travel, which he did with much success in regard to the natural history and antiquities of Dalmatia and the other tracts visited by him.   He was not only a naturalist and learned man, but also a poet and author of verses on love and friendship.   He wrote many papers on the geology of different parts of Northern Italy.   Having accompanied Desmarest in his excursion through the volcanic parts of that region, he adopted the views of the French geologist as to the origin of basalt, but he indulged his fancy in supposing the heat caused by the eruptions of the Vicentin to have been so great as to raise the temperature of the Adriatic to such a degree as to permit tropical species to live in its waters.   His *Mémoires pour servir à l'Histoire Naturelle et principalement à l'Oryctographie de l'Italie et des pays adjacents* were published in two volumes at Paris in 1802.

[2] See *postea*, p. 254.

[3] For notices of these geologists, see *postea*, pp. 255-258.

blatant band, urged on its way by Werner, opposed these doctrines. Although the controversy raged through Desmarest's life, he took, as I have said, no share in it. He made an occasional allusion to the disorder and confusion that had been introduced into a question which in itself was simple enough to those who knew how to look at the actual facts. He asked reproachfully what would become of natural history and mineralogy, if every question were treated as that concerning Basalt had been ? And he wrote somewhat scornfully of the authors who, without having ever undertaken any researches of the kind themselves, ventured in discussing those of others to indulge in unfounded hypotheses.[1] When any belated straggler from the enemy's camp came to consult Desmarest on the subject in dispute, the old man would content himself with the answer, "Go and see."

Leaving this controversy for subsequent consideration in connection with its later developments, I will pass from the subject for the present, for the purpose of calling attention in the following chapter to a contemporary event which was one of the most interesting features in the scientific life of the latter half of the eighteenth century—the rise of the spirit of scientific travel.

[1] See the article "Basalte" in vol. iii. of the *Géographie Physique*, published 1809.

CHAPTER VI

OF all the physical events that happened in the latter
half of the eighteenth century, there was probably none
so fruitful in fostering, among the civilized countries
of the world, an emulation in discovery and research,
as the transit of Venus, which occurred in the summer
of 1769. To that event we owe the voyages of Cook,
and all the rich harvest of results which they added
to our knowledge of the geography of the globe.
What England did on the ocean, it was reserved for
Russia to rival on the land. The Empress Catherine
II. had been irritated by the sarcastic remarks made
by a French astronomer who had travelled to Russia
to observe the previous transit of Venus in 1763, and
she is even said to have been at the trouble of refuting
them herself. At all events, she resolved to do without foreign assistance for the second transit. Determined that the work should be done thoroughly, and in
such a way as to redound to the glory of her reign, she
commissioned the Academy of Sciences of St. Petersburg to organize the expedition. This undertaking
was conceived in a truly imperial spirit. Not only

were astronomers sent out for the more immediate objects of the research, but advantage was taken of the occasion to despatch a competent band of observers for the purpose of penetrating into every region of the vast empire, and making known its condition and resources.

The instructions drawn up for the guidance of the explorers were of the most exhaustive kind. Accurate observations were to be made in the geography and meteorology of each region visited, the positions of the principal places were to be astronomically determined, the nature of the soils, the character of the waters, and the best means of reclaiming the waste places were to be accurately observed. The travellers were to enquire into the rocks and minerals, and to attend to the outer forms and internal composition of the mountains. They were further to carry on careful researches among the plants and animals of each territory, and, in short, to obtain as much accurate information as possible in every department of natural history. Nor were the social problems of life forgotten. The expedition was further instructed to pay special attention to the various races of mankind met with in the journeys, and to report on their manners, customs, religions, forms of worship, languages, traditions, monuments and antiquities. They were likewise enjoined to take note of the condition of agriculture, of the maladies that affected man and beast, and the best remedies for them, of the cultivation of bees and silk-worms, the breeding of cattle and sheep, and generally of the occupations, arts, and industries of each province.

A survey of this complete nature, carried over so

M

vast a region as the Russian Empire, demanded much
skill, labour and time. It was fortunately entrusted
to a man in every way qualified for the task—Pierre
Simon Pallas (1741-1811). The whole expedition
comprised seven astronomers and geometers, five
naturalists and several assistants. Starting from St.
Petersburg in June 1768, they traversed the vast
empire to its remotest bounds, making many journeys
in every direction. After six years of unwearied
labour, and almost incredible suffering and privation,
during which Pallas had from time to time sent home
accounts of his more important observations, he returned in July 1774.

Never before had so large a store of observations
in all departments of natural history, extending over
so wide a region of the earth's surface, been gathered
in so brief a time. Pallas wrote his results in German
(his native language, for he was born at Berlin), and
sent them home as they were ready. They were
published at St. Petersburg between 1772 and 1776,
in three quarto volumes. Translated into French,
the work afterwards appeared at Paris during the
years from 1788 to 1793,[1] in five handsome quartos,
with a folio atlas of plates.

Pallas was an accomplished naturalist, and made
some original and valuable contributions to zoology.
But it is only with his geological work that we are
here concerned. One of the geological questions
which especially interested him was the occurrence of
the remains of huge pachyderms in the superficial

[1] Another edition of this translation appeared in 8 volumes 8vo,
and was reprinted at Bâle in 1806.

deposits of the north of Siberia. These remains, as far back as the later years of the seventeenth century, had been known to exist, for a trade in the ivory tusks of fossil elephants from the Siberian coasts and rivers had before that time been carried on. The actual bones of these animals were subsequently disinterred by observers capable of describing their mode of occurrence, so that Pallas had his curiosity much excited by the accounts which had already been published. There was still much to be found out regarding these strange relics of the frozen north, and Pallas determined to investigate the subject in the fullest detail. He kept his eye open for every trace of fossils of any kind, and one of the most valuable parts of his labours is to be seen in the precision with which he chronicles every fossiliferous locality. But the most astonishing feature of his journeys in this respect was the proofs he obtained of the almost incredible number of bones and tusks of the huge pachyderms. The whole vast basin of Siberia lying to the east of the Ural mountains, and north of the Altai chain to the shores of the Arctic Ocean, was found by him to be, as it were, strewn with these remains. He noticed that the bones belonged to species of elephant, rhinoceros and buffalo, and in one case he saw parts of the carcase of a rhinoceros still retaining its leather-like skin and its short hairs. From the abundance of hair on some parts of the skin of these animals, he inferred that the rhinoceros of Siberia could live in a more temperate climate than its living representatives now enjoy.

But undoubtedly the most important contribution made by Pallas to geological investigation is to be found in his memoir on the formation of mountains and the changes that have taken place on the globe, particularly with regard to the Empire of Russia.[1] The highest mountains, he remarked, are composed of granite, with various schists, serpentine, grits, and other bedded masses in vertical or highly inclined positions. These formed his Primitive band, and in his opinion were older than the creation of organized beings, for no trace of organic remains was to be found in any part of them.

The primitive schistose band of the great chains is immediately succeeded by the calcareous band, which consists first of solid masses of limestone, either containing no marine productions or only slight traces of them. The thick beds of limestone are placed at high angles and parallel to the direction of the chain, which is also generally that of the schistose band. As they recede from the line of the mountains, the limestones rapidly sink down into a horizontal position, and soon appear full of shells, corals and other marine organisms. These upheaved limestones form the Secondary mountains of Pallas. A third series of rocks, which seemed to him to be the record of some of the latest revolutions of the globe, consists of sandstones, marls, and various other strata, forming a chain of lower hills in front of the limestone range. To this series of deposits he gave the name of Tertiary mountains.[2]

[1] *Act. Acad. Sci. Imp. Petropolit.* 1777, pp. 21-64.

[2] A threefold classification of the rocks was also made by Arduino in Northern Italy and by Lehmann in Germany, as will be more particularly referred to in the following chapter.

These geological terms, thus proposed by Pallas, were not of course used by him in their more precise modern definition. We know, for example, that his Tertiary mountains consisted mainly of the younger Palæozoic sediments which are now called Permian, and that with these ancient formations he included the much younger sands and clays that inclose the remains of mammoth, rhinoceros and other extinct mammals.

The main value of his observations lies in his clear recognition of a geological sequence in passing from the centre to the outside of a mountain-chain. He saw that the oldest portions' were to be found along the axis of the chain, and the youngest on the lower grounds on either side. He recognized also that the sea had left abundant proofs of its former presence on the land, he thought that its level had never been more than 100 fathoms higher than at present, and he supposed that the elevation of the mountains had been caused by commotions of the globe.[1]

We now pass from the Ural chain, which served Pallas as his type of mountain-structure, to another and more famous group of mountains, where, during the same period, another not less zealous explorer was at work. The labours of De Saussure among the Alps mark an epoch, not only in the investigation of the history of the globe, but in the relations of civilized mankind to the mountains which diversify the surface of the land.

Up till towards the end of the eighteenth century

[1] See the summary of Pallas's views given by D'Archiac in his *Cours de Paléontologie Stratigraphique*, p. 159, 1862. For a fuller exposition consult *Journal de Physique*, xiii. (1779), pp. 329-350.

mountain-scenery was usually associated in men's minds with ideas of danger, and repulsion. Every reader of English literature will remember passages, alike among poets and prose-writers, wherein the strongest abhorrence is expressed for the high, rugged and desolate regions of the earth. These tracts, which seemed at that time to have in themselves no attractions, were generally looked upon as best seen from a distance, and not to be entered or traversed save on the direst compulsion.

The first step in the breaking down of this pre-judice, which we all now laugh at, was made by the scientific researches of Horace-Benedict de Saussure (1740-1799), from which we may date the rise of the modern spirit of mountaineering. He it was who first taught the infinite charm and variety of mountain-scenery, the endless multiplicity of natural phenomena there to be seen, and the enthusiasm which the mountain-world will awaken in the heart of every responsive climber. How few among the thousands who every year repair to the Alps, the Pyrenees, the Caucasus, or who find their way to the peaks of the Rocky Mountains and the Sierra Nevada, are aware of the debt they owe to the great geologist of Geneva !

De Saussure was born in that city in the year 1740. His career at college was so distinguished that at twenty years of age he became a candidate for a pro-fessorship of mathematics, and at two-and-twenty ob-tained one of philosophy. Trained in physical science, he acquired habits of exactitude in observation and reasoning, which stood him in good stead in the scientific life to which he eventually devoted himself. Botany was his first love, and after a long and fruitful devotion to other parts of the domain of science, it was to plants that he turned again at last in the closing years of his life. Amidst his laborious campaigns in the Alps, the plants of the mountains never lost their charm for him. Among the highest crests, surrounded by all that is most impressive in Nature, and occupied with the profoundest problems in the history of the globe, he would carefully gather the smallest flower and mark it with pleasure in his notebook.[1]

De Saussure's attitude towards his native mountains may be inferred from a few of the sentences with which he prefaces his immortal work. "It is the study of mountains which above all else can quicken the progress of the theory of the earth or geology. The plains are uniform, and allow the rocks to be seen only where these have been excavated by running water or by man. The high mountains, on the other hand, infinitely varied in their composition as in their forms, present gigantic natural sections wherein the order, the position, the direction, the thickness and the nature of the different formations of which they are composed, as well as the fissures which traverse them, can be seen with the greatest clearness and at one view. Nevertheless, to no purpose are these facilities of observation offered, if those who propose to study the question do not know how to consider these grand objects as a whole and in their widest relations. The sole object of most

[1] Cuvier, " Éloge de Saussure," *Éloges*, vol. i. p. 411.

travellers who call themselves naturalists is to collect curiosities ; they walk, or rather they crawl, with their eyes fixed on the ground, picking up little bits here and there, without aiming at any general observations. They are like an antiquary who at Rome, with the Pantheon and the Colosseum in front of him, should scrape the ground to seek for pieces of coloured glass without ever casting his eyes on the architecture of these superb edifices. It is not that I advise the neglect of detailed observations. On the contrary, I look upon them as the only basis of solid knowledge. But while we gather these details, I desire that we should never lose sight of the great masses, and that we should always make a knowledge of the great objects and their relations, our aim in studying their small parts.

"But to observe these mighty masses we must not content ourselves with following the high-roads, which nearly always wind through the valleys, and which never cross the mountains, save by the lowest passes. We must quit the beaten tracts, and climb to the lofty summits, whence the eye can take in at one sweep a multiplicity of objects. Such excursions are toilsome, I admit ; we must relinquish carriages, and even horses, endure great fatigue, and expose ourselves sometimes to considerable danger. Many a time the naturalist, when almost within reach of a summit on which he eagerly longs to stand, may doubt whether he has still strength enough left to reach it, or whether he can surmount the precipices which guard its approaches. But the keen fresh air which he breathes makes a balm to flow in his veins that restores him, and the expectation of the great panorama which he will enjoy, and of the new truths which it will display to him, renews his strength and his courage. He gains the top. His eyes, dazzled and drawn equally in every direction, at first know not where to fix themselves. By degrees he grows accustomed to the great light, makes choice of the objects that should chiefly occupy his attention, and determines the order to be followed in observing them. But what words can describe the sensations or the ideas with which the sublime spectacle fills the soul of the philosopher. Standing as it were above the globe, he seems to discover the forces that move it, at least he recognizes the principal agents that effect its revolutions."

De Saussure spent his life among the scenes he so enthusiastically described, studying the meteorology no less than the geology of the Alps. As regards the geological structure of mountains and the origin of their component rocks, however, he seems hardly to have advanced beyond the ideas of Pallas. He believed, with Werner, that the central granite had resulted from deposition and crystallization in the waters of a primeval ocean. The vertical or highly inclined limestones, and other strata flanking the granite, were for a long time regarded by him as still in the position in which they were originally deposited. It was only when he found among these strata layers of sand and rounded pebbles that he was driven to admit that there had been some disturbance of the earth's surface.

Like Pallas and his contemporaries generally, De Saussure never attempted to set down his observations of the distribution of the rock-formations upon a map, nor, though he had before him the excellent sections constructed by Lehmann, to which reference will be made in the following chapter, did he give definite expression to his ideas of the mutual relations of the rocks by constructing a horizontal section even of the most general and diagrammatic kind. It is thus a somewhat laborious task to gather from his *Voyages dans les Alpes* what precisely were the opinions he held in regard to tectonic questions. To him, however, so far as I have been able to discover, we owe the first adoption of the terms geology and geologist. This science had formed a part of mineralogy, and subsequently of physical geography. The earliest writer who dignified it with the name it now bears was the first great explorer of the Alps.[1]

De Saussure's theoretical views underwent some modification during the prolonged period occupied by the publication of his work, though they seem never

---

[1] In the year 1778 there appeared at the Hague the first imperfect edition of De Luc's *Lettres Physiques et Morales sur les Montagnes,* in the introduction to which the author states that for the science that treats of the knowledge of the earth he employs the designation of Cosmology. The proper word, he admits, should have been Geology, but he "could not venture to adopt it because it was not a word in use" (Preface, p. viii.). In the completed edition of his work, published the next year, he repeats his statement as to the use of the term Cosmology, yet he uses Geology in his text notwithstanding (vol. i. pp. 4, 5). In the same year (1779), De Saussure employs the term Geology in his first volume without any explanation or apology, and alludes to the geologist as if he were a well-known species of natural philosopher. (See his *Discours Préliminaire,* pp. vii., ix., xiv., xvi.)

to have advanced much, notwithstanding his constantly increasing experience and the enormous amount of observations amassed by him regarding the rocks of the mountains.

His first quarto volume appeared in 1779, the second in 1786, the third and fourth in 1796. There was thus an interval of fifteen years during which, with unwearied industry, he continued to traverse the Alps from end to end, and to multiply his notes regarding them. Yet he does not seem ever to have reached any broad conceptions of stratigraphical succession, or of orographical structure. When he came upon strata crumpled and doubled over upon themselves, he thought of crystallization in place as the cause of such irregularities. The idea of subterranean disturbance would sometimes occur to him, but for many years he dismissed it with an expression of his incredulity, remarking that "if the underground fires had been able to upraise and overturn such enormous masses, they would have left some trace of their operation, but that after the most diligent search he had been unable to discover any mineral or stone which might even be suspected to have undergone the action of these fires."[1] He had thus no conception of any operation of nature other than that of volcanoes, which could produce great disturbances of the terrestrial crust. Not only had he met with no trace of any igneous rock in the Alps, but the granite veins which he found traversing a schist, and which he at once regarded as throwing light on the origin of that rock, were believed by him to be almost

[1] *Voyages dans les Alpes,* vol. iii. (1796) p. 107.

demonstrably due to infiltration, as the granite itself
had in his opinion been formed from crystallization
in the waters of the ancient ocean.[1]

Even when he found the vertical conglomerate of
Valorsine, and recognized that it must have been
originally deposited horizontally, he refrained from
hazarding a conjecture as to the reason of its position.
"We are still ignorant," he says, "by what cause
these rocks have been tilted. But it is already an
important step, among the prodigious quantity of
vertical strata in the Alps, to have found certain
examples which we can be perfectly certain were formed
in a horizontal position."[2]

An important part of De Saussure's work among
the Alps deserves special recognition. Profoundly impressed by the power of running water in the sculpture
of the mountains, he ridiculed the notion that the
valleys had been carved out by the sea. He showed
conclusively that they could only have been excavated
by melted snow, rain and rivers. He appealed to any
map that might first come to hand in corroboration
of his opinion that the valley-system of a country
is intimately connected in origin with the system of
drainage.[3] Hutton quotes largely from the *Voyages
dans les Alpes* in support of this doctrine, which he
made so essential a part of his *Theory of the Earth*,
and which he derived from the illustrious geologist
of Switzerland.

It is interesting to notice that, among the agenda
which De Saussure inserted at the close of his last

[1] Vol. i. pp. 533 *et seq.*   [2] Vol. ii. § 690.
[3] Vol. ii. § 920.

volume, as the fruit of his long experience, he gives a chapter of suggestions as to what should be looked for in regard to organic remains among the rocks. Some of these suggestions are full of sagacity, and show that, though he had not followed them in his own researches, he recognized the importance of the advice he was giving. One of his admonitions was " to ascertain whether certain shells occur in the older rocks but not in the later, and whether it is possible by their means to fix the relative ages and eras of appearance of the different species." Another recommendation is " to compare exactly the fossil bones, shells, and plants with their living analogues and to determine whether they differ from these." [1]

One of the most interesting features of De Saussure's work is exhibited in the care with which he equipped himself for the study of the rocks of the region that he undertook to examine and describe. Petrography was at that time in a very embryonic condition. Linnaeus and Wallerius had made a beginning in the definition of rocks, but Werner's labours had hardly begun. The Swiss naturalist set himself with his usual ardour to the study, into which he introduced his accustomed order and precision. Among other aids in his researches, he devised a series of experiments in fusion, in order to determine for himself the probable origin of different rocks, and especially to enable him to decide whether certain varieties could be produced by the melting of others. It will be remembered that Desmarest had propounded the doctrine that the basalts of Auvergne had been formed by the fusion of the

[1] Vol. iv. p. 505.

underlying granite by volcanic fire. De Saussure, when he began to study these questions, was astonished to discover how little had been done in the way of experimental research into the nature of rocks. He selected various Swiss granites, and found that in no instance could he reduce them by fusion into basalt. In case there might be any deficiency in the granites of his own country, he tried the effects of a high temperature on pieces of granite which he had himself collected in Auvergne, but equally without success. He then experimented on a granite containing abundant schorl, and obtained a black vesicular glass sprinkled with the white grains of infusible quartz. He next took specimens of different porphyries, and though he got a compact black enamel, nothing appeared in the least resembling basalt, whence he concluded that it could not be from the natural fusion of such rocks as these that basalt was derived.[1]

These experiments are especially interesting, as they mark the earliest beginnings of experimental geology. The results obtained from them were negative, and De Saussure did not advance further along the path he had thus opened into a domain which was destined in future to become so fruitful. But his name must ever be had in honour for the share he took in establishing the use of direct experiment in the elucidation of geological problems. He did not live to put in practice the directions which he left for the further exploration of the Alps by those who should come after him. A disease, which perhaps took its rise from the fatigues and privations of his life among the

[1] Vol. i. p. 122-127.

mountains, began to increase upon him after his fiftieth year. It was aggravated by anxiety on account of the effect of the French Revolution on his private resources. After three successive strokes of paralysis he died in 1799 at the age of fifty-nine years.

De Saussure was the first and most illustrious of that distinguished band of geologists which Switzerland has furnished to the ranks of science. To his inspiration and example we owe the labours of Merian, Escher von der Linth, Studer, Favre, and the later and living observers who have so diligently and successfully unravelled the complicated structure of the Alps. His descriptions of a great mountain-chain form admirable models of careful observation and luminous narrative. Though he did not add much to the advancement of geological theory, he contributed largely to the stock of ascertained fact, which was so needful as a basis for theoretical speculation. The data which he collected became thus of the utmost service to those who had to work out the principles of geology. To Hutton, for example, they supplied many admirable illustrations of the geological processes on which he based his *Theory of the Earth*. It was under the guidance of the great Swiss observer that the Scottish philosopher stood in imagination on the summit of the Alps, and watched from that high tower of observation the ceaseless decay of the mountains, the never-ending erosion of the valleys, and that majestic evolution of topography which he so clearly portrayed. Among the illustrious men who contributed to plant the foundations of geology, an honoured place must always be assigned to De Saussure.

CHAPTER VII

HISTORY of the Doctrine of Geological Succession. Arduino, Lehmann, Füchsel, Werner.

IN the gradual growth of knowledge regarding the history of our globe, it is surprising how late men were in realising that this knowledge must be based not on mere speculation, but on patient investigation of what evidence can be gathered from the structure of the planet itself. Slowly and laboriously the truth was reached that the rocks which form the terrestrial crust bear witness to the passage, not of one or two, but of a whole series of revolutions, that these changes occupied vast intervals of time, and that while they varied indefinitely in their local effects from one region to another, they were but incidents in one vast onward march of development which embraced the whole globe within its influence. What we now know as the doctrine of geological succession, in other words, the history of the evolution of the earth, during a prolonged series of ages up to the present time, took shape with extreme slowness, each generation adding a little to the basis of fact and to the superstructure of inference.

There were in especial two lines of investigation along which progress could be made. On one of these, the various masses of rock that are visible over the surface of the globe had to be studied with a view to the determination of their origin and sequence. On the other line, the details of these rock-masses, and more particularly of the sedimentary series, had to be worked out, and their organic contents to be noted, in order to ascertain how far the living creatures of older times differed from those of the present. The former of these two branches of research naturally came to be pursued first. It is by far the more obvious of the two, and considerable progress had to be made in it before the very possibility of the second line of enquiry could be recognised and pursued.

We have seen that with all his sagacity and insight, Guettard gave no indication that he had any ideas as to the chronological relations of the various groups of strata which he included in his "bands." Neither he nor his contemporaries ventured to draw geological sections. We have found that even De Saussure and Pallas, though they saw that the rocks of the central part of the mountain-chains are older than those of their flanks, did not definitely express their ideas on this subject in graphic form. Desmarest had clearly perceived the evidence for a long sequence of volcanic eruptions in Central France, but he never applied this evidence towards an elucidation of the general history of the globe as a whole. Buffon too had vividly realised the pregnant idea that the earth has passed through a long evolutional history whereof the monuments are to be gathered from the structure of the

N

planet itself. But though he worked out this idea with great logical acumen and brilliant rhetoric, he had only a slender groundwork of ascertained fact on which to base his pictures of the successive stages through which the earth has passed. Such a ground-work could not be laid down without much patient detailed observation of the rocks, and a comparison of the records afforded by them in different countries. Yet even in Buffon's time the first seeds of Strati-graphy had been sown which, before the end of the eighteenth century, were to germinate in so wide an expansion of geological theory.

In tracing the history of the idea of a chronological sequence among the rocks of the earth's crust it is interesting to mark its independent origination in different countries. In regions where minerals, more especially coal-seams, had long been worked it was familiar knowledge that a certain definite order could be traced among the rock-formations. Thus in Eng-land, prolonged mining in the coal-fields led to a clear recognition not only of a local order of arrangement, but of a sequence which might be capable of wide application. The first writer in England whose obser-vations on this subject deserve to be cited is John Strachey, who contributed two papers to the *Philosophi-cal Transactions* in the years 1719 and 1725, in which he recognised the sequence of the geological formations in the south-west of the country, enumerating in their proper order the various leading subdivisions of the stratigraphical series from the Coal to the Chalk. He likewise recorded the important fact that while the Coal-strata are all more or less inclined, the overlying formations from the Red Marl upwards lie horizontally across their edges.[1]

In Italy the name of Giovanni Arduino (1713-1795) is deservedly held in honour for the share which during his long life he took in upholding the reputation of the illustrious Italian school of geology. Born near Verona, he became inspector of mines in Tuscany and finally professor of Mineralogy and Metallurgy at Venice. Among his contributions to science it may be noted that he classified the rocks of the north of Italy as Primitive, Secondary, Tertiary and Volcanic. The first of these divisions included the schists and associated masses which occupy the core of the mountains and contain no organic remains. The second comprised limestones, marls, shales and other stratified sedimentary materials, many of which are crowded with fossils. The third was made up of generally looser detritus, derived from the disintegration of the other rocks, and sometimes full of remains of terrestrial plants and animals. The volcanic group consisted of lavas and tuff accumulated by repeated eruptions and inundations of the sea. Thus to Arduino geology is indebted for the threefold classification of the rocks of the earth's crust, which amid all the changes of nomenclature, has survived down to the present time.

Johann Gottlob Lehmann (died 1767) published at Berlin in 1756 a little duodecimo volume, roughly printed on poor paper, extending to 240 pages, and bearing the title *Versuch einer Geschichte von Flötz-Gebürgen*, etc. This unpretending treatise must be ranked as one of the classics of geological literature.

[1] *Phil. Trans.* xxx. (1719) p. 968 ; xxxi. p. 395.

It gives the results of the author's own observations
among the rocks of the Harz and the Erzgebirge.
Like Arduino he recognized three orders of mountains.
1st, Those which appeared coeval with the making of
the world; 2nd, those which arose from a general
alteration of the ground; and 3rd, those which have
been formed from time to time by local accidents.
The first order is distinguished not only by the
greater height of its members, but by their internal
structure. The rocks are less various, their strata
are not horizontal but vertical or inclined, and their
layers are neither so weak nor so multifarious as those
of the other groups. Nor are they mere superficial
deposits, but they plunge down into unknown depths
into the earth's interior. The second order, or Flötz-
gebirge, are of much younger date, and have arisen
from the successive deposit of sediments from water
that once covered their sites, these sediments being
now seen in flat sheets or strata, piled above each
other to no great height. Lehmann showed that
these sedimentary deposits contain abundant petrifactions, such as remains of wild animals, shells, plants
and trees. He gave a number of sections to show the
order in which the strata succeed each other, remarking
that the coarser sediments were generally lowest, while
limestone came at the top. His profiles of the succession of strata showed a remarkable grasp of some
of the essential features of tectonic geology. It is
singular that these suggestive examples should not
have had more imitators during the latter half of
the eighteenth century. Nothing could be more
precise and distinct than Lehmann's demonstration

of the stratified nature and aqueous origin of the younger formations of the earth's crust, or his proofs that the strata succeed each other in a definite order in the region with which he was acquainted.

Contemporary with Lehmann, and though less frequently quoted, worthy of a still higher place in the bede-roll of geological worthies was George Christian Füchsel (1722-1773).[1] This remarkable man was the son of a baker in Ilmenau, at the northern foot of the Thuringian Forest. He studied at the Universities of Jena and Leipzig, and having from an early date addicted himself to minerals and rocks, he was lucky enough to find a seam of coal at Mühlberg, near Erfurt, and still more fortunate to receive from the proprietor of the ground a reward of 200 crowns for the discovery. At Erfurt he took his degree of Doctor of Medicine, and eventually became physician to the Prince of Rudolstadt. He lived to the age of only fifty-one, and died in the year 1773.

His position at Rudolstadt was favourable for the cultivation of his taste for geological pursuits. To the south rose the ancient rocks of the Thuringer Wald, flanked by the great series of Permian and Triassic formations, regularly superposed upon each other, and cut out into valleys by the rivers that drain the mountain range. In the year 1762, when he was forty years of age, he published one of the

[1] For the personal data here given I am indebted to a brief notice by C. Keferstein in the *Journal de Géologie*, vol. ii. (1830), p. 191, and to his account of Füchsel in his *Geschichte und Litteratur der Geognosie* (1840), p. 55 *seq.*

most remarkable treatises which up to that time had
been devoted to the description of the actual structure
and history of the earth. It was in Latin, and, under
the title of "A History of the Earth and the Sea,
based on a History of the Mountains of Thuringia,"
appeared in the *Transactions of the Electoral Society
of Mayence*, established at Erfurt.[1] It was illustrated
with a geological map and sections of the country.
Eleven years later he published in German a *Sketch of
the most Ancient History of the Earth and Man*, which
contained a further development of his geological
views.[2]

These views were founded on the author's own
observations in the region where he had been born
and passed his life. He recognized as clearly as
Lehmann, and with more accuracy of detail, the
sequence of stratified rocks resting in gently-inclined
strata against the older upturned masses of the
mountains. He noted the position of the Coal with
its exotic plants, followed by the copper-bearing shales,
Zechstein, mottled sandstone, marls, gypsum, and
finally the Muschelkalk.

Taking no limited or parochial view of the phenomena that presented themselves before his eyes, he
connected the history of his little principality with
that of the whole globe. In the order of succession

[1] "Historia terrae et maris, ex historia Thuringiae per montium
descriptionem erecta" (*Trans. Elect. Soc. Mayence*, vol. ii. pp.
44-209). The map was the first detailed geognostical and petrographical map of a large district in Germany, and the sections
were excellent for their time.

[2] *Entwurf zu der ältesten Erd- und Menschengeschichte*, 275 pages,
8vo, 1773.

of the rocks around him, he saw the records of a series of changes which the earth had once undergone. These changes were conceived by him to have been of no abnormal kind, but to have resembled those which might quite possibly occur now, for, in his opinion, our planet had always presented phenomena similar to those of the present time. He saw that the existing dry land was in large measure formed of strata that had once been laid down on the floor of the sea, like the sandstones, marls and limestones with which he was familiar. Rising from underneath these strata, the older and inclined rocks of the mountains appeared to him as the relics of a more ancient continent, which had in like manner been built up of marine sediments. He believed that the tilted, highly-inclined positions of these rocks were due to their having tumbled down into the hollow interior of the earth.

Füchsel, with much sagacity, not only interpreted the origin of individual strata, but divined that a continuous series of strata of the same composition constitutes a formation, or the record of a certain epoch in the history of the globe, thus anticipating a doctrine which afterwards took a prominent place in the system of Werner. All these sediments were originally deposited horizontally. Where they have been placed in inclined positions, the alteration was, in his opinion, to be attributed to some subsequent disturbance, such as the effects of earthquakes or oscillations of the ground. To earthquakes also he assigned the production of the rents which, being filled from above, now form veins in the rocks. It was his opinion that the earthy passage-beds between formations mark intervening periods of disturbance.

The Muschelkalk in Füchsel's district forms the highest of the Secondary formations, and is succeeded by the various alluvial deposits. These youngest accumulations, containing only terrestrial remains, were looked upon by him as having arisen from the action of a great deluge.

This singularly shrewd observer deserves further to be remembered for the place which he assigned to organic remains in his theoretical views of the past history of the earth. He clearly recognized these objects as relics of once living things. He saw that the Coal was distinguished by its land-plants, the Zechstein by its gryphites, the Muschelkalk by its ammonites; further, that some formations contained only marine remains, others only terrestrial, and thus that the latter point to the neighbourhood of ancient land, while the former indicate the presence of the sea.

The clear and detailed evidence brought forward by Lehmann and Füchsel, that the materials of the terrestrial crust had not been thrown down at random, but succeeded each other in a certain definite order, and contained a record of former processes and changes, like those in progress now, ought to have given at once a great forward impetus to the study of the history of the earth. Lehmann's volume, however, was not in itself attractive, and Füchsel's first essay, though by far the most detailed and philosophical treatise on the subject that had yet appeared, was written in Latin, and buried in the publications of an obscure Society. Füchsel himself lived quietly in a little town, with no disciples to spread his doctrines, so that his very name remained hardly known even in Germany, while other and much inferior writers achieved a wide reputation. His writings seem to have dropped out of sight, until they were unearthed and brought to notice fifty-seven years after his death by Keferstein. The seed sown in Germany by Lehmann and Füchsel was thus long in springing into abundant growth. During the remainder of the century the idea of geological succession was proclaimed, indeed, from the housetops, but it was so mingled with fanciful hypothesis, that its truth and real value were almost lost sight of.

We come now to the time of the advent of a man who bulks far more largely in the history of geology than any of those with whom up to the present we have been concerned—a man who wielded an enormous authority over the mineralogy and geology of his day. Through the loyal devotion of his pupils, he was elevated even in his lifetime into the position of a kind of scientific pope, whose decisions were final on any subject regarding which he chose to pronounce them. During the last quarter of the eighteenth century, by far the most notable figure in the ranks of those who cultivated the study of minerals and rocks was unquestionably Abraham Gottlob Werner (1749-1817).

The vast influence which this man wielded arose mainly from his personal gifts and character, and especially from the overmastering power he had of impressing his opinions upon the convictions of his hearers. It was an influence of a curiously mingled kind. From one point of view, Werner appears to us as the enthusiastic teacher, drawing men from all countries under his spell, and kindling in them much of his own zeal for the study of minerals and rocks. In another aspect, he stands out as the dogmatic theorist, intolerant of opinions different from his own, training his pupils in an artificial and erroneous system, and sending them out into the world not patiently to investigate nature, but to apply everywhere the uncouth terminology and hypothetical principles which he had taught them.

Though he himself mixed but little publicly in the dispute, he was directly the cause of the keen controversy over the origin of basalt, the echoes of which had hardly ceased when some of the older geologists of our day were born. I have myself known a number of men who remembered well the acrimony of the warfare, and some of whom even played the part of combatants in the struggle. Werner had a large following. He was undoubtedly the most popular teacher of the science of minerals and rocks in his time. His services to mineralogy were great, and have always been freely admitted. By the partiality of his pupils and friends he was also raised to the highest eminence as a teacher of geology, and was even looked up to as the founder of that science. The noise of conflict, and the plaudits of enthusiastic disciples have now long been silent. We can calmly consider what Werner did, in what state he found the science of the rocks, and in what condition he left it. As the result of my own investigation in this subject I have been compelled to arrive at the conclusion that, although he did great service by the precision of his lithological characters and by his insistence on the doctrine of geological succession, yet that as regards geological theory, whether directly by his own teaching, or indirectly by the labours of his pupils and followers, much of his influence was disastrous to the higher interests of geology. The career of such a man, so full of contradictions, so preponderant in the studies to which it was devoted, and so momentous in its effects upon the progress of science in his own generation, merits the careful consideration of all who would realise how geology has gained its present place.

Werner was born on 25th September 1749 at Wehrau on the Queiss in Upper Lusatia.[1] His ancestors had been engaged in the iron industry of that region of Germany for some 300 years. His father was inspector of Count Solms' foundry, and at one time it seemed as though the future mineralogist were to carry on, in the same profession, the traditions of the family. From infancy he was familiar with stones. When still hardly able to speak, it was one of his favourite amusements to break down pieces of sandstone and marl. After he had begun to learn his alphabet, his father, as a reward for proficiency in his lessons, would allow him to look over a small collection of minerals which he kept in a box, and

[1] For the biographical details given in this sketch I am indebted partly to the " Kurzer Nekrolog Abraham Gottlob Werners," by K. A. Blöde, in the *Memoirs of the Mineralogical Society of Dresden*, vol. ii. (1819), p. 249, and partly to the *Éloge* on Werner by Cuvier. Blöde, who had access to family documents, gives 1749 as the year of Werner's birth ; Cuvier and other authorities make it 1750.

would talk to him about them, their origin and their uses. Late in life Werner could vividly recall the very minerals that were the playthings of his child-hood—various ores and spars, as well as some varieties of which his father did not know the names. When he could read, his favourite books were lexicons of mining and manufactures, wherein he specially selected the articles on mineralogy. His tendencies, thus early shown, were further fostered by his father, who in hours of leisure would entertain him with stories of the mines.

In his tenth year the boy went to school at the old fortified town of Bunzlau in Silesia, and after a few years returned in 1764 to assist his father and become controller of the smelting houses at Wehrau. But the aspirations he had formed to devote himself to minerals seem at last to have grown too strong to be resisted, so that after doing his duty at the foundries for five years, he resolved to betake himself in 1769 to the Mining Academy of Freiberg, which had been founded two years before, and of the attractions of which he had no doubt heard much. Amid what was there thoroughly congenial to him, he threw himself with enthusiasm into the work of the school, not only availing himself of all the formal instruction in the art of mining to be had from the teachers, but visiting all the chief Saxon mines, especially those of most importance in the Freiberg district, descending the shafts, joining in the manual labour of the miners, and thus making himself master of the whole art of mining, below ground as well as above. His zeal and capacity were soon recognized

by the officials at Freiberg, and before he had been
long there he was offered a place in the Saxon Corps
of Mines. He was not unwilling to accept the
appointment, but determined first of all to prosecute
a wider range of study for a few years at the
University of Leipzig.

Accordingly, after some two years spent in mining
pursuits, Werner went to Leipzig in the spring of
the year 1771, and for the next two years devoted
himself almost entirely to the study of law. In his
third and last year at the University, he seems to
have taken up a miscellaneous series of subjects,
especially modern languages, but he settled down at
last to the prosecution of his first love—mineralogy ;
and with such industry and enthusiasm did he pursue
his study, that while in his twenty-fifth year, and still
a "student of the science and law of mining," he
published his first essay—a little duodecimo of 300
pages, on the external characters of minerals.[1] We
can imagine the astonishment and delight of the lovers
of mineralogy when they first got hold of this treatise,
and found there, instead of the miscellaneous, isolated,
and heterogeneous observations to which they were
accustomed, an admirably ordered method and a clear
marshalling and co-ordination of facts, such as had
never before been seen in mineralogical literature.

On leaving the University of Leipzig, Werner went
back to his home by the Queiss. It seemed as though
the authorities at Freiberg, who at one time were so

---

[1] "Von den aüsserlichen Kennzeichen der Fossilien, abgefasst von
Abraham Gottlob Werner, Der Bergwerks-Wissenschaften und
Rechte Beflissenen," Leipzig, 1774.

anxious to secure his services, had now forgotten his existence. He had heard nothing more of the proposal to engage him, and he began to arrange his plans for the future. But the officials, though slow in their movements, had not lost sight of him. They had made note of his progress at Leipzig, and especially of his admirable little book, and at last in February 1775, to his own astonishment, Werner received a call from them to become Inspector and Teacher of Mining and Mineralogy in the Freiberg Mining Academy at a yearly stipend of 300 thalers. He thus attained before he was twenty-six the position in which he spent the rest of his life and achieved his great fame. For some forty years he continued in the same appointment. By his genius he raised the Mining School from a mere local seminary, founded for the training of a few Saxon miners, to the importance of a great academy or university, to which as in mediaeval times, his renown as a teacher drew pupils from all corners of the civilized world. Men advanced in years, as well as youths, sometimes even men of science already distinguished, betook themselves to the acquisition of German that they might attend the lectures of the great oracle of geology.

The life of such a man, seldom tempted to stir from home, immersed in the daily discharge of the duties of his office, and only varying from year to year the subject of his prelections, offers little incident to the biographer. Moreover, though he precociously began so young as an author, he wrote merely a few short treatises and papers in journals, thus leaving hardly any personal memorial behind him. It is from the writings of his pupils that we chiefly learn what manner of man he was, and what were the special characteristics of his teaching.

From the portrait of him prefixed to one of his works,[1] we gather that his large keen eyes looked out beneath a broad and high forehead, over which his hair was dressed in the formal wig-fashion of the day, and turned up in large curls on either side. The round, smooth-shaven face had, as its most conspicuous feature, a mouth in which, while the firm lips denoted decision of character, the upward curve on either side, combined with a slight dimpling of the cheeks, gave the impression of great sweetness of disposition, with a touch of humour, and a certain degree of timidity. There is moreover a notable trimness of person, indicative of the exceeding orderliness of his whole nature.

His personal charm must have been altogether remarkable. Cuvier tells us with what paternal fondness Werner was accustomed to treat his pupils. There was no sacrifice of time or energy which he would not make for their sake, even his slender purse was at their service, if they ever stood in need of pecuniary help. When the students crowded round him, so that only a portion of them could conveniently see and hear his demonstrations, he would divide them and repeat his lecture.[2]

[1] *New Theory of the Formation of Veins.*   Translated by Charles Anderson, M.D.   Edinburgh, 1809.

[2] There is an enthusiastic account of Werner as a teacher by one of his pupils, C. A. Böttiger : " Uber Werners Umgang mit seinen Schülern,"—*Auswahl. Gesellsch. Mineralog. Dresden*, Band ii. p. 305 (1819).

His manner of discourse also was so attractive and stimulating that he riveted the attention of his pupils, incited them to pursue the studies that he loved, and fired them with a desire to apply his methods.   Ostensibly he had to teach mineralogy—a science which in ordinary hands can hardly be said to evoke enthusiasm.   But Werner's mineralogy embraced the whole of Nature, the whole of human history, the whole interests and pursuits and tendencies of mankind. From a few pieces of stone, placed almost at random on the table before him, he would launch out into an exposition of the influence of minerals and rocks upon the geography and topography of the earth's surface.   He would contrast the mountainous scenery of the granites and schists with the tamer landscapes of the sandstones and limestones.   Tracing the limits of these contrasts of surface over the area of Europe, he would dwell on their influence upon the grouping and characteristics of the nations.   He would connect, in this way, his specimens with the migration of races, the spread of languages, the progress of civilization.   He would show how the development of the arts and industries of life had been guided by the distribution of minerals, how campaigns, battles, and military strategy as a whole, had been dependent on the same cause.   The artist, the politician, the historian, the physician, the warrior were all taught that a knowledge of mineralogy would help them to success in their several pursuits.   It seemed as if the most efficient training for the affairs of life were obtainable only at the Mining School of Freiberg.

By such continual excursions into domains that

might have been thought remote enough from the dry study of minerals, and by the clear and confident method, playful vivacity and persuasive eloquence with which they were conducted, Werner roused his hearers to a high pitch of enthusiasm. No teacher of geological science either before or since has approached Werner in the extent of his personal influence, or in the breadth of his contemporary fame.

Let us now inquire what were the leading characteristics of his doctrines, and what permanent influence they exerted upon the progress of the science of his time. His brilliance and discursiveness might attract and retain large audiences, but his lectures must have possessed more solid and enduring qualities, which inspired his disciples to devote their lives to the studies into which he introduced them, and filled them with the ardour of devoted proselytes.

The first feature to which we may direct our attention, distinguishable in every part of his life and work, was his overmastering sense of orderliness and method. This habit of mind became in him a true passion. He is said to have bought books, rather to arrange them systematically than to read them. He observed the details of social etiquette as punctiliously as the characters of minerals, but with one remarkable exception, to which I shall afterwards allude ; and he would deliberate over the arrangement of a dinner with as much gravity as over that of his library or his cabinet.

We cannot take up any of Werner's writings without at once noting this prominent peculiarity of his mind. Every fact, every proposition is definitely

o

classified and ticketed, and even when he has little or
nothing to say under any particular subdivision, the
subdivision is nevertheless placed in its due niche all
the same.

This methodical habit proved of the greatest service
to the cause of mineralogy. When Werner entered
upon his mineralogical studies, the science of minerals
was an extraordinary chaos of detached observations
and unconnected pieces of knowledge. But his very
first essay began to put it into order, and by degrees
he introduced into it a definite methodical treatment,
doing for it very much what Linnaeus had done some
years before for botany. Like that great naturalist, he
had to invent a language to express with precision the
characters which he wished to denote, so that mineralogists everywhere could recognise them. For this
purpose he employed his mother tongue, and devised
a terminology which, though artificial and cumbrous,
was undoubtedly of great service for a time. Uncouth
in German, it became almost barbarous when translated
into other languages. What would the modern English-speaking student think of a teacher who taught
him, as definite characters, that a mineral could be
distinguished as " hard, or semi-hard," " soft or very
soft," as " very cold, cold, pretty cold, or rather cold,"
as " fortification-wise bent," as " indeterminate curved
lamellar," as " common angulo-granular," or as " not
particularly difficultly frangible " ? [1]

Werner arranged the external characters of minerals
in so methodical a way, that they could readily be

[1] These terms are all taken from the Wernerian system as expounded in English by Werner's pupil, Jameson (note on next page).

applied in the practical determination of species. Yet strangely enough he neglected the most important of them all—that of crystalline form. From the individual minerals, he proceeded to the consideration of their distribution, and the character and origin of the different rocks in which they occur. To this branch of inquiry he gave the name of geognosy, or knowledge of the earth, and he defined it as the science which reveals to us in methodical order the terrestrial globe as a whole, and more particularly the layers of mineral matter whereof it consists, informing us of the position and relations of these layers to each other, and enabling us to form some idea of their origin. The term geology had not yet come into use, nor would either Werner or any of his followers have adopted it as a synonym for the "geognosy" of the Freiberg school. They prided themselves on their close adherence to fact as opposed to theory. One of them, with pointed reference to the writings of Hutton and Playfair, which had appeared shortly before, wrote: "We should form a very false conception of the Wernerian geognosy were we to believe it to have any resemblance to those *monstrosities* known under the name of *Theories of the Earth.* . . . Armed with all the *facts* and inferences contained in these visionary fabrics, what account would we be able to give of the mineralogy of a country, if required of us, or of the general relations of the great masses of which the globe is composed?"[1] The geognosts

[1] Jameson, "Elements of Geognosy," forming vol. iii. of his *System of Mineralogy,* p. 42. The italics in this quotation are in the original.

boasted of the minuteness and precision of their master's system, and contrasted the positive results to which it led with what they regarded as the vague conclusions and unsupported or idle speculations of other writers. Werner arranged the crust of the earth into a series of "formations", which he labelled and described with the same precision that he applied to the minerals in his cabinet. He taught that these formations were to be recognised all over the world, in the same order and with the same characters. The students whom he sent forth naturally believed that they carried with them, in this sequence, the key that would unlock the geological structure of every country.

But never in the history of science did a stranger hallucination arise than that of Werner and his school, when they supposed themselves to discard theory and build on a foundation of accurately-ascertained fact. Never was a system devised in which theory was more rampant; theory, too, unsupported by observation, and, as we now know, utterly erroneous. From beginning to end of Werner's method and its applicacations, assumptions were made for which there was no ground, and these assumptions were treated as demonstrable facts. The very point to be proved was taken for granted, and the geognosts, who boasted of their avoidance of speculation, were in reality among the most hopelessly speculative of all the generations that had tried to solve the problems of the theory of the earth.

Werner's first sketch of his plan of the structure of the earth's crust and the succession of the rocks that compose it appeared as a thin quarto of only 28 pages, published at Dresden in the year 1787.[1] It was descriptive rather than theoretical, and was marked by all its author's precision and orderliness of statement. It contained the essence of his system in its simplest form. In later years, as we shall see, further experience compelled him to enlarge and modify the system, but without changing the fundamental conceptions on which it was founded. The modifications, however, were not embodied by Werner in any later edition of his work. They were given by him from time to time in his lectures, and gradually became known from the writings of his students. One of the most devoted and distinguished of these followers was Robert Jameson, who afterwards became Professor of Natural History in the University of Edinburgh. He was mainly instrumental in introducing the Wernerian doctrines into Britain, and continued for a number of years to be their most ardent supporter. In many respects the fullest accounts of Werner's views are to be found in the various works of the Edinburgh Professor, and I shall cite some further passages from them in the present chapter.

One of the fundamental postulates of the Wernerian doctrines was the existence of what were termed universal formations. When he elaborated his system, Werner had never been out of Saxony and the immediately adjacent regions. His practical knowledge of the earth was, therefore, confined to what he could

---

[1] *Kurze Klassification und Beschreibung der verschiedenen Gebirgsarten,* von A. G. Werner, Bergakademie Inspector, und Lehrer der Bergbaukunst und Mineralogie zu Freiberg.   Dresden, 1787.

see there, and so little was then known of the geological structure of the globe as a whole, that he
could not add much to his acquaintance with the
subject by reading what had been observed by others,
though there can be little doubt that he stood
greatly indebted to Lehmann and Füchsel. With this
slender stock of acquirement, he adopted the old idea
that the whole globe had once been surrounded with
an ocean of water, at least as deep as the mountains
are high, and he believed that from this ocean
there were deposited by chemical precipitation the
solid rocks which now form most of the dry land.
He taught that these original formations were universal, extending round the whole globe, though not
without interruption, and that they followed each
other in a certain order. He affirmed that the first-
formed rocks were entirely of chemical origin, and

he called them Primitive, including in them granite,
which was the oldest, gneiss, mica-slate, clay-slate,
serpentine, basalt, porphyry, and concluding with
syenite as the youngest. Succeeding these came what
he afterwards separated as the Transition Rocks,
consisting chiefly of chemical productions (greywacke,
greywacke-slate and limestone), but comprising the
earliest mechanical depositions, and indicating the
gradual lowering of the level of the universal ocean.
Still newer, and occupying, on the whole, lower positions, marking the continued retirement of the waters,
were the Floetz Rocks, composed partly of chemical,
but chiefly of mechanical sediments, and including
sandstone, limestone, gypsum, rock-salt, coal, basalt,
obsidian, porphyry, and other rocks. Latest of all

came the Alluvial series, consisting of recent loams, clays, sands, gravels, sinters, and peat.

This system was not put forward tentatively as a suggestion towards a better comprehension of the history of the earth. It was announced dogmatically as a body of ascertained truth, about which there could be no further doubt or dispute. Let me quote by way of illustration a few sentences from Werner's *Theory of Veins*, where he definitely expresses his opinions on these matters. "In recapitulating the state of our present knowledge," he observes, "it is obvious that we know with certainty that the floetz and primitive mountains have been produced by a series of precipitations and depositions formed in succession from water which covered the globe. We are also certain that the fossils which constitute the beds and strata of mountains were dissolved in this universal water and were precipitated from it; consequently the metals and minerals found in primitive rocks, and in the beds of floetz mountains, were also contained in this universal solvent, and were formed from it by precipitation. We are still further certain that at different periods, different fossils have been formed from it, at one time earthy, at another metallic minerals, at a third time some other fossils. We know, too, from the position of these fossils, one above another, to determine with the utmost precision which are the oldest, and which the newest precipitates. We are also convinced that the solid mass of our globe has been produced by a series of precipitations formed in succession (in the humid way); that the pressure of the materials, thus accumulated, was not the same

throughout the whole ; and that this difference of
pressure and several other concurring causes have
produced rents in the substance of the earth, chiefly
in the most elevated parts of its surface. We are
also persuaded that the precipitates taking place from
the universal water must have entered into the open
fissures which the water covered. We know, moreover, for certain, that veins bear all the marks of
fissures formed at different times ; and, by the causes
which have been assigned for their formation, that
the mass of veins is absolutely of the same nature as
the beds and strata of mountains, and that the nature
of the masses differs only according to the locality of
the cavity where they occur. In fact, the solution
contained in its great reservoir (that excavation which
held the universal water) was necessarily subjected to
a variety of motion, whilst that part of it which was
confined to the fissures was undisturbed, and deposited
in a state of tranquillity its precipitate."[1]

It would be difficult to cite from any other modern
scientific treatise a series of consecutive sentences
containing a larger number of dogmatic assertions, of
which almost every one is contradicted by the most
elementary facts of observation. The habit of confident affirmation seems to have blinded Werner to
the palpable absurdity of some of his statements.
When, for example, he speaks of the great reservoir
or excavation which held the universal water, what
idea could have been present to his mind ? If the
primeval ocean, as he asserted, surrounded the whole

[1] *Neue Theorie von der Entstehung der Gängen*, chap. vii. § 68 (1791).
English translation by Anderson, p. 110 (1809).

globe, and was as deep as the mountains are high, where was the excavation ? As an acute writer in the *Edinburgh Review* pointed out, the excavation spoken of by Werner " can mean nothing else than the convexity of the solid nucleus round which the universal water was diffused. To call this convexity an excavation, is to use such a freedom with language as can only be accounted for by the perplexity in which every man, of whatever talents, must find himself involved when he attempts to describe a whole, of which the parts are inconsistent with one another."[1]

The theory of a primeval universal ocean that overtopped the mountains, which formed the basis of Werner's teaching, led in every direction to such manifest contradictions and absurdities, that we need a little patience and some imagination to picture to ourselves how it could have been received and fervently believed in by men of intelligence, to whom the facts of the earth's structure were not wholly unknown. It was claimed for Werner that the doctrine of a universal and gradually subsiding ocean, though it had been taught long before his time, was first demonstrated by him to be true, (1) because he found the older strata occupying the highest eminences, and the younger coming in at successively lower levels, down to the modern alluvia of the plains and the sea-shore,[2] and (2) because the primitive and loftiest rocks are entirely formed of chemical precipitations, those of

---

[1] *Edin. Review*, xviii. p. 90 (1811).

[2] But as has been shown in a previous chapter, this idea had been clearly enunciated long before by Buffon and was recognized by Werner's German predecessors.

mechanical origin not appearing until a much later period, and becoming increasingly abundant down to the present time, when they constitute almost all the deposits that are now taking place.[1]

One of the most obvious questions that would arise, we might suppose, in the mind of any student of ordinary capacity to whom the theory was propounded, would be how did the deep primitive ocean disappear. Steno, Leibnitz, and other older writers had conjectured that the waters found their way into vast caverns in the earth's interior. Such a conjecture, however, was not suited to the taste of the true Wernerian, who would allow no speculation, but took his stand on a basis of ascertained fact. Well, we may be curious to know how he disposed of the difficulty. Yet we shall search in vain through Wernerian literature for any serious grappling with this obvious, and one would have thought formidable, objection to the doctrine. Werner himself appears to have inclined to the belief that the waters vanished into space. He thought it possible that " one of the celestial bodies which sometimes approach near to the earth may have been able to withdraw a portion of our atmosphere and of our ocean."[2] But if once the waters were abstracted, how were they to be brought back again, so as to cover all the hills on which his highest Floetz formations were deposited ?

---

[1] Jameson's *Geognosy*, p. 78. Werner's followers, from the prominence they gave to the sea in their geognosy, were styled Neptunists, while those of Hutton, who dwelt on the potency of the earth's internal fire, were dubbed Plutonists or Vulcanists.

[2] See D'Aubuisson's *Géognosie*, i. p. 414 (1819).

The most famous of the English followers of Werner, Jameson, honestly asked the question, "What has become of the immense volume of water that once covered and stood so high over the whole earth?" His answer may be cited as thoroughly characteristic of the mental attitude of a staunch Wernerian. "Although," he says, "we cannot give any very satisfactory answer to this question, it is evident that the theory of the diminution of the water remains equally probable. We may be fully convinced of its truth, and are so, although we may not be able to explain it. To know from observation that a great phenomenon took place, is a very different thing from ascertaining how it happened."[1] I do not suppose that in the whole literature of science a better illustration could be found of the advice—"When you meet with an insuperable difficulty, look it steadfastly in the face —and pass on."

One might have thought that having disposed of the universal ocean, even in this rather peremptory fashion, the Wernerians would have been in no hurry to call it back again, and set the same stupendous and inexplicable machinery once more going. But the exigencies of their theory left them no choice. Having determined, as an incontrovertible fact, that certain rocks had been deposited as chemical precipitates in a definite order from a universal ocean, when these philosophers, as their knowledge of Nature increased, found that some of these so-called precipitates occurred out of their due sequence and at much higher altitudes than had been supposed, they were compelled to bring

[1] Jameson, *op. cit.* p. 82.

back the universal ocean, and make it rise high over hills from which it had already receded. Not only had they to call up the vasty deep, but they had to endow it with rapid and even tumultuous movement, as it swept upwards over forest-clothed lands. Having raised it as high as their so-called Floetz formations extended, and having allowed its waters to settle and deposit precipitates of basalt and greenstone, they had to hurry it away again to the unknown regions where it still remains. This, forsooth, was the system that discarded hypothesis, and rested proudly on an irrefragable foundation of demonstrable fact.

In another notable respect the crudeness of the Wernerian sytem and its disregard of the most familiar facts in nature are shown by its classification of so many diverse kinds of rocks as chemical precipitates from a hypothetical universal ocean. Chemistry was then sufficiently far advanced to prove the absurdity of this dogma. Even if the ocean had been a mass of boiling water, it could not have held all these rocks in solution, and have deposited them as successive precipitates. But the Wernerian geognosts scouted the idea that the globe and its outer envelopes, ever had a high temperature. They seem never to have tried to reason out the chemical reactions involved in their theory of solution and precipitation, nor to have formed any conception of the causes which could have led to the successive deposition of the various precipitates. That the ocean could not have been a strong solution of mineral substances when the so-called chemical precipitates of the Transition Rocks were deposited, but must have had a composition

not greatly dissimilar to what it possesses now might
have been suggested to these theorists by the occurrence of the abundant remains of animal life in many
of the rocks—a fact of which they ultimately became
well aware.

A further singular characteristic of the Wernerian
school was the position it took up with regard to the
evidence for disturbances of the earth's crust, and for
the universality and potency of what is now termed
igneous action. A hundred years before Werner's
time Steno had pointed to the inclined and broken
strata of Northern Italy as evidence of dislocation of
the crust. The Italian observers, and especially Moro,
familiar with the phenomena of earthquakes and volcanoes, had been impressed by the manifest proofs
of the potency of the internal energy of the earth
upon its outer form. But these early adumbrations
of the truth were all brushed aside by the oracle of
Freiberg. I have tried to imagine the current of
thought by which Werner was led to this crowning
absurdity of his system, and I think we may trace it
in the history of his relation to the basalt hills of
Saxony. The question is of some interest, not only
as a curious piece of human psychology, but because
it was on this very point of the origin of basalt that
the Wernerian ship finally struck and foundered.

The year after his appointment as teacher of
mineralogy, Werner visited the famous Stolpen, one
of the most picturesque castle-crowned basalt hills
of Saxony, to which I have already referred in connection with Agricola's revival of the old word
" basalt." He had probably by this time begun to

form in his mind a more or less definite picture of chemical precipitation from aqueous solution, as applied to the history of rock-masses. But be this as it may, he was aware that basalt, by not a few observers before his time, had been claimed as a rock of volcanic origin. How far he had then made up his mind as to the formation of that rock must remain in doubt. But he tells us himself that at the Stolpen he " found not a trace of volcanic action, nor the smallest proof of volcanic origin. So I ventured publicly to assert and prove that all basalts could certainly not be of volcanic origin, and that to these non-volcanic rocks the Stolpen mass undoubtedly belongs. Though at first I met with much opposition, yet soon several geognosts came over to my views. These views gained special importance from the observations which I made in 1777 on the old subterranean fire in the coal-field that lies around the hills of basalt and porphyry-slate in the middle of Bohemia, and the consequent pseudo-volcanic hills that have arisen there. After further more matured research and consideration, I hold that no basalt is volcanic, but that all these rocks, as well as the other Primitive and Floetz rocks, are of aqueous origin."[1]

[1] *Kurze Klassification und Beschreibung der Verschiedenen Gebirgsarten*, 1787, p. 25. Later in the same year (1787) he visited a little eminence near Scheibenberg in the Erzgebirge, and found there a cake of basalt lying on clay and sand, and thought he could trace these materials passing into each other. Whereupon he announced as a " new discovery" that all basalt is of aqueous origin, and constitutes, with clay, sand and wacke, one single formation which originally extended far and wide over the primitive and floetz rocks, but has in course of time been worn away, leaving only cappings on the hills.—Keferstein, *Geschichte der Geognosie*, p. 69.

Thus ten years of reflection had only served to make him more positive in maintaining an opinion which the most ordinary observation in his own Saxony ought to have enabled him to disprove and reject. He had not only asserted that basalt is a chemical precipitate, but had placed it among his primitive rocks.

When we remember the long and patient labours of Desmarest before he announced his conclusions regarding the volcanic origin of basalt, we cannot but wonder at the audacity of Werner in discarding these conclusions without comment, and announcing an entirely opposite opinion, rapidly formed on the slender evidence of one or two isolated patches of basalt. It was not as if he claimed to apply his explanation merely to those few cases which he had himself examined; he swept all the basalts of the earth's surface into his net. His view had not even the merit of originality, for, as we have seen, Guettard, among others, had held the opinion that basalt is of aqueous origin. But, announced as a new discovery, with all the authority of the great Freiberg professor, it commanded attention and met with wide acceptance. Even from the time of its promulgation, however, it awakened some opposition, and it became the subject of bitter controversy for fully a generation. Only a month after Werner proclaimed his discovery he was answered by J. K. W. Voigt of Weimar, who maintained the volcanic nature of the very examples cited by the professor.[1] Werner replied, and was

[1] *Bergmänn. Journ.* 1788, 1789, 1791, pp. 185, 347, etc. See also Hoffmann's *Geschichte der Geognosie* (1838), p. 117.

again answered, but soon retired from the combat and devoted his energies to strengthen his theory. As an instance of the wide interest taken in the question, I may mention that even at Berne, where there are no basalts, nor any other traces of volcanic action, the Society of Naturalists of that town offered a prize of twenty-five thalers for the best essay in answer to the question, "What is Basalt: Is it volcanic or is it not?" The successful competitor, after elaborately reviewing all the arguments brought forward by the Vulcanists, pronounced in favour of Werner's views.[1] Werner himself made two contributions to the discussion, one giving his theory of volcanoes,[2] and the other his matured views upon basalt.[3]

Volcanoes and volcanic action, if they were regarded as betokening any potent kind of reaction between the interior and the exterior of our planet, were utterly antagonistic to Werner's conception of the structure and history of the earth. In a world which had entirely resulted from the precipitations and depositions of an ocean of water, there was obviously no place for internal fire. In the system which Werner had so laboriously devised, it was imperatively necessary to treat volcanoes as modern and accidental phenomena, which never entered into the process of the formation of the crust of the earth. Accordingly, in his earliest sketch of his classification of rocks, he placed volcanic rocks among the latest of the whole series. And this

[1] J. F. W. Widenmann, Höpfner's *Magazin für die Erdkunde*, iv. (1789), p. 135.

[2] Höpfner's *Magazin für die Erdkunde*, iv. (1789), p. 239.

[3] *Bergmännisches Journal*, 1789, i. p. 252. See also p. 272.

view he maintained to the last. That volcanic action had been in progress from the very beginning of geological time, and that it had played an important part in building up the framework of the land in many countries all over the globe, were ideas that seem never to have occurred to him.

We have seen how old was the notion that volcanoes, or "burning mountains," arose from the combustion of subterranean beds of coal. Werner adopted this opinion, which suited his system, and was quite in congenial surroundings there. In 1789, two years after the appearance of his little *Kurze Klassification*, he definitely announced, in one of the papers above referred to, what he called the "highly probable conjecture that most, if not all, volcanoes arise from the combustion of underground seams of coal."[1] The coal might be set on fire by spontaneous combustion, and the most vigorous volcanoes would be those starting on the thickest masses of coal. In order to support this belief, it was necessary to furnish evidence of the existence of deposits of coal around volcanoes. And much research and ingenuity were displayed in collecting all the known examples. Not only coal, but every kind of natural inflammable substance was pressed into service, and made to do duty as fuel for the subterranean fires.

It was also obviously needful to maintain that volcanoes must be comparatively modern phenomena. We are told that "it was only after the deposition of the immense repositories of inflammable matter in the Floetz-trap that volcanoes could take place;

[1] See the paper just cited in Höpfner's *Magaz.* iv. (1789), 240.

P

they are therefore to be considered as new occurrences in the history of Nature. The volcanic state appears to be foreign to the earth." [1]

The similarity of basalt to many undoubtedly volcanic rocks had long been noticed, and could not escape the observant eyes of Werner. But he did not therefore infer basalt to be of volcanic origin. He had already established, as one of the indisputable canons of geognosy, that basalt was precipitated from chemical solution in a universal ocean. The way in which he accounted for the resemblance between basalt and lava must be regarded as a signal proof of his ingenuity. He announced that volcanoes not only occur where there are seams of coal, but where these are covered by sheets of basalt and wacke, and that eruptions of lava take place when these overlying rocks are melted by the combustion of the coal. He thus provided himself with a triumphant answer to any objector who felt inclined to question his dictum as to the origin of basalt. If the rock occurred on isolated hill tops, it was a member of the Floetz-trap formation produced by universal chemical precipitation. If it was found in the condition of lava, the original precipitate had been fused by the burning of underlying seams of coal.

With so flexible a theory to defend and apply, it can be understood how the pupils of the Freiberg school scouted the notion that volcanoes were of any real geognostical importance, and how they had a ready

---

[1] Jameson's *Geognosy*, p. 96. Werner could, not claim even originality for this absurd doctrine, for it had been adopted by Buffon before the Saxon professor was born (*ante*, p. 93).

answer to any opponent, or a prompt explanation of any apparent difficulty in the acceptance of their master's teaching. If any one claimed that basalt was of volcanic origin, he was at once confidently assured that this was an entire mistake, for the great law-giver of Freiberg had pronounced it to be a chemical precipitate from water. If he ventured to quote the columnar structure as in favour of his view, he was told that he ought to know that lava never assumed this structure,[1] and that "rocks which have been formed or altered by the action of heat are most distinctly different from those that constitute the great mass of the crust of the globe."[2] If he brought to the unabashed Wernerian a piece of obsidian, and asked whether such a rock should not be admitted to be a volcanic glass, "Nothing of the kind," would have been, in effect, the immediate reply. "It is true that the rock does resemble 'completely melted stony substances, and occurs in volcanic countries,' but the notion that it is itself of volcanic origin is quite unfounded, 'because obsidian has never been observed accompanying lava, because it is connected with basalt, and because it contains a considerable portion of water of composition, which is never the case with true volcanic rocks.'"[3] If the questioner, still unconvinced, presumed to present a piece of pumice, pointing to its froth-like structure and its presence in volcanic countries as evidence of its former fusion, the answer would have been an equally prompt and decided negative. Let me quote the actual words of a Wernerian in

[1] Jameson, *op. cit.* p. 58.   [2] *Op. cit.* p. 74.
[3] *Op. cit.* p. 196.

reply. " It was formerly the general opinion that pumice was a volcanic product, because it frequently occurs in countries conjectured to be of igneous formation. It is now ascertained to be an aquatic product, from the following facts : 1, It alternates with Neptunian rocks, as basalt and porphyry ; 2, it is most distinctly stratified ; 3, it passes into obsidian and pearlstone, and is thus connected with basalt, pitchstone, etc. ; 4, it contains water of composition, which is never the case with true volcanic rocks ; 5, it has never been observed to flow in streams from the crater or sides of a volcano, and no one ever saw it forming a stream in countries containing extinct volcanoes." [1]

Well might the inquirer retire in despair from such an encounter. In vain would he have sought an explanation of the origin of the vesicular structure of the rock, or have asked how this structure could ever have originated from an aqueous solution. He would probably have been plied with a few more " facts " of equal veracity, and a few more examples of reasoning in a circle. But he would never succeed in extracting an expression of doubt, or an admission that the *ipse dixit* of the Freiberg professor could for a moment be called in question.

The same attitude which Werner assumed towards volcanoes was consistently maintained by him in his treatment of the proofs of disturbances in the terrestrial crust. He seems never to have realized that any reservoir of energy is stored up in the interior of our globe. It was part of his teaching that the spheroidal form of the planet furnished one of the proofs of a primeval

[1] Jameson, *op. cit.* p. 196.

universal ocean. He admitted that the crust had been abundantly cracked, but in these cracks he saw no evidence of any subterranean action. His own statement of his views on this subject is sufficiently explicit, and I quote his words : " When the mass of materials of which the rocks were formed by precipitation in the humid way, and which was at first soft and movable, began to sink and dry, fissures must of necessity have been formed, chiefly in those places where the greatest quantity of matter has been heaped up, or where the accumulation of it has formed those elevations which are called mountains."[1] He gave no explanation of the reason why the precipitates of his universal ocean should have gathered more thickly on one part of the bottom than on another. It was enough for himself and his disciples that he was convinced of the fact.

As all rents in the earth's crust were thus mere superficial phenomena resulting from desiccation and the slipping down of material from the sides of mountains, so it was conceived by Werner that, when they were filled up, the mineral matter that was introduced into them could only come from above. He drew no distinction in this respect between what are now called " mineral veins " and " intrusive veins." Veins of granite, of basalt, of porphyry, of quartz, of galena, or of pyrites were all equally chemical precipitates from an overlying sea. He does not appear to have seen any difficulty in understanding how the desiccation and rupture of the rocks were to take place, if the sea still covered them, or how, if they were exposed to the air and evaporation, he was to raise the level of the ocean

[1] *Theory of Veins*, § 39.

again so as to cover them, and fill up their rents with
new precipitates.

Werner's original scheme of classification of the
rocks of the earth's crust had at least the merit of
clearness and simplicity. Though he borrowed his
order of sequence partly from Lehmann and Füchsel,
he worked it into a scheme of his own regarding the
origin of the rocks and their successive production
from a universal ocean. Tracing in the arrangement
of the rocks of the earth's crust the history of an
original oceanic envelope, finding in the masses of
granite, gneiss, and mica-schist the earliest precipitations from that ocean, and recognising the successive
alterations in the constitution of the water as witnessed
by the series of geological formations, Werner launched
upon the world a bold conception which might well
fascinate many a listener to whom the laws of chemistry
and physics, even as then understood, were but little
known. Unfortunately the conception was based entirely on the imagination, and had no real foundation
in observation or experiment.

Werner adopted the leading ideas of his system in
an early part of his career when his personal experience
was extremely limited. And having once adopted
them, he maintained them to the last. His methodical
mind demanded some hypothesis that would allow him
to group, in definite and genetic connection, all the
facts then known regarding the structure of the earth's
crust. His first sketch of a classification of rocks
shows by its meagreness how slender at that time
was his practical acquaintance with rocks in the field.
The whole of the Primitive formations enumerated

by him are only twelve in number, and some of these were confessedly rare.   As years went on, he intercalated new varieties, introduced the division of Transition rocks, and was compelled to reduplicate some of his primitive formations by having to find places also for them among the Floetz series.

Yet with all these shiftings to and fro, the apparent symmetry and conspicuous method of the system were retained to the end.   No Saxon mine could have had its successive levels more regularly planned and driven, than the crust of the earth was parcelled out among the various Wernerian universal formations.   Each of these had its definite chronological place.   When you stood on granite, you knew you were at the base and root of all things mundane.   When you looked on a hill of Floetz-trap you saw before you a relic of one of the last acts of precipitation of the ancient universal ocean.

But Nature has not arranged her materials with the artificial and doctrinaire precision of a mineralogical cabinet.   Werner's system might temporarily suffice for the little part of the little kingdom of Saxony which, when he promulgated his views, he had imperfectly explored.   But as his experience widened and new facts accumulated, the modifications to which I have referred were so serious that they might well make the author of the system pause, and raise in his mind some doubts whether the fundamental conception on which the system was based could possibly be true.[1]

[1] D'Aubuisson, a loyal and favoured pupil of the Saxon Professor, remarks that " Werner has continued from year to year to modify, and even to recast, some parts of his doctrine, while his disciples,

It was eventually found, for instance, that some granite overlies instead of underlying the slates of the Primitive series; that some greenstones, instead of occurring among the Primitive rocks, lie in the Floetz division; that there are ever so many horizons for porphyry, which was at first believed to be entirely Primitive. These contradictions were surmounted by affixing such adjectives as "oldest" or "newest" to the several appearances of the same rock, or by numbering them according to their various horizons. Thus there were oldest and newest granites, oldest and newer serpentine, and first, second, and third porphyry formations.

This patching up of the system may have saved it in appearance, but a moment's reflection will show us that it was fatal to Werner's fundamental doctrine of a series of successive chemical precipitates from a universal ocean, which by the deposition of these precipitates was gradually altering its constitution. The modifications rendered necessary by fresh discovery proved that the supposed definite sequence did not exist. In fact, as was well said by a critic at the time, they were mere "subterfuges by which the force of facts was evaded."[1] They were devised for the purpose of bolstering up a system which was entirely artificial, and to the erroneousness of which new facts were continually bearing witness.

It was claimed for Werner that he first established the doctrine of geological succession in the earth's

following his teaching, in proportion as their observations have multiplied, have added, and are continually adding new improvements to his system."—*Traité de Géognosie* (1819), preface, p. xvi.

[1] *Edinburgh Review*, vol. xviii. (1811), p. 95.

crust. We have seen that the idea was already supplied to him by Lehmann and Füchsel, and it is now evident that, by working into it his notion of universal aqueous precipitates, he introduced an element of hypothesis which threw back for some years the progress of sound geology. What was true in the doctrine was borrowed from his predecessors, what was his own consisted largely of unwarranted assumption. He undoubtedly did enormous service by his precise definitions and descriptions of rocks, and by dwelling on the fact that there was an observable order of succession among them, even though he mistook this order in some important particulars, and entirely misinterpreted its meaning and history. The full significance of geological succession was not understood until it was worked out independently in England and France by a rigid collection of facts and on a palæontological basis, as I shall describe in a later chapter.

Werner's writings are so few and slight that his disciples and admirers continually expressed their sorrow that he would leave so little behind him save his world-wide fame. His natural dislike of the pen increased with his years. He would discourse eloquently on many subjects, but could never bring himself to write fully on any one. Usually when he went to lecture he would retire for a quarter of an hour to arrange his ideas, and when he appeared before his audience he brought with him only some scraps of paper, with a few words scribbled on them. He never wrote a single lecture. If this abstinence from the use of the pen saved him from scientific controversy it did not secure him undisturbed repose. With all his efforts after the placid life of a philosopher, there was one subject that not unnaturally stirred his wrath —the unwarranted publication, or at least circulation of his lectures and theories. As he did not publish them himself, and as there was a widespread desire to become acquainted with them, manuscript copies of notes of his lectures were widely circulated, as a kind of mercantile speculation. This was bad enough, but he heard of an intention to print and publish them. So he took an opportunity of cautioning the world that, while willing to shut his eyes on the past, he could not tolerate any such conduct in future, that he was himself engaged in revising his works on the several branches of science he professed, and that they would " forthwith appear one after another, enriched by his latest observations and discoveries." [1]   But the revision was never made, and the publications never appeared.

Werner's repugnance to writing in any form increased with his years. By degrees he ceased to write letters, even when the dearest friend begged for a reply, and at last, to save himself from the reproach of this neglect, he allowed the letters which he received to remain unopened. Cuvier tells how once an author, desiring to consult some of the learned men of the day concerning a work which he proposed to publish, circulated his voluminous manuscript among them. The precious parcel disappeared in the circuit. After endless seeking, it was disinterred in Werner's room from underneath some hundreds of others. He never

[1] *New Theory of the Formation of Veins*, 1791, preface.

answered the Academy of Sciences of Paris when it conferred on him the very high distinction of electing him one of its eight foreign associates, and he might never have heard of the affair had he not come across the mention of it in some almanack. " But," says Cuvier, " we forgave him when we heard that about the same time a messenger sent express by his sister from Dresden had been kept waiting, at the professor's expense, for two months for a mere signature to some pressing family document."

Save for the occasional irritation caused by rumours of the unwarranted reproduction of his lectures, Werner's life appears to have passed quietly in the midst of the work which he loved and the pupils and friends who looked up to him with veneration and affection. His health was never robust, and the effort of lecturing proved sometimes a great strain upon his energy. After a discourse in which he would pour forth his ideas with the full flow of his exuberance, the bodily and mental effort would be so great that he would have to change his clothes even to his inner raiment. He tried to preserve both body and mind in an equable frame. Among his little foibles was the care he took never to expose himself to a draught. He kept himself out of controversy, and eventually refrained even from reading the journals, and from knowing what was said in the outer world about himself and his opinions. In this tranquil life he might perhaps have prolonged his days, had not his feelings been deeply stirred by the misfortunes which, during the Napoleonic wars, had befallen Saxony, his adopted home. He took these trials so much to heart that they led to a series of internal complications, from which he died at Dresden, in the arms of his sister, on 30th June 1817, in the sixty-eighth year of his age.

Whether the regrets loudly expressed by his contemporaries that Werner published so little were justified, may perhaps be open to doubt. If his fame had to rest on his written works, or even on his teaching as expounded by his pupils, it could never have grown so great, nor, judging from what we know of his views in maturer life, can we suppose that any account of them by himself would really have added to his reputation, or have contributed materially to the advancement of science. It was not his writings, nor even his opinions and theories in themselves, that gave him his unquestioned authority among the geologists of his time. His influence and fame sprang mainly from the personality of the man. His unwearied enthusiasm and eager zeal in the furtherance of his favourite studies, his kindness and helpfulness, his wide range of knowledge, and the vivacity, perspicuity, and eloquence with which he communicated it, his absolute confidence in the solidity of his theoretical doctrines—these were the sources of his power rather than the originality and importance of his own contributions to geology. His followers, indeed, captivated by the precision of his system and its apparent applicability in any and every country, claimed for him the highest place in the ranks of those who had studied the history of the earth. But the exaggeration of their claim was amply shown by the rapidity with which the Wernerian doctrines began to fall into disrepute even before the death of their author.

CHAPTER VIII

In tracing the influence of Werner's teaching upon the progress of geological inquiry, we must begin by the full and frank acknowledgment that when all objections and qualifications have been made regarding his theoretical opinions, the momentous fact remains that by his personal example and contagious enthusiasm he rendered a vast service to the science. He awakened a far more widespread interest in the ancient history of the earth than had ever before existed, and even where his pupils found reason eventually to abandon many of the doctrines which he had taught them, they still retained their devotion to the studies for which he had kindled in them so ardent a zeal. "It was to his irresistible influence," as Cuvier has well remarked, "that the world owes those authors who have treated so fully of minerals, and those indefatigable observers who have so fully explored the globe. The Karstens and the Wiedemanns in the cabinet, the Humboldts, the Von Buchs, the D'Aubuissons, the Hermanns, the Freieslebens, at the summit of the Cordilleras, in the midst of the flames of Vesuvius and of Etna, in the deserts of Siberia, in the depths of the mines of Saxony, of Hungary, of Mexico, of Potosi, have been borne onward by the spirit of their master ; they have brought back to him the honour gained by their labours ; and we may say of him, what was never truthfully said before, save of Linnaeus, that Nature everywhere found herself interrogated in his name."

Besides this general impetus to the pursuit of geology, Werner left on the science of his time and country that bias towards the mineralogical and petrographical side which has ever since so honourably distinguished German geological investigation, and which in our own day has culminated in the masterpieces of Roth, Groth, Zirkel, Rosenbusch, and many other notable writers. Again, his constant advocacy of the doctrine of geological succession kept the interest and importance of the problem before the world, and helped to prepare the way for the great advances which have since been made in that department of the science. But his theoretical views on this subject, and the comparative neglect of organic remains in his system, tended to retard in his own country the fuller development of stratigraphy, which was making even during his lifetime such rapid strides in England and France.

As it was the exigencies of Saxon mining industry that started the Mining School of Freiberg, so the teaching there had necessarily constant reference to the underground operations of the district. Much of

Werner's practical acquaintance with the relations and structure of rock-masses was derived from what he learnt at the mines. It was only natural, therefore, that he should have inculcated upon his pupils the vast importance of subterranean exploration in unravelling the structure of the earth. The devout Wernerian put mines before mountains as a field for geological investigation.[1] Indeed the whole system of the Freiberg school, with its limited knowledge, its partial view of things, its dogmatism and its bondage to preconceived theory, is suggestive rather of the dim lamplight and confined outlook of a mine than of constant and unfettered contact with the fresh and open face of Nature.

These characteristics of Werner's teaching were keenly felt by some of the more clear-sighted of his contemporaries, who, though they recognised his genius and the vast services he had rendered to mineralogy by solid achievement, as well as by the enthusiasm he had excited in many hundreds of pupils, yet felt that in regard to geological progress his influence had become retrogressive and obstructive. This judgment was forcibly expressed in the article which appeared in the *Edinburgh Review* in the year 1811 from which some citations have been given in the foregoing pages. I have reason to believe that this article was from the pen of Dr. W. H. Fitton, who afterwards became one of the leaders of English geology. A few sentences from it may here be quoted.

" The Wernerian school obstructs the progress of discovery. The manner in which it does so is plain.

[1] See, for example, Jameson, *op. cit.* p. 43.

By supposing the order already fixed and determined when it is really not, further inquiry is prevented, and propositions are taken for granted on the strength of a theoretical principle, that require to be ascertained by actual observation. It has happened to the Wernerian system, as it has to many other improvements ; they were at first inventions of great utility ; but being carried beyond the point to which truth and matter of fact could bear them out, they have become obstructions to all further advancement, and have ended with retarding the progress which they began with accelerating. This is so much the case in the instance before us, that when a Wernerian geognost, at present, enters on the examination of a country, he is chiefly employed in placing the phenomena he observes in the situations which his master has assigned to them in his plan of the mineral kingdom. It is not so much to describe the strata as they are, and to compare them with rocks of the same character in other countries, as to decide whether they belong to this or that series of depositions, supposed once to have taken place over the whole earth ; whether, for example, they be of the Independent Coal or the Newest Floetz-trap formation, or such like. Thus it is to ascertain their place in an ideal world, or in that list of successive formations which have nothing but the most hypothetical existence :—it is to this object, unfortunately for true science, that the business of mineralogical observation has of late been reduced." [1]

So long as the great master at Freiberg lived, the loyalty of his attached pupils naturally kept them

[1] *Edin. Review*, vol. xviii. (1811), art. 3, pp. 96, 97.

from openly rejecting his doctrines, even when they could no longer accept them. His death in 1817 was felt by many of them to bring a relief from the despotism which he had so long exercised.[1] And from that time his system declined in favour even in Germany.

It was one of the most singular episodes in the history of geological science that the first serious check to the triumphal march of Wernerianism through Europe came from two of Werner's most distinguished pupils, D'Aubuisson and Von Buch, and that their first opposition to their master's teaching was inspired by that very volcanic tract in Central France to which Desmarest had so long before appealed in vain. Let us see how, in this instance, the whirligig of time brought in his revenges.

Jean François D'Aubuisson de Voisins (1769-1819) was born in the south of France on 16th April, 1769. After receiving his early education in his own country, he spent some years as a diligent student at the Mining School of Freiberg. For four consecutive years, he tells us, he was in the most favourable circumstances for mastering the Wernerian doctrines, inasmuch as the illustrious teacher honoured him with particular attention, and in the course of many conversations unfolded to him the principles of his science, and traced for him the path that would lead him to the

---

[1] One of Jameson's ablest pupils, Ami Boué, trained in the Wernerian faith, confessed, but with evident reluctance, and "as a truth which others may be unwilling to make public," that Werner's death had greatly contributed to the progress of geology in Germany.— *Journ. Phys.* xciv. (1822), p. 298.

establishment of a true geognosy.[1]   While still pursuing his studies in Saxony, D'Aubuisson took up
the question of the basalts of that kingdom, travelled
over all their scattered hills, and at last wrote a treatise
upon them, which appeared in Paris in 1803.   In this
little volume of 170 pages the Wernerian doctrine as
to the origin of basalt is not only accepted but treated
as if it were incontestable.   In one passage, indeed, the
author guards himself by saying that his conclusions
have reference only to the basalts which he himself
has seen, and that if some day he can visit Auvergne
and the Vivarais, he perhaps may be better able to
discuss the question more generally, and to appreciate
what has been written on the other side.[2]   His essay
was presented to the Institute of Sciences, and the two
referees, Haüy and Ramond, to whom it was submitted,
appended to their favourable report on it a most
judicious piece of advice to the young author.   "A
subject," they say, "where the analogies already
hazarded have led to more than one mistake, demands the utmost caution in their use, and in a field
which the two parties dispute foot by foot, every step
should be justified by an observation and marked by
a fact.   Citizen D'Aubuisson has never seen either
active or extinct volcanoes.   Living till now in the
midst of aqueous formations, we should like him to
visit places where fire has manifested its empire.   We
would especially desire that he should see the basalts of
Auvergne, which another disciple of Werner [Leopold

[1] *Traité de Géognosie* (1819), vol. i. preface, p. xv.
[2] *Mémoire sur les Basaltes de la Saxe*, Paris, 1803, pp. 97, 100, 101.

von Buch] has just visited. That the citizen D'Aubuisson knows how to observe, is shown by his published
works, even if the memoir we have now been considering were not ample enough proof, and the interest of
his observations cannot be recognised in a manner
more useful to science than by encouraging him to
continue them."

D'Aubuisson lost no time in following the advice
thus given to him. He went to Auvergne and
found the basaltic rocks there lying on granite,
which in some valleys could be seen to be more
than 1200 feet thick. If these basaltic rocks were
lavas, they must, according to the Wernerian doctrine, have resulted from the combustion of beds of
coal. But how could coal be supposed to exist under
granite, which was the first chemical precipitate of a
primeval ocean ? Such an infra-position was incon-
ceivable, and thus an apparent confirmation of the
Freiberg view of the aqueous origin of basalt was
at first obtained. But a very short time sufficed to
stagger the young geologist. He saw the perfect
craters with their rugged lava-streams, which he
followed along their branches into the valleys. It
was impossible to resist this evidence. "The facts
which I saw," he says, "spoke too plainly to be
mistaken ; the truth revealed itself too clearly before
my eyes, so that I must either have absolutely refused
the testimony of my senses in not seeing the truth, or
that of my conscience in not straightway making it
known. There can be no question that basalts of
volcanic origin occur in Auvergne and the Vivarais.
There are found in Saxony, and in basaltic districts

generally, masses of rock with an exactly similar groundmass, which enclose exactly and exclusively the same crystals, and which have exactly the same structure in the field. There is not merely an analogy, but a complete similarity; and we cannot escape from the conclusion that there has also been an entire identity in formation and origin."[1]

The frank and courageous Wernerian read his recantation before the Institute of France the year after his work on the Saxon basalts appeared.[2] Still retaining his profound admiration for Werner, he nevertheless relinquished one after another the peculiar tenets of the Freiberg school, and became so impartial a chronicler of geological progress, that in his remarkably able *Treatise on Geognosy*, though inclining, on the whole, to his master's system, he did not entirely

---

[1] *Géognosie*, vol. ii. pp. 603, 605. Ch. Keferstein wrote a learned disquisition on Basalt entitled "Beiträge zur Geschichte und Kenntniss des Basaltes, und der ihm verwandten Massen," which is contained in the *Neue Schriften der Naturforschenden Gesellschaft zu Halle*, Band ii. 1819. The last part of the Memoir (pp. 139-250) consists of a review of the various opinions which up to that time had been expressed in regard to the nature of the rock, and contains copious references to authorities.

[2] "Sur les volcans et les basaltes de l'Auvergne," read to the Institute of Sciences in 1804; *Journ. de Physique*, tom. lviii. p. 427, lix. p. 367, lxxxviii. (1819), p. 432; *Soc. Philom. Bull. Paris*, 1804, p. 182. It is an indication of the slowness of the transmission of scientific news in those days that in the English translation of D'Aubuisson's *Basalts of Saxony*, which appeared at Edinburgh in 1814—that is, eleven years after the original—the translator states that he had heard of the author's having modified his views regarding the basalts of Auvergne, but that he was not aware that he had expressed any change of opinion in respect of those of Saxony.

adopt it, but presented his facts and inferences in such a manner that, as he himself claimed, even a follower of Hutton would hardly find a few paragraphs which he would wish to modify. D'Aubuisson lived into his seventy-third year, and died in 1819.

We turn now to the story of Leopold von Buch (1774-1853), the most illustrious geologist that Germany has produced. He came of a good family, which as far back as the twelfth century held an important position in the district of Altmark. His father, an ambassador in the Prussian service, had a family of six sons and seven daughters. Leopold, the sixth son, born on 25th April 1774, passed through a short course of mineralogical and chemical teaching at Berlin, and then went to Freiberg at the age of sixteen, to place himself under the guidance of Werner. He lived mostly under that great teacher's roof for three years, having for part of the time as his companion Alexander von Humboldt, with whom he then began a lifelong friendship. From Freiberg, where he drew in the pure Wernerian inspiration, he proceeded to the University of Halle, and later to that of Göttingen. For a brief period he held an appointment in the mining department of Silesia, but he soon abandoned the trammels of official employment, and having a sufficient competence for life, dedicated himself heart and soul to independent geological research. He was by far the most eminent of all the band of active propagandists who, issuing from Freiberg, spread themselves over Europe to illumine the benighted natives with the true light of Wernerianism.

Von Buch's earlier writings were conceived after the strictest rules of his master's system. In his first separate work, a mineralogical description of Landeck, he proclaimed, among other orthodox tenets of the Freiberg school, his adhesion to the aqueous origin of basalt, collected all the instances he could find of organic remains in that rock, and boldly affirmed that "it cannot be denied that Neptunism opens up to the spirit of observation a far wider field than does the volcanic theory."[1]

In the year 1797 Von Buch had his first view of the Alps, and in the following year began his more distant journeys, passing into Austria, and thence into Italy, where he spent a considerable time among the volcanic districts. In 1802 he published the first of two volumes descriptive of these early travels. It was appropriately dedicated to Werner, and expressed his continued adhesion to the Wernerian faith. "Every country and every district," he remarks, "where basalt is found furnishes evidence directly opposed to all idea that this remarkable rock has been erupted in a molten condition, or still more that each basalt hill marks the site of a volcano."[2] Before the second volume appeared, the writer of that sentence had an opportunity of visiting Auvergne. His conversion there appears to have been as rapid as that of

[1] *Gesammelte Schriften*, vol. i. p. 68.

[2] *Geognostische Beobachtungen auf Reisen durch Deutschland und Italien*, Berlin, i. (1802), p. 126. It is a curious fact that A. von Humboldt also began his geological career among the basalts of Germany, and published in 1790 a little tract of 126 pages, entitled *Mineralogische Beobachtungen über einige Basalte am Rhein*.

D'Aubuisson, but his announcement of it was much
more sensational. It was in the spring of 1802 that
he went to Central France, but owing to various
accidents the second volume of his travels did not
appear until the year 1809.[1] He had made no secret,
however, of his change of opinion, for in the winter
following his French tour, a letter from him was published, recommending a geologist who wanted to see
volcanoes to choose Auvergne rather than Vesuvius
or Etna.[2] His views were thus well known to Haüy
and Ramond when they recommended D'Aubuisson
to betake himself to the same volcanic region.

When his fuller account of his rambles in Auvergne
appeared, its very first sentence betrayed a curious
ignorance or forgetfulness of the literature of the
subject. "Here we are," he says, "in a region about
which the naturalists of France have talked so much,
to which they have persistently referred us, but which
they have never yet described to us." It is difficult
to believe that Von Buch had never seen Desmarest's
papers and accompanying maps. Yet throughout the
whole account which he gives of his excursions he does
not once refer to them, but writes as if he were almost

[1] The descriptions of Auvergne are contained in an Appendix to
vol. ii., consisting of *Mineralogische Briefe aus Auvergne an Herrn
Geh. Ober-Bergrath Karsten*, p. 227 (1809).

[2] *Journal des Mines*, vol. xiii. 1802-1803, p. 249. Boué, in an
obituary notice of Von Buch, says picturesquely that "in the year
1798 the learned geognost left Germany a Neptunist and came home
in 1800 a Vulcanist." His conversion, though as complete, was
not quite so rapid, for even after his visit to Italy and Central
France, though he gave up some parts of the Wernerian system, he
still clung tenaciously to others which he afterwards abandoned.

the first geologist who had ever made any detailed and exact observations in the country.[1]

Nothing could be more explicit than Von Buch's testimony to the volcanic origin of the basalts of Auvergne. The marvellous cone and crater of the Puy de Pariou excited, as they well might, his astonishment and admiration. " Here," he says, " we find a veritable model of the form and degradation of a volcano, such as cannot be found so clearly either at Etna or Vesuvius. Here at a glance we see how the lava has opened a way for itself at the foot of the volcano, how with its rough surface it has rushed down to the lower grounds, how the cone has been built above it out of loose slags which the volcano has ejected from its large central crater. We *infer* all this also at Vesuvius, but we do not always *see* it there as we do at the Puy de Pariou." [2]

Perhaps the most interesting passages in Von Buch's brightly-written letters are to be found at the end. The obviously volcanic origin of the rocks in Auvergne, and their position immediately above a mass of granite through which the craters had been opened, had evidently powerfully impressed his mind. With all these recent vivid experiences, he reflects upon his earlier wanderings among the basalt hills of Germany, and, as if taking his readers into his inner confidence, he declares that " it is impossible to believe in a

---

[1] He refers indeed several times to Montlosier's *Essai sur les Volcans d'Auvergne*, which he calls an excellent work. In one passage he actually credits this author with some of the most important generalisations made by Desmarest. (*Geog. Beobacht.*, pp. 279, 280.)

[2] *Op. cit.* p. 240.

particular or local formation of basalt, or in its flowing out as lava, when we know what the relations of this rock are in Germany, and when we remember how many different kinds of rocks are there associated with basalt as essential accompaniments, how these rocks form with basalt a connected whole which is absolutely inconsistent with any notion of volcanic action—a peculiar coal formation, entirely distinct from any other, only found with basalt and entirely enclosed among basaltic rocks, often even a peculiar formation of limestone." [1]

This was the one side of the picture. He could not yet break entirely the Wernerian bonds that held him to the beliefs he had imbibed at Freiberg. He could not bring himself to admit that all that his master had taught him as to the origin of basalt, all that he had himself so carefully noted down from his extended journeys in Germany, was radically wrong. He, no doubt, felt that it was not merely a question of the mode of origin of a single kind of stone. The whole doctrine of the chemical precipitation of the rocks of the earth's crust was at stake. If he surrendered it at one point, where was he to stop? We cannot wonder, therefore, that he still refused to permit himself to question the truth of the Wernerian faith in so far as the old basalts of Saxony and Silesia were concerned. He comforted himself with the belief that they at least, with all their associated sedimentary strata, must have been deposited by water.

But when he turns round again to the clear evidence displayed in Central France, he asks, " Is it the fault of

[1] *Op. cit.* p. 309.

the geologist in Auvergne that the arguments which are
powerful in Germany have no effect on him here, even
though he does not dispute them? May he not be
allowed in retort to ask whether the principles which so
obviously arise from the phenomena in Central France
are not also applicable to the German basalts? At all
events, he may contend, we see very little connection
between these basalts and ours as regards relations of
structure. Would you have us give up our convictions
as to the principles which give grandeur, consistency,
and simplicity to the explanation of our Auvergne
mountains, and adopt views founded on relations
which are not to be seen here?"[1]

Well might Von Buch conclude by saying that he
"stands perplexed and embarrassed." Whatever he
may think of the basalts of Auvergne, he will not
allow the Vulcanist to wrest his admissions to any
general conclusion with regard to the German basalts.
"Opinions are in opposition which only new observations can remove."

Von Buch's faith in the Wernerian interpretation of
volcanoes and basalt-hills had a rude shaking from his
excursions in Italy and Central France. His next
great journey taught him that Werner's scheme of
geological succession could not be maintained. Before
his volume descriptive of the Italian tour was published,
he had started for Norway, where he remained hard at
work for no less than two years. Among the vast mass
of important observations which he made, one that
must have greatly impressed him was that in which
he satisfied himself that the rocks in the Christiania

[1] *Op. cit.* p. 310.

district could not be arranged according to the Wernerian plan which there completely broke down. Von Buch found a mass of granite lying among fossiliferous limestones which were manifestly metamorphosed, and were pierced by veins of granite, porphyry, and syenite. Such observations did not lead him, any more than those in Central France, to a formal renunciation of Wernerianism. But they enabled him to take a wide and independent view of Nature, and gradually to emancipate himself from the narrower views in which he had been trained at Freiberg.[1]

Von Buch's memorable investigation of the proofs of the recent uprise of Scandinavia contributed still further to expand his geological horizon. When he announced that the whole of the continent of Sweden from Frederikshald to Abo is now slowly rising above the sea, he did as much as any Vulcanist of his day in support of the theory of the earth promulgated by Hutton.

A further emancipation from the tenets of Freiberg was displayed by a series of papers on the mountain-system of Germany, wherein Von Buch gave the first clear description of the geological structure of Central Europe. He declared that the more elevated mountains had never been covered by the sea, as Werner had taught, but were produced by successive ruptures and uplifts of the terrestrial crust. In 1824 he produced a geological map of the whole of Germany in forty-two sheets, the first large map of its kind to illustrate a great area of the European continent, and a signal monument of its author's unwearied research

[1] See his "Reise nach Norwegen und Lappland," *Gesammelte Schriften*, vol. ii. p. 109.

and of his geological acumen.   For more than sixty years this distinguished man continued to enrich geological literature with memoirs contributed to scientific societies and journals, and with independent works. His earliest writings stamped him as an observer of great sagacity and independence, and his reputation rose higher every year, until he came to be the acknowledged leader of geological science in Germany. Pressing forward into every department of the science, he illuminated it with the light of his penetrating intellect.   From the North Cape to the Canary Islands there was hardly a region that he did not personally explore, and not many that he did not describe. With ceaseless industry and exhaustless versatility, he ranged from the structure of the Alps to that of the Cystideans, from the distribution of volcanoes to that of Ammonites, from the details of minerals and rocks to the deepest problems in the history of the globe.[1]

His influence in his time was great.   Though he began as a Wernerian, he gradually and almost unconsciously passed into the ranks of the Vulcanists.   In no respect did he show his independence and love of truth more than in his long and enthusiastic researches among volcanoes.   No vulcanist could have worked out more successfully than he did the structure and history of the Canary Islands.

Among the leaders of geology in the first half of this

---

[1] Von Buch's collected writings form four large closely-printed octavo volumes.   The Royal Society's Catalogue assigns 153 separate papers to him.   For a biographical account of Von Buch see the sketch by W. Haidinger in *Jahrb. k. k. geol. Reichsanst.* Band iv. (1853), p. 207, and the notices prefixed to his collected works.

century there was no figure more familiar all over Europe than that of Von Buch.   Living as a bachelor, with no ties of home to restrain him, he would start off from Berlin, make an excursion to perhaps a distant district or foreign country, for the determination of some geological point that interested him, and return, without his friends knowing anything of his movements.   He made most of his journeys on foot, and must have been a picturesque object as he trudged along, stick in hand.   He wore knee-breeches and shoes, and the huge pockets of his overcoat were usually crammed with note-books, maps, and geological implements.   His luggage, even when he came as far as England, consisted only of a small baize bag, which held a clean shirt and silk stockings.   Few would have supposed that the odd personage thus accoutred was one of the greatest men of science of his time, an honoured and welcome guest in every learned society of Europe.   He was not only familiar with the writings of the geologists of his day, but knew the men personally, visited them in their own countries, and with many of them kept up a friendly and lively correspondence. He had an extensive knowledge of the languages of Europe, and had read widely not only in his own subjects, but in allied sciences, in history, and in literature, ancient and modern.   Kindly, frank, outspoken, and fearless, he was beloved and honoured by those who deserved his friendship, and dreaded by those who did not.   With tender self-sacrifice he would take his blind brother every year to Carlsbad, and with endless benefactions did he brighten the lives of many who survived to mourn his loss.   He died on 4th March 1853, in

the seventy-ninth year of his age.   A fitting monument
to his memory was raised by subscriptions from all over
Europe.   In the picturesque region of Upper Austria,
not far from Steyer, a granite boulder 16 feet high that
had been borne by a former glacier from the Alps was
chosen as his cenotaph.   The stone, chiselled into a flat
surface, bears inscribed upon it, with the reverence of
admirers in Germany, Belgium, France, England, and
Italy, the immortal name of Leopold von Buch.[1]

While D'Aubuisson and Von Buch were, even in
Werner's lifetime, emancipating themselves from the
tenets of the Freiberg School, various other observers,
without definitely becoming controversialists, were providing a large body of material which eventually proved
of great service in the establishment of a sound geology.
Chief among them were those who devoted themselves
with such ardour to the study of the Italian volcanoes.
One of the most active and interesting of their number
was Gratet de Dolomieu (1750-1801), who, born in
Dauphiné, died at the early age of fifty-one, after a
strangely eventful life.   At the age of 25 he published
some works on science, for which he was elected a
correspondent of the Academy of Sciences of Paris.   He
thereafter took to geological and mineralogical exploration, making his journeys on foot, with a bag on his
back, and a hammer in his hand, and studying successively
the minerals and rocks of Portugal, Spain, Sicily, the

[1] An account of the movement for the preparation of this monument will be found in *Das Buch-Denkmal,* a pamphlet by Ritter von
Hauer and Dr. Hörnes, published in Vienna in 1858.   It gives
a portrait of Von Buch, and a view of the monument, with a
map showing the position of the site.

Lipari Islands, the Pyrenees, the Alps, the Apennines, Central France, and the Vosges. He made extensive collections of specimens, and published many memoirs descriptive of the regions he visited. His attention was especially drawn to the active and extinct volcanoes of the Mediterranean basin. As far back as 1776 he made the announcement that he had found in Portugal evidence of volcanoes older than certain mountains of limestone—a statement which he supplemented in 1784 with further evidence from Sicily, proving the intercalation of ancient lavas among stratified deposits.[1] To this important discovery further reference will be given on a later page.

Among his other writings allusion may here be made to his little volume on the Lipari Isles, to the paper in which, following Desmarest, he described the old volcanoes of Central France, and to his " Memoire sur les Iles Ponces."[2] Though his theoretical views were not always sound, he was a careful and indefatigable observer, and provided copious material towards the establishment of the principles of geology. To him more than perhaps to any of his contemporaries is science indebted for recognising and enforcing the connection of volcanoes with the internal heat of the globe.

Faujas de St. Fond (1742-1819) did excellent service by his splendid folio on the old volcanoes of the Vivarais and the Velay—a work lavishly illustrated with engravings, which, by showing so clearly the association of columnar lavas with unmistakable

---

[1] *Journ. de Phys.* xxiv., Septembre 1784, p. 191.
[2] *Journ. des Mines*, vol. vii. (1798), pp. 393-405.

volcanic cones, ought to have done much to arrest
the progress of the Freiberg doctrine of the aqueous
origin of basalt.[1]   The same good observer undertook
a journey into the Western Isles of Scotland towards
the end of the eighteenth century,[2] when that region
was much less easily visited than it now is, and convinced himself of the volcanic origin of the basalts
there, thus adding another important contribution to
the literature of volcanic geology.

Spallanzani (1729-1799), the illustrious professor of
Pavia, Reggio, and Modena, born in 1729, devoted
his earlier life to animal and vegetable physiology,
and was fifty years of age before he began to turn
his attention to geological questions.   But from that
period onward he made many journeys in the basin of
the Mediterranean from Constantinople to Marseilles.
Of especial interest were his minute and picturesque
descriptions of the eruptions of Stromboli, which at
not a little personal risk he watched from a crevice
in the lava.   His *Travels in the Two Sicilies and in
some Parts of the Apennines* contained a mass of careful
observations among the recent and extinct volcanoes of
Italy.[3]

Another Italian vulcanist well worthy of remembrance was Scipio Breislak (1748-1826) who, born in
Rome and destined for the church, showed so strong a
bent for scientific pursuits that he was eventually made
professor of natural philosophy and mathematics at

[1] *Recherches sur les Volcans éteints du Vivarais et du Velay,* folio, 1778.

[2] *Voyage en Angleterre, en Écosse, et aux Iles Hébrides,* 2 vols. 8vo,
1797.

[3] *Viaggi alle due Sicilie,* 1792-93.

Ragusa, whence he passed to the Collegio Nazareno at Rome. His fondness for geological studies led to his appointment by Napoleon "Inspecteur des poudres et salpêtres" in the kingdom of Italy, which gave him the opportunity of making himself personally acquainted with the geology of a large part of his native country. Powerful as an advocate for the Vulcanist doctrines in opposition to the prevailing Neptunism of his time, he wrote some excellent monographs on the geology of different parts of Italy, particularly of the Campania ; also an Introduction to Geology, of which a French version was published in 1812, and a more important treatise which, translated into French from his Italian manuscript, was published at Milan in three volumes in 1818. The attitude which Breislak took towards the Freiberg School may be inferred from his remark— " I respect the standard raised by Werner, but the flag of the marvellous and mysterious will never be that which I shall choose to follow." [1]

Reference has been made in an earlier chapter (p. 159) to F. D. de Reynaud, Comte de Montlosier (1755-1838) who is chiefly known as a distinguished French publicist. He went into exile at the time of the French Revolution, but ultimately returned to France, and in the end became a member of the Chamber of Peers where, even when he had passed his eightieth year, he continued to be one of the most assiduous orators. He was the author of many political writings, but deserves mention here for the small treatise which he published in 1789 and which, as we

[1] *Introduzione alla Geologia*, 2 vols. 8vo, 1811.

have seen, proved useful to Von Buch in Auvergne. Montlosier, being an Auvergnat proprietor, had from his boyhood been familiar with the physical features of that interesting region. His *Essai* gives a lively account of the volcanic district from his own personal rambles, but it contains nothing of importance that is not to be found in the earlier writings of Desmarest, whose views he adopts, but without citing him as his authority. The last chapter of the *Essai* is devoted to a discussion of the nature of volcanic force, which the author regarded as something distinct from the " fire," and perhaps of the nature of electricity, " the energy whereof is increased under ground by chance encounter with certain antagonistic materials." He was at all events convinced that " neither coal, nor bitumen, nor any of the other substances known to us can possibly be the principle of volcanic force, which acts indifferently upon everything it meets with."

So long as the crude conception prevailed that volcanic action was due to the combustion of beds of coal or other inflammable materials, it was an obvious consequence that the production of volcanoes should be regarded as a comparatively modern feature in the history of our planet. Not until thick forests had flourished on the earth's surface, and had been buried deep under accumulations of sediment, could any subterranean conflagrations be expected to arise. But there was yet another influence which could not but retard the recognition of evidence of ancient volcanic eruptions preserved among the strata of the earth's crust. Hutton and his school, whose contributions to geological progress will be described in the next chapter, while they vigorously contended for the igneous origin of the "whinstone" (basalt) rocks, in opposition to the teachings of the Neptunists, looked upon these rocks as "not of volcanic, nor of aqueous, but certainly of igneous origin," having been "formed, in the bowels of the earth, of melted matter poured into the rents and openings of the strata."[1] So intent were the Plutonists on collecting all the evidence they could find in favour of the deep-seated and intrusive origin of these masses, that they naturally neglected or explained away, in accordance with their own theory, the cases where there was no evidence of intrusion. The Neptunists, on the other hand, seized upon these very cases in support of their contention that sheets of basalt regularly inter-stratified with aqueous deposits must themselves have been precipitated from solution in water. The disputants on neither side perceived that a third and entirely distinct explanation of the facts could be given. If the strata of sedimentary materials were accumulated under water, as was universally admitted, might not the sheets of basalt and other presumably volcanic materials have been erupted upon the floor of that water, whether sea or lake, so as to alternate with the normal deposits of sediment?

Already two acute observers had led the way towards this, the true solution of the apparent contradiction, though neither school of combatants would accept their explanation. Desmarest, as we have seen, (p. 166) had declared as far back as 1775, that traces

[1] Playfair's *Illustrations of the Huttonian Theory*, §§ 234, 239.

of ancient subaqueous volcanic eruptions have been preserved among the sedimentary strata that overlie the granite of Auvergne. A year or two later, Dolomieu pointed out the evidence for the contemporaneous interstratification of volcanic sheets among ordinary marine deposits. He first directed attention to the subject in 1776, and brought forward still more clearly in 1784 proofs of ancient eruptions preserved in a series of marine limestones.[1] He showed that in the Val di Noto in Sicily such limestones, abounding in large corals and shells, attain a considerable thickness and lie in horizontal beds of white rock, alternating with numerous intercalations of dark volcanic material. He found in one section eleven such prominent alternations, though if he had included the layers not more than an inch thick, this number would have been doubled. The volcanic material varied from band to band, two-thirds consisting of fragmental detritus, and the remainder of sheets of basalt, sometimes regularly columnar. The most abundant constituent was a black sand or tuff, which had been laid down in thin layers, with the coarsest particles at the bottom. Some of the bands consisted of a conglomerate made up of blocks of different lavas cemented together in a calcareous or argillaceous matrix. In all the limestones Dolomieu found volcanic fragments to be generally present. He observed that the basalt-sheets sometimes lie directly on a floor of limestone, sometimes on a layer of aggregated cinders, and that in the former case the two rocks are inter-

[1] "Sur les Volcans éteints du Val di Noto en Sicile," *Journ. de Physique*, xxv., Septr. 1784, p. 191.

mingled along the junction-plane. He rightly reasoned that these facts demonstrate the contemporaneous discharge of volcanic products over the sea-bottom, at the time when the limestones were in process of accumulation. He found a difficulty, however, in explaining how the basalts could have flowed so far as perhaps ten leagues, without becoming solid, and he thought that the vents from which the eruptions proceeded in such long succession must have rapidly risen above sea-level, otherwise their fires would have been speedily extinguished by the rush of the water down into their craters. The submarine volcanic series of younger Tertiary age in Sicily is now well known from the labours of subsequent observers, but it is not always pointed out that the credit of the original discovery of it belongs to Dolomieu.

Playfair was fully acquainted with the arguments of the French geologist, and refers to them with characteristic candour. He brings forward what he considers "insuperable objections" to them—objections which in the light of present knowledge are easily removable—but he frankly admits the value of Dolomieu's explanation of the facts by granting that "it makes a considerable approach to a true theory, and that the submarine volcanoes of Dolomieu have an affinity to the unerupted lavas of Dr. Hutton."[1]

The long continuance of the Huttonian prejudice in favour of these "unerupted lavas" can hardly be better illustrated than by reference to the *Description of the Western Islands of Scotland*, by John

[1] *Illustrations*, § 243.

Macculloch (1773-1835), published in 1819. This now classic work undoubtedly gave a great impetus to geological progress, especially in the department of the science which deals with the igneous rocks. The number and striking character of the illustrations which it afforded of the truly eruptive nature of these rocks did much to strengthen the Plutonist cause throughout the world. Yet though the region described included the great basalt-plateaux of the Inner Hebrides, with what we now recognise to be their abundant evidence of the superficial outpouring of streams of basic lava and showers of volcanic ashes, in continuous sequence, as clearly exposed along hundreds of miles of sea-precipices, no reader of Macculloch's volumes would be likely to gather from them that any such record of prolonged volcanic activity is to be found in the West of Scotland. Even so late as the year 1832, K. C. von Leonhard, in his ample monograph on *Die Basalt-Gebilde*, fully describes the volcanic features of these rocks as displayed in Auvergne, the Eifel and other districts, but when he comes to deal with the sheets of basalt intercalated among the strata of the Earth's crust, he is chiefly careful to mark their connection with dykes, and the proofs they furnish that they have been injected into and have altered the contiguous strata. It would almost appear that if in the earlier years of last century a Vulcanist had maintained the contemporaneity of a basalt-sheet with the sedimentary deposits among which it lay, he would have run some risk of being regarded as having gone over to the Neptunist camp.

Notwithstanding the lessons so clearly taught by

Desmarest from the structure of Auvergne, and by
Dolomieu from that of the Val di Noto, many years
had to pass away before it began to be generally
realised that all the sheets of igneous material intercalated among the sedimentary formations of the
terrestrial crust are not plutonic intrusions, but that
not a few of them are unquestionably lavas and
ashes, thrown out by once active volcanoes, either
under the sea or on land. Only by slow steps of
investigation was the truth at last ascertained and
admitted that volcanic action has been abundant all
over the globe, from the earliest geological times, and
that a record of its successive phases has been preserved among the rocks.

When at last the controversy as to the origin of
basalt, and the eruptive character of the so-called
"Trap-rocks" had been settled, and men were able,
apart from the disputes of the rival schools, to look at
these rocks impartially, with the view of learning what
record they have to contribute to the history of the
earth, it was fitting that progress in this subject should
begin to be made in Britain—a portion of the earth's
surface which, for its size, contains a fuller chronicle
of past volcanic activity than any other land hitherto
examined. A brief outline of the early stages of this
research within the British Isles will show how slowly
yet how securely the foundation stones in this department of geology were laid.

Among the followers of the Wernerian faith who
early emancipated themselves from Werner's doctrines
regarding volcanic rocks, an honourable place must
be assigned to Ami Boué (1794-1881). Born in

Hamburg, but of Swiss parentage and old French descent, he was sent for his medical education to the University of Edinburgh, where he graduated as M.D. in the year 1816. But his strong bent towards natural history pursuits led him to take up geology, in which he was trained after the Wernerian system by Jameson. He rambled far and wide over Scotland, and formed his own conclusions as to the origin and age of many of the igneous rocks so abundantly developed in that country. Leaving Edinburgh, he settled for a time in Paris, and while there, wrote an excellent treatise in French, with the title of *Essai Géologique sur l'Écosse*, which though it bears no date, appears to have been published in the year 1820. In many respects this remarkable work was far in advance of its time, particularly in regard to the views expressed in it regarding the trappean rocks. Boué's acute eyes recognised the volcanic nature of the great series of " roches feldspathiques et trappéennes " of central Scotland, which he claimed to mark eruptions in the time of the Old Red Sandstone. He boldly introduced for the first time, into the geological table for that country, a division entitled " Terrain Volcanique," wherein he included not only the younger basalts of the Inner Hebrides which had been described by Faujas St. Fond, Macculloch and others, but also the basalts, andesites, trachytes, tuffs and other rocks intercalated in the Carboniferous system.

On the other hand, Charles Daubeny (1795-1867) another pupil of Jameson, who afterwards wrote an excellent treatise on volcanoes, could so late as 1821

still speak of granite passing into sandstone, of " fire
and water, although such opposite agents, having in
some instances, produced effects nearly, if not altogether identical," and of the probability that what is
now known to be a typical and admirable series of
alternations of basalt-lavas with tuffs and sedimentary
fossiliferous strata, was entirely the product of aqueous
deposition.[1]

But in the third and fourth decades of the nineteenth century a number of independent observers had
their attention aroused by the intercalation of rocks
which they could only regard as volcanic, among the
older stratified formations of Britain. In his singularly
suggestive volume entitled *Researches in Theoretical
Geology*, published in 1831, Henry Thomas De la Beche
(1796–1855) expressed, though cautiously, his opinion
that some at least of the " trappean " rocks associated
with the lower parts of the " grauwacke series " in
different countries of Europe, appear to have been
contemporaneous with the strata among which they lie,
" precisely as a bed of lava may flow over a sandy

[1] Letters to Professor Jameson, *Edin. Phil. Journ.*, 1820-21. In
Conybeare's Introduction to Conybeare and Phillips' *Outlines of the
Geology of England and Wales*, published in 1822, regretful reference
is made to the " excessive addiction to theoretical speculations " on
the part of the zealous rival partizans of the Huttonian and
Wernerian systems at Edinburgh. The author refrains from pro-
nouncing any judgment on the controversy as to the origin of
the Trap rocks, being desirous " to keep these conjectural speculations entirely distinct from that positive knowledge, acquired from
observation, which is as yet the only certain portion of geological
science." One can see that, in spite of this laudable caution,
Conybeare's sympathies were rather in favour of the igneous
views.

bottom and afterwards be covered up by a deposit of
sand or mud." He had himself observed considerable
accumulations of "comminuted trappean matter" among
the greenstones and porphyries of the older grauwacke
of Devon and Cornwall, and was inclined to believe
them to represent volcanic ashes ejected at the time
that the associated sediments were in course of deposition. He was thus led to suppose "that there
had been ejections of igneous matter into the atmosphere or beneath shallow water, and consequently that
we might expect to discover similar facts among the
other fossiliferous rocks, under favourable circumstances
and in different parts of the world." [1]

While these observations were in progress in the
south of England, another series on a larger scale was
advancing in the Lake District of the north. In that
mountainous tract Adam Sedgwick (1785-1873) had
spent some years, tracing the intricate structure of the
ground, and had found a great group of green slates
and porphyries, comprising fine compact slates with
coarse granular concretionary masses and breccias or
pseudo-breccias; likewise amorphous, semi-columnar,
prismatic porphyries, which did not take the form of
dykes nor altered the limestone that rests upon them.
He therefore "inferred that the whole group is of

[1] *Op. cit.* pp. 384, 385. The "ashes" here referred to are of
Middle Devonian age. He also recognised the probable con-
temporaneous eruption of the trappean rocks associated with the
much younger red conglomerate of South Devon which may be
Permian. *Geological Manual,* 1831, p. 389. The progress of the
Geological Survey in later years enabled De la Beche to add
fresh details regarding the Lower Silurian volcanic rocks of Southern
Wales. *Mem. Geol. Survey,* vol. i. (1846) pp. 29-36.

one formation which has originated in the simultaneous action of aqueous and igneous causes long continued."[1]

Sedgwick next turned his attention to the complicated geological structure of the mountainous region of North Wales, and after great labour succeeded in unravelling it. Among the important additions to geological science made by him at this time was the recognition of the intercalation of vast masses of igneous rocks among the ancient sedimentary series (Cambrian and Lower Silurian) of that region. He distinguished trappean conglomerates, contemporaneous sheets of "felstone-porphyry" and "felstone," and found the two classes of aqueous and igneous rocks so interlaced that they could not be separated and were regarded by him as of contemporaneous origin. He likewise noted the presence of later intrusions of "greenstone" and other trappean masses. Thus the existence of a vast complex of ancient Palæozoic lavas, tuffs, and breccias was introduced into geological literature.[2]

While the Woodwardian Professor was at work

[1] *Proc. Geol. Soc.* vol. i. p. 248 (5th January, 1831) and p. 400 (2nd May, 1832).

[2] *Proc. Geol. Soc.* ii. (1838) pp. 678-9; iii. (1841) p. 548; iv. (1843) p. 215. *Quart. Journ. Geol. Soc.* i. (1843) pp. 8-17; iii. (1846) p. 134. In the last cited paper Professor Sedgwick speaks of at least ninety hundredths of the trappean rocks of North Wales being of contemporaneous origin with their associated strata; but he regards them all as essentially "subaqueous or plutonic." He shows how they have been involved in all the latter plication of the region, and how they may be used as recognisable and well-defined stratigraphical platforms.

in North Wales his friend Roderick Impey Murchison
(1792-1871) was engaged on the borders of the
Principality in attacking the sedimentary (grauwacke)
strata that emerge from under the base of the Old Red
Sandstone, as will be more particularly noticed in
Chapter XIII. He had not advanced far in this
investigation before he in turn was confronted with
many examples of what were evidently igneous rocks,
intercalated among the stratified formations to which
he was more specially directing his attention. In one
of his papers, read before the Geological Society in
1824, he shows at what an early period in his inquiries
he had detected proofs of true volcanic masses associated with these formations. He there remarks " that as
some of the porphyritic and felspathic rocks alternate
conformably with strata of marine origin, containing
organic remains of a very early period, and as some of
the layers in which such remains are imbedded have
a base of true volcanic matter, the date of the origin of
this class of rock is thereby fixed. These conformable
alternations of trap and marine sediment establish a
direct analogy between their mode of production and
those replications of volcanic ejections and marine
deposit which are now going on beneath the present
seas ; whilst they further explain the manner in which,
in times of the highest geological antiquity, the porphyry-
slates were arranged in parallel laminæ with the sedimentary accumulations of that age. The existence of
certain strata containing organic remains, yet possessing
a matrix composed in great measure of the same
materials as the adjacent ridges of trap-rock, has
strengthened the inference that some of the ebullitions

of these submarine volcanoes were contemporaneous
with the period in which these animals lived and died,
the finer volcanic ejections having, it is presumed, led
to the formation of the volcanic sandstone."[1]

In Scotland, after the war between the Plutonists and
the Neptunists had ceased, a period of calm, almost of
stagnation ensued, so far at least as regarded the investigation of igneous rocks. While it was now generally
conceded that these rocks had really resulted from the
action of subterranean causes, the old Huttonian idea
still prevailed that they had all been injected among
the strata at some depth beneath the surface. Even
so late as 1834 when Hay Cunningham, a pupil of
Jameson, began to prepare the materials for his essay
on "The Geology of the Lothians,"[2] he failed to
distinguish between the intrusive and contempor-
aneously intercalated sheets of igneous rock, although
each series is admirably developed in the region which
he had to investigate and describe. In the year 1839
there was published by far the most important treatise
that had yet been devoted to the description of any portion of the ancient volcanic rocks of Britain—the *Sketch
of the Geology of Fife and the Lothians* by Charles
Maclaren. In this classic work the structure of two
groups of hills—Arthur's Seat and the Pentlands—was
worked out in ample detail, and the volcanic history of
each of them was admirably traced. In the one case,

---

[1] *Proc. Geol. Soc.* ii. (1834) p. 92. Fuller discussion of the subject,
with ample local details, was given in his *Silurian System*, which was
published at the end of 1838. See especially pp. 225, 258, 268,
287, 317, 324 and 401.

[2] *Mem. Wernerian Soc.* vol. vii.

the successive outflows of a series of "claystone" "clinkstone" and "porphyry" lavas, from subaqueous craters or fissures, belonging to the time of the Old Red Sandstone, was demonstrated by conclusive proofs. In the other, the combination of subterranean injection and superficial outflow from a crater of Lower Carboniferous age was clearly shown, together with evidence of alternations of basalt-lavas with volcanic tuffs, succeeded by prolonged denudation and a subsequent renewal of volcanic activity on the same site. The author, by appeals to the known behaviour of modern volcanoes, illustrated each main feature in the history of these ancient centres of eruption. His convincing and suggestive essay ought to have immediately stimulated the investigation of the subject in other parts of the same region, where innumerable examples of the phenomena, on even a more striking scale, remained still unknown or misunderstood. But Maclaren did not himself continue his volcanic researches, nor for nearly twenty years did any one arise to take up again the work which he had so well begun.

The Geological Survey in Wales developed with great detail the history of the igneous rocks which had been briefly noticed by Sedgwick and Murchison. Subsequently the extension of the Survey to Scotland in 1854 brought to light the remarkable fulness of the volcanic record in that kingdom. Gradually this record has been deciphered for the whole of the British Isles, which are now found to include a singularly varied and prolonged succession of volcanic rocks, extending through Palæozoic time and another wide-spread and complicated series dating from the older part of the Tertiary period.[1]

It is unnecessary to trace the progress of investigation in other countries regarding the volcanic action of former geological periods. In Germany, the lavas and tuffs of Devonian and Permian age have long been made familiar by many able writers. In France, besides the complicated history of the Tertiary volcanic history which, first sketched in broad outline by Desmarest, has been followed into the minutest details by Fouqué, Michel Lévy, Boule and other observers, a great series of Palæozoic eruptions has been brought to light by Barrois. In the United States also, a long and complicated volcanic record, dating from older Tertiary time, has been made known by the geologists of the various surveys which have been extended over the Western States and Territories. And thus the present active volcanoes of the globe have been shown to be the latest in a series which can be traced backwards into the remotest geological periods.

We have seen in the course of these chapters that volcanoes and earthquakes were assumed, even as far back as the time of the ancient Greeks and Romans, to be connected phenomena arising from one common cause, but that no attempt was made during all the subsequent centuries either by close observation or well-devised experiment to discover what this active cause might be. The prevalent opinion was that which looked upon subterranean wind as the main

[1] I have given a full account of this volcanic history in my *Ancient Volcanoes of Great Britain*, 2 vols., 1897.

agent of commotion, aided by the collapse of the roofs or sides of underground caverns. When the disturbance of the air in these recesses reached a maximum of intensity its friction or that of falling masses of loosened rock set fire to combustible materials, and eventually the wind and hot vapours forced their way with violence to the surface in volcanic explosions. That earthquakes are common in volcanic districts had been recognised from the earliest times, but they had been experienced also in regions where there were no active volcanoes. In the latter case they were regarded as volcanic convulsions which had not succeeded in opening a vent above ground. But down to the middle of the eighteenth century no real progress had been made in the solution of the problem of their origin.

The year 1750 was remarkable for the number of earthquakes which at that time affected the west of Europe, and which caused some alarm in the south of England. The Royal Society collected and published the narratives of many observers, and likewise some lucubrations on the " philosophy of earthquakes." The same century was distinguished for its great activity and rapid advance in the investigation of electricity. This new and still mysterious force, so stupendous, sudden and swift in its operation, seemed to some minds to offer a probable explanation of the phenomena of earthquakes. The earliest writer who tried to picture to himself the manner in which electricity acts in the process seems to have been Dr. Stukeley, who contributed several communications on the subject to the *Philosophical Transactions* of the Royal Society.

He " did not enter into the common notion of struggles between subterraneous winds, or fires, vapours or waters, that heaved up the ground like animal convulsions ; but always thought it was an electrical shock, exactly of the same nature as those, now become very familiar in electrical experiments." In one passage he remarks that, owing to peculiar meteorological conditions, a wide extent of country is sometimes brought into a highly electrified state and that if then a " non-electric cloud " should discharge its contents, in a heavy shower of rain, " an earthquake must necessarily ensue." In another part of the same essay he refers to " a black sulphureous cloud " which comes " at a time when sulphureous vapours are rising from the earth in greater quantity than usual ; in which combined circumstances, the ascending sulphureous vapours in the earth may probably take fire and thereby cause an earth-lightning, which is at first kindled at the surface, and not at great depths, as has been thought ; and the explosion of this lightning is the immediate cause of an earthquake." [1]

Of a very different stamp from these crude speculations was an essay by the Rev. John Michell (1724-1793) read before the Royal Society in the spring of the year 1760. During the decade that had elapsed since the " earthquake year " of 1750, western Europe had not ceased to be shaken, and there had happened the great Lisbon earthquake of 1st November 1755—the most extensive and disastrous catastrophe which had ever been recorded.

[1] *Phil. Trans.* vol. xlvi. (1750), pp. 643, 676.

The keenest interest was consequently aroused in the subject of earthquakes, and numerous reports from eye-witnesses of the effects of that great disturbance were printed in the 49th volume of the *Philosophical Transactions*. Among the various papers Michell's "Essay on the Causes and Phenomena of Earthquakes" stands out conspicuously as by far the most important contribution to this branch of science that had yet appeared in any language or country. Starting on the assumption that earthquakes are due to the sudden access of large quantities of water to subterranean fires, whereby vapour is produced in sufficient quantity and elastic force to give rise to the shock, the author proceeds to adduce facts and arguments in support of this hypothesis. In the course of the discussion he points to the frequency of earthquakes in the neighbourhood of active volcanoes, and to their usual occurrence as accompaniments of volcanic eruptions. He states that the motion of the ground in earthquakes is partly tremulous and partly propagated by waves which, succeeding each other at intervals, generally travel much further than the tremors. He sees no difficulty in believing that subterranean fires may continue to burn for long periods without the access of air, and he adopts the idea that the spontaneous combustion of subterranean pyritous strata among inflammable materials may be the cause of the fires of volcanoes. If the vapours raised from these fires, and finding an outlet at volcanic vents, are powerful enough to convulse the surrounding region to a distance of ten or twenty miles, what may we not expect from them when they are confined under ground and prevented from escaping ? When the roof above one of the volcanic fires falls into the molten mass below it, all the water contained in the fissures and cavities would be precipitated into the fire and be almost instantly raised into vapour, which, by its first effort, would form a cavity between the melted matter and the superincumbent rock. This rock would thus be first compressed, and then, on recovery, dilated, producing a vibratory motion at the surface of the ground, and partially occasioning the noise that accompanies an earthquake, though this may also be due to the grating of the parts of the earth together during the wave-like motion through them. The waves propagated through the earth are largest above their source of origin, and gradually diminish until they may only be detected by the motion of sheets of water and objects suspended from a height, as hanging branches and lamps in churches.

Michell further remarks that while earthquakes are frequent in mountainous districts, they are usually less extensive there than those which originate under the sea, and he thinks that far more extensive fires may exist below the ocean than on land, where the mass of material lying above them is less. In seeking to find the focus of origin of an earthquake, this acute writer points out that if lines be drawn in the direction of the observed track of the earth-waves through all the places affected, "the place of their common inter-section must be nearly the place sought." He shows that the great Lisbon earthquake had its origin under the Atlantic, somewhere between the latitudes of Lisbon and Oporto. While admitting that a sufficient number of accurate data had not then been collected to permit any satisfactory computation of the depth of origin of earthquakes, which might considerably vary, he yet thought that "some kind of guess might be formed concerning it," and in illustration of such a "random guess" he supposed that the depth at which the Lisbon earthquake took its origin "could not be much less than a mile, or a mile and a half, and probably did not exceed three miles."

From this brief summary of his opinions it will be seen that Michell still laboured under the popular and time-honoured delusion that volcanoes take their rise from the combustion of inflammable strata below ground, and that he attributed earthquakes exclusively to the influence of these subterranean fires. Realising that the sudden development of large bodies of vapour within the terrestrial crust might start the disturbances of earthquakes, he made a great onward step in showing that successive waves would be generated in that crust, and would travel outwards, in constantly diminishing amplitude until they finally died away. It was the first time that this conception of earthquake motion had been laid before the world. Michell, however, appears to have assumed the propagation of the vapour to be the cause of the wave-like motion of the ground. He speaks of the vapour "raising the earth in a wave as it passes along between the strata, which it may easily separate in an horizontal direction." He refers to "the wave at the surface of the earth occasioned by the passing of the vapour under it," and states that "the shortest way that the vapour could pass from near Lisbon to Loch Ness was under the ocean." But with all his limitations we may yet rank him as the great pioneer of the modern science of Seismology.[1]

It was not until about the middle of last century that scientific methods and instrumental research began to be seriously applied to the study of earthquake phenomena, and the modern science of Seismology came into being. Alexis Perry of Dijon had rendered important service by laboriously collecting statistics of earthquakes from all countries and of all ages back to the early centuries of our era. But it is more especially to the labours of Robert Mallet (1810–1881) that we owe the initial impetus which has led to such valuable results in recent years. In 1846 he published a paper "On the Dynamics of Earthquakes,"[2] which, as he himself says of it, was "the first attempt to bring the phenomena of the earthquake within the range of exact science, by reducing to system the enormous mass of disconnected and often discordant and ill-observed facts which the multiplied

---

[1] Michell was specially distinguished as an astronomer. After serving various offices at the University of Cambridge, where he had graduated as fourth wrangler, he became rector first of St. Botolph's, Cambridge, and for the last twenty-six years of his life, of Thornhill in Yorkshire. He was a Fellow of the Royal Society, and author of a number of remarkable papers on astronomical subjects. His essay on earthquakes may have led to his being appointed in 1762 to the Woodwardian Professorship of Geology at Cambridge, but it appears to be his only contribution to geological science. Not only does it treat of the subject of its title, but it gives an excellent account of the tectonic arrangement of the stratified formations, to which further reference will be made in a later chapter.

[2] *Trans. Roy. Irish Acad.* vol. xxi. (1846), p. 51.

narratives of earthquakes present, and educing from these, by an appeal to the established laws of the higher mechanics, a theory of earthquake motion." In this his earliest contribution to the subject he announced his famous definition of that motion as " the transit of a wave of elastic compression in any direction, from vertically upwards, to horizontally, in any azimuth, through the surface and crust of the earth, from any centre of impulse or from more than one, and which may be attended with tidal and sound waves dependent upon the former, and upon circumstances of position as to sea and land." This epoch-making essay was followed by his paper on the " Observation of Earthquake Phenomena " contributed to the Admiralty *Manual of Scientific Enquiry* in 1849, and thereafter by a voluminous series of Reports published by the British Association for the Advancement of Science from 1850 to 1858. These Reports included a Catalogue of recorded earthquakes from 1606 B.C. to A.D. 1850, and a full discussion of the facts and theory of earthquake phenomena.

Mallet's enthusiasm in the study of these phenomena received a vivid stimulus from the occurrence of the Neapolitan earthquake of December 1857—the third in point of extent and severity hitherto experienced in Europe. Under the auspices of the Royal Society, he was enabled to visit the scene of devastation in southern Italy, shortly after the calamity, and to make careful observations of the effects upon buildings and upon the surface of the ground. The results of his investigation formed the subject of his work in two volumes *The First Principles of Observational Seis-*

mology (*Great Neapolitan Earthquake of* 1857). Mallet further contributed to our knowledge of the transmission of waves of shock through the earth's crust by exploding gunpowder and measuring the rate at which the shock travels through different kinds of materials, such as loose sand, on the one hand, and solid granite, on the other.

The subsequent progress of seismology belongs to a later time than falls within the limits marked out for treatment here. The science has made a great advance since Mallet's time, more particularly as a consequence of the greater perfection of instrumental observation, and of the labours of Professor John Milne and the native observers in Japan—a region where earthquakes are frequent and sometimes of great violence. Such is the general interest in the subject that observing stations, furnished with good self-registering seismographs, are now to be found in many parts of both hemispheres, and such is the sensitiveness of these instruments that every severe earthquake is detected and registered even at the antipodes of the region from which it originates.

CHAPTER IX

Rise of the modern conception of the theory of the Earth. Hutton, Playfair.

WHILE the din of geological warfare resounded across Europe, and the followers of Werner, flaunting the Neptunist flag in every corner of the continent, had succeeded in making the system promulgated from Freiberg almost supplant every other, a series of quiet and desultory researches was in progress, which led to the establishment of some of the fundamental principles of modern geology. We have now to turn our eyes to the northern part of the British Isles, and to trace the career of a man who, with singular sagacity, recognising early in life the essential processes of geological change, devoted himself with unwearied application to the task of watching their effects, and collecting proofs of their operation, and who combined the results of his observation and reflection in a work which will ever remain one of the great classics of science. In following the course of his researches, we shall see another illustration of the influence of environment on mental tendencies, and mark how the sea-shores and mountains, the glens and lowlands of Scotland have given form and colour to the development of geological theory.

James Hutton (1726-1797) was born in Edinburgh on the 3rd June 1726, and was educated at the High School and University of that city.[1] His father, a worthy citizen there, had held the office of City Treasurer, but died while the son was still young, to whom he left a small landed property in Berwickshire. While attending the logic lectures at the University, Hutton's attention was arrested by a reference to the fact that, although a single acid suffices to dissolve the baser metals, two acids must combine their strength to effect the solution of gold. The professor, who had only used this illustration in unfolding some general doctrine, may or may not have made his pupil a good logician, but he certainly made him a chemist, for from that time the young student was drawn to chemistry by a force that only became stronger as years went on. When at seventeen years of age he had to select his profession in life, he was placed as an apprentice in a lawyer's office. But genius is irrepressible, and amid the drudgery of the law the young clerk's chemistry not infrequently came to the surface. He would be found amusing himself and his fellow-apprentices with chemical experiments, when he should have been copying papers or studying legal proceedings,

[1] For the biographical details in this sketch I am indebted to the admirable "Biographical Account of Dr. James Hutton" by his friend and illustrator, Playfair. This was first printed in the *Transactions of the Royal Society of Edinburgh*, and will be found in vol. iv. of Playfair's collected works

so that finally his master, seeing that law was evidently not his bent, released him from his engagement, and advised him to seek some other employment more suited to his turn of mind.

Hutton accordingly, after a year's drudgery at law, made choice of medicine as the profession most nearly allied to chemistry, and most likely to allow him to indulge his predilection for science. For three years he prosecuted his medical studies at Edinburgh, and thereafter, as was then the custom, repaired to the Continent to complete his professional training. He remained nearly two years in Paris, pursuing there with ardour the studies of chemistry and anatomy. Returning to Scotland by way of the Low Countries, he took the degree of Doctor of Medicine at Leyden in September 1749.

But the career of a physician seems to have grown less attractive to him as the time came on for his definitely settling in life. He may have been to some extent influenced by the success of certain chemical researches which he had years before begun with a friend of kindred tastes—researches which had led to some valuable discoveries in connection with the nature and production of sal ammoniac, and which appeared to offer a reasonable prospect of commercial success. In the end he abandoned all thought of practising medicine, and resolved to apply himself to farming. He was a man never disposed to do things by halves. Having made up his mind in favour of agriculture as his vocation, he determined to take advantage of the best practical instruction in the subject then available. Accordingly in 1752 he betook himself to Norfolk, lived with a Norfolk farmer, and entered with all the zest of a young man of six-and-twenty into the rural sports and little adventures which, in the intervals of labour, formed the amusement of his host and his neighbours.

It appears to have been during this sojourn in East Anglia that Hutton's mind first definitely turned to mineralogy and geology. He made many journeys on foot into different parts of England. In Norfolk itself there was much to arouse his attention. Every here and there, the underlying White Chalk came to the surface, with its rows of fantastically-shaped black flints. To the east, lay the Crag with its heaps of sea-shells, stretching over many miles of the interior. To the north, the sea had cut a range of cliffs in the Boulder-clay which, with its masses of chalk and its foreign stones, presented endless puzzles to an inquirer. To the west, the shores of the Wash showed the well-marked strata of Red Chalk and Car-stone, emerging from underneath the White Chalk of the interior.

Hutton tells, in one of his letters written from Norfolk, that he had grown fond of studying the surface of the earth, and was looking with anxious curiosity into every pit or ditch or bed of a river that fell in his way.

After spending about two years in Norfolk, he took a tour into Flanders, with the view of com-paring the husbandry there with that which he had been studying in England. But his eyes were now turned to what lay beneath the crops and their soils, and he took note of the rocks and minerals of the districts through which he passed. At last, about the end of the summer of 1754, he settled down on his own paternal acres in Berwickshire, which he cultivated after the most approved methods. For fourteen years he remained immersed in rural pursuits, coming occasionally to Edinburgh and making, from time to time, an excursion to some more distant part of the kingdom. His neighbours in the country probably looked upon him only as a good farmer, with more intelligence, enterprise, culture and knowledge of the world than were usual in their society, and displaying a playful humour and liveliness of manner which must have made his companionship extremely pleasant. Probably not one of the lairds and farmers in the South of Scotland, who met him at kirk and market, had the least suspicion that this agreeable neighbour of theirs was a man of surpassing genius, who at that very time, amidst all the rural pursuits in which he seemed to be absorbed, was meditating on some of the profoundest problems in the history of the earth, and was gathering materials for such a solution of these problems as had never before been attempted.

The sal ammoniac manufacture had proved successful, and from 1765 Hutton became a regular co-partner in it. His farm, now brought into excellent order, no longer afforded him the same interest and occupation, and eventually he availed himself of an opportunity of letting it to advantage. He determined about the year 1768 to give up a country life and establish himself in Edinburgh, in order that, with uninterrupted leisure, he might devote himself entirely to scientific pursuits.

The Scottish capital had not yet begun seriously to suffer from the centripetal attractions of London. It was the social centre of Scotland, and retained within its walls most of the culture and intellect of that ancient kingdom. Hutton, from his early and close connection with Edinburgh, had many friends there, and, on his return for permanent residence, was received at once into the choicest society of the town. One of his most intimate associates was Dr. Joseph Black, the famous chemist to whom we owe the discovery of carbonic acid. This sympathetic friend took the keenest interest in Hutton's geological theories, and was able to contribute to their formation and development. Hutton himself acknowledges that one of his doctrines, that of the influence of compression in modifying the action of heat, was suggested by the researches of Dr. Black. The chemist's calm judgment and extensive knowledge were always at the command of his more impulsive geological friend, and doubtless proved of essential service in guiding him in his speculations.

Another of Hutton's constant and intimate associates was John Clerk of Eldon, best known as the author of a work on naval tactics, and the inventor of the method of breaking the enemy's line at sea, which led to so many victories by the fleets of Great Britain. A third member of his social circle, who may be alluded to here, was the philosopher and historian Adam Ferguson, a man of remarkable force of character, who, to his various literary works, which were translated into French and German, added the distinction of a diplomatist, for in 1778-1779 he acted

as Secretary of the Commission sent across the Atlantic
by Lord North to try to arrange the matters in dispute
between the mother country and her North American
colonies.

When Hutton found himself in these congenial
surroundings, with ample leisure at his command,
he appears to have turned at once to his first love
in science, by betaking himself to chemical experiment.   Even without the testimony of his biographer,
we have only to look at his published works to be
impressed by his unwearied industry, and by the extraordinarily wide range of his studies.   Though up to
the time of his settling in Edinburgh he had published
nothing, he had read extensively.   There were hardly
any of the sciences, except the mathematical, to which
he did not turn his attention.   He was a diligent
reader of voyages, travels and books of natural history,
carefully storing up the facts which seemed to him to
bear on the problems of the earth's history.   He not
only prosecuted chemistry and mineralogy, but distinguished himself as a practical meteorologist by his
important contribution to the theory of rain.   He
wrote a general system of physics and metaphysics in
one quarto volume, and no fewer than three massive
quartos were devoted by him to *An Investigation of
the Principles of Knowledge, and of the Progress of Reason
from Sense to Science and Philosophy.*   At the time of
his death he was engaged upon a treatise on the
Elements of Agriculture.

Hutton was thus no narrow specialist, wrapped
up in the pursuit of one circumscribed section of
human inquiry.   His mind ranged far and wide

over many departments of knowledge. He took the keenest interest in them all, and showed the most vivid sympathy in their advancement. His pleasure in every onward step made by science and philosophy showed itself in the most lively demonstrations. " He would rejoice," we are told by Playfair, " over Watt's improvements on the steam-engine, or Cook's discoveries in the South Seas, with all the warmth of a man who was to share in the honour or the profit about to accrue from them. The fire of his expression, on such occasions, and the animation of his countenance and manner, are not to be described ; they were always seen with great delight by those who could enter into his sentiments ; and often with great astonishment by those who could not."

While so much was congenial to his mental habits in the friendly intercourse of Edinburgh society, there was not less in the scenery around the city that would stimulate his geological proclivities. He could not take a walk in any direction without meeting with illustrations of some of the problems for the solution of which he was seeking. If he turned eastward, Arthur's Seat and Salisbury Crags rose in front of him, with their memorials of ancient volcanic eruptions. If he strolled westward, the ravines of the Water of Leith presented him with proofs of the erosive power of running water, and with sections of the successive sea-bottoms of the Carboniferous period. Even within the walls of the city, the precipitous Castle Rock bore witness to the energy with which in ancient times molten material had been thrust into the crust of the earth.

No more admirable environment could possibly have inspired a geologist than that in which Hutton now began to work more sedulously at the study of the former changes of the earth's surface. But he went far afield in search of facts, and to test his interpretation of them. He made journeys into different parts of Scotland, where the phenomena which engaged his attention seemed most likely to be well displayed. He extended his excursions likewise into England and Wales. For about thirty years, he had never ceased to study the natural history of the globe, constantly seeking to recognise the proofs of ancient terrestrial revolutions, and to learn by what causes they had been produced. He had been led to form a definite theory or system which, by uniting and connecting the scattered facts, furnished an intelligible explanation of them. But he refrained from publishing it to the world. He had communicated his views to one or two of his friends, perhaps only to Dr. Black and Mr. Clerk, whose judgment and approval were warmly given to him. The world, however, might have had still a long time to wait for the appearance of his dissertation, had it not been for the interest that he took in the foundation of the Royal Society of Edinburgh, which was incorporated by Royal Charter in 1783.[1] At one of

[1] The Royal Society had been preceded by the Philosophical Society, out of which it sprang. Edinburgh at that time was famous for the number of its clubs and convivial meetings, at some of which Black and Hutton were constant companions. Various anecdotes have been handed down of these two worthies and their intercourse, of which the following may suffice as a specimen. "These attached friends agreed in their opposition to the usual vulgar prejudices, and frequently discoursed together upon the absurdity of many generally

the early meetings of this Society he communicated a concise account of his Theory of the Earth, which appeared in the first volume of the *Transactions*. This essay was afterwards expanded, with much ampler details of observations and fuller application of principles to the elucidation of the phenomena, and the enlarged work appeared in two octavo volumes in the year 1795 with the title of *Theory of the Earth, with Proofs and*

received opinions, especially in regard to diet. On one occasion they had a disquisition upon the inconsistency of abstaining from feeding on the testaceous creatures of the land, while those of the sea were considered as delicacies. Snails, for instance—why not use them as articles of food ? They were well known to be nutritious and wholesome—even sanative in some cases. The epicures, in olden time, esteemed as a most delicious treat the snails fed in the marble quarries of Lucca. The Italians still hold them in esteem. The two philosophers, perfectly satisfied that their countrymen were acting most absurdly in not making snails an ordinary article of food, resolved themselves to set an example ; and accordingly, having procured a number, caused them to be stewed for dinner. No guests were invited to the banquet. The snails were in due season served up ; but, alas ! great is the difference between theory and practice—so far from exciting the appetite, the smoking dish acted in a diametrically opposite manner, and neither party felt much inclination to partake of its contents. Nevertheless, if they looked on the snails with disgust, they retained their awe for each other; so that each conceiving the symptoms of internal revolt peculiar to himself, began, with infinite exertion to swallow in very small quantities the mess which he internally loathed. Dr. Black at length broke the ice, but in a delicate manner, as if to sound the opinion of his messmate, ' Doctor, do you not think that they taste a little—a very little—queer ?' ' D—— queer, D—— queer, indeed ; tak them awa', tak them awa'!' vociferated Dr. Hutton, starting up from table and giving full vent to his feelings of abhorrence."—*A Series of Original Portraits*, by John Kay (commonly known as Kay's *Edinburgh Portraits*), vol. i. p. 57.

T

Illustrations. After Hutton's death his friend Playfair published in 1802 his classical *Illustrations of the Huttonian Theory.* We are thus in possession of ample information of the theoretical views adopted by Hutton, and of the facts on which he based them. Before considering these, however, it may be convenient to follow the recorded incidents of his quiet and uneventful life, that we may the better understand the manner in which he worked, and the nature of the material by which he tested and supported his conclusions.

It was one of the fundamental doctrines of Hutton's system that the internal heat of the globe has in past time shown its vigour by the intrusion of large masses of molten material into the crust. He found many examples of these operations on a small scale in the neighbourhood of Edinburgh and in the lowlands of Scotland. But he conceived that the same effects had been produced in a far more colossal manner by the protusion of large bodies of granite. This rock, which Werner had so dogmatically affirmed to be the earliest chemical precipitate from his primeval ocean, was surmised by Hutton to be of igneous origin, and he believed that, if its junctions with the surrounding strata were examined, they would be found to furnish proofs of the correctness of his inference. The question could be easily tested in Scotland, where, both in the Highlands and among the Southern Uplands, large bodies of granite had long been known to form important groups of mountains. Accordingly, during a series of years, Hutton undertook a number of excursions into various parts of his native country, and returned from each of them laden with fresh illustrations of the truth of the conclusions at which he had arrived. At one time he was busy among the roots of the Grampian Hills, at another he was to be seen scouring the lonely moorlands of Galloway, or climbing the precipices and glens of Arran. His visit to Glen Tilt has been made memorable by Playfair's brief account of it.[1] He had conjectured that in the bed of the river Tilt actual demonstration might be found that the Highland granite has disrupted the surrounding schists. Playfair describes how " no less than six large veins of red granite were seen in the course of a mile, traversing the black micaceous schistus, and producing, by the contrast of colour, an effect that might be striking even to an unskilful observer. The sight of objects which verified at once so many important conclusions in his system, filled him with delight ; and as his feelings, on such occasions, were always strongly expressed, the guides who accompanied him were convinced that it must be nothing less than the discovery of a vein of silver or gold that could call forth such strong marks of joy and exultation."

Another of Hutton's fundamental generalisations was tested in as vivid and successful a manner. He taught that the ruins of an earlier world lie beneath the secondary strata, and that where the base of these strata can be seen, it will be found to reveal, by what is now known as an unconformability, its relation to the older rocks. He had at various points in Scotland satisfied himself by actual observation that this relation holds good. But he determined to verify it

[1] Hutton's account is in the portion of the third volume of his *Theory* referred to in a note on p 297.

once more by examining the junction of the two groups of rock along the coast where the range of the Lammermuir Hills plunges into the sea. Accompanied by his friend Sir James Hall, whose property of Dunglass lay in the immediate neighbourhood, and by his colleague and future biographer, Playfair, and favoured with calm weather, he boated along these picturesque shores until the unconformable junction was reached. The vertical Silurian shales and grits were found to protrude through, and to be wrapped round by, the red sandstone and breccia. " Dr. Hutton," Playfair writes, " was highly pleased with appearances that set in so clear a light the different formations of the parts which compose the exterior crust of the earth, and where all the circumstances were combined that could render the observation satisfactory and precise. On us who saw these phenomena for the first time, the impression made will not easily be forgotten. The palpable evidence presented to us of one of the most extraordinary and important facts in the natural history of the earth, gave a reality and substance to those theoretical speculations which, however probable, had never till now been directly authenticated by the testimony of the senses. We often said to ourselves, what clearer evidence could we have had of the different formation of these rocks, and of the long interval which separated their formation, had we actually seen them emerging from the bosom of the deep ? . . . The mind seemed to grow giddy by looking so far into the abyss of time ; and while we listened with earnestness and admiration to the philosopher who was now unfolding to us the order and series of these wonderful events, we became sensible how much further reason may sometimes go than imagination can venture to follow."

Hutton's lithe active body betokened the unwearied vigour of his mind. His high forehead, firmly moulded features, keen observant eyes, and well-shaped, rather aquiline nose, marked him out at once as a man of strong intellect, while the gentleness that beamed in his face was a reflex of the kindliness of his nature. His plain dress, all of one colour, gave a further indication of the unostentatious simplicity of his character.

His mode of life was in harmonious keeping with these personal traits. After working in his study during the day he would invariably pass the evening with his friends. "A brighter tint of gaiety and cheerfulness spread itself over every countenance when the doctor entered the room ; and the philosopher who had just descended from the sublimest speculations of metaphysics or risen from the deepest researches of geology, seated himself at the tea-table, as much disengaged from thought, as cheerful and gay, as the youngest of the company." His character was distinguished by its transparent simplicity, its frank openness, its absence of all that was little or selfish, and its overflowing enthusiasm and vivacity. In a company he was always one of the most animated speakers, his conversation full of ingenious and original observation, showing wide information, from which an excellent memory enabled him to draw endless illustrations of any subject that might be discussed, where, "when the subject admitted of it, the witty and the ludicrous never failed to occupy a considerable place."

Though his partnership in the chemical work brought him considerable wealth, it made no difference in the quiet unostentatious life of a philosopher, which he had led ever since he settled in Edinburgh. A severe attack of illness in the summer of 1793 greatly reduced his strength, and though he recovered from it and was able to resume his life of activity, a second attack of the same ailment in the winter of 1796 terminated at last fatally on the 26th March, 1797, when he was in his seventy-first year.

Hutton's claim to rank high among the founders of geology rests on no wide series of writings, like those which Von Buch poured forth so copiously for more than two generations. Nor was it proclaimed by a host of devoted pupils, like those who spread abroad the fame of Werner. It is based, so far at least as geology is concerned, on one single work,[1] and on the elucidations of two friends and disciples.

On the 7th of March and 4th of April, 1785, Hutton read to the Royal Society of Edinburgh his Memoir on a " Theory of the Earth ; or an Investigation of the Laws observable in the Composition, Dissolution and Restoration of Land upon the Globe." Extending to no more than 96 quarto pages, it was written in a quiet, logical manner, with no attempt at display but with an apparent anxiety to state the author's opinions as tersely as possible.

---

[1] The first sketch and the expansion of it into two octavo volumes may be regarded as practically one work, so far as the originality of conception is concerned.

Probably no man realised then that this essay would afterwards be regarded as marking a turning-point in the history of geology. For some years it remained without attracting notice from friend or foe.[1]

For this neglect various causes have been assigned. The title of the Memoir was perhaps unfortunate. The words "Theory of the Earth" suggested still another repetition of the endless speculations as to the origin of things, of which men had grown weary. System after system of this kind of speculation had been proposed and had dropped into oblivion; and no doubt many of his contemporaries believed Hutton's "Theory" to be one of the same ill-fated brood. His friend Playfair admits that there were reasons in the construction of the Memoir itself why it should not have made its way more speedily into notice. Its contents were too condensed, and contained too little explanation of the grounds of the reasoning. Its style was apt to be prolix and obscure. It appeared, too, in the *Transactions* of a learned society which had only recently been founded, and whose publications were hardly yet known to the general world of science.

---

[1] It does not appear to be generally known that Desmarest, departing from his usual practice of not noticing the work of living writers, wrote a long and careful notice of Hutton's Memoir of 1785 in the first volume of his *Géographie Physique*, published in 1794-1795. He disagrees with many of Hutton's views, such, for instance, as that of the igneous origin of granite. But he generously insists on the value of the observations with which the Scottish writer had enriched the natural history of the earth and the physical geography of Scotland. "It is to Scotland," he says, "that Hutton's opponent must go to amend his results and substitute for them a more rational explanation" (p. 750).

At last, after an interval of some five years, De Luc assailed the "Theory" in a series of letters in the *Monthly Review* for 1790 and 1791. So far as we know, Hutton published no immediate reply to these attacks. He had often been urged by his friends to publish his entire work on the Theory of the Earth, with all the proofs and illustrations which had been accumulating in his hands for so many years. He delayed the task, however, until, during the convalescence from his first severe illness, he received a copy of a strenuous attack upon his system and its tendencies by Richard Kirwan, a well-known Irish chemist and mineralogist of that day.[1]

This assailant not only misconceived and misrepresented the views which he criticized, but charged their author with atheistic opinions. Weakened as he was by illness, Hutton, with characteristic energy, the very day after he received Kirwan's paper, began the revision of his manuscript, and worked at it until he was able to send it to the press. It appeared in 1795, that is, ten years after the first sketch of the subject had been given to the Royal Society of Edinburgh. Besides embodying that sketch, it gave a much fuller statement of his conclusions, and an ampler presentation of the facts and observations on which they were founded. It formed two octavo volumes. Playfair tells us that a third volume,

---

[1] "Examination of the Supposed Origin of Stony Substances," read to the Royal Irish Academy, 3rd February, 1793, and published in vol. v. of their *Transactions*, p. 51. For a crushing exposure of Kirwan's mode of attack see Playfair's *Illustrations of the Huttonian Theory*, §§ 119, 418.

necessary for the completion of the work, remained in manuscript.[1]

If Hutton's original sketch was defective in style and arrangement, his larger work was even more unfortunate in these respects. Its prolixity deterred readers from its perusal. Yet it is a vast storehouse of acute and accurate observation and luminous deduction, and it deserves to be carefully studied by every geologist who wishes to comprehend the history of his own science.

Fortunately for Hutton's fame and for the onward march of geology, the philosopher numbered among his friends the illustrious mathematician and natural philosopher, John Playfair (1748-1819), who had been closely associated with him in his later years, and was intimately conversant with his geological opinions. Gifted with a clear penetrating mind, a rare faculty of orderly logical arrangement, and an English style of altogether remarkable precision and elegance, he was of all men best fitted to let the world know what it owed to Hutton. Accordingly, after his friend's death, he determined to prepare a more popular and perspicuous account of Hutton's labours. He gave in this work, first a clear statement of the essential principles of Hutton's system, and then a series of notes or essays upon different parts of the

---

[1] A portion of this precious manuscript containing six chapters (iv.-ix.) came into the possession of Leonard Horner, F.R.S., who presented it to the Geological Society of London. It remained hardly noticed in the library of the Society until 1899, when at my solicitation the Society printed and published it. This is the only portion of the MS. now known to exist.

system, combining in these a large amount of original observation and reflection of his own.   His volume appeared in the spring of 1802, just five years after Hutton's death, with the title of *Illustrations of the Huttonian Theory of the Earth*.   Of this great classic it is impossible to speak too highly.   After the lapse of a century it may be read with as much profit and pleasure as when it first appeared.   For precision of statement and felicity of language it has no superior in English scientific literature.   To its early inspiration I owe a debt which I can never fully repay. Upon every young student of geology I would impress the advantage of reading and re-reading, and reading yet again this consummate masterpiece.   How different would geological literature be to-day if men had tried to think and write like Playfair !

There are thus three sources of information as to Hutton's geological system—his first sketch of 1785, his two octavo volumes of 1795, with the portion of the third volume published in 1899 and Playfair's *Illustrations* of 1802.[1]   Let us now consider what were his fundamental doctrines.

Although he called his system a Theory of the Earth, Hutton's conceptions entirely differed from those of the older cosmogonists, who thought themselves bound to begin by explaining the origin of things, and who proceeded on a foundation of hypothesis to erect a more or less fantastic edifice of mere speculation.   He, on the contrary, believed that it is

[1] To these may be added the memoirs by Sir James Hall which appeared after Hutton's death and from which some interesting particulars may be gleaned as to the master's opinions.

the duty of science first to try to ascertain what evidence there is in the earth itself that will throw light
upon the history of the planet. Instead of invoking
conjecture and hypothesis, he proceeded from the
very outset to collect the actual facts, and to marshall
these in such a way as to make them tell their own
story. Unlike Werner, he had no preconceived theory
about the origin of rocks, with which all the phenomena of nature had to be made to agree. His theory
grew so naturally out of his observations that it
involved no speculation in regard to a large part
of its subject.

Hutton started with the grand conception that the
past history of our globe must be explained by what
can be seen to be happening now, or to have happened
only recently. The dominant idea in his philosophy is
that the present is the key to the past. We have
grown so familiar with this idea, it enters so intimately
into all our conceptions in regard to geological questions, that we do not readily realise the genius of
the man who first grasped it with unerring insight,
and made it the chief corner-stone of modern geology.

From the time of his youthful rambles in Norfolk,
Hutton had been struck with the universal proofs
that the surface of the earth has not always been as
it is to-day. Everywhere below the covering of soil
he found evidence of former conditions, entirely unlike
those visible now. In the great majority of cases,
he noticed that the rocks there to be seen consist of
strata, disposed in orderly arrangement parallel with
each other. Some of these strata are formed of
pudding-stone, others of sandstone, of shale, of lime-

stone, and so forth, differing in many respects from each other, but agreeing in one essential character, that they are composed of fragmentary or detrital material, derived from rocks older than themselves. He saw that these various strata could be exactly paralleled among the accumulations now taking place under the sea. The pudding-stones were, in his eyes, only compacted gravels, the sandstones were indurated sand, the limestones were in great part derived from the aggregation of the remains of marine calcareous organisms, the shales from the consolidation of mud and silt. The wide extent of these strata, forming, as they do, most of the dry land, seemed to him to point to the sea as the only large expanse of water in which they could have been deposited.

Thus corroborating the deductions of previous observers, the first conclusion of the Scottish philosopher was that the greater part of the land consists of compacted sediment which, worn away from some pre-existing continents, was spread out in strata over the bed of the sea. He realised that the rocks thus formed are not all of the same age, but, on the contrary, bear witness to a succession of revolutions. He acknowledged the existence of a series of ancient rocks which he called Primary, not that he believed them to be the original or first-formed rocks in the structure of the planet, but that they were the oldest that had then been discovered. They included the various schists and slates which Werner claimed as chemical precipitates, but in which Hutton could only see the hardened and altered mechanical sediments of a former ocean. Above them, and partly formed out of them, came the Secondary strata that constitute the greater part of the land.

But all these sedimentary deposits have passed from their original soft condition into that of solid stone. Hutton attributed this change to the action of subterranean heat. In his day, the chemistry of geology was exceedingly imperfect, though in Hutton's hands it was greatly less erroneous than in those of Werner. The solubility of silica, for instance, and its capacity for being introduced in aqueous solution into the minutest crevices and pores of a rock, were not known. It need not, therefore, surprise us to find that in the Huttonian conception the flints in chalk were injected into the rock in a molten state, and that the agate of fossil wood bore marks of igneous fusion. Hutton did not realise to what an extent mere compression could solidify the materials of sedimentary strata, nor how much may be done, by infiltration and deposition between the clastic grains, towards converting originally loose detritus into the most compact kind of stone. But there was one kind of compression which though not perhaps at first obvious, was clearly perceived by him in its geological relations. Following out ideas suggested to him by Black, he saw that the influence of heat upon rocks must be largely modified by pressure. The more volatile components, which would be speedily driven off by a high temperature at the surface of the earth, might be retained under great pressure below that surface. Hutton conceived that limestone might even be fused in this way, and yet still keep its carbonic acid. This idea was ridiculed at the time, but its truth was

confirmed afterwards by Hall's experiments, to which
I shall allude in the sequel.

The next step in Hutton's reasoning was that
whereby he sought to account for the present position
of the strata which, originally deposited under the sea,
are now found even on mountain-crests 15,000 feet
above sea-level. We have seen how Werner looked on
his vertical primitive strata as having been precipitated
from solution in that position, and as having been
uncovered by the gradual subsidence and disappearance
of the water. Hutton attacked the problem in a
different fashion. He saw that if the exposure of
the dry land had been due merely to the subsidence
of the sea, it would involve no change in the positions
of the strata relatively to each other. What were
first deposited should lie at the bottom, what were
last deposited, at the top ; and the whole should retain
their original flatness.

But the most cursory examination was, in his
opinion, sufficient to show that the actual conditions in
nature were entirely different from any such arrangement. Wherever he went, he found, as Steno had
done, proofs that the sedimentary strata, now forming
most of the land, had in large measure lost the
horizontal or gently inclined position in which sedimentary deposits are normally accumulated. He saw
them often inclined, sometimes placed on end, or even
stupendously contorted and ruptured. It was manifestly absurd, as De Saussure had shown in the Alps,
to suppose that pebbles in vertical beds of conglomerate could ever have been deposited in such
positions. And if some of the vertical strata could thus

be demonstrated to have been originally horizontal or nearly so, there could be no reason for refusing to concede that the same alteration had happened to the other vertical strata, even although they might not afford such obvious and convincing proofs of it.   As Steno had long before pointed out, no stratum could have ended off abruptly at the time of its formation, unless against a cliff or slope that arrested its detrital materials from drifting further, nor could it have been accumulated in plicated layers.   But nothing is more common than to find strata presenting their truncated ends to the sky, while in some districts they are folded and crumpled, like piles of carpets.   Not only so, but again and again, they are found to be sharply dislocated, so that two totally different series are placed parallel to each other.

Hutton recognised that these changes, which were probably brought about at different periods, must be attributed to some great convulsions which, from time to time, have shaken the very foundations of the earth. He could prove that, in some places, the Primary rocks had in this way been broken up and placed on end before the Secondary series was laid down, for, as on the Berwickshire Coast, he had traced the older vertical strata overlain and wrapped round by the younger horizontal deposits, and had also observed, from the well-worn fragments of the former enclosed in the latter, that the interval of time represented by the break between them must have been of considerable duration.

Having been led by this train of observation and deduction, to the demonstration of former gigantic disturbances, by which the bed of the sea had been upheaved and its hardened sediments had been tilted, plicated and fractured, in order to form the existing dry land, Hutton had next to look round for some probable cause for these phenomena.   He inferred that the convulsions could only have been produced by some force that acted from below upward, but was so combined with the gravity and resistance of the mass to which it was applied, as to create a lateral and oblique thrust that gave rise to the contortions of the strata. (He did not pretend to be able to explain the nature and operation of this subterranean force, though he believed it to be essentially due to the effects of heat.) Far from sharing the ancient misconception that volcanoes are due to the combustion of inflammable substances, he connected them with the high internal temperature of the globe, and regarded them as " spiracles to the subterranean furnace in order to prevent the unnecessary elevation of land, and fatal effects of earthquakes." [1]

Unlike Werner, Hutton saw that while no mere combustion of inflammable substances could account for this high temperature of the subterranean regions, the actual conditions involved must be so far different from ordinary combustion as not improbably to require no circulation of air, nor any supply of carbonaceous or other materials as fuel. The nucleus of the globe might accordingly " be a fluid mass, melted, but unchanged by the action of heat."

In this way, appealing at every step to the actual facts of nature, Hutton built up the first part of his

[1] *Theory of the Earth*, vol. i. p. 146. It will be remembered that a similar opinion was expressed by Strabo.

immortal Theory. Most of the facts cited by him were more or less familiar to men ; and some of the obvious inferences to be drawn from them had been deduced by other observers before his time. But no— one until then had grouped them into a coherent system by which the earth became, as it were, her own interpreter. The very obviousness and familiarity of his doctrine at the present time, when it has become the groundwork of modern geology, are apt to blind us to the genius of the man who first conceived it, and worked it into a harmonious and luminous whole.

In the course of his journeys in Scotland, Hutton had come upon many examples of rocks that were not stratified. Some of these occurred among the Primary masses ; others were observable in the Secondary series. Reflecting on the probable reaction of the heated interior of the globe upon its outer cooler shell or crust, he had come to the conclusion that many, if not all, of these unstratified rocks were to be regarded as material that had once been in a molten condition, and had been injected from below during some of the great convulsions indicated by the disturbed strata. He distinguished three principal kinds of such intrusive rocks—" Whinstone," under which term he included a miscellaneous series of dark, heavy, somewhat basic rocks, now known as dolerites, basalts, diabases and andesites ; Porphyry, which probably comprised such rocks as felsite, orthophyre and quartz-porphyry ; and Granite, which, though the term was generally used by him in its modern sense, embraced some rocks of more basic character.

He showed that the whinstones correspond so

closely to modern lavas in structure and composition, that they may be regarded as probably also of volcanic origin. But, as was discussed in Chapter VIII. (p. 259), he did not suppose that they had actually been erupted at the surface, like streams of lava. He found them to occur sometimes in vertical veins, known in Scotland as *dykes*, a term now universal in English geological literature, and sometimes as irregular bosses, or interposed as sheets between the strata. He believed these rocks to be masses of subterranean or unerupted lava, but as we have seen, the grounds on which he reached this conclusion were not always such as the subsequent progress of inquiry has justified. The deduction was itself in many cases correct, but the reasoning that led up to it, was partly fallacious. Hutton argued, for instance, that the carbonate of lime, so commonly observable in his "Whinstones" indicated that the rock had been fused deep within the earth, under such pressure as to keep that mineral in a molten state, without the loss of its carbonic acid. Like other mineralogists of his day, he was not aware that the calcite of the amygdales has been subsequently introduced in aqueous solution into the steam-cavities, and that the diffused lime-carbonate in the body of the rocks generally results from their partial decomposition by infiltrating water. Much more accurate were his observations that whinstone has greatly indurated the strata into which it has been injected, even involving and fusing fragments of them, and reducing carbonaceous substances, such as coal, to the condition of coke or charcoal; that it has sometimes been intruded among the strata with such violence as to shift, upraise, bend and otherwise disturb them, and that it can be seen to have been thrust abruptly into one continuous succession of strata, which, above and below it, are exactly alike, and have obviously been at one time in contact with each other.

Granite, as Hutton pointed out, differs in many important respects from "whinstone," more particularly in its position, for it was then believed to lie beneath all the known rocks, rising to higher elevations and sinking to greater depths than any other material in the crust of the earth. Yet though he admitted its infraposition, he differed from the Neptunists in regard to its relative antiquity. He believed it to be younger than the strata which rest upon it, for he regarded it as a mass that had once been melted and had been intruded among the rocks with which it is now found associated. He supported this conclusion by various arguments, chief among which was one based on the occurrence of veins that diverge from the granite and ramify through the surrounding rocks, diminishing in width as they recede from their parent mass (p. 291).

Properly to appreciate the value of these doctrines in regard to the development of a sound geological philosophy, we must bear in mind what were the prevalent views entertained on the subject when Hutton worked out his theory. We have seen that granite, generally regarded as an aqueous formation, was affirmed by Werner to have been the first precipitate that fell to the bottom from his universal ocean. H. B. De Saussure, who had seen more of granite and its relations to other rocks than Werner, or

indeed than any other geologist of his time, remained
up to the last a firm believer in the aqueous origin of
that rock.   Even after the death of the great Swiss
geologist, Cuvier, sharing his opinions on these
matters, proclaimed as late as the year 1810 his
belief that De Saussure overthrew the doctrine of
central fire, or of a source of heat within the earth's
interior, demonstrated granite to be the oldest rock,
and proved it to have been formed in strata that
were deposited in water.[1]   Nobody before Hutton's
time had been bold enough to imagine a series of
subterranean intrusions of molten matter.   Those who
adopted his opinion on this subject were styled
Plutonists, and were looked upon as carrying out the
Vulcanist doctrines to still greater extravagance, "attributing to the action of fire widely-diffused rocks which
nobody had till then ever dreamt of removing from
the domain of water."[2]

According to the Huttonian theory, fissures and
openings which have from time to time arisen in the
external crust of the earth have reached down to the
intensely hot nucleus.   Up these rents the molten
material has ascended, forming veins of whinstone
underground, and, where it has reached the surface,
issuing there in the form of lava and the other
phenomena of volcanoes.   Every geologist recognises
these generalisations as part of the familiar teachings
of modern geology.

We have seen that Werner made no distinction,
as regards origin, between what we now call mineral-

[1] Cuvier, " Éloge de De Saussure," *Éloges,* i. p. 427.
[2] Cuvier, *Op. cit.* ii. p. 363.

veins and the dykes and veins of granite, basalt or other eruptive rocks. He looked upon them all as the results of chemical precipitation from an ocean that covered the rocks in which fissures had been formed. Hutton, in like manner, drew no line between the same two well-marked series of veins, but regarded them all as formed by the introduction of igneous material. Though more logical than Werner, he was, as we now know, entirely in error in confounding under one denomination two totally distinct assemblages of mineral matter. Werner correctly referred veins of ores and spars to deposition from aqueous solution, but was completely mistaken in attributing the same origin to veins of massive rock. Hutton, on the other hand, went as far astray in regard to his explanation of mineral veins, but he made an important contribution to science in his insistence upon the truly intrusive nature of veins of granite and whinstone.

There was another point of difference between the views of Werner and of Hutton in regard to mineral veins. One of the undoubted services of the Freiberg professor was his clear demonstration than veins could be classified according to their directions, that this arrangement often sufficed to separate them also according to age and material, those running along one parallel, and containing one group of minerals, being intersected by, and therefore older than, another series following a different direction, and consisting of other metals and vein-stones. This important distinction found no place in Hutton's system. To him it was enough that he was able to show that certain veins known to him were intrusive masses of igneous origin.[1]

In the Huttonian theory we find the germ of the Lyellian doctrine of metamorphism. Hutton, having demonstrated that granite is not an aqueous but an igneous rock, further showed that the " Alpine schistus," (which included sandstones, shales and slates, as well as crystalline schists), being stratified, could not be original or primitive, but had been deposited like recent sediments, and had been invaded and altered by the granite. A passage from his chapter, "On the Primary Part of the Present Earth " may be quoted in illustration of the sagacity of his judgment on this subject : " If, in examining our land, we shall find a mass of matter which had been evidently formed originally in the ordinary manner of stratification, but which is now extremely distorted in its structure and displaced in its position,—which is also extremely consolidated in its mass and variously changed in its composition,—which, therefore, has the marks of its original or marine composition extremely obliterated, and many subsequent veins of melted mineral matter interjected, we should then have reason to suppose that here were masses of matter which, though not different in their origin from those that are gradually deposited at the bottom of the ocean, have been more acted upon by subterranean heat and the ex-

---

[1] In Playfair's *Illustrations*, however, the successive origin of mineral veins is distinctly affirmed, § 226. Reference is there made to the coincidence between the prevalent direction of the principal Cornish veins and the general strike of the strata, and to the intersection of these by the cross-courses at nearly right angles.

panding power, that is to say, have been changed in a greater degree by the operations of the mineral kingdom."[1] Hutton here compresses into a single, though somewhat cumbrous, sentence the doctrine to which Lyell in later years gave the name of metamorphism.

Hutton's vision not only reached far back into the geological past, it stretched into the illimitable future, and it embraced also a marvellously broad yet minute survey of the present. From his early youth he had been struck with the evidence of incessant decay upon the surface of the dry land. With admirable insight he kept hold of this cardinal fact, and followed it fearlessly from mountain-top to sea-shore. Wherever we may go, on each variety of rock, in every kind of climate, the doom of dissolution seemed to him to be written in ineffaceable characters upon the whole surface of the dry land. No sooner was the bed of the ocean heaved up into mountains, than the new terrestrial surface began to be attacked. Chemical and mechanical agents were recognised as concerned in this disintegration, though the precise nature and extent of their several operations had not then been studied. The general result produced by them, however, was never appreciated by any observer more clearly than by Hutton. From the coast, worn into stack and skerry and cave, by the ceaseless grinding of the waves, he had followed the progress of corrosion up to the crests of his Scottish hills. No rock, even the hardest, could escape, though some resisted more stubbornly than others.

[1] *Theory of the Earth*, vol. i. pp. 375, 376. This passage may serve also as an illustration of Hutton's peculiar style of composition.

The universality of this terrestrial waste had been more or less distinctly perceived by other writers, as has been pointed out in previous pages. But Hutton saw a meaning in it which no one before him had so vividly realised. To his eye, while the whole land undergoes loss, it is along certain lines traced by running water that this loss reaches its greatest amount. In the channels of the streams that carry off the drainage of the land he recognised the results of a constant erosion of the rocks by the water flowing over them. As the generalisation was beautifully expressed by Playfair : " Every river appears to consist of a main trunk, fed from a variety of branches, each running in a valley proportioned to its size, and all of them together forming a system of valleys, communicating with one another, and having such a nice adjustment of their declivities, that none of them join the principal valley, either on too high or too low a level, a circumstance which would be infinitely improbable if each of these valleys were not the work of the stream that flows in it.

" If, indeed, a river consisted of a single stream without branches, running in a straight valley, it might be supposed that some great concussion, or some powerful torrent, had opened at once the channel by which its waters are conducted to the ocean ; but, when the usual form of a river is considered, the trunk divided into many branches, which rise at a great distance from one another, and these again subdivided into an infinity of smaller ramifications, it becomes strongly impressed upon the mind that all these channels have been cut by the waters themselves ; that they have been slowly dug out by the washing and erosion of the land ; and that it is by the repeated touches of the same instrument that this curious assemblage of lines has been engraved so deeply on the surface of the globe."[1]

The whole of the modern doctrine of earth-sculpture is to be found in the Huttonian theory. We shall better appreciate the sagacity and prescience of Hutton and Playfair, if we remember that their views on this subject were in their lifetime, and for many years afterwards, ignored or explicitly rejected, even by those who accepted the rest of their teaching. Hall, their friend and associate, could not share their opinions on this subject. Lyell too, who adopted so much of the Huttonian theory and became the great prophet of the Uniformitarian school, never would admit the truth of Hutton's doctrine concerning the origin of valleys. Nor even now is that doctrine universally accepted. It was Jukes who in 1862 revived an interest in the subject, by showing how completely the valley system in the south of Ireland was due to the action of the rivers.[2] Ramsay soon after followed with further illustrations of the principle.[3] Later effective support to Hutton's teaching has been given by the geologists of the United States, who, among the comparatively undisturbed strata of the Western

[1] *Illustrations of the Huttonian Theory*, p. 102. It will be remembered that the subaerial excavation of valleys was first demonstrated in ample detail by Desmarest from Auvergne, and subsequently by De Saussure from the Alps. The doctrine was afterwards sustained by Lamarck. See chap. xi.

[2] *Quart. Journ. Geol. Soc.* xviii. (1862).

[3] *The Physical Geology and Geography of Great Britain*, 1863.

Territories, have demonstrated, by proofs which the most sceptical must accept, the potency of denudation in the production of the topography of the land.

To the Huttonian school belongs also the conspicuous merit of having been the first to recognise the potency of glaciers in the transport of detritus from the mountains. Playfair, in his characteristically brief and luminous way, proclaimed at the beginning of last century that "for the removing of large masses of rock the most powerful engines without doubt which nature employs are the glaciers, those lakes or rivers of ice which are formed in the highest valleys of the Alps, and other mountains of the first order. . . . Before the valleys were cut out in the form they now are, and when the mountains were still more elevated, huge fragments of rock may have been carried to a great distance ; and it is not wonderful if these same masses, greatly diminished in size, and reduced to gravel or sand, have reached the shores or even the bottom of the ocean."[1] Here the conception of the former greater extension of the glaciers was foreshadowed as a possible or even probable event in geological history. Yet for half a century or more after Playfair's time, men were still speculating on the probability of the transport of the erratics by floating icebergs during a submergence of Central Europe under the sea,—an hypothesis for which there was not a particle of evidence. No geologist now questions the truth of Playfair's suggestion.

In the whole of Hutton's doctrine he rigorously guarded himself against the admission of any principle

[1] *Illustrations*, p. 388.

which could not be founded on observation. He made
no assumptions. Every step in his deductions was
based upon actual fact, and the facts were so arranged
as to yield naturally and inevitably the conclusion
which he drew from them. Let me quote from the
conclusion of his work a few sentences in illustration of
these statements. In the interpretation of Nature, he
remarks, " no powers are to be employed that are not
natural to the globe, no action to be admitted of except
those of which we know the principle, and no extraordinary events to be alleged in order to explain a
common appearance. The powers of Nature are not
to be employed in order to destroy the very object
of those powers ; we are not to make Nature act
in violation to that order which we actually observe,
and in subversion of that end which is to be perceived
in the system of created things. In whatever manner,
therefore, we are to employ the great agents, fire and
water, for producing those things which appear, it
ought to be in such a way as is consistent with the
propagation of plants and the life of animals upon
the surface of the earth. Chaos and confusion are
not to be introduced into the order of Nature, because
certain things appear to our practical views as being
in some disorder. Nor are we to proceed in feigning
causes when those seem insufficient which occur in our
experience."[1]

No geologist ever lived among a more congenial
and helpful group of friends than Hutton. While
they had a profound respect for his genius, they were
drawn towards him by his winning personality, and

[1] *Theory of the Earth*, vol. ii. p. 547.

he became the centre of all that was bright, vivacious and cheerful in that remarkable circle of eminent men. If he wanted advice and assistance in chemical questions, there was his bosom-friend Joseph Black, ever ready to pour out his ample stores of knowledge, and to test every proposition by the light of his wide experience and his sober judgement. If he needed companionship and assistance in his field journeys, there was the sagacious Clerk of Eldin, willing to join him, to examine his evidence with judicial impartiality, and to sketch for him with an artistic pencil the geological sections on which he laid most stress. If he felt himself in need of the counsel of a clear logical intellect, accustomed to consider physical problems with the precision of a mathematician, there was the kindly sympathetic Playfair, ever prompt and pleased to do him a service. With such companions he discussed his theory in all its bearings. Their approval was ample enough for his ambition. He was never tempted to court publicity by frequent communications to learned societies, or the issue of independent works treating of his geological observations and discoveries. But for the establishment of the Royal Society of Edinburgh, he might have delayed for years the preparation of the first sketch of his theory, and had it not been for the virulent attacks of Kirwan, he might never have been induced to finish the preparation of his great work. He was a man absorbed in the investigation of Nature, to whom personal renown was a matter of utter indifference, contented and happy in the warm regard and sympathetic appreciation of the friends whom he loved.

CHAPTER X

Among the friends with whom Hutton associated in Edinburgh there was one to whom allusion has already been made, but who demands more special notice here, seeing that to him a distinguished place must be assigned among the founders of geology. To Sir James Hall of Dunglass we owe the establishment of experimental research as a powerful aid in the investigation and solution of geological problems.[1] Inheriting a baronetcy and a landed estate in East Lothian, not far from the picturesque cliffs of St. Abb's Head, and possessed of ample leisure for the prosecution of intellectual pursuits, he was led to interest himself in geology. His father, a man of scientific tastes, became acquainted with Hutton when the future philosopher was a farmer in the neighbouring county of Berwick. From these early days Hutton found the hospitality of Dunglass always open to him. It will be remembered that the famous

---

[1] The previous experiments of De Saussure have already been referred to (*ante* p. 189) but they were not continued and led to no satisfactory conclusions.

visit to the rocks on the coast at Siccar Point, described by Playfair, was made with Sir James from that house.

At first Sir James Hall could not bring himself to accept Hutton's views. "I was induced," he tells us, "to reject his system entirely, and should probably have continued still to do so, with the great majority of the world, but for my habits of intimacy with the author, the vivacity and perspicuity of whose conversation formed a striking contrast to the obscurity of his writings. I was induced by that charm, and by the numerous original facts which his system had led him to observe, to listen to his arguments in favour of opinions which I then looked upon as visionary. After three years of almost daily warfare with Dr. Hutton on the subject of his theory, I began to view his fundamental principles with less and less repugnance."[1]

As his objections diminished, Hall's interest in the details of the system increased. His practical mind soon perceived that some of the principles, which Hutton had established by reasoning and analogy, might be brought to the test of direct experiment. And he urged his friend to make the attempt, or allow him to carry out the necessary researches. The proposal received little encouragement from the philosopher. Hutton believed that the scale of Nature's processes was so vast that no imitation of them, on the small scale of a laboratory, could possibly lead to any reliable results, or as he afterwards expressed himself in print, "there are superficial reasoning men who, without

[1] *Trans. Roy Soc. Edin.* vi. (1812), pp. 71-186.

truly knowing what they see, think they know those regions of the earth which can never be seen, and who judge of the great operations of the mineral kingdom from having kindled a fire and looked into the bottom of a little crucible." [1]

Sir James Hall, notwithstanding his veneration for his master, could not agree with him in this verdict. He was confirmed in his opinion by an accident which had occurred at Leith glass-works, where a large mass of common green glass, that had been allowed to cool slowly, was found to have lost all the properties of glass, becoming opaque, white, hard and crystalline. Yet a piece of this substance, when once more melted and rapidly cooled, recovered its true vitreous characters. Hall's shrewd instinct at once applied this observation to the Huttonian doctrine of the igneous origin of granite and other rocks. It had been objected to Hutton's views that the effect of great heat on rocks was to reduce them to the condition of glass, but that granite and whinstone, being crystalline substances, could never possibly have been melted. Yet here, in this glass-house material, it could be demonstrated that a thoroughly molten glass could, by slow cooling, be converted into a crystalline condition, and could be changed once more by fusion into glass. Hutton had overlooked the possibility that the results of fusion might be modified by the rate of cooling, and Hall at once began to test the matter by experiment. He repeated the process by which the devitrified glass had been accidentally obtained at the glass-house, and found that he could

[1] *Theory of the Earth,* vol. i. p. 251.

at will produce, from the same mass of bottle glass, either a glass or a stony substance, according to the rate at which he allowed it to cool.

Sir James was too loyal a friend and too devoted an admirer of the author of the *Theory of the Earth* to pursue these researches far during the philosopher's lifetime. " I considered myself as bound," he tells us, "in practice to pay deference to his opinion, in a field which he had already so nobly occupied, and I abstained during the remainder of his life from the prosecution of experiments which I had begun in 1790." [1]

The death of Hutton in 1797 allowed the laird of Dunglass to resume the experiments on which he had been meditating during the intervening years. Selecting samples of " whinstones," that is, intrusive dolerites and basalts, from the dykes and sills in the Carboniferous strata around Edinburgh, he reduced them in the reverberatory furnace of an iron-foundry to the condition of perfect glass. Portions of this glass were afterwards re-fused and allowed to cool very slowly. There was thus obtained " a substance differing in all respects from glass, and in texture completely resembling whinstone." This substance had a distinctly crystalline structure, and Hall gave it the name of *crystallite*, which had been suggested by the chemist, Dr. Hope.

Before he was interested in the defence of the Huttonian theory, Sir James had made a journey into

---

[1] For Hall's papers see *Trans. Roy. Soc. Edin.* iii. (1790), p. 8 ; v. (1798), p. 43 ; vi. (1812), p. 71 ; vii. (1812), pp. 79, 139, 169 ; x. (1825), p. 314.

Italy in the year 1785, visiting Vesuvius, Etna, and the Lipari Isles, and having for part of the time the advantage of the company of Dolomieu. He could not help being much struck with the resemblance between the lavas of these volcanic regions and the familiar " whinstones " of his own country. So close was this resemblance in every respect that he felt " confident that there was not a lava in Mount Etna to which a counterpart might not be produced from the whinstones of Scotland." At Monte Somma he noted the abundant " vertical lavas " which, in bands from two to twelve feet broad, run up the old crater-wall. These bands seemed to him at the time " to present only an amusing variety in the history of volcanic eruptions," and, like Dolomieu and Breislak, he looked on them as marking the positions of rents which, formed in the mountain during former volcanic explosions, had been filled in from above by the outflow of lava down the outer fissured surface of the cone. Subsequent reflection, however, led him to reconsider this opinion, and to realise that these " vertical lavas " were " of the utmost consequence in geology, by supplying an intermediate link between the external and subterraneous productions of heat. I now think," he remarks, " that though we judged rightly in believing those lavas to have flowed in crevices, we were mistaken as to their direction ; for instead of flowing downwards, I am convinced they have flowed upwards, and that the crevices have performed the office of pipes, through which lateral explosions have found a vent." He had observed, also, that the outer margins of some of these dykes,

x

in contact with the surrounding rock, were vitreous, while the central parts presented the ordinary lithoid texture. This difference, he saw, was fully explained by his fusion experiments. The lava having risen in a cold fissure, and having been suddenly chilled along its outer surface, consolidated there as glass, while the inner parts, which had cooled more slowly, took a crystalline structure.

These observations are of historic interest in the progress of volcanic geology. Hall had sagaciously found the true interpretation of volcanic dykes, and he at once proceeded to apply it to the explanation of the abundant dykes of Scotland. He thus brought to the support of Hutton's doctrine of the igneous intrusion of these rocks a new and strong confirmation from the actual crater of a recent volcano.

When engaged upon his fusion experiments with Scottish whinstones, it occurred to Hall to subject to the same processes specimens of the lavas which he had brought from Vesuvius and Etna. The results which he thus obtained were precisely similar to those which the rocks from Scotland had yielded. He was able to demonstrate that lavas may be fused into a perfect glass, and that this glass, on being re-melted and allowed to cool gradually, passes into a stony substance not unlike the original lava. In this manner, the close agreement between modern lavas and the ancient basalts of Scotland was clearly proved, while their identity in chemical composition was further shown by some analyses made by Dr. Robert Kennedy. Sir James Hall had thus the satisfaction of showing that a fresh appeal to direct experiment and observation furnished further powerful support to some of the disputed doctrines in the theory of his old friend Hutton.[1]

There was another and still more important direction in which it seemed to this original investigator that the Huttonian doctrines might be subjected to the test of experiment. It was an important feature in these doctrines that the effects of heat upon rocks must differ very much according to the pressure under which the heat is applied. Hall argued, like Hutton, that within the earth's crust the influence of great compression must retard the fusion of mineral substances, and retain within them ingredients which, at the ordinary atmospheric pressure above ground, are rapidly volatilized. He thus accounted for the retention of carbonic acid by calcareous rocks, even at such high temperatures as might melt them. Here then was a wide but definite field for experiment, and Hall entered it with the joy of a first pioneer. As soon as he had done with his whinstone fusions, he set to work to construct a set of apparatus that would enable him to subject minerals and rocks to the highest obtainable temperatures in hermetically closed tubes. For six or seven years, he continued his researches, conducting more than 500 ingeniously devised experiments. He enclosed carbonate of lime in firmly secured gun-barrels, in porcelain tubes, in tubes bored through solid iron, and thereafter exposed it to the highest temperatures which he could obtain.

[1] "Experiments on Whinstone and Lava," read before the Royal Society of Edinburgh 5th March and 18th June 1798, *Trans. Roy. Soc. Edin.* vol. v. p. 43.

He was able to fuse the carbonate without the loss
of its carbonic acid, thus practically demonstrating the
truth of Hutton's contention. He obtained from
pounded chalk a substance closely resembling marble.
Applying these results to the Huttonian theory, he
contended that the effects shown by his experiments
must occur also on a great scale at the roots of
volcanoes ; that subterranean lavas may melt limestone ; that where the molten rock comes in contact
with shell-beds, it may either drive off their carbonic acid or convert them into limestone, according
to the heat of the lava and the depth under which
it acts ; and that his experiments enabled him to
pronounce under what conditions the one or the
other of these effects would be produced. He concluded that having succeeded in fusing limestone
under pressure, he could adduce in that single result
" a strong presumption in favour of the solution
which Dr. Hutton has advanced of all the geological
phenomena ; for the truth of the most doubtful
principle which he has assumed has thus been established by direct experiment."[1]

Hardly less striking were Hall's experiments in

[1] "Account of a series of experiments showing the effects of compression in modifying the action of heat," read to the Royal
Society of Edinburgh, 3rd June 1805.—*Trans. Roy. Soc. Edin.* vi.
p. 71. The same ingenious observer subsequently instituted a series
of experiments to imitate the consolidation of strata. By filling an
iron vessel with brine and having layers of sand at the bottom, he was
able to keep the lower portions of the sand at a red heat, while the
brine at the top was not too hot to let the hand be put into it. In
the end the sand at the bottom was found compacted into sandstone.
Op. cit. x. (1825), p. 314.

illustration of the processes whereby strata, originally horizontal, have been thrown into plications. His machine for contorting layers of clay is familiar to geological students from the illustrations of it given in text-books.[1] He showed how closely the convolutions of the Silurian strata of the Berwickshire coast could be experimentally imitated by the lateral compression of layers of clay under considerable vertical pressure. In this, as in his other applications of experiment, he led the way, and laid the foundation on which later observers have built with such success.[2]

There was thus established at Edinburgh a group of earnest and successful investigators of the history of the earth, who promulgated a new philosophy of geology, based upon close observation and carefully devised experiment. Among these men there was only one teacher—the gentle and eloquent Playfair ; but his functions at the University were to teach mathematics and natural philosophy. He had thus no opportunity of training a school of disciples who

[1] *Trans. Roy. Soc. Edin.* vol. vii. p. 79 and Plate iv. As already remarked, Hall differed from his master and from Playfair in regard to their views on the efficacy of subaerial denudation. He preferred to invoke gigantic debacles of water rushing over the land, and to these he attributed the transport of large boulders and the smoothing and striation of rocks, now referred to the action of glaciers and ice-sheets.

[2] The most illustrious of Hall's successors, A. Daubrée, has made generous recognition of the importance of the work of the early master. Daubrée's own studies in experimental geology are a monument of patient, skilful and original research, and well sustain the high reputation of the French school of geologists.

might be sent forth to combat the errors of the
dominant Wernerianism. He did what he could in
that direction by preparing and publishing his admirable " Illustrations," which were widely read, and, as
Hall has recorded, exerted a powerful influence on
the minds of the most eminent men of science of
the day.

But another influence, strongly antagonistic to the
progress of the Huttonian philosophy, was established
in Edinburgh at the very time when the prospect
seemed so fair for the creation of a Scottish school
which might do much to further the advance of
sound geology. Robert Jameson (1774-1854), whose
influence and writings have been referred to in Chapter VIII., had studied for nearly two years at
Freiberg under Werner. After two more years spent
in continental travel, full of enthusiasm for his
master's system, he had returned to the Scottish
capital in 1804, when he was elected to the Chair
of Natural History in the University. His genial
personal character, and his zeal for the Freiberg faith
soon gathered a band of ardent followers around
him. He had much of Werner's power of fostering
in others a love of the subjects that interested himself. Travelling widely over Scotland, from the
southern borders to the furthest Shetland Isles, he
everywhere saw the rocks through Saxon spectacles.
From the very beginning, the books and papers
which he wrote were drawn up after the most approved Wernerian method, pervaded by the amplest
confidence in that method, and by hardly disguised
contempt for every other. Nowhere indeed can the

peculiarities of the Wernerian style be seen in more typical perfection than in the writings of the Edinburgh professor.[1]

In the year 1808, Jameson founded a new scientific association in Edinburgh, which he called the "Wernerian Natural History Society," with the great Werner himself at the head of its list of honorary members. So far as geology was concerned, the original aim of this institution appears to have been to spread the doctrines of Freiberg. I know no more melancholy contrast in geological literature than is presented when we pass from the glowing pages of Playfair, or the suggestive papers of Hall, to the dreary geognostical communications in the first published Memoirs of this Wernerian Society. On the one side, we breathe the spirit of the most enlightened modern geological philosophy, on the other we grope in the darkness of a Saxon mine, and listen to the repetition of the familiar shibboleths, which even the more illustrious of Werner's disciples were elsewhere beginning to discard.

The importation of the Freiberg doctrines into Scotland by an actual pupil of Werner, carried with it the controversy as to the origin of basalt. This question, it might have been thought, had been practically settled there by the writings of Hutton, Playfair, and Hall, even if it had not been completely solved by

---

[1] See, for instance, the way in which he dismisses the observations of Faujas de St. Fond on Scottish rocks, and the unhesitating declaration that there is not in all Scotland the vestige of a volcano.— *Mineralogy of the Scottish Isles* (1800), p. 5. He never loses an opportunity of a sneer at the "Vulcanists" and "fire-philosophers."

Desmarest, Von Buch, D'Aubuisson, and others on
the Continent. But the advent of Jameson rekindled
the old fires of controversy. The sections of the rocks
laid open among the hills and ravines around Edinburgh, which display such admirable illustrations of
eruptive action, were confidently appealed to alike by
the Plutonists and the Neptunists. Jameson carried
his students to Salisbury Crags and Arthur Seat, and
there demonstrated to them that the so-called igneous
rocks were manifestly merely chemical precipitates in
the "Independent Coal formation." The Huttonians
were ready to conduct any interested stranger to the
very same sections to prove that the whinstone was
an igneous intrusion. There is a characteristic anec-
dote told of one of these excursions in an article
by Dr. W. H. Fitton in the *Edinburgh Review*. One
of the Irish upholders of the aqueous origin of basalt,
Dr. Richardson, had attained some notoriety from
having found fossils in what he called basalt at Port-
rush, on the coast of Antrim. His discovery was
eagerly quoted by those who maintained the aqueous
origin of that rock, and though eventually Playfair
showed that the fossils really lie in Lias shale, which
has been baked into a flinty condition by an intrusive
basaltic sheet, this explanation was not accepted by the
other side, and the fossiliferous basalt of Antrim continued to be cited as an indubitable fact by the zealous
partizans of Werner. While these were still matters
of controversy Dr. Richardson paid a visit to Scotland, chiefly with reference to fiorin grass, in which he
was interested. The writer in the *Edinburgh Review*
tells us that he was asked by Sir James Hall, to meet

Dr. Hope and the Irish geologist. "It was arranged that the party should go to Salisbury Crags, to show Dr. Richardson a junction of the sandstone with the trap, which was regarded as an instructive example of that class of facts. After reaching the spot, Sir James pointed out the great disturbance that had taken place at the junction, and particularly called the attention of the doctor to a piece of sandstone which had been whirled up during the convulsion and enclosed in the trap. When Sir James had finished his lecture, the doctor did not attempt to explain the facts before him on any principle of his own, nor did he recur to the shallow evasion of regarding the enclosed sandstone as contemporaneous with the trap ; but he burst out into the strongest expressions of contemptuous surprise that a theory of the earth should be founded on such small and trivial appearances ! He had been accustomed, he said, to look at Nature in her grandest aspects, and to trace her hand in the gigantic cliffs of the Irish coast ; and he could not conceive how opinions thus formed could be shaken by such minute irregularities as those which had been shown to him. The two Huttonian philosophers were confounded ; and, if we recollect rightly, the weight of an acre of fiorin and the number of bullocks it would feed formed the remaining subjects of conversation." [1]

It is not needful to follow into further detail the history of the opposition encountered by the Huttonian theory of the earth. Some of the bitterest antagonists of Hutton hailed from Ireland. Besides Richardson, with his fossiliferous basalt, there was Kirwan, President

[1] *Edinburgh Review*, No. lxv. 1837, p. 9.

of the Royal Irish Academy, whose ungenerous attacks stung Hutton into the preparation of his larger treatise. In England and on the Continent another determined opponent was found in the versatile and prolific De Luc. But though these men wielded great influence in their day, their writings have fallen into deserved oblivion. They are never read save by the curious student, who has leisure and inclination to dig among the cemeteries of geological literature.

The gradual progress of the Huttonian school and the concomitant decay of Wernerianism at Edinburgh, are well indicated by the eight volumes of *Memoirs* published by Jameson's Wernerian Society, which ranged from 1811 to 1839, an interval of less than a generation. The early numbers might have emanated from Freiberg itself. Not a sentiment is to be found in them of which Werner himself would not have approved. How heartily, for example, Jameson must have welcomed the concluding sentence of a paper by one of the ablest of his associates when, after a not very complimentary allusion to Hutton's views about central heat, the remark is made—"He who has the boldness to build a theory of the earth without a knowledge of the natural history of rocks, will daily meet with facts to puzzle and mortify him." [1] The fate which this complacent Wernerian here predicted for the followers of Hutton, was now surely and steadily overtaking his own brethren. One by one the faithful began to fail, and, as we have seen, those who had gone out to preach the faith of Freiberg came back

[1] The Rev. John Fleming, *Mem. Wer. Soc.* vol. ii. (1813), p. 154.

convinced of its errors, and of the truth of much which they had held up to scorn in the tenets of the Plutonists. Even among Jameson's own students, as already noticed (*ante*, pp. 241, 263), defections began to appear in the early decades of last century. His friends might translate into English, and publish at Edinburgh, tracts of the most orthodox Wernerianism, such as Werner's *Treatise on Veins*, or Von Buch's *Description of Landeck*, or D'Aubuisson's *Basalts of Saxony*. But his pupils, who went farther afield, who came into contact with the distinct current of opposition to some of the doctrines of the Freiberg school that was now setting in on the Continent, who began seriously to study the igneous rocks of the earth's crust, and who found at every turn facts that could not be fitted into the system of Freiberg, gradually, though often very reluctantly, went over to the opposite camp. Men like Ami Boué would send to Jameson notes of their travels, full of what a staunch Wernerian could not but regard as the rankest heresy.[1] But the Professor with great impartiality printed these in the Society's publications. And so by degrees the *Memoirs* of the Wernerian Society ceased to bear any trace of Wernerianism, and contained papers of which any Huttonian might have been proud to be the author.[2]

One important result of the keen controversies

---

[1] See *Mem. Wer. Soc.* vol. iv. (1822), p. 91.

[2] See, for example, the papers by Hay Cunningham in vols. vii. and viii. In an Address to the Geological Society in 1828 Fitton alluded to the universal adoption in Britain of " a modified volcanic theory, and the complete subsidence, or almost oblivion of the Wernerian and Neptunian hypotheses." *Proc. Geol. Soc.* i. p. 55.

between the Vulcanist and Neptunist schools in Europe is to be found in the appeal that was necessitated to Nature herself for a solution of the disputed problems. The days of mere theorizing in the cabinet or the study had now passed away. Everywhere there was aroused a spirit of inquiry into the evidence furnished by the earth itself as to its history. The main theoretical principles of the science had been established, so far as related to geological processes and their influence in the structure of the terrestrial crust. But the palæontological side of geology had still to be opened up. The fruitful doctrine of stratigraphy remained to be developed and applied to the elucidation of the grand record of geological history. How this doctrine, which has done more than any other for the progress of geological investigation, was worked out will be the subject of the next four chapters.

CHAPTER XI

THAT the rocks around and beneath us contain the
record of terrestrial revolutions before the establishment of the present dry land, was an idea clearly
present to the minds of the early Italian geologists,
and, having been so eloquently enforced by Buffon,
was generally admitted, before the end of the
eighteenth century, by all who interested themselves
in minerals and rocks. The Neptunists and Vulcanists might dispute vigorously over their respective
creeds, but they all agreed in maintaining the doctrine
of a geological succession. Werner made this doctrine
a cardinal part of his system, and brought it into
greater prominence than it had ever held before his
time. His sequence of formations from granite, at
the base, to the youngest river-gravel or sea-formed
silt, betokened, in his view, a gradual development of
deposits, which began with the chemical precipitates
of a universal ocean, and ended with the modern
mechanical and other accumulations of terrestrial surfaces, as well as of the sea-floor. But, as we have

seen, the lithological characters on which he based the discrimination of his various formations proved to be unreliable. Granite was soon found not always to lie at the bottom. Basalt, at first placed by him among the oldest formations, turned up incontinently among the youngest. He and his disciples were consequently obliged to alter and patch the Freiberg system, till it lost its simplicity and self-consistence, and was still as far as ever from corresponding with the complex order which nature had followed. Obviously the Wernerian school had not found the key to the problem, though it had done service in showing how far a lithological sequence could be traced among the oldest rocks.

Hutton's views on this question were in some respects even less advanced than Werner's. He realized, as no one had ever done so clearly before him, the evidence for the universal decay of the land. At the same time, he perceived that unless some compensating agency came into play, the whole of the dry land must eventually be washed into the sea. The upturned condition of the Primary strata, which had once been formed under the sea, furnished him with proofs that in past time the sea-floor has been upheaved into land. Without invoking any fanciful theory, he planted his feet firmly on these two classes of facts, which could be fully demonstrated. To his mind the earth revealed no trace of a beginning, no prospect of an end. All that he could see was the evidence of a succession of degradations and upheavals, by which the balance of sea and land and the habitable condition of our globe were perpetuated.

Hutton was unable to say how many of these revolutions may be chronicled among the rocks of the earth's crust.[1] Nor did he discover any method by which their general sequence over the whole globe could be determined.

A totally new pathway of investigation had now to be opened up. The part that had hitherto been played by species of minerals and rocks was henceforth to be taken by species of plants and animals. Organic remains, imbedded in the strata of the earth's crust, had been abundantly appealed to as evidence of the former presence of the sea upon the land, or as proofs of upheaval of the sea-floor. But they were now to receive far closer attention, until they were found to contain the key to geological history, to furnish a basis by which the past revolutions of the globe could be chronologically arranged and accurately described, and to cast a flood of light upon the history and development of organised life upon the surface of the earth.

Apart altogether from questions of cosmogony or of geological theory, some of the broad facts of stratigraphy could not but, at an early time, attract attention. In regions of little-disturbed sedimentary rocks, the superposition of distinct strata, one upon another, was too obvious to escape notice. A little travel with observant eyes would enable men to see that the same kinds of strata, accompanied by the

---

[1] Playfair thought that the revolutions may have been often repeated, and that our present continents appear to be the third in succession, of which relics may be observed among the rocks.— *Works,* vol. iv. p. 55.

same topographical characters, ranged from district to district, across wide regions. We have found that it was in countries of regular and gently-inclined stratified rocks that Lehmann and Füchsel made their observations, which paved the way for the development of the idea of palæontological succession. We have now to trace the growth of this idea, and the discovery that organic remains furnish the clue to the relative chronology of the strata in which they are imbedded.

The fact that different rocks contain dissimilar but distinctive fossils had been noted by various observers long before its geological significance was perceived. Thus, as far back as 1671, we find Martin Lister affirming, in a letter already cited (p. 76), that "quarries of different stone yield us quite different sorts or species of shells not only one from another (as those Cockle-stones of the iron-stone quarries of Adderton, in Yorkshire, differ from those found in the lead-mines of the neighbouring mountains, and both these from the cockle-quarrie of Wansford Bridge, in Northamptonshire; and all three from those to be found in the quarries about Gunthrop and Beauvour Castle, etc.), but, I dare boldly say, from anything in nature besides, that either the land, salt or freshwater doth yield us." [1]

Again, John Strange writing in 1779 remarks that

[1] *Phil. Trans.* vol. vi. p. 2283. Greenough in his *Critical Examination of the First Principles of Geology*, 1819, (p. 284), in quoting this passage, adds that Lister had "followed the course of the Chalk Marl over an extensive tract of country by mere attention to its fossils," but no reference is given to the authority for this statement.

" the *Gryphites* oyster is not only found abundantly in the lower part of Monmouthshire and about Purton Passage, but also extends in considerable aggregates along the neighbouring midland counties ; having myself traced them, either in gravel or limestone, through Gloucestershire, Worcestershire, Warwickshire and Leicestershire, occupying in like manner the lower parts of those counties, under the hills."[1] It would thus appear that the outcrop of the Lias had been traced, by means of its fossils, across a great part of England some years before William Smith began his labours.

There were two regions of Europe well fitted to furnish any competent inquirers with the evidence for establishing, by means of fossil organic remains, this supremely important section of modern geology. In France, the Secondary and Tertiary formations lie in undisturbed succession, one above another, over hundreds of square miles. They come to the surface, not obscured under superficial deposits, but projecting their escarpments to the day, and showing, by their topographical contours, the sharply defined limits of their several groups. Again, in England, the same formations cover the southern and eastern parts of the country, displaying everywhere the same clear evidence of their arrangement. Let us trace the progress of discovery in each of these regions. To a large extent this progress was simultaneous, but there is no evidence that the earlier workers in the one country were aware of what was being done in the other.

[1] *Archæologia*, vol. vi. (1782), p. 36.

To the Abbé J. L. Giraud-Soulavie (1752-1813) the merit must be assigned of having planted the first seeds from which the magnificent growth of strati-graphical geology in France has sprung. Among other works, he wrote a *Natural History of Southern France* in seven volumes, of which the first two appeared in the year 1780. He gave much of his attention to the old volcanoes of his native country, and devoted several of his volumes entirely to their description. But his chief claim to notice here lies in a particular chapter of his work which, he tells us, was read before the Royal Academy of Sciences of Paris on 14th August 1779.[1] In describing the cal-careous mountains of the Vivarais, he divided the limestones into five epochs or ages, the strata in each of which are marked by a distinct assemblage of fossil shells. The first of these ages, he declared, was represented by limestone containing organic remains with no living analogues, such as ammonites, belemnites, terebratulæ, gryphites, etc. Having no more ancient strata in the district, the Abbé called this oldest limestone primordial. His second age was indicated by limestone, in which the fossils of the preceding epoch were still found, but associated with some others now living in our seas. Among the new forms of life that appeared in these secondary strata he enumerated chamas, mussels, comb-shells, nautili, etc. These, he said, inhabited the sea, to-gether with survivors from the first age, but the latter at the end of the second age disappeared.

[1] *Histoire Naturelle de la France Méridionale*, tome i. 2ᵐᵉ partie, chap. viii. p. 317.

Above their remains other races established themselves, and carried on the succession of organised
beings.

The third age was one in which the shells were of
recent forms, with descendants that inhabit the present
seas.   The remains of these shells were found in a
soft white limestone, but not a trace of ammonite,
belemnite, or gryphite was to be seen associated with
them.   Among the organisms named by the Abbé
were limpets, whelks, volutes, oysters, sea-urchins,
and others, the number of species increasing with the
comparative recentness of the formation. He thought,
like Werner, that the most ancient deposits had been
accumulated at the highest levels, when the sea covered
the whole region, and that, as the waters sank,
successively younger formations were laid down at
lower and lower levels.

From the occurrence of worn pebbles of basalt in
the third limestone, Giraud-Soulavie inferred that volcanic eruptions had preceded that formation, and that
an enormous duration of time was indicated by the
erosion of the lavas of these volcanoes, and the
transport and deposit of their detritus in the white
limestone.

The fourth age in the Vivarais was represented by
certain carbonaceous shales or slates, containing the
remains of primordial vegetation to which it was
difficult to discover the modern analogues.   Giraud-
Soulavie believed that he could observe among these
slates a succession of organic remains similar to that
displayed by the limestones, those strata which lay on
the oldest marble containing ammonites, while the

most recent enclosed, but only rarely, unknown plants
mingled with known forms. It would thus appear
that the deposits of the so-called fourth age were
more or less equivalents of those of the three calcareous ages.

The fifth age was characterised by deposits of
conglomerate and modern alluvium, containing fossil
trees, together with bones and teeth of elephants and
other animals. "Such is the general picture," the
Abbé remarks, " presented by our old hills of the
Vivarais, and of the modern plains around them.
The progress of time and, above all, of increased
observation will augment the number of epochs which
I have given, and fill up the blanks ; but they will
not change the relative places which I have assigned to
these epochs." [1]   He felt confident that if the facts
observed by him in the Vivarais were confirmed in
other regions, a historical chronology of fossil and
living organisms would be established on a basis of
incontestible truth.   In his last volume, replying to
some objections made to his opinions regarding the
succession of animals in time, he contends that the
difference between the fossils of different countries is
due not to a geographical but to a chronological cause.
"The sea," he says, " produces no more ammonites,
because these shells belong to older periods or other
climates.   The difference between the shells in the
rocks rests on the difference in their relative antiquity,
and not on mere local causes.   If an earthquake were
to submerge the ammonite-bearing rocks of the
Vivarais beneath the Mediterranean, the sea returning

[1] *Op. cit.* p. 350.

to its old site would not bring back its old shells. The course of time has destroyed the species, and they are no longer to be found in the more recent rocks."[1]

The sagacity of these views will at once be acknowledged. Yet they seem to have made, for a time, no way either in France or elsewhere. The worthy Abbé, though a good observer and a logical reasoner, was a singularly bad writer. At the end of the eighteenth century a wretched style was an unpardonable offence even in a man of science.[2] Whatever may have been the cause, Giraud-Soulavie has fallen into the background. His fame has been eclipsed, even in France, by the more brilliant work of his successors. Yet, in any general survey of geological progress, it is only just to acknowledge how firmly he had grasped some of the fundamental truths of stratigraphical geology, at a time when the barren controversy about the origin of basalt was the main topic of geological discussion throughout Europe.

We have seen that the distinctness, regularity, and persistence of the outcrops of the various geological formations of the Paris basin suggested to Guettard the first idea of depicting on maps the geographical distribution of rocks and minerals. The same region and the same features of topography and structure inspired long afterwards a series of researches that contributed in large measure to the establishment of the principles of geological stratigraphy. No fitter birthplace could be found in Europe for the rise of

---

[1] *Op. cit.* tome vii. (1784), p. 157.
[2] D'Archiac, *Géologie et Paléontologie*, 1866, p. 145.

this great department of science. Around the capital
of France, the Tertiary and Secondary formations are
ranged in orderly sequence, group emerging from
under group, to the far confines of Brittany on the
west, the hills of the Ardennes and the Vosges on
the east, and the central plateau on the south. Not
only is the succession of the strata clear, but their
abundant fossils furnish a most complete basis for
stratigraphical arrangement and comparison.

Various observers had been struck with the orderly
sequence of rocks in this classic region. Desmarest
tells us that the chemist G. F. Rouelle (1703-1770)
was so impressed with its symmetry of structure that,
though he never wrote anything on the subject, he
used to discourse on it to his students at the Jardin
des Plantes, of whom Desmarest himself appears to
have been one. He would enlarge to them upon the
significance of the masses of shells imbedded in the
rocks of the earth's surface, pointing out that these
rocks were not disposed at random, as had been
supposed. He saw that the shells were not the
same in all regions, that certain forms were always
found associated together, while others were never
to be met with in the same strata or layers. He
noticed, as Guettard had done before him, that in
some districts the fossil shells were grouped in exactly
the same kind of arrangement and distribution as on
the floor of the present sea—a fact which, in his
eyes, disproved the notion that these marine organisms
had been brought together by some violent deluge ;
but which, on the other hand, showed that the present
land had once been the bottom of the sea, and had been

laid dry by some revolution that took place without producing any disturbance of the strata. Rouelle recognised a constant order in the arrangement of the shells. Thus, immediately around Paris, he found certain strata to be full of screw shells (*Turritella*, *Cerithium*, etc.), and to extend to Chaumont, on the one side, and to Courtagnon near Rheims, on the other. He pointed to a second deposit, or "mass" as he called it, full of belemnites, ammonites, gryphites, etc. (Jurassic), forming a long and broad band outside the eastern border of the Chalk, and stretching north and south beyond that formation up to the old rocks of the Morvan. Desmarest's account of his teacher's opinions was published in the third year of the Republic.[1] It is thus evident that Rouelle had formed remarkably correct views of the general stratigraphy of the Paris basin probably long before 1794.

Desmarest himself published many valuable observations regarding the rocks of the Paris basin in separate articles in his great *Géographie Physique*. Lamanon had written on the gypsum deposits of the region, which he regarded as marking the sites of former lakes, and from which he described and figured the remains of mammals, birds and fishes. Noting the alternations of gypsum and marls, he traced what he believed to be the limits of the sheets of freshwater in which they were successively deposited. Still more precise was the grouping adopted by Lavoisier (1743-1794). This great man, who, if he had not given himself up to chemistry, might have become one of

[1] *Géographie Physique* (*Encyclopédie Méthodique*), tome i. (1794), pp. 409-431.

the most illustrious among the founders of geology, was, as already stated (p. 115), associated early in life with Guettard in the construction of mineralogical maps of France. As far back as the year 1789, he distinguished between what he called littoral banks and pelagic banks, which were formed at different distances from the land, and were marked by distinct kinds of sediment and peculiar organisms. He thought that the different strata, in such a basin as that of the Seine, pointed to very slow oscillations of the level of the sea, and he believed that a section of all the stratified deposits between the coasts and the mountains would furnish an alternation of littoral and pelagic banks, and would reveal by the number of strata the number of excursions made by the waters of the ocean. Lavoisier accompanied his essay with sections which gave the first outline of a correct classification of the Tertiary deposits of the Paris region. His sketch was imperfect, but it represented in their true sequence the white Chalk supporting the Plastic Clay, lower sands, Calcaire Grossier, upper sands and upper lacustrine limestone.[1]

A few years later, a more perfect classification of these Tertiary deposits was published by Coupé, but without sufficiently detailed observations to convince his contemporaries that the work was wholly reliable.[2]

[1] *Mém. Acad. Roy. Sciences* (1789), p. 350, pl. 7. This memoir of Lavoisier on modern horizontal strata and their disposition is fully noticed by Desmarest in the first volume of his *Géographie Physique*, p. 783. Lavoisier's distinction between pelagic and littoral organisms and deposits was afterwards adopted by Lamarck (*postea*, p. 355).

[2] *Journ. de Physique*, tome lix. (1804), pp. 161-176.

The Tertiary formations of the great basin of the Seine were destined not only to furnish a vast impetus to the development of stratigraphical geology, but to provide the first broad scientific basis for the foundation of the science of Palæontology. In this momentous development of geological science two names stand out with conspicuous prominence among those who carried on the work—Lamarck and Cuvier.

Jean-Baptiste-Pierre-Antoine de Monet, Chevalier de Lamarck (1744-1829) came of an ancient but somewhat decayed family, and was born in a village of Picardy, as the eleventh and youngest child of the Seigneur de Béarn.[1] The ancestral patrimony having become too slender to provide a living for the boy, he was designed for the church, and was sent to begin his studies under the Jesuits of Amiens. But since for centuries his ancestors had been soldiers, and he had three brothers in the army, he could not bring himself to settle down finally to the peaceful life of an ecclesiastic. The death of his father in 1760 gave him an opportunity of leaving his books and joining the French forces that were then engaged in the disastrous war which began in 1756. With no other passport than a letter of introduction from a lady in his neighbourhood to the Colonel of the Beaujolais regiment, he set out for the seat of war, mounted on a sorry nag, and attended by a poor

[1] For the biographical details of Lamarck's life I am indebted to Cuvier's *Éloge* of him in the *Recueil des Éloges Historiques*, vol. iii. p. 179, and to the excellent volume by Mr. A. S. Packard, *Lamarck, the Founder of Evolution: His Life and Work*, 1901.

lad of his village. He arrived at the camp immediately before an attack was to be made on the allied army under Prince Ferdinand of Brunswick.

In this attack, known as the battle of Willingshausen (14th July 1761), which ended in the signal defeat of the French, young Lamarck at last found himself in charge of his company, whereof all the officers had been killed in the action, and which was left behind unnoticed in the confusion of the retreat. The oldest grenadier of the band counselled him to retire, but the youthful volunteer, with characteristic courage, refused to move without orders from the post that had been assigned to them. Not without some risk and difficulty he and the remnant of his company were at last relieved and withdrawn. He was at once rewarded for his valour by being made an officer by the Commander-in-Chief. Further promotion followed, and after the peace he passed some time in garrison duty. The enforced leisure of this kind of life, and the seclusion rendered necessary by a severe accident, led him to return to some of the studies, more particularly to botany, which had interested him during his stay at the College.

Seeing at last no prospect of a satisfactory future in the army he resolved to try his fortune elsewhere, and to qualify himself for the medical profession. Having, however, an annual allowance of no more than 400 francs, he eked out his slender income by working for a portion of his time in the office of a banker. His medical education is said to have extended over four years. But he does not seem ever to have taken up the practice of the profession, though the scientific training he then received must have been an excellent prelude to his subsequent career.

Lamarck, from his early love for plants, threw himself with all the ardour of his enthusiastic and indomitable nature into the study of botany, insomuch that at the age of 24 he abandoned everything else to be able to devote himself to its pursuit. He worked under Bernard de Jussieu at the Jardin des Plantes, and made botanical excursions round Paris with Rousseau. He was eventually appointed Keeper of the Herbarium of the Royal Gardens at the miserable salary of 1000 francs, afterwards increased to 1800. Yet his first published essay showed that he was not entirely engrossed in botanical studies. Not improbably the high garret in the Quartier Latin, which he had tenanted as a student, and which commanded a wide view of the sky, had given him occasion to watch the movements of the clouds and other phenomena of meteorology. At all events, in the year 1776, when he was 32 years of age, he presented to the Academy of Sciences a memoir " On the Vapours of the Atmosphere," which was well received, and proved to be the first of a long series of contributions from him to meteorological science.

After ten years of earnest botanical study Lamarck published in 1778 his *Flore Française* in three volumes. In this work he gave a succinct description of all the wild plants of the country, arranged in accordance, not with the Linnaean system of nomenclature, but with a classification which he had himself devised. This treatise, at the special instance of Buffon, was printed at the expense of the Government and it at once placed its author in a prominent position among the naturalists of the day. Buffon's friendship proved a valuable aid to him in various ways, and doubtless helped to secure his speedy election into the Academy of Sciences. But he still remained exceedingly poor, and had a hard struggle to support himself and the family that was now growing up around him.

From the time of the appearance of the *Flore Française* Lamarck continued for fifteen years to work mainly at botanical subjects, contributing papers to the Memoirs of the Academy of Sciences, and producing the successive botanical volumes in the great *Encyclopédie Méthodique*. These labours had raised him into the front rank of botanists, but they did not make the tenure of his appointment so secure that he had not to defend his position. He was compelled to publish a statement of the nature and importance of the duties he had to perform, and at the same time he urged that more ample provision should be made for the scientific work of the Museum and Garden. The National Convention took up the matter, and in the summer of 1793 reorganised and enlarged the establishment. Of the twelve new chairs then founded, the botanical appointments were naturally bestowed on the two senior distinguished botanists of the staff, Jussieu and Desfontaines, while Lamarck was offered one of the chairs of zoology. When it is remembered that he was now verging on 50 years of age, and that he had never paid much attention to zoological matters, but had given up his time and energies to botany, one may well feel astonishment at the courage of the man in accepting the appointment and resolving to make himself master of another science. The title of his chair was "Professor of Zoology; of insects, of worms and of microscopic animals," and the annual stipend 2868 livres or about £115 sterling. Having made up his mind to undertake the new duties, he threw himself with such courage and zeal into them, that before many years he was acclaimed as an even more accomplished and original zoologist than he had been a botanist. Yet he continued to find time for excursions into physical science. He went on for a succession of years publishing meteorological reports, which may be regarded as in some respects forerunners of the weather-charts of recent times. He also entered the lists against the prevalent chemical and physical opinions of the day, propounding some extraordinary views which had no experimental basis and were generally regarded as too eccentric to require refutation.

In the course of his zoological studies Lamarck was led directly and indirectly to make important contributions towards the advance of geology. In dealing with the invertebrata, especially with the mollusca, he studied and described the varied assemblage of fossil shells so abundantly and perfectly preserved among the Tertiary deposits of the Paris basin. Correlating the living with the extinct forms, he was enabled to present a far broader and more accurate picture of the invertebrate division of the animal kingdom than had ever before been attempted. Cuvier has been claimed as the great founder of vertebrate Palæontology; Lamarck may with at least equal justice be regarded as the founder of the invertebrate half of the science. His researches among the shells of the Paris basin furnished, as we shall see, an accurately determined basis on which Cuvier and Brongniart could work out the stratigraphy of that region.

But Lamarck's original and philosophical genius could not be confined within the limits of the mere determination of new genera and species. From the contemplation of these details, he advanced into broad generalisations among the higher problems of biology. He propounded views in organic evolution which, though received at the time with ridicule and subsequently with neglect, have in later years been revived, and meet now with a constantly increasing degree of acceptance. His *Philosophie Zoologique* has become a classic in biological literature, while his great work the *Animaux Sans Vertèbres*, which appeared in seven volumes between 1815 and 1822, marks a memorable epoch in the march of natural history, and will ever remain one of the glories of French science.

Though Lamarck wrote little on geology, the extent to which he had pondered over the problems of the science, which in his time had hardly taken definite shape, is well illustrated by the little volume which he published in 1802 under the title of *Hydrogéologie*.[1]

[1] The full title of this little known but extremely interesting treatise is as follows : "Hydrogéologie, ou Recherches sur l'influence qu'ont les eaux sur la surface du globe terrestre ; sur les causes de l'existence du bassin des mers, de son déplacement et de son transport successif sur les différentes points de la surface de ce globe ; enfin sur les changemens que les corps vivans exercent sur la nature et l'état de cette surface. Par J. B. Lamarck, Membre de l'Institut National de France, Professeur-Administrateur au Muséum d'Histoire

The object of this work was to propose and attempt to solve four problems, the solution of which must constitute the foundation of any true theory of the earth. 1st. What are the natural effects of the movements of the terrestrial waters on the surface of the globe? 2nd. Why is the sea confined to a basin and within limits that always separate it from the projecting dry land? 3rd. Has the basin of the sea always existed as we now see it, and if not, what is the cause that led to its being elsewhere, and why is it not there still? 4th. What is the influence of living organisms on the mineral substances of the earth's surface and crust, and what are the general results of this influence?

1. Lamarck realised more clearly than most of his contemporaries, the part played by terrestrial waters on the surface of the land. He recognised that nothing can ultimately resist the alternating influence of wetness and drought, combined with that of heat and cold, and that the disintegration of mineral substances by these atmospheric conditions prepares the way for the erosive action of running water in all its various forms. As the result of this action, plains are hollowed out into ravines, and these are widened into valleys. The spaces between rivers are worn into ridges, which in course of time become high crests.

Naturelle &c." Paris, An X (1802). It is interesting to note that this volume and Playfair's *Illustrations of the Huttonian Theory* were published in the same year, and to contrast the opinions of the two writers. In all that relates to the organic world, the French naturalist had a far wider outlook than the Scottish philosopher, while on the other hand, the latter showed a truer insight into most of the physical problems of geology with which he dealt.

If the surface of the land had been at first a vast plain, yet at the end of a certain time, through the operation of its water-courses, it would have lost that aspect, and would ultimately come to be traversed with mountains like those with which we are familiar.

In these deductions, the French philosopher re-echoed the principles established by De Saussure, Desmarest and Hutton. But he carried them to an extreme which may possibly have raised a prejudice against them. He declared that every mountain which has not been erupted by volcanic action or some other local catastrophe, has been cut out of a plain, so that the mountain-summits represent the relics of that plain, save in so far as its level has been lowered in the general degradation. Geologists have accepted this explanation for the systems of mountains which, having no internal or tectonic structure peculiar to themselves, appear to have been carved out of ancient tablelands. Lamarck, however, though he speaks of local catastrophes, seems to have had no conception of any widespread cause whereby the terrestrial crust has from time to time been folded and driven upwards into vast chains of mountains. He admits that in many mountains the component strata are often vertical or highly inclined. But he will not on that account believe in any universal catastrophe, such as had been demanded by many previous writers, and was still loudly advocated in his own time by his fellow-countryman Cuvier. He considers that the inclination of the strata may be due partly to the natural slope of the surface on which the sediments were originally deposited, like the talus-slopes of mountains, partly and frequently to many kinds of accidents, such as arise from local subsidence. But he enters into no further detail, and shows no personal knowledge of the real structure of a true mountain-chain.

The task of the fresh waters, according to this thinker, is thus two-fold ; to erode the dry land, thereby producing valleys and mountains, and to spread the detritus over plains, before finally sweeping it out to sea, where it tends towards the filling up of the sea-basins.

2. In attempting to solve his second problem Lamarck ventured far beyond his depth in regard to the physics of the earth, and broached some crude ideas, based on no reliable evidence, but directly contrary to such facts regarding the ocean as were known in his time.   He conceived the ocean-basin to owe its existence and preservation to the perpetual oscillation of the tides, and partly also to a general westerly movement of the water.   He supposed the tidal oscillation to be a gigantic force which has actually eroded the basin and now prevents it from being shallowed, through the deposit of land-derived sediment, by continually scouring this sediment out and casting it up along the more sheltered shores of the land. Since the sea does not cover the whole globe, but is gathered into its vast basin, the centre of gravity of the earth does not strictly coincide with what Lamarck called its "centre of form."   Owing to the shifting of the ocean-bed westward, he thought that the centre of gravity is simultaneously displaced and slowly makes a revolution round the centre of form.   In these speculations the great naturalist displayed a singular

misapprehension of the effects of the tides, and made
no allowance for any movement of the terrestrial crust.

3. The same limited acquaintance with the facts
which were needed for the solution of his difficulties
is not less conspicuous in the way in which he dealt
with his third problem. He thinks that in spite of
the tidal oscillations which seem to retard the deposit
of sediment over the sea-floor, the basin of the ocean
might eventually be filled up, or that at least the sea
would rise above its present mean level, if some
unceasingly active cause did not counteract this tendency. Looking around at the margin of the land
in different quarters of the globe, he sees what seems
to him evidence that the waters of the ocean are
subject to a continual impulse which drives them
from east to west, due, he believed, to the influence
chiefly of the moon, but partly also of the sun. He
does not show, however, in what form this impulse is
imparted otherwise than in the tidal wave. The
eastern coasts of the continents appear in his eyes to
be wasted by the attacks of the sea, while the western
shores, being sheltered from these attacks, receive
deposits of sediment. He looks on the Gulf of
Mexico as a vast hollow, dug out of the land by the
westerly advance of the Atlantic. The eastern side
of Asia, with its chains of islands and the passage
opened for the marine currents between these islands
and Australia, appeals to his mind as a striking
example of the truth of his generalisation, while the
eastern side of America is hardly less confirmatory,
although the sea has not yet cut through the Isthmus
of Panama.

Much more interesting and satisfactory is Lamarck's fresh demonstration, from authentic and irrefragable evidence, of the long accepted truth that the sea has once covered many parts of the surface of the globe from which it has long disappeared. This evidence rests on the occurrence of organic remains, and in dealing with it he evidently feels himself at home with his subject, and launches warmly into its discussion. The term "fossil," as we have seen (p. 215), had been indiscriminately applied to any mineral substance dug out of the earth, but Lamarck now for the first time definitely restricts it to the "still recognisable remains of organised bodies."[1] After citing a number of examples of the occurrence of such remains in the heart of mountains, at great heights above the sea and in different widely separated parts of the globe, he proceeds to dwell on the importance of fossils as monuments that furnish one of the chief means of ascertaining the revolutions which our globe has undergone. He urges naturalists to study fossil shells, to compare them with their analogues in our present seas, to investigate carefully where each species is found, the banks formed of them, the different layers which these banks may display, and other associated features. He points out, as Lavoisier had done before him (p. 344), that among fossil shells some are pelagic and some littoral, and that they even occasionally include terrestrial and fluviatile forms. These last would, in his opinion, be much more numerous had not their greater fragility led to their being generally broken and destroyed before they could be washed into the sea.

[1] *Hydrogéologie*, p. 55.

Discussing the cause of the former long-continued sojourn of the sea on so many parts of the surface of the land, he inquires whether we are to invoke the occurrence of the Deluge or some great catastrophes, as had so often been done in the past, and as continued to be done for many years afterwards by Cuvier. He will admit such an extraordinary cause if it be granted to have endured for the vast periods of time which the accumulation of thick and regular deposits of marine remains must have required. But he would rather seek for some explanation that will be more in accordance with the observed order of Nature. He was thus a follower of the Huttonian theory.

And here the great naturalist breaks forth in a tone that reminds one of the language of his Greek prototype, Aristotle : " In this globe which we inhabit, everything is subject to continual and inevitable changes. These arise from the essential order of things, and are effected with more or less rapidity or slowness, according to the varying nature or position of the objects implicated in them. Nevertheless they are accomplished within a certain period of time. For Nature, time is nothing, and is never a difficulty; she always has it at her disposal, and it is for her a means without bounds, wherewith she accomplishes the greatest as well as the least of her tasks." " Oh, how vast is the antiquity of our earth ! and how small are the ideas of those who assign to the existence of this globe a duration of six thousand and some hundreds of years from its beginning to our own days ! " " Losing trace of what has once existed, we can hardly believe nor even conceive the immensity of our planet's age. Yet how much vaster still will this antiquity appear to man when he shall have been able to form a just conception of the origin of living creatures, as well as of the causes of their gradual development and improvement, and above all when he shall perceive that time and the requisite conditions having been necessary to bring into existence all the living species now actually to be seen, he himself is the final result and actual climax of this development of which the ultimate limit, if such there be, can never be known."[1]

With such a limitless vista of past time to contemplate, Lamarck could indulge in unfettered speculation on the secular displacement of the ocean basin, and the concomitant submergence of the land. Inappreciably slow though the mutation might be, he believed it to be part of the regular order of nature, proceeding without interruption until every part of the dry land had in succession become the bed of the sea. In this slow westerly movement, the ocean seemed to him to have travelled round the globe, not once but perhaps many times, every part of the land becoming first the shore, and then passing under the scour of the great oceanic waters until at last reduced to form the bottom of the marine abysses. He thought that this displacement of the basin of the sea, by producing a constantly variable inequality in the terrestrial radii, causes a shifting of the centre of gravity of the globe as well as of the two poles, and that as this variation, markedly irregular though

[1] *Op. cit.* pp. 67, 88, 89.

it be, appears not to be confined within definite
limits, probably every point on the surface of our
planet may have successively passed through all the
different terrestrial climates.[1]

Though his theory of the interchange of land and
sea cannot be accepted, it is impossible to read without admiration Lamarck's marshalling of the facts on
which he relied, and his acute reflections on the deductions to be drawn from the characters and probable
habitats of organic remains. He points out the importance of distinguishing pelagic from littoral shells,
each series being usually found in distinct beds, the
one marking deep water the other former shore-lines.
Every part of the earth's surface that has once been
overspread by the sea has had twice a zone of
littoral shells and once a deposit of pelagic shells,
making three distinct and successive formations,
representing the passage of a vast lapse of time.
No sudden catastrophe is admissible as an explanation
of the facts ; such an event would have jumbled the
organisms together and would have broken the more
delicate shells, which have nevertheless been admirably
preserved in great numbers among the other fossils.
Again, the bivalves, with which many of the limestones are crowded, would not so commonly have
retained their valves in contact, unless they had lived
and died where their remains are found. In
Lamarck's opinion a large part of the calcareous
material, now to be found on the surface and within
the crust of the earth, has been derived from once
living organisms. He will not admit the propriety

[1] *Op. cit.* p. 87.

of the term "primitive," applied by mineralogists to the more ancient limestones. Though all trace of organic structure may have disappeared from these strata, he nevertheless believes them to have had an organic origin, and he can indicate the process by which the organic structures might be destroyed. He even goes so far as to affirm that such calcareous matter did not exist in the primitive earth, but like other animal and vegetable substances, only came into existence when it was secreted by living organisms.

4. To the treatment of the fourth problem Lamarck devotes nearly as much space as to the other three taken together, tempted doubtless to this greater discursiveness by the opportunity to re-state and develop his peculiar views in physics and chemistry, and to claim for the subject a far more important place in scientific investigation than his contemporaries seemed disposed to admit. Without entering here into his controversy, it may be sufficient to note the more important geological observations and deductions wherein the author was either wholly or partly in the right, and where he led the way in a line of inquiry wherein much still remains to be accomplished.

The crust of the earth, conjectured by Lamarck to be perhaps 3 or 4 leagues thick (13 to 17 kilometres or 8 to $10\frac{1}{2}$ English miles), was pictured by him to be, as regards its outer part, in a continual state of alteration ; ceaselessly worked over by the various forms of water, by the displacements and alternate passages of the ocean-basin, by the continual deposits of all kinds formed by living organisms on its exposed portions ; further by the changes, the upheavals, the accumulations, the subsidences and excavations produced in its thickness by volcanoes and earthquakes. Under these manifold influences it must certainly have undergone, in its condition and in the nature of its parts, variations which but for these different causes could never have taken place. All composite bodies tend to decay into their component constituents. Yet the visible crust of the earth consists almost entirely of compound materials. How is this fact to be accounted for ? There must be, he thought, some other potent force in Nature which acts antagonistically to the tendency towards the resolution of combinations into their component constituents, and he believed this force to be supplied by living organisms, or by what he calls the *Pouvoir de la Vie*. Having long watched the operations of living plants and animals, he saw that the organic action of living bodies unceasingly forms combinations of substances, which, without this action, would never have come into existence. From this well-founded observation, however, he leaped to the astounding generalisation that " the compound mineral substances, which are to be found in almost every part of the outer crust of the globe and form most of its composition, while at the same time they are continually modifying it by the changes they undergo, are all, without exception, the result of the remains and debris of living bodies." He had broached this view more than eighteen years earlier and he now complains that so striking a truth, only discoverable by observation, should have been rejected and apparently scorned by the very men who ought to have been the first to welcome it. We can hardly wonder, however, that his contemporaries should have refrained from treating this speculation as a serious contribution to science.

And yet though the conclusion was wholly untenable, it must in justice to Lamarck be admitted that he perceived in this matter, far more vividly than any other naturalist of his time, the importance of the part played by plants and animals in effecting geological changes by decomposing mineral matter, and thus modifying the surface of the earth and providing fresh materials for its crust. No one before his day had been able to follow so clearly the successive stages through which organic remains pass until they become crystalline stone, presenting no trace of their original organic structure. He distinguished between the consolidation of stratified rocks through the deposit of fine sediment (*Lapidescence par sédimens*), and through permeation by some cementing material (*Lapidescence par infiltration*).[1] He showed that agates and petrifactions are examples of the results of such infiltration, but he came to the singular conclusion that the " elementary earth," " vitreous earth," or silica of the chemists, has been so potent an agent in infiltration that it constitutes the base

[1] In this department of his subject Lamarck held much more accurate opinions than Hutton and Playfair, who were so carried away by their view of the efficacy of underground heat, as to believe that flints and agates had been injected in a molten state into the rocks in which they are now found.

of all the earths and stones of every sort, in short, of solid matter everywhere.

When he thus threw aside as error all that had then been ascertained as to the chemistry of minerals, he found no difficulty in accounting for all rocks as the results of the decay of organic bodies. He looked on granite, for example, not as the "primitive" rock which mineralogists had called it, nor as directly connected with the material that forms the interior of the globe, but as due to the transport of the decaying debris of organisms by rivers, and to the accumulation of this detritus on the floor of the sea. He believed that all argillaceous materials come from the decay of plants and all calcareous materials from the remains of animals, and that from these two chief sources the most important and abundant earthy and stony bodies are derived, all the other mineral substances being only mixtures or modifications of these. Even metals appeared to him divisible into two series, according as their earthy base has been supplied by animals or by plants. Here again he generalised from the undoubted precipitation of some metallic salts by organic matter to the production of all metallic substances from the same cause. His discussion ends with a pungent attack on the chemists of his day and their methods, and he declares that though all the world may believe them, he is content to be alone in his disbelief.

There can be little doubt that this spirit of opposition to many of the prevalent opinions of the time, together with the apparent extravagance of some of his doctrines, conspired to detract from the position and influence to which Lamarck's splendid abilities and achievements justly entitled him among his contemporaries. During the last ten years of his long life he suffered from total blindness, and had to rely on the affectionate devotion of his eldest daughter for the completion of such works as he had in progress before his eyesight failed. The world is becoming more conscious now of what it owes to the genius of this illustrious naturalist. Among those students of science who have most reason to cherish his memory, geologists should look back gratefully to his services in starting the science of Palæontology, in propounding the doctrine of evolution and in affirming with great insight some of the fundamental principles of modern geology.

Returning now to the Paris basin, we may take note that not until the year 1808 was the Tertiary stratigraphy of this district worked out in some detail, so as to furnish a foundation for the establishment of a general system of stratigraphical geology in France. This task was accomplished by two men who have left their mark upon the history of the science, Cuvier and Brongniart.

Georges Chrétien Leopold Dagobert Cuvier (1769-1832) came of an old Protestant family in the Jura, which in the sixteenth century had fled from persecution and had settled at Montbéliard, then the chief town of a little principality belonging to the Duke of Würtemberg. He was born at that place on 23rd August 1769, and after a singularly brilliant career at school and at the Caroline Academy of Stuttgart, became tutor in a Normandy family living near Fécamp. He had been drawn into the study of natural history,

when a mere child, by looking over the pages of
Buffon, and had with much ardour taken to the
observation of insects and plants.   In Normandy,
the treasures of the sea were opened to him.
Gradually ˙ his dissections and descriptions, though
not published, came to the notice of some of the
leading naturalists of France, and he was eventually
induced to come to Paris, where, after filling various
appointments, he was elected to the chair of Comparative Anatomy in 1795.

Cuvier's splendid career belongs mainly to the
history of biology.   We are only concerned here in
noting how he came to be interested in geological
questions.   He tells himself that some *Terebratulæ*
from the rocks at Fécamp suggested to him the idea
of comparing the fossil forms with living organisms.
When he settled in Paris, he pursued this idea,
never losing an opportunity of studying the fossils
to be found in the different collections.   He began
by gathering together as large a series as he could
obtain of skeletons of living species of vertebrate
animals, as a basis for the comparison and determination of extinct forms.   As a first essay in the new
domain which he was to open up to science, he read
to the Institute, at the beginning of 1796, a memoir
in which he demonstrated that the fossil elephant
belonged to a different species from either of the
living forms.   Two years later, having had a few
bones brought to him from the gypsum quarries of
Montmartre, he saw that they indicated some quite
unknown animals.   Further research qualified him
to reconstruct the skeletons, and to demonstrate their

entire difference, both specifically and generically, from
any known creatures of the modern world. He was
thus enabled to announce the important conclusion
that the globe was once peopled by vertebrate animals
which, in the course of the revolutions of its surface,
have entirely disappeared.

These discoveries, so remarkable in themselves, could
not but suggest many further inquiries to a mind
so penetrating and philosophical as that of Cuvier.
He narrates how he was pursued and haunted by
the desire to know why these extinct forms disappeared, and how they had come to be succeeded
by others. It was at this point that he entered
upon the special domain of geology. He found that
besides studying the fossil bones in the cabinet, it
was needful to understand, in the field, the conditions under which they have been entombed and
preserved. He had himself no practical acquaintance with the structure and relations of rocks, but
he was fortunate in securing the co-operation of a
man singularly able to supply the qualifications in
which he was himself deficient.

Alexandre Brongniart (1770-1847) Cuvier's associate,
was a year younger than the great anatomist. Born
in Paris, he began his career early in life by endeav-
ouring to improve the art of enamelling in France.
Thereafter he served in the medical department of
the army until he was attached to the Corps of Mines,
and was made director of the famous porcelain factory
of Sèvres. He had long given his attention to
minerals and rocks, and was eventually appointed
professor of mineralogy at the Museum of Natural

History. But his tastes led him also to study zoology.
Thus, among his labours in this field, he worked out
the zoological and geological relations of Trilobites.
There was consequently in their common pursuits, a
bond of union between him and Cuvier. They had
both entered upon a domain that was as yet almost
untrodden ; and each brought with him knowledge
and experience that were needful to the other.

Accordingly they engaged in a series of researches
in the basin of the Seine, which continued for some
years. Cuvier relates that during four years he made
almost every week an excursion into the country
around Paris, for the sake of studying its geological
structure. Particular attention was given to two
features,—the evidence of a definite succession among
the strata, and the distinction of the organic remains
contained in them. At last the results of these investigations were embodied in a joint memoir by
Cuvier and Brongniart, which first appeared in the
year 1808.[1]

The two naturalists continued their researches with
great industry during the following years. An account
of these additional observations was read by them
before the Institute in April 1810, and was published
as a separate work with a map, sections, and plate of
fossils in 1811.[2] Referring afterwards to this conjoint
essay and its subsequent enlargement, Cuvier generously
wrote that though it bore his name, it had become

[1] *Journal des Mines*, tome xxiii. (1808), p. 421.

[2] *Essai sur la Géographie Minéralogique des Environs de Paris, avec une
Carte géognostique et des Coupes de terrain*, 4to, 1811. An enlarged
edition of this separate work appeared in 1822.

almost entirely the production of his friend, from the
infinite pains which, ever after the first conception of
their plan, and during their various excursions, he
had bestowed upon the thorough investigation of all
the objects of the inquiry, and in the preparation of
the essay itself.[1] Brongniart's experience as a mining
engineer would naturally make him fitter than Cuvier
for the requirements of stratigraphical research.

It is not necessary for our present purpose to trace
the development of view shown by these observers
during the three years that elapsed between the appearance of their first sketch and that of their illustrated
quarto memoir. It will be enough to note the general
characters of their first essay, and to see how far in
advance it was of anything that had preceded it.

After briefly describing the limits and general features of the Seine basin, the authors proceed to show
that the formations which they have to consider were
deposited in a vast bay or lake, of which the shores
consisted of Chalk. They point out that the deposits
took place in a certain definite order, and can be easily
recognised by their lithological and palæontological
characters throughout the district. They classify
them first broadly into two great groups, which they
afterwards proceed to subdivide into minor sections.
The first of these groups, covering the Chalk of the
lower grounds, consists partly of the plateau of limestone without shells, and partly of the abundantly
shell-bearing Calcaire Grossier. The second group
comprises the gypseo-marly series, not found uniformly
distributed, but disposed in patches.

[1] *Discours sur les Révolutions de la Surface du Globe*, 6th edit. p. 294.

Starting from the Chalk of the north of France, the two observers succinctly indicate the leading characters of that deposit, its feeble stratification, chiefly marked by parallel layers of dark flints, the varying distances of these layers from each other, and the distinctive fossils. Putting together the organisms they had themselves collected, and those previously obtained by Defrance, they could speak of fifty species of organic remains known to occur in the Chalk—a small number compared with what has since been found. The species had not all been determined, but some of them, such as the belemnites, had been noted as different from those found in the "compact limestone," or Jurassic series.

From the platform of Chalk, Cuvier and Brongniart worked their way upward through the succession of Tertiary formations. At the base of these, and resting immediately on the Chalk, came the Plastic Clay—a deposit that in many respects presented strong contrasts to the white calcareous formation underneath it. It showed no passage into that formation, from which, on the contrary, it was always abruptly marked off, and it yielded no organic remains. The two geologists accordingly drew the sound inference that the clay and the chalk must have been laid down under very different conditions of water, and they believed that the animals which lived in the first period did not exist in the second. They likewise concluded that the abrupt line of junction between the two formations might indicate a long interval of time, and they inferred, from the occurrence of an occasional breccia of chalk fragments at the base of the clay, that the chalk was already solid when the clay was deposited.

The next formation in ascending order was one of sand and the Calcaire Grossier. It was shown to consist of a number of bands or alternations of limestone and marl; following each other always in the same order, and traceable as far as the two observers had followed them. Some of the strata might diminish or disappear, but what were below in one district were never found above in another. "This constancy in the order of superposition of the thinnest strata," the writers remark, "for a distance of at least 12 myriametres (75 English miles), is in our opinion one of the most remarkable facts which we have met with in the course of our researches. It should lead to results for the arts and for geology all the more interesting that they are sure."

One of the most significant parts of the essay is the account it gives of the method adopted by the explorers to identify the various strata from district to district. They had grasped the true principle of stratigraphy, and had applied it with signal success. The passage deserves to be quoted from its historical importance in the annals of science : "The means which we have employed, among so many limestones, for the recognition of a bed already observed in a distant quarter, has been taken from the nature of the fossils contained in each bed. These fossils are generally the same in corresponding beds, and present tolerably marked differences of species from one group of beds to another. It is a method of recognition which up to the present has never deceived us.

" It must not be supposed, however, that the difference in this respect between one bed and another is as sharply marked off as that between the chalk and the limestone. The characteristic fossils of one bed become less abundant in the bed above and disappear altogether in the others, or are gradually replaced by new fossils, which had not previously appeared."[1]

The authors then proceed to enumerate the chief groups of strata composing the Calcaire Grossier, beginning at the bottom and tracing the succession upward. It is not necessary to follow them into these details. We may note that, even at that time, the prodigious richness of the lower parts of this formation in fossil shells had been shown by the labours of Defrance, who had gathered from them no fewer than 600 species, which had been described by Lamarck. It was remarked by Cuvier and Brongniart that most of these shells are much more unlike living forms than those found in the higher strata. These observers also drew, from the unfossiliferous nature of the highest parts of the formation, the inference that during the time when the Calcaire Grossier was deposited slowly, layer after layer, the number of shells gradually diminished until they disappeared, the waters either no longer containing them or being unable to preserve them.

The gypseous series which succeeds offered to Cuvier and Brongniart an excellent example of what Werner termed a " formation," inasmuch as it presents a succession of strata markedly different from each other, yet evidently deposited in one continuous

[1] *Journal des Mines*, xxiii. p. 436.

sedimentation. Cuvier had already startled the world by his descriptions of some of the extinct quadrupeds entombed in these deposits. In calling attention to the occurrence of these animals, the authors refer to the occasional discovery of fresh-water shells in the same strata, and to the confirmation thereby afforded to the opinion of Lamanon and others, that the gypsum of Montmartre and other places around Paris had been deposited in fresh-water lakes.

They saw the importance of a thin band of marl at the top of the gypseous series which, in spite of its apparent insignificance, they had found to be traceable for a great distance. Its value arose partly from its marking what would now be called a lithological horizon, but even more from its stratigraphical interest, inasmuch as it served to separate a lacustrine from a marine series. All the shells below this seam were found to be fresh-water forms. Those in the seam itself were species of *Tellina*, and all those in the strata above were, like that shell, marine. The two geologists, struck by the marked difference of physical conditions represented by the two sections of the gypseous series, had tried to separate it into two formations, but had not carried out the design.

Higher up in the series, above a group of sands and marine sandstones, an unfossiliferous siliceous limestone, and a sandstone formation without shells, Cuvier and Brongniart found a widespread fresh-water siliceous limestone or millstone, specially characterised by containing *Limnea*, *Planorbis*, and other lacustrine shells.

The youngest formation which they described was the alluvium of the valleys, with bones of elephants and trunks of trees.

Subsequent research has slightly altered and greatly elaborated the arrangement made by Cuvier and Brongniart of the successive Tertiary formations of the Paris basin. But although the subdivision of the strata into definite stratigraphical and palæontological platforms has been carried into far greater detail, the broad outlines traced by them remain as true now as they were when first sketched a century ago. These two great men not merely marked out the grouping of the formations in a limited tract of country. They established on a basis of accurate observation the principles of palæontological stratigraphy. They demonstrated the use of fossils for the determination of geological chronology, and they paved the way for the enormous advances which have since been made in this department of science. For these distinguished labours they deserve an honoured place among the Founders of Geology. Cuvier's contributions to zoology, palæontology, and comparative anatomy were so numerous and important that his share in the establishment of correct stratigraphy is apt to be forgotten. But his name must ever be bracketed with that of Brongniart for the service rendered to geology by their conjoint work among the Tertiary deposits of the Paris basin.

Although Cuvier's researches among fossil animals, and the principles of comparative anatomy which he promulgated, contributed powerfully towards the

foundation and development of vertebrate palæontology as a distinct department of biology, his services
to geology proper may be looked upon as almost
wholly comprised in the joint essay with Brongniart.
Geology indeed had much fascination for him, and
he wrote a special treatise on it entitled *A Discourse
on the Revolutions of the Surface of the Globe*.[1] In
this work he maintains the opinion that the past
history of the earth has been marked by the occurrence of many sudden and widespread catastrophes,
exceeding in violence anything we can imagine at the
present day, whereby the surface of the land has been
overwhelmed by the sea, and its inhabitants have been
destroyed. Briefly reviewing the usual action of rain
and frost, brooks and rivers, the sea and volcanoes,
he comes to the conclusion that the former revolutions were so stupendous that " the thread of Nature's
operations was broken by them, that her progress was
altered, and that none of the agents which she employs

---

[1] In its first form it was prefixed to the *Recherches sur les Ossemens
Fossiles* as a Preliminary Discourse on the Theory of the Earth (1821).
It was afterwards published separately as the *Discours sur les Révolutions
de la surface du Globe* (1826). The work showed no marked advance in geological progress. Yet it went through six editions in the
author's lifetime, the latest (6th) corrected and augmented by him
appearing in 1830. The versions published in England were edited
and copiously annotated by Prof. Jameson of Edinburgh, whose notes
to the early editions supply some curious samples of his adherence to
Wernerianism. Cuvier was also the author of a Report on the Progress of the Natural Sciences, presented to the Emperor Napoleon in
1808, in which he expressed various vague and indefinite opinions on
geological questions. In his earlier years his geological bias was
decidedly towards Wernerianism (see the references in his *Éloge* on
De Saussure already cited, p. 308).

to-day could have sufficed for the accomplishment of her ancient works."[1]

The contrast between these opinions and those of Lamarck on the same subject could not fail to impress the minds of their contemporaries. Cuvier was a Cataclysmist, Lamarck an Evolutionist. The former by his brilliant style, his social charm, and his influential position commanded the attention of the world, so that his geological volume, though views which it specially advocated have long since been abandoned, went through a number of successive editions, besides being translated into English and German. It became, indeed, one of the chief portals through which the ordinary reader of the day made his acquaintance with the science of geology. Lamarck's little *Hydrogéologie*, on the other hand, met with no such success. Though in many respects, in spite of its occasional extravagance, a more philosophical treatise than Cuvier's, it never reached a second edition, has never been reprinted, and has almost sunk out of sight.

Notwithstanding the prominence assigned by Cuvier to great cataclysms in the past history of our planet, he recognised that there has been, on the whole, an upward progress among the races of animals that have successively flourished upon the earth. The oviparous quadrupeds, for instance, preceded the viviparous. But, unlike Lamarck, he set his face against evolution, and refused to admit that the existing races can be modifications of ancient forms, brought about by local circumstances, change of climate or other causes; for if any such evolution had taken place, he claimed

[1] *Discours Préliminaire*, p. xiii.

that some evidence of it should have been found in the shape of intermediate forms in the rocks. He regarded species as permanent, though varieties might arise. He offered a detailed argument to prove, from physical facts and from the history of nations, that the present continents are of modern date, and he entered into an elaborate refutation of the alleged antiquity of some peoples. He believed, with De Luc and Dolomieu, in opposition to the opinions so well expressed by Lamarck, that if any conclusion has been well-established in geology, it is that a great and sudden catastrophe befell the surface of the earth some five or six thousand years ago, whereby the countries inhabited by man were devastated and their inhabitants were destroyed. At that time portions of the sea-floor were upraised to form the present dry land. But the rocks show that this land had previously been inhabited, if not by man, at least by land-animals, and thus that one preceding revolution, if not more, had submerged these tracts and swept away their population.

But it was the relation of such terrestrial revolutions to the organic world which chiefly attracted the great French naturalist. He could foresee the deeply interesting problems that awaited solution in regard to the alternation of sedimentary materials and the succession of organic remains in the great series of stratified formations, and he concludes his discourse with these eloquent words : " What a noble task it would be were we able to arrange the objects of the organic world in their chronological order, as we have arranged those of the mineral world. Biology would thereby gain much. The development of life, the succession of its forms, the precise determination of those organic types that first appeared, the simultaneous birth of certain species and their gradual extinction— the solution of these questions would perhaps enlighten us regarding the essence of the organism as much as all the experiments that we can try with living species. And man, to whom has been granted but a moment's sojourn on the earth, would gain the glory of tracing the history of the thousands of ages which preceded his existence and of the thousands of beings that have never been his contemporaries." [1]

Cuvier's brilliant career is well known, but I am only concerned at present with those parts of it which touch on geological progress. In 1802, the year in which Lamarck's *Hydrogéologie* appeared, he became perpetual Secretary of the Institute of France, and it was in this capacity that he composed that remarkable series of *Éloges* in which so much of the personal history of the more distinguished men of science of his time is enshrined. Eloquent and picturesque, full of knowledge and sympathy, these biographical notices form a series of the most instructive and delightful essays in the whole range of scientific literature. They include sketches of the life and work of De Saussure, Pallas, Werner, Desmarest, Sir Joseph Banks, Haüy, and Lamarck.

Five years after the appearance of the earliest conjoint memoir by Cuvier and Brongniart, the structure of the country which they described was still further explored and elucidated by a man who afterwards

[1] From the first edition of the *Discours Préliminaire*, 1821.

rose to fill an important place among the geologists
of Europe—J. J. d'Omalius d'Halloy (1783-1875).
In 1813 this able observer read to the Institute a
memoir on the geology of the Paris basin and the
surrounding regions.[1] It corrected and extended the
work of his predecessors among the Tertiary formations, but its interest for our present purpose centres
mainly in its important contribution to the stratigraphy
of the Secondary rocks. He recognised the leading
subdivisions of the Cretaceous series, and actually
showed the extent of the system upon a map. He
likewise ascertained the stratigraphical relations and
range of the Jurassic system, which he called the
" old horizontal limestone," and which he correctly
depicted in its course outside the Chalk. His little
map, with its clear outlines and colours, is of historical
importance as being the first attempt to construct a
true geological map of a large tract of France. It
was not a mere chart of the surface rocks, like
Guettard's, but had a horizontal section, which showed
the Jurassic series lying unconformably upon the edges
of the Palæozoic slates, and covered in turn by the
Gault and the Chalk.

[1] *Ann. des Mines*, i. (1817), p. 251.   He was the author of
numerous subsequent memoirs on the geology of Belgium and the
north of France, as well as of several excellent text books of the
science.

CHAPTER XII

WHILE in France it was the prominence and richly
fossiliferous character of the Tertiary strata which
first led to the recognition of the value of fossils in
stratigraphy, and to the definite establishment of the
principles of stratigraphical geology, in England a
similar result was reached by a study of the Secondary
formations, which are not only more extensively
developed there than the younger series, but display
more clearly their succession and persistence. But
in both countries the lithological sequence, being the
more obvious, was first established before it was confirmed and extended by a recognition of the value
of the evidence of organic remains.

Early in the eighteenth century Strachey published
the succession of formations from the Coal to the
Chalk (p. 194). Michell in 1760 gave a clear account of the stratified arrangement of the sedimentary
formations, describing their general characters and the
persistence of these characters for great distances, and

showing that while on the flat ground the strata remain nearly level, they gradually become inclined as they approach the mountains.[1] He pointed out that the mountains are formed generally of the lower or older rocks, while the more level ground lies usually on the upper and nearly horizontal strata. He remarked further that the same sets of strata, in the same order, are generally met with in crossing Britain towards the sea, the direction of the ridge being towards the north-north-east and south-south-west. That he was familiar with the broad features of the succession of the geological formations in England, from the Coal-measures of Yorkshire up to the Chalk, is shown by an interesting table which seems to have been drawn up by him about 1788 or 1789, and which was published after his death.[2]

Michell enables us to form a clear conception of his views by the following illustration. "Let a number of leaves of paper," he remarks, "of several different sorts or colours, be pasted upon one another; then bending them up into a ridge in the middle, conceive them to be reduced again to a level surface, by a plane so passing through them as to cut off all the part that has been raised. Let the middle now be again raised a little, and this will be a good general representation of most, if not all, large tracts of mountainous countries, together with the parts adjacent, throughout the whole world. From this formation of the earth it will follow that we ought to meet with the same kinds of earths, stones, and minerals, appearing at the surface in long

[1] *Phil. Trans.* vol. li. (1760), part ii. p. 582, *et seq.*
[2] *Phil. Mag.* vol. xxxvi. p. 102, and lii. p. 186.

narrow slips, and lying parallel to the greatest rise of
any long ridge of mountains ; and so, in fact, we find
them."

Contrast this clear presentation of the tectonic
structure of our mountains and continents with the
confused and contradictory explanation of the same
structure subsequently promulgated from Freiberg.
Michell clearly realised that the rocks of the earth's
crust had been laid down in a definite order, that
they had been uplifted along the mountain axes,
that they had been subsequently planed down, and
that their present disposition in parallel bands was
the result partly of the upheaval and partly of the
denudation.

Another English observer, whose name may be
mentioned here, is John Whitehurst (1713-1788) who
published in 1778 an "Inquiry into the Original
State and Formation of the Earth." This work was
the last effort of the fantastic English School of
Cosmogonists. Amid absurd speculations as to the
condition of Chaos and other equally visionary topics,
he wrote well on organic remains, and showed that he
clearly grasped the stratigraphical succession of the
formations in Derbyshire and other parts of England.
" The strata invariably follow each other," he remarks,
" as it were, in alphabetical order," and though they
may not be alike in all parts of the earth, nevertheless, " in each particular part, how much soever they
may differ, yet they follow each other in a regular
succession."

While the stratigraphical sequence of the geological
formations in England was thus partially realised by

few pioneers, its final establishment was the work of William Smith (1769-1839)—usually known as he "Father of English geology." He definitely arranged the rocks in their true order from the Killas eries (Cambrian and Silurian) of Wales up to the Tertiary groups of the London basin. More particularly he determined the subdivisions of the Secondary, or at least of the Jurassic (Oolitic) rocks, and established their order, which has been found applicable not only to England but to the rest of Europe. No more interesting chapter in scientific annals can be found than that which traces the progress of this remarkable man, who, amidst endless obstacles and hindrances, clung to the idea which had early taken shape in his mind, and who lived to see that idea universally accepted as the guiding principle in the investigation of the geological structure, not of England only, but of Europe and of the globe.

William Smith came of a race of yeoman farmers who for many generations had owned small tracts of land in Oxfordshire and Gloucestershire.[1] He was born at Churchill, in the former county, on 23rd March 1769, the same year that gave birth to Cuvier. Before he was eight years old he lost his father. After his mother married for the second time, he seems to have been largely dependent upon an uncle

[1] The biographical details are derived from the *Memoirs of William Smith, LL.D.*, by his nephew and pupil, John Phillips, 1844. The biographer (1800-1874) became himself a leading geologist in England and for the last eighteen years of his active and useful life was the genial Reader and Professor of Geology in the University of Oxford.

for education and assistance. The instruction obtainable at the village school was of the most limited kind. With difficulty the lad procured means to purchase a few books from which he might learn the rudiments of geometry and surveying. Already he had taken to the observing and collecting of stones, particularly of the well-preserved fossils whereof the Jurassic rocks of his neighbourhood were full. He came to be interested in questions of drainage and other pursuits connected with the surface of the land, and in spite of want of encouragement, made such progress with his studies that at the age of eighteen he was taken as assistant to a surveyor. But he had no education beyond that of the village school and what he had been able to acquire through his own reading. This early defect crippled, to the end of his life, his efforts to make known to the world the scientific results he obtained.

Smith's capacity and steady powers of application were soon appreciated in the vocation upon which he had entered. Before long he was entrusted with all the ordinary work of a land surveyor, to which were added many duties that would now devolve upon a civil engineer. From an early part of his professional career, his attention was arrested by the great variety among the soils with which he had to deal, and the connection between these soils and the strata underlying them. He had continually to traverse the red ground that marks the position of the Triassic marls and sandstones in the south-west and centre of England, and to pass thence across the clays and limestones of the Lias, or to and fro among the freestones and shales of the Oolites. The contrasts of these different kinds of rock, the variations in their characteristic scenery, and the persistence of feature which marked each band of strata gave him constant subjects of observation and reflection.

By degrees his surveying duties took him farther afield, and brought him in contact with yet older formations, particularly with the Coal-measures of Somerset and their dislocations. At the age of four-and-twenty, he was engaged in carrying out a series of levellings for a canal, and had the opportunity of confirming a suspicion, which had been gradually taking shape in his mind, that the various strata with which he was familiar, though they seemed quite flat, were really inclined at a gentle angle towards the east, and terminated sharply towards the west, like so many "slices of bread and butter." He took the liveliest interest in this matter, and felt convinced that it must have a far deeper meaning and wider application than he had yet surmised.

His first start on geological exploration took place the following year (1794) when, as engineer to a canal that was to be constructed, he was deputed to accompany two of the Committee of the Company in a tour of some weeks duration, for the purpose of gaining information respecting the construction, management, and trade of other lines of inland navigation. The party went as far north as Newcastle, and came back through Shropshire and Wales to Bath, having travelled 900 miles on their mission. The young surveyor made full use of the opportunities which this journey afforded him. He had by this time satisfied himself that the stratigraphical succession, which he had worked out for a small part of the south-west of England, had an important bearing on scientific questions, besides many practical applications of importance. But it needed to be extended and checked by a wider experience. "No journey, purposely contrived," so he wrote, "could have better answered my purpose. To sit forward on the chaise was a favour readily granted; my eager eyes were never idle a moment; and post-haste travelling only put me upon new resources. General views, under existing circumstances, were the best that could have been taken, and the facility of knowing, by contours and other features, what might be the kind of stratification in the hills is a proof of early advancement in the generalisation of phenomena.

"In the more confined views, where the roads commonly climb to the summits, as in our start from Bath to Tetbury, by Swanswick, the slow driving up the steep hills afforded me distinct views of the nature of the rocks; rushy pastures on the slopes of the hills, the rivulets and kind of trees, all aided in defining the intermediate clays; and while occasionally walking to see bridges, locks, and other works, on the lines of canal, more particular observations could be made.

"My friends being both concerned in working coal, were interested in two objects; but I had three, and the most important one to me I pursued unknown to them; though I was continually talking about the rocks and other strata, they seemed not desirous of knowing the guiding principles or objects of these remarks; and it might have been from the many hints, perhaps mainly on this subject, which I made in the course of the journey, that Mr. Palmer jocosely recommended me to write a book of hints." [1]

We can picture the trio on this memorable journey—the young man in front eagerly scrutinizing every field, ridge, and hill along each side of the way, noting every change of soil and topography, and turning round every little while, unable to restrain his exuberant pleasure as his eye detected one indication after another of the application of the principles he had found to hold good at home, and pointing them out with delight to his two sedate companions, who looked at him with amusement, but with neither knowledge of his aims nor sympathy with his enthusiasm.

For six years William Smith was engaged in setting out and superintending the construction of the Somersetshire Coal Canal. In the daily engrossing cares of these duties it might seem that there could be little opportunity for adding to his stores of geological knowledge, or working out in more detail the principles of stratigraphy that he had already reached. But in truth these six years were among the most important in his whole career. The constant and close observation which he was compelled to give to the strata that had to be cut through in making the canal, led him to give more special attention to the organic remains in them. From boyhood he had gathered fossils, but without connecting them definitely with the succession of the rocks that contained them.

[1] *Memoirs*, p. 10.

2 B

He now began to observe more carefully their distribution, and came at last to perceive that, certainly
among the formations with which he had to deal,
"each stratum contained organized fossils peculiar to
itself, and might, in cases otherwise doubtful, be
recognized and discriminated from others like it, but
in a different part of the series, by examination of
them."[1]

It was while engaged in the construction of this
canal that Smith began to arrange his observations
for publication. He had a methodical habit of writing out his notes and reflections, and dating them.
But he had not the art of condensing his material,
and arranging it in literary form. Nevertheless, he
could not for a moment doubt that the results which
he had arrived at would be acknowledged by the
public to possess both scientific importance and practical value. Much of his work was inserted upon
maps, wherein he traced the position and range of
each of the several groups of rock with which he had
become familiar. He had likewise ample notes of
local sections, and complete evidence of a recognisable succession among the rocks. Not only could he
identify the strata by their fossils, but he could point
out to the surveyors, contractors, and other practical
men with whom he came in contact, how useful in
many kinds of undertakings was the detailed knowledge which he had now acquired. In agriculture,
in mining, in road-making, in draining, in the construction of canals, in questions of water-supply, and
in many other affairs of everyday life, he was able

[1] *Memoirs*, p. 15.

to prove that his system of observation possessed great practical utility.

In the year 1799, his connection with the Canal Company came to an end. He was thereafter compelled to put his geological knowledge to commercial use, and to undertake the laborious duties of an engineer and surveyor on his own account. Eventually he found considerable employment over the whole length and breadth of England, and showed singular shrewdness and originality in dealing with the engineering questions which came before him. He was a close observer of nature, and his knowledge of natural processes stood him in good stead in his professional calling. If he had to keep out the sea from low ground, he constructed his barrier as nearly as possible like those which the waves themselves had thrown up. If he was asked to prevent a succession of landslips, he studied the geological structure of the district and the underground drainage, and drove his tunnels so as to intercept the springs underneath. His nephew and biographer tells us that his engagements in connection with drainage and irrigation involved journeys of sometimes 10,000 miles in a year.

Such continuous travelling to and fro across the country served to augment enormously his minute personal acquaintance with the geological structure of England. He made copious notes, and his retentive memory enabled him to retain a vivid recollection even of the details of what he had once seen. But the leisure which he needed in order to put his materials together seemed to flee from him. Year after year passed away; the pile of manuscript rose higher, but no progress was made in the preparation of the growing mass of material for publication.

In the year 1799, William Smith made the acquaintance of the Rev. Benjamin Richardson, who, living in Bath, had interested himself in forming a collection of fossils from the rocks of the neighbourhood. Looking over this collection, the experienced surveyor was able to tell far more about its contents than the owner of it knew himself. Writing long afterwards to Sedgwick, Mr. Richardson narrated how Smith could decide at once from what strata they had respectively come, and how well he knew the lie of the rocks on the ground. "With the open liberality peculiar to Mr. Smith," he adds, "he wished me to communicate this to the Rev. J. Townsend of Pewsey (then in Bath), who was not less surprised at the discovery. But we were soon much more astonished by proofs of his own collecting, that whatever stratum was found in any part of England, the same remains would be found in it and no other. Mr. Townsend, who had pursued the subject forty or fifty years, and had travelled over the greater part of civilized Europe, declared it perfectly unknown to all his acquaintance, and, he believed, to all the rest of the world. In consequence of Mr. Smith's desire to make so valuable a discovery universally known, I without reserve gave a card of the English strata to Baron Rosencrantz, Dr. Müller of Christiania, and many others, in the year 1801."[1]

The card of the English strata referred to in this letter was a tabular list of the formations from the Coal up to the Chalk, with the thicknesses of the several

[1] *Memoirs*, p. 31.

members, an enumeration of some of their characteristic fossils, and a synopsis of their special lithological peculiarities and scenery. This table was drawn up in triplicate by Mr. Richardson, at Smith's dictation, in the year 1799, each of the friends and Mr. Townsend taking a copy. Smith's copy was presented by him to the Geological Society of London in 1831.

Though not actually published, this table obtained wide publicity. It showed that the fundamental principles of stratigraphy had been worked out by William Smith alone, and independently, before the end of the eighteenth century. He had demonstrated, as his friend and pupil Farey testified, "that the fossil productions of the strata are not accidentally distributed therein, but that each particular species has its proper and invariable place in some particular stratum ; and that some one or two or more of these species of fossil shells may serve as new and more distinctive marks of the identity of most of the strata of England."[1] Had Smith's table been printed and sold it would have established his claim to priority beyond all possibility of cavil. But even without this technical support, his place among the pioneers of stratigraphy cannot be gainsaid.

Notwithstanding the abundant professional employment which he obtained, Smith never abounded in money. So keenly desirous was he to complete his investigation of the distribution of the strata of England, for the purpose of constructing a map of the country, that he spent as freely as he gained, walking, riding, or posting in directions quite out of the way

[1] See note on p. 394.

of his business. "Having thus emptied his pockets for what he deemed a public object, he was forced to make up, by night-travelling, the time he had lost, so as not to fail in his professional engagements."

Stimulated by the kindly urgency of his friend Richardson, who alarmed him by pointing out that if he did not publish his observations, some one else might anticipate him, Smith was prevailed upon to draw up a prospectus of a work in which he proposed to give a detailed account of the various strata of England and Wales, with an accompanying map and sections. A publisher in London was named, and the prospectus was extensively circulated ; but it led to nothing.

Eventually Smith established himself in London as the best centre for his professional work, and in 1805 he took a large house there, with room for the display of his collections and maps, which were open to the inspection of any one interested in such matters. Among his materials he had completed a large county map of Somersetshire, as a specimen of what might be done for the different counties of England. This document seems to have been exhibited at the Board of Agriculture, and a proposal was made that he should be permanently attached to the corps of engineers then engaged in surveying the island. But the idea never went farther. Not until thirty years later was it revived by De la Beche, and pressed with such perseverance as to lead in the end to the establishment of the present Geological Survey of Great Britain.

From 1799, when Smith first contemplated the publication of his observations, every journey that he took was as far as possible made subservient to the completion of his map of England. At last, but not until the end of the year 1812, he found a publisher enterprising enough to undertake the risk of engraving and publishing this map. The work was begun in January 1813, and was published in August 1815.[1] It was appropriately dedicated to Sir Joseph Banks, President of the Royal Society, who had encouraged and helped the author.

William Smith's map has long since taken its place among the great classics of geological cartography. It was the first attempt to portray on such a scale not merely the distribution, but the stratigraphy of the formations of a whole country. Well might D'Aubuisson say of it that "what the most distinguished mineralogists during a period of half a century had done for a little part of Germany, had been undertaken and accomplished for the whole of England by one man; and his work, as fine in its results as it is astonishing in its extent, demonstrates that England is regularly divided into strata, the order of which is never inverted, and that the same species of fossils are found in the same stratum even at wide distances."[2]

But it is not so much as a cartographical achievement that Smith's great map deserves our attention at present. Its appearance marked a distinct epoch in stratigraphical geology, for from that time some of what are now the most familiar terms in geological nomenclature passed into common use. Smith had no scholarship; he did not even cull euphonious terms

---

[1] For the title and description of the map see p. 452, where reference will be found to the map of G. B. Greenough.

[2] *Traité de Géognosie* (1819), tome ii. p. 253.

from Greek or Latin lexicons ; he was content to take
the rustic or provincial names he found in common
use over the districts which he traversed. Hence were
now introduced into geological literature such words
as London Clay, Kentish Rag, Purbeck Stone, Car-
stone, Cornbrash, Clunch Clay, Lias, Forest Marble.

By ingeniously colouring the bottom of each formation a fuller tint than the rest, Smith brought the
general succession of strata conspicuously before the
eye. Further, by the aid of vertical tables of the
formations and a horizontal section from Wales to
the vale of the Thames, he was able to give the details
of the succession which, for some twenty-four years,
he had been engaged in unravelling in every part of
the kingdom.

Of especial value and originality was his clear subdivision of what is now known as the Jurassic system.
He did for that section of the geological record what
Cuvier and Brongniart had done for the Tertiary series
of Paris. After the first copies of the map had been
issued, he was able still further to subdivide and
improve his classification of these strata, introducing
among the new bands, Crag, Portland Rock, Coral
Rag, and Kellaways Stone.[1]

In the memoir accompanying the map, the tabular
arrangement of the strata drawn up in 1799 was
inserted, with its column giving the names, so far as
he knew them, of the more characteristic fossils of
each formation.

To the laborious researches of William Smith we
are thus indebted for the first attempt to distinguish

[1] Phillips, *Memoirs*, p. 146.

the various subdivisions of the Secondary rocks, from the base of the New Red Sandstone up to the Chalk, and for the demonstration that these successive platforms are marked off from each other, not merely by mineral characters, but by their peculiar assemblages of organic remains. From his provincial terminology come the more sonorous names of Purbeckian, Portlandian, Callovian, Corallian, Bathonian, Liassic, which are now familiar words in every geological text-book.

In his eagerness to make his map as complete and accurate as was possible to him, Smith spent so freely of his hardly-earned income that he accumulated no savings against the day of trial, which came only too soon. He had been induced to lay down a railway on a little property which early in life he had purchased near Bath, with the view of opening some new quarries and bringing the building-stone to the barges on the canal. Unfortunately the stone, on the continuance and quality of which the whole success of the enterprise rested, failed. It became necessary to sell the property, and thereafter the sanguine engineer was left with a load of debt under which most men would have succumbed. Struggling under this blow, he was first compelled to part with his collections of fossils, which were acquired by the Government and placed in the British Museum. Next he found himself no longer able to bear the expense of the house in London which he had occupied for fifteen years. Not only so, but hard fate drove him to sell all his furniture, books and other property, keeping only the maps, sections, drawings and piles of manuscript which were so precious in his own eyes, but for which nobody would have been likely to give him anything. For seven years he had no home, but wandered over the north of England, wherever professional engagements might carry him. His income was diminished and fluctuating, yet even under this cloud of trial he retained his quiet courage and his enthusiasm for geological exploration.

That a man of Smith's genius should have been allowed to remain in this condition of toil and poverty has been brought forward as a reproach to his fellow-countrymen. It may be doubted, however, whether a man of his strong independence of character would have accepted any pecuniary assistance, so long as he could himself gain by his own exertions a modest though uncertain income. It is not that his merits were unrecognised in England, though perhaps the appreciation of them was tardier than it might have been. In 1818 a full and generous tribute to his merits was written by Fitton, and appeared in the *Edinburgh Review* for February in that year.[1] But though his fame was thus well established, his financial position remained precarious. He had gradually formed a consulting practice as a mineral and geological surveyor in the north of England, and he

---

[1] At the end of 1817 there seems to have been some inquiry as to priority of discovery in regard to Smith's work. In the following March, Mr. John Farey contributed to Tilloch's *Philosophical Magazine* a definite statement of Smith's claims, showing that the fundamental facts and principles he had established had been freely made known by him to many people as far back as 1795, and that Farey himself, on 5th August 1807, had published an explicit notification of Smith's discoveries and conclusions as to fossil shells in the article on Coal in Rees' *Cyclopedia*.

eventually settled at Scarborough. From 1828 to
1834 he acted as land-steward on the estate of
Hackness in the same district of Yorkshire. In
1831 he received from the Geological Society the
first Wollaston Medal, and the President of the
Society, Adam Sedgwick, seized the occasion to pro-
claim, in fervid and eloquent words, the admiration
and gratitude of all the geologists of England towards
the man whom he named "the father of English
geology." Next year a pension of £100 from the
Crown was conferred upon him. Honours now came
to him in abundance. But his scientific race was
run. He continued to increase his piles of manuscript, but without methodically digesting them for
publication. He died on 28th August 1839, in the
seventy-first year of his age.

William Smith was tall and broadly built, like the
English yeomen from whom he came. His face
was that of an honest, sagacious farmer, whose broad
brow and firm lips betokened great capacity and
decision, but would hardly have suggested the enthusiastic student of science. His work, indeed, bears
out the impression conveyed by his portrait. His
plain, solid, matter-of-fact intellect never branched
into theory or speculation, but occupied itself wholly
in the observation of facts. His range of geological
vision was as limited as his general acquirements. He
had reached early in life the conclusions on which
his fame rests, and he never advanced beyond them.
His whole life was dedicated to the task of extending
his stratigraphical principles to every part of England.
But this extension, though of the utmost importance

to the country in which he laboured, was only of secondary value in the progress of science.

Besides his great map of England, Smith published also a series of geological maps, on a larger scale, of the English counties, comprising in some instances much detailed local information. He likewise issued a series of striking horizontal sections (1819) across different parts of England, in which the succession of the formations was clearly depicted. These sections may be regarded as the complement of his map, and as thus establishing for all time the essential features of English stratigraphy, and the main out-lines of the sequence of the Secondary formations for the rest of Europe. In another publication, *Strata Identified by Organized Fossils* (1816), he gave a series of plates, with excellent engraved figures of charac-teristic fossils from the several formations. He adopted in this work the odd conceit of having the plates printed on variously coloured paper, to corre-spond with the prevalent tint of the strata from which the fossils came. He had no palæontological knowledge, so that the thin quarto, never completed, is chiefly of interest as a record of the organisms that he had found most useful in establishing the succession of the formations.

There is yet another name that deserves to be remembered in any review of the early efforts to group the Secondary formations—that of Thomas Webster (1773-1844).[1] As far back as 1811, this clever artist

[1] Webster was born in the Orkney Islands, received his education at Aberdeen, and came early in life to London. He practised as an architect, and made journeys in England during which he devoted

and keen-eyed geologist began a series of investigations of the coast-sections of the Isle of Wight and
of Dorset, and continued them for three years. They
were published in 1815, the same year that Smith's
map made its appearance.[1] They were thus independent of that work. Webster had already studied the
Tertiary formations of the Isle of Wight and had published a remarkable memoir upon them in which he
recognised their alternations of fresh-water and marine
strata,[2] as had been done in the Paris basin. He now
threw into tabular arrangement the whole succession of
strata from the upper fresh-water (Oligocene) group
through the Lower Tertiary series to the Kimmeridge
shale in the Jurassic system. He clearly defined each
of the leading subdivisions of the Cretaceous series,
and prepared the way for the admirable later and more
detailed work of William Henry Fitton (1780-1861)[3]

much time to geological enquiry. In 1826 he became House-secre-
tary and Curator to the Geological Society, and in 1841 was appointed
Professor of Geology in University College, London.

[1] See Englefield's *Isle of Wight* (1815), p. 117.

[2] *Trans. Geol. Soc.* vol. ii. This and his other memoirs are classic
contributions to the Secondary and Tertiary geology of England.

[3] Fitton, though of English lineage, was born in Dublin. After
distinguishing himself at Trinity College there, he at first proposed to
enter the church, but his predilection for natural science turned him
into medicine, and he finally took the degree of M.D. and for some
years practised as a physician in Northampton. Early in life he
studied at Edinburgh, and acquired there under Jameson a love of
geological pursuits. Eventually, having married a lady possessed of
ample means, he retired from his profession, and established himself
in London, where his house became one of the scientific centres of his
time. From 1817 down to the middle of last century he continued
at intervals to contribute articles to the *Edinburgh Review* on the

to whom we are indebted for the first detailed and accurate determination of the succession of strata and their distinctive fossils, from the base of the Chalk down into the Oolites, in the south of England and the neighbouring region in France. More particularly he showed the relations and importance of the Greensand formations, his memoirs on which are now among the classics of English geology.

In concluding this sketch of the early progress of stratigraphical geology in Britain I may refer to the important influence exerted by the Geological Society of London which was founded in 1807 " to investigate the mineral structure of the Earth." At that time the warfare between the Neptunists and Plutonists still continued, but there were many men, interested in the study of geological subjects, who were weary of the conflict of hypotheses, and who would fain devote their time and energy to the accumulation of facts regarding the ancient history of the globe, rather than to the elaboration of theories to explain them. A few such enquirers formed themselves into the Geological Society, and soon attracted others around them until, in a few years, they had established an active institution which became a centre for geological research and discussion, published the contributions of its

progress of his favourite science. These essays showed him to be an able and elegant writer, who was not only conversant with all the advances in the geology of the day, but having also an intimate acquaintance with the history and literature of the science, was able by his criticism to exercise a guiding influence on his contemporaries. His researches among the Greensand formations, on which his fame rests as an original observer, were continued for twelve years from 1824 to 1836.

members in quarto volumes, and eventually was incorporated by Royal Charter as one of the leading scientific bodies of the country. This society, which has been the parent of others in different countries, continues to flourish, and its publications, extending over nearly a century, contain a record of original researches which have powerfully helped the progress of all branches of geology. Besides their papers issued by the society, some of the early members published separate works which greatly advanced the cause of their favourite science. Among these early independent treatises perhaps the most important was the *Outlines of the Geology of England and Wales* by W. D. Conybeare (1787-1857) and W. Phillips (1775-1828) which appeared in 1822. In this excellent volume all that was then known regarding the rocks of the country, from the youngest formations down to the Old Red Sandstone, was summarised in so clear and methodical a manner as to give a powerful impulse to the cultivation of geology in England.

From the outline given in this and the previous Chapter, it will be seen that during the last two decades of the eighteenth and the first four of the nineteenth century, great progress was made in the study of the stratigraphy of the Secondary and Tertiary formations of France and England, while the principle of the application of the evidence of organic remains to the identification of these formations from district to district was everywhere applied with signal success. From the youngest alluvial deposits down through the whole series of sedimentary rocks to the Carboniferous system, the clue had been obtained and put to use whereby the stratigraphical order could be satisfactorily established from one country to another. A prodigious impetus was now given to the study of geology. The various stratified formations, arranged in their true chronological sequence, were seen to contain the regular and decipherable records of the history of our globe, which could be put together with at least as much certainty as faded manuscripts of human workmanship. The organic remains contained in them were found to be not random accumulations, heaped together by the catastrophes of bygone ages, but orderly chronicles of old sea-floors, lake-bottoms, and land-surfaces. The centre of gravity of geology was now rapidly altered, especially in Western Europe. Minerals and rocks no longer monopolized the attention of those who interested themselves in the crust of the earth. The petrified remains of former plants and animals ceased to be mere curiosities. Their meaning as historical documents was at last realised. They were seen to have a double interest, for while they told the story of the successive vicissitudes which the surface of the earth had undergone, from remote ages down to the present, they likewise unfolded an altogether new and marvellous panorama of the progress of life upon that surface. They had hitherto shared with minerals and rocks the usage of the term "fossil." As their importance grew, they were discriminated as "organized fossils." But the rising tide of awakened interest, following Lamarck's lead, swept away the qualifying participle, and organic remains became sole possessors of the term, as if they were the only objects dug out of the earth that were any longer worthy to be denominated fossils.

While the whole science of geology made gigantic advances during the nineteenth century, by far the most astonishing progress sprang from the recognition of the value of fossils. To that source may be traced the prodigious development of stratigraphy over the whole world, the power of working out the geological history of a country, and of comparing it with the history of other countries, the possibility of tracing the synchronism and the sequence of the geographical changes of the earth's surface since life first appeared upon the planet. To the same source, also, we are indebted for the rise of the science of Palæontology, and the splendid contributions it has made to biological investigation. In the midst of the profusion, alike of blossom and of fruit, let us not forget the work of those who sowed the seed of the abundant harvest which we are now reaping. Let us remember the early suggestive essays of Guettard, the pregnant ideas of Lehmann and Füchsel, the prescient pages of Giraud-Soulavie, the brilliant work of Lamarck, Cuvier and Brongniart, and the patient and clear-sighted enthusiasm of William Smith.

To another feature in the rapid advance of geology after these pioneers had gone to their rest, brief allusion must here be made. The amount of ascertained fact regarding the structure and history of the earth was every year increasing at so rapid a rate that it became necessary to prepare digests of it, for the use of those who wished to be informed on these subjects or to keep pace with the advance of knowledge. Hence

arose in different countries, text-books, manuals and
other general treatises wherein an account was given of
the facts and principles of geological science. The
earlier works of this kind were in some cases a mere
reproduction of the system taught by Werner at Freiberg.   Such were the *Lehrbuch der Mineralogie* (1801-
1803) of F. A. Reuss and the *Treatise on Geognosy*
(1808) by R. Jameson which formed the third volume
of the first edition of his *System of Mineralogy*.   The
citations which have been made in Chapter VII. from
the Edinburgh Professor's volume may serve as illustrations of the Wernerian geognosy.   But the great
advance made by the science during the first three
decades of last century, consequent on the development
of stratigraphy and the construction of geological maps
led to a complete change in the method of treatment
adopted in the text-books.   In the excellent *Traité de
Géognosie* of J. F. d'Aubuisson de Voisons the transition
from Neptunianism to more modern and scientific views
is well displayed.   In Germany various treatises appeared in which the newer developments of geology
were discussed, the most voluminous and exhaustive
being the admirable *Lehrbuch* of C. F. Naumann.   In
Belgium the *Élémens de Geologie* of Omalius d'Halloy
and his *Abrégé* went through successive editions, and did
good service in spreading a knowledge of the science.
In Italy the works of Breislak already cited (p. 257)
especially his *Institutions Géologiques* (Milan and Paris
1818) were useful additions to geological literature.

    In England the *Outlines* of Conybeare and Phillips,
already noticed, deserves a special commendation.
Nine years later the *Manual of Geology* by H. T.

De la Beche appeared (1831) and at once established
for itself a world-wide reputation for its ample and
clear presentation of the science. It was translated
into French and German, and an edition of it was
also published in the United States. De la Beche's
other works, more particularly his *Researches in Theoretical Geology* (1831) and his *How to observe in
Geology* (1835), which showed his remarkable range
of acquirement, his scientific insight and his wide
practical acquaintance with rocks in the field, were
important contributions to the science. But of all the
English writers of general treatises on geology, the first
place must undoubtedly be assigned to Charles Lyell
(1797-1875) who exercised a profound influence on the
geology of his time in all English-speaking countries.
Adopting the principles of the Huttonian theory, he
developed them until the original enunciator of them
was nearly lost sight of. With unwearied industry he
marshalled in admirable order all the observations that
he could collect in support of the doctrine that the
present is the key to the past. With inimitable luci-
dity he traced the operation of existing causes, and
held them up as the measure of those which have acted
in bygone time. He carried Hutton's doctrine to its
logical conclusion, for not only did he refuse to allow
the introduction of any process which could not be
shown to be a part of the present system of Nature, he
would not even admit that there was any reason to
suppose the degree of activity of the geological agents
to have ever seriously differed from what it has been
within human experience. He became the great high
priest of Uniformitarianism—a creed which grew to be

almost universal in England during his life, but which never made much way in the rest of Europe, and which in its extreme form is probably now held by few geologists in any country.   Lyell's *Principles of Geology* will, however, always rank as one of the classics of geology, and must form an early part of the reading of every man who would wish to make himself an accomplished geologist.   The last part of this work was ultimately published as a separate volume, with the title of *Elements of Geology*, in which a large space was devoted to an account of the stratified fossiliferous formations. This treatise, diligently kept up to date by its author, continued during his life-time to be the chief English exposition of its subject, and the handbook of every English geologist.

Lyell's function was mainly that of a critic and exponent of the researches of his contemporaries, and of a philosophical writer thereon, with a rare faculty of perceiving the connection of scattered facts with each other, and with the general principles of science.   As Ramsay once remarked to me, " We collect the data, and Lyell teaches us to comprehend the meaning of them."   But Lyell, though he did not, like Sedgwick and Murchison, add new chapters to geological history, nevertheless left his mark upon the nomenclature and classification of the geological record.   Conceiving, as far back as 1828, the idea of arranging the whole series of Tertiary formations in four groups, according to their affinity to the living fauna, he established, in conjunction with Deshayes, who had independently formed a similar opinion, the well-known classification into Eocene, Miocene, and Pliocene.   The first of these terms was proposed for strata containing an extremely small proportion of living species of shells ; the second for those where the percentage of recent species was considerable, but still formed the minority of the whole assemblage, while the third embraced the formations in which living forms were predominant. The scheme was a somewhat artificial one, and the original percentages have had to be modified from time to time, but the terms have kept their place, and are now firmly planted in the geological language of all corners of the globe.

CHAPTER XIII

Progress of Stratigraphical Geology—The Transition or Greywacke formation resolved by Sedgwick and Murchison into the Cambrian, Silurian and Devonian systems. The Primordial Fauna of Barrande. The pre-Cambrian rocks first begun to be set in order by Logan.

THE determination of the value of fossils as chronological documents has done more than any other discovery to change the character and accelerate the progress of geological inquiry. No contrast can be more striking than the difference between the condition of the science before and after that discovery was made. Before that time, while the Wernerian classification of the rocks of the earth's crust prevailed, there was really little stimulus to investigate these rocks in their chronological relations to each other. They were grouped, indeed, in a certain order, which was believed to express their succession in time, but their identification from one country to another proceeded on no minute study of their internal structure, their fossil contents, or their tectonic relations. It was thought enough if their mineral characters were determined so that they could be placed in one or other of the divisions of the Freiberg system. Hence, as was pointed in an earlier chapter, when an orthodox disciple of Werner had relegated a mass of deposits to the Transition series, or the Floetz or the Independent Coal-formation, as the case might be, he considered that all that was really essential had been ascertained, and his interest in the matter came practically to an end.

But the extraordinary awakening which resulted from the labours of Soulavie, Lamarck, Cuvier, Brongniart and William Smith, invested the strata with a new meaning. As stratigraphical investigations multiplied, the artificiality and inadequacy of the Wernerian arrangement became every day more apparent. Even more serious than the attacks of the Vulcanists, and the disclosure of eruptive granites and porphyries among the Transition rocks, were the discoveries made among the fossiliferous stratified formations. It was no longer possible to crowd and crush these rocks within the narrow limits of the Wernerian system, even in its most modified and improved form. The necessity for expansion and for adopting a perfectly natural nomenclature and classification, based upon the actually observed facts, as these were successively ascertained, made itself felt especially in England and in France. Hence arose the curiously mongrel terminology which is now in use. Certain formations were named from some prominent mineral in them, such as Carboniferous. Others were discriminated by some conspicuous variety of rock, like the Cretaceous series. Some took their names from a characteristic structure, like Oolitic, others from their relative position in the whole series, as in the case of Old Red Sandstone and New Red Sandstone. Certain terms betrayed the country of their origin, as did William Smith's English provincial names, like Gault, Kellaways Rock, and Lias.

The growth of the present stratigraphical nomenclature is thus eminently characteristic of the early rise and progress of the study of stratigraphy in Europe. Precisians decry this inartificial and haphazard language, and would like to introduce a brand new harmonious and systematic terminology. But the present arrangement has its historical interest and value, and so long as it is convenient and intelligible, I do not see that any advantage to science would accrue from its abolition. The method of naming formations or groups of strata after districts where they are typically developed has long been in use and has many advantages, but it has not supplanted all the original names, and I for. my part hope that it never will.

With regard to what are now known as the Tertiary and Secondary formations, the Wernerian " Floetz," under which they were all comprised, soon sank into disuse.[1]   But there was a long pause before the strata of older date were subjected to the same diligent study.

[1] One of the latest adaptations of the word was that of Keferstein in his *Tabellen über die vergleichende Geologie* (1825).   He frankly threw over Wernerianism, but stuck to the pre-Wernerian Floetz, which he arranged in five subdivisions.   (1) Youngest Floetz,— alluvium, etc.; (2) Tertiary Floetz,—marls, gypsum, etc., of Paris, Brown coal; (3) Younger Floetz, or Chalk rocks,—Chalk, Jura Limestone, Greensand; (4) Middle Floetz, or Muschelkalk—Lias, Keuper marl, Bunter sandstone, Zechstein; (5) Old Floetz, or Mountain Limestone—Coal, Mountain Limestone.

For this delay various good reasons may be assigned. We have seen that William Smith's researches went down into the Coal-measures, but he had only a general and somewhat vague idea of the sequence of the rocks beneath that formation. In the table accompanying his map (1812) he placed below the Coal the Derbyshire Limestone followed by Red and Dunstone, Killas or Slate and lastly Granite, Syenite, and Gneiss. Some of these rocks were known to be fossiliferous, but in general, throughout Western Europe, they had been so disturbed and dislocated that they no longer presented the proofs of their sequence in the same orderly manner as had led to the recognition of the succession of the younger formations.

It will be remembered that in his original scheme of classification Werner grouped some rocks as Primitive (*uranfängliche*), and classed together as Floetz the whole series of stratified formations between these and the alluvial deposits. Further experience led him to separate an intermediate group between the Primitive and the Floetz, which he denominated Transition. He considered that this group was "deposited during the passage or transition of the earth from its chaotic to its habitable state."[1] He recognised that it contains the earliest organic remains, and believed it to include the oldest mechanical deposits. He subdivided the Transition rocks rather by mineral characters than by ascertained stratigraphical sequence. The hardened variety of sandstone called greywacke formed by far the most important member of the whole series, and

[1] Jameson's *Geognosy*, p. 145 (1808).

was believed by Werner to mark a new geognostic period when, instead of chemical precipitates, mechanical accumulations began to appear.

The two Wernerian terms Transition and Greywacke survived for some years after the commencement of the great stratigraphical impulse in the early years of last century. They formed a kind of convenient limbo or No-man's Land, into which any group of rocks might be thrown which obstinately refused to reveal its relations with the rest of the terrestrial crust. Down to the base of the Carboniferous rocks, or even to the bottom of the Old Red Sandstone, the chronological succession of geological history seemed tolerably clear. But beneath and beyond that limit, everything betokened disorder. It appeared well-nigh hopeless to expect that rocks so broken and indurated, generally so poor in fossils, and usually so sharply cut off from everything younger than themselves, would ever be made to yield up a connected and consistent series of chapters to the geological record.

And yet these chapters, if only they could be written, would be found to possess the most vivid interest. They would contain the chronicles of the earlier ages of the earth's history, and might perhaps reveal to man the geography of the first dry land, the sites of the most ancient seas, the positions of the oldest volcanoes, the forms of the first plants and animals that appeared upon the planet. There was thus inducement enough to attack the old rocks that contained within their stony layers such precious memorials.

It is not that the Transition rocks were entirely neglected. The keen interest awakened in fossils led to renewed search among the fossiliferous members of that ancient series. A large number of organic remains had been collected from Devonshire, Wales, the Lake District, Rhineland, the Eifel, France, Sweden, Norway, Russia, as well as from New York and Canada. These fossils were distinct from those of the Secondary formations, and they were obviously distributed, not at random, but in groups which reappeared at widely separated localities.[1] As yet, however, no clue had been found to their stratigraphical sequence. Specimens from what are now known as Cambrian, Silurian, Devonian, and even Lower Carboniferous strata were all thrown together as coming from the undefined region of the Greywacke or Transition rocks. A task worthy of the best energy of the most accomplished geologist lay open to any man bold enough to undertake to introduce among these rocks the same stratigraphical method which had reduced the Secondary and Tertiary formations to such admirable order, and had furnished the means of comparing and correlating these formations from one region to another. This

[1] The amount and nature of the information in existence regarding the Transition rocks or Greywacke, at the time when Murchison entered upon their investigation, may be gathered from the summaries contained in the contemporary general treatises on Geology. Even as late as the spring of 1833, Lyell, after devoting about 300 pages to the Tertiary formations, dismissed the Palæozoic series in twelve lines (*Principles of Geology*, vol. iii. (1833), p. 326). One of the fullest of the early descriptions of the older fossiliferous rocks, with copious lists of fossils, will be found in the first edition of De la Beche's *Geological Manual* (1831), p. 433, under the head of "Grauwacke Group." But no attempt is there made to arrange the rocks stratigraphically, and the fossil lists comprise organisms from all the older Palæozoic formations without discrimination of their horizons.

task was at last accomplished by two men, working independently of each other in Wales and the border counties of England. Murchison and Sedgwick, whose observations on ancient volcanic action have already been referred to, carried the principles of Cuvier, Brongniart, and William Smith into the chaos of old Greywacke, and succeeded in adding the Devonian, Silurian and Cambrian chapters to the geological record, thus establishing a definite order among the oldest fossiliferous formations, and completing thereby Palæozoic stratigraphy.

Roderick Impey Murchison, who was born in Rossshire in 1792, belonged to a family that had lived for centuries among the wilds of the north-western Highlands of Scotland, and had taken part in much of the rough life of that remote and savage region.[1] Entering the army when he was only fifteen years of age, he served for a time in the Peninsular war, and carried the colours of his regiment at the battle of Vimieira. During the subsequent retreat to Corunna he narrowly escaped being taken prisoner by the French. On the conclusion of the Napoleonic wars, seeing no longer any prospect of military activity or distinction, he quitted the army, married, and for some years devoted himself with ardour to fox-hunting, in which his love of an open-air life and of vigorous exercise could have full gratification. But he was made for a nobler kind of existence than that of a mere Nimrod. His wife, a woman of cultivated tastes, had led him to take much interest in art and

[1] The biographical details are taken from my *Life of Sir Roderick I. Murchison*, 2 vols. 8vo, 1875.

antiquities, and when Sir Humphry Davy, who also recognised his qualities, urged him to turn his attention to science, she strenuously encouraged him to follow the advice. He at last sold his hunters, came to London, and began to attend lectures on chemistry and geology at the Royal Institution.

Murchison was thirty-two years old before he showed any interest in science. But his ardent and active temperament spurred him on. His enthusiasm being thoroughly aroused, his progress became rapid. He joined the Geological Society, and having gained the goodwill of Buckland, went down to Oxford for his first geological excursions under the guidance of that genial professor. He then discovered what field-geology meant, and learnt how the several parts of a landscape depend for their position and form upon the nature of the rocks underneath. He returned to London with his zeal aflame, burning to put into practice the principles of observation he had now been taught. He began among the Cretaceous formations around his father-in-law's home in Sussex, but soon extended his explorations into Scotland, France and the Alps, bringing back with him at the end of each season a bundle of well-filled note-books from which to prepare communications for the Geological Society. These early papers, meritorious though they were, do not call for any special notice here, since they marked no new departure in geological research, nor added any important province to the geological domain.

During six years of constant activity in the field, Murchison, together with Sedgwick, worked out the structure of parts of the west and north of Scotland,

and toiled hard in disentangling the complicated
structure of the eastern Alps ; he also rambled with
Lyell over the volcanic areas of Central and Southern
France. Thereafter he determined to try whether the
"interminable greywacke," as he called it, could not
be reduced to order and made to yield a stratigraphical
sequence, like that which had been so successfully
obtained among younger formations. At the time
when be began, that is, in the summer of 1831,
absolutely nothing was known of the succession of
rocks below the Old Red Sandstone. It was an
unknown land, a pathless desert, where no previous
traveller had been able to detect any trace of a practic-
able track towards order, or any clue to a system of
arrangement that would enable the older fossiliferous
rocks of one country to be paralleled, save in the
broadest and most general way, with those of another.

Starting with his "wife and maid, two good grey
nags and a little carriage, saddles being strapped behind
for occasional equestrian use," Murchison made his
way into South Wales. In that region, as was well
known, the stratigraphical series could be followed
down into the Old Red Sandstone, and within the
frame or border of that formation, greywacke was
believed to extend over all the rest of the Principality.
Let me quote a few sentences in which Murchison
describes his first entry into the domain with which his
fame is now so inseparably linked. " Travelling from
Brecon to Builth by the Herefordshire road, the gorge
in which the Wye flows first developed what I had not
till then seen. Low terrace-shaped ridges of grey rock,
dipping slightly to the south-east, appeared on the

opposite bank of the Wye, and seemed to rise quite conformably from beneath the Old Red Sandstone of Herefordshire. Boating across the river at Cavansham Ferry, I rushed up to these ridges, and, to my inexpressible joy, found them replete with Transition fossils, afterwards identified with those at Ludlow. Here then was a key, and if I could only follow this out on the strike of the beds to the north-east, the case would be good."[1]

With unerring instinct Murchison had realised that if the story of old Greywacke was ever to be fully told, a beginning must be made from some known and recognisable horizon. It would have been well-nigh useless to dive into the heart of the Transition hills, and try to work out their complicated structure, for even if a sequence could then have been determined, there would have been no means of connecting it with the already ascertained stratigraphical series, unless it could be followed outwards to the Old Red Sandstone. But by commencing at the known base of that series, every fresh stage conquered was at once a definite platform added to what had already been established.

The explorer kept along the track of the rocks for many miles to the north. No hunter could have followed the scent of the fox better than he did the outcrop of the fossiliferous strata, which he saw to come out regularly from under the lowest members of the Old Red Sandstone. Directed to the Wye by Buckland, he had the good-fortune to come at once upon some of the few natural sections where the order

[1] *Life*, vol. i. p. 182.

of the higher Transition rocks of Britain, and their relations to the overlying formations, can be distinctly seen. He pursued the chase northwards until he lost the old rocks under the Triassic plains of Cheshire. "For a first survey," he writes, "I had got the upper grauwacke, so called, into my hands, for I had seen it in several situations far from each other, all along the South Welsh frontier, and in Shropshire and Herefordshire, rising out gradually and conformably from beneath the lowest member of the Old Red Sandstone. Moreover, I had ascertained that its different beds were characterized by peculiar fossils, . . . a new step in British geology. In summing up what I saw and realised in about four months of travelling, I may say that it was the most fruitful year of my life, for in it I laid the foundation of my Silurian system. I was then thirty-nine years old, and few could excel me in bodily and mental activity."[1]

Not only did the work of these four momentous months mark a new step in British geology. It began the lifting of the veil from the Transition rocks of the whole globe. It was the first successful foray into these hitherto intractable masses, and prepared the way for all that has since been done in deciphering the history of the most ancient fossiliferous formations, alike in the Old World and in the New.

Contenting himself with a mere announcement of his chief results at the first meeting of the British Association, held in York in 1831, Murchison gave a brief outline of his subdivisions of the Upper

[1] *Op. cit.* pp. 183, 192. .

Greywacke to the Geological Society in the spring of 1833.[1]   He continued to toil hard in the field, mapping on the ground his various formations, and making careful sections of their relations to each other. Every fresh traverse confirmed the general accuracy of his first observations, and supplied him with further illustrations of the persistence and distinctness of the several groups into which he had subdivided the Greywacke.   At the beginning of 1834, he was able to present a revised and corrected table of his stratigraphical results, each formation being defined by its lithological characters and organic remains, and the subdivisions being nearly what they still remain.[2]   The Ludlow rocks are shown to pass upward into the base of the Old Red Sandstone, and downward into the Wenlock group, which in turn is succeeded below by the Horderley and May Hill rocks, followed by the Builth and Llandeilo flags. By the summer of 1835, at the instigation of Élie de Beaumont and other geological friends, he had made up his mind as to the name that should be given to this remarkable assemblage or system of formations which he had disinterred from out of the chaos of Greywacke.   Following the good rule that stratigraphical terms are most fitly formed on a geographical basis with reference to the regions wherein the rocks are most typically developed, he had looked about for some appropriate and euphonious term that would comprise his various formations and connect them with that borderland of England

[1] *Proc. Geol. Soc.* vol. i. (1833), p. 474.
[2] *Ibid.* vol. ii. (1834), p. 11.

and Wales where they are so copiously displayed.
This territory was in Roman times inhabited by
the tribe of the Silures, and so he chose the term
Silurian—a word that is now familiar to the geologists of every country.[1]

At the same time Murchison published a diagrammatic section of his classification which, except in one
particular, has been entirely sustained by subsequent
investigation.   He there groups the whole series of
formations as the Silurian system, which he divides
into Upper and Lower, drawing the line of separation
where it still remains.   In the upper section come the
Ludlow and Wenlock rocks ; in the lower the Caradoc
and Llandeilo.   The base of the series, however, is
made to rest unconformably on a series of ancient
slaty greywackes.   No such base exists, for the Llandeilo
group passes downward into a vast series of older
sediments.   At that time, however, both Murchison
and Sedgwick believed that a strongly marked separation lay between the Silurian System and the rocks
lying to the west of it.

Murchison used to maintain, with perfect justice,
that he had succeeded in his task, because he had
followed the method which had led William Smith
to arrange so admirably the Secondary formations of
England.   He was able to show that, apart from mere
lithological differences, which might be of only local
value, his formations were definitely characterized, each
by its peculiar assemblage of organic remains.   If
Smith's labours had not only brought the Mesozoic
rocks of England into order, but had furnished a

[1] *Phil. Mag.* July 1835, p. 48.

means of dealing in like fashion with the rocks of the same age in other countries, there seemed no reason why the palæontological succession, found to distinguish the greywacke in England and Wales, should not be equally serviceable among the Transition rocks of Europe and even of America. And if this result should be achieved, Murchison might fairly claim that he had added a series of new and earlier chapters to the geological history of the globe.

The various brief communications to the Geological Society, after the first discoveries in 1831, though they had made geologists familiar with the main results of Murchison's work, only increased their desire to know the detailed observations on which his generalisations were founded, and more particularly to have complete information as to the assemblages of organic remains which he had discovered. Previous collections from the Transition rocks were generally of little service for stratigraphical purposes, because those of widely separate horizons had all been mixed together. But Murchison's specimens had been carefully gathered, with the view of sustaining his classification, and for the purpose of forming a basis of comparison between the Transition rocks of Britain and those of other countries. Early in the course of his wanderings along the Welsh border, he had been urged to prepare a full and more generally accessible account of his labours than was offered in the publications of a learned Society. Accordingly, adding this task to his other engagements, he toiled at the making of a big book, until at last, towards the end of the year 1838, that is, about seven years from the time when he broke ground by the banks of the Wye, he published his great work, *The Silurian System*, a massive quarto of 800 pages, with an atlas of plates of fossils and sections, and a large coloured geological map.

The publication of this splendid monograph forms a notable epoch in the history of modern geology, and well entitles its author to be enrolled among the founders of the science. For the first time, the succession of fossiliferous formations below the Old Red Sandstone was shown in detail. Their fossils were enumerated, described and figured. It was now possible to carry the vision across a vast series of ages, of which hitherto no definite knowledge existed, to mark the succession of their organisms, and thus to trace backward, far farther than had ever before been possible, the history of organised existence on this globe.

It has already been pointed (*ante* p. 268) that while carefully working out the stratigraphy of the region, Murchison had come upon various masses of eruptive rock, some of which he recognised as intrusive, while others he saw to be lavas and ashes that had been ejected over the floor of the ancient ocean. In this way he was able to present a picture of extraordinary interest, in which the geologist could mark the position of the old seas, trace the distribution of their organisms, and note the sites of their volcanoes.

Even before the advent of his volume, the remarkable results which he had succeeded in obtaining had become widely known, and had incited other observers all over the world to attack the forbidding domain of Greywacke. In France, his classification had been adopted, and applied to the elucidation of the older fossiliferous rocks by Élie de Beaumont and Dufrénoy, who were then engaged in constructing their geological map of that country (p. 456). In Turkey it had been similarly made available by Boué and De Verneuil. Forchhammer had extended it to Scandinavia. Featherstonhaugh and Rogers had applied it in the United States. Thus within a few years, the Silurian system was found to be developed in all parts of the world, and Murchison's work furnished the key to its interpretation.

Let us now turn to the researches that were in progress by another great master of English geology, simultaneously with those of Murchison. Adam Sedgwick belonged to a family that had been settled for 300 years or more in the Dale of Dent, a picturesque district which lies along the western border of Yorkshire. To the end of his long and active life his heart ever turned with fondness to the little valley where he first saw the light, and to the kindly dalesmen among whom he spent his boyhood. He remained to the end a true dalesman himself, with all the frankness of nature, mirthfulness and loyalty, so often found among the natives of these pastoral uplands. He was born in the year 1785, his father being the Vicar of Dent. After receiving his school education at the neighbouring little town of Sedbergh, he went to Trinity College, Cambridge, which thenceforth became his home to the end of his life. At the age of thirty-three he was elected to the Woodwardian Professorship of Geology. Up to that time, however, he had shown no special interest in geological pursuits, and though he may have read a little on the subject, his knowledge of it was probably not greater than that of the average college Fellow of his day. But his appointment as Professor awakened his dormant scientific proclivities, and he at once threw himself with all his energy and enthusiasm into the duties of his new vocation. Gifted with mental power of no common order, which had been sedulously trained in a wide range of studies, possessing a keen eye for the geological structure of a region, together with abundant bodily prowess to sustain him in the most arduous exertions in the field, eloquent, witty, vivacious, he took at once the place of prominence in the University which he retained to the last, and he came with rapid strides to the front of all who in that day cultivated the infant science of geology in England.

What little geology Sedgwick knew, when he became a professor of the science, seems to have been of a decidedly Wernerian kind. He began his geological writings with an account of the primitive ridge and its associated rocks in Devon and Cornwall. His earliest paper might have been appropriately printed in the first volume of the *Memoirs of the Wernerian Society*. In later years, referring to his Neptunist beginnings, he confessed that "for a long while I was troubled with water on the brain, but light and heat have completely dissipated it," and he spoke of "the Wernerian nonsense I learnt in my youth."[1] It was by his own diligent work in the field that he came to a true perception of geological principles. His excursions carried him all over England, and enabled him to

[1] *Life and Letters of Adam Sedgwick*, by J. W. Clark and T. M'K. Hughes, vol. i. p. 284.

bring back each season a quantity of specimens for his museum, and a multitude of notes from which he regaled the Cambridge Philosophical Society with an account of his doings. Eventually he joined the Geological Society of London, and found there a wider field of action. After a time, Murchison also became a fellow of that Society, and he and Sedgwick soon formed a close intimacy. This friendship proved to be of signal service to the cause of geological progress. The two associates were drawn towards the same departments of investigation. They began their co-operation in the year 1827 by a journey through the west and north of Scotland, and from that time onward for many years they were constantly working together in Britain and on the Continent of Europe.

It would be interesting, but out of place here, to linger over the various conjoint labours of these two great pioneers in Palæozoic geology. We are only concerned with what they did, separately and in conjunction, towards the enlargement of the geological record and the definite establishment of the Palæozoic systems. Sedgwick began his work among the older fossiliferous formations by attacking the rugged and complicated region of Cumberland and Westmoreland, commonly known as the Lake District, and in a series of papers communicated to the Geological Society he worked out the general structure of that difficult tract of country. Though fossils had been found in the rocks, he did not at first make use of them for purposes of stratigraphical classification. He ascertained the succession of the great groups of strata by noting their lithological characters. One of the

most remarkable features of his investigation has been
above referred to (p. 266)—the recognition of volcanic
rocks intercalated among the ancient marine sediments
of the Lake District.   These rocks, since so fully
worked out, and now known as the "Borrowdale
Volcanic Series," of Lower Silurian age, were first
assigned to their true origin by Sedgwick, who thus
made an important contribution to the progress of
volcanic geology.

By a curious coincidence, Sedgwick and Murchison
both broke ground in Wales during the summer of
1831.   But while Murchison determined to work his
way downward, from the known horizons of the Old
Red Sandstone of South Wales into the greywacke
below, Sedgwick, with characteristic dash, made straight
for the highest, ruggedest and most complicated tract
of North Wales.   Returning to the same ground the
following year, he plunged into the intricacies of the
older Palæozoic rocks, and succeeded in disentangling
their structure, tracing out their flexures and dislocations, and ascertaining the general sequence of their
principal subdivisions.   It was a splendid achievement,
which probably no other man in England at that time
could have accomplished.

But valuable as this work was, as a contribution to
the elucidation of the tectonic geology of a part of
Britain, it had not yet acquired importance in general
stratigraphy.   In the first place, Sedgwick's groups
of strata were mere lithological aggregates.   They
possessed as yet no distinctive characters that would
allow of their being adopted in the interpretation of
other countries, or even in distant parts of Britain.

They contained fossils, but these had not been made use of in defining the subdivisions. There was thus neither a basis for comparison with other regions, nor for the ascertainment of the true position of the North Welsh rocks in the great territory of Greywacke. In the second place, there was no clue to the connection of these rocks with any known formation, for they were separated from everything younger than themselves by a strong unconformability. The Carboniferous and Old Red Sandstone strata were found to lie on the upturned edges of the older masses, and it was impossible to say how many intervening formations were missing.

Murchison's researches, on the other hand, brought to light the actual transition from the base of the Old Red Sandstone into an older series of fossiliferous formations underneath. There could, therefore, be no doubt that part at least of his Silurian system was younger than Sedgwick's series in North Wales. And as he found what appeared to be older strata emerging from underneath his system, and seeming to stretch indefinitely into the heart of Wales, he naturally believed these strata to be part of his friend's domain, and at first left them alone. Such, too, was Sedgwick's original impression. The two fellow-workers had not drawn a definite boundary between their respective territories, but they agreed that the Silurian series was less ancient than the rocks of North Wales.

As a distinct name had been given to what they believed to be the younger series, Murchison urged his associate to choose an appropriate designation for what they regarded as the older, and in the summer of 1835 the term " Cambrian " was selected.[1]   By this time Murchison had learnt that no hard and fast line was to be drawn between the bottom of the Silurian and the top of the Cambrian series.   " In South Wales he had traced many distinct passages from the lowest member of the ' Silurian system ' into the underlying slaty rocks now named by Professor Sedgwick the Upper Cambrian."   Sedgwick, on the other hand, confessed that neither in the Lake District nor in North Wales was the stratigraphical succession unbroken, and that in these regions it was impossible to tell " how many terms are wanting to complete the series to the Old Red Sandstone and Carboniferous Limestone."[2] He adopted a threefold subdivision into Lower, Middle, and Upper Cambrian, but this classification rested merely on mineral characters, no attempt having yet been made by him to determine how far each of his subdivisions was defined by distinctive fossils.

Eventually it was ascertained that the organic remains in the upper part of the Cambrian system were the same as those found in the Lower Silurian formations as defined by Murchison.   It became obvious that the one series was really the equivalent of the other, and that they ought not to be classed under separate names. The officers of the Geological Survey, working from the clearly defined Silurian formations, could draw no line between these and those of North Wales, which Sedgwick had classed as Cambrian.   Finding the same

[1] From "Cambria," the old name of Wales.   Brit. Assoc. August 1835, *Phil. Mag.* vol. vii. (December 1835), p. 483, "On the Silurian and Cambrian Systems" by A. Sedgwick and R. I. Murchison.
[2] *Op. cit.*

fossils in both, they felt themselves constrained to class them all under the same designation of Silurian. Murchison, of course, had no objection to the indefinite extension of his system. Sedgwick, however, after some delay, protested against what he considered to be an unjustifiable appropriation of territory which he had himself conquered. And thus arose a misunderstanding between these two old comrades, which deepened ere long into a permanent estrangement.

It is not my intention to enter here into the details of this unhappy controversy.[1] My only object in referring to it is to point out how far we are indebted to Sedgwick for the establishment of the Cambrian system. He eventually traced through a part of the Welsh border a marked unconformability between the Upper Silurian formations and everything below them, and he proposed that his Cambrian system should be carried up to that physical break, and should thus include Murchison's Lower Silurian formations. But as these formations had been defined stratigraphically and palæontologically before he had been able to get his fossils from North Wales examined, they obviously had the right of priority. And the general verdict of geologists went in favour of Murchison.

While this dispute was in progress in Britain, a remarkable series of investigations by Joachim Barrande (1799-1883) had made known the extraordinary abundance and variety of Silurian fossils in Bohemia. This distinguished observer not only recognised the equivalents of Murchison's Upper and

[1] I have already given a full and, I believe, impartial account of it in my *Life of Murchison.*

Lower Silurian series, but found below that series a
still older group of strata, characterized by a different
assemblage of fossils, which he termed the first or
Primordial fauna.   It was ascertained that representatives of this fauna occur in Wales among some of
the divisions of Sedgwick's Cambrian system, far below
the Llandeilo group which formed the original base
of the Silurian series.   Eventually, therefore, since
the death of the two great disputants, there has been
a general consensus of opinion that the top of the
Cambrian system should be drawn at the upper limit
of the Primordial fauna.[1]

By this arrangement, Sedgwick's name is retained for
an enormously thick and varied succession of strata
which possess the deepest interest, because they contain the earliest records yet discovered of organised
existence on the surface of our globe.   It was Sedgwick who first arranged the successive groups of strata
in North Wales, from the Bala and Arenig rocks
down into the depths of the Harlech anticline.   His
classification, though it has undergone some slight
modification, remains to this day essentially as he left
it.   And thus the name which he selected for his
system, and which has become one of the household
words in geological literature, remains with us a
memorial of one of the most fearless, strenuous, gentle

[1] It has been proposed by Professor Lapworth that the strata named
by Murchison Lower Silurian and claimed by Sedgwick as Upper
Cambrian, should be taken from both and be given a new name,
"Ordovician."   But this proposal is fair to neither disputant.   By
all the laws that regulate scientific priority, the strata which were
first separated by Murchison and distinguished by their fossils, should
retain the name of Lower Silurian which he gave them.

and lovable of all the master minds who have shaped geological science into its present form.

By the establishment of the Cambrian and Silurian systems a vast stride was made in the process of reducing the chaos of Greywacke into settled order. But there still remained a series of rocks in that chaos which could not be claimed as either Cambrian or Silurian, and did not yield fossils which would show them to be Carboniferous. Before any dispute arose between Sedgwick and Murchison as to the respective limits of their domains in Wales, they were led to undertake a conjoint investigation which resulted in the creation of the Devonian system. The story of the addition of this third chapter to early Palæozoic history may be briefly told.

It had long been known that Greywacke or Transition rocks cover most of the counties of Devon and Cornwall. Closer examination of that region had shown that a considerable tract of Greywacke, now known as Culm-measures, contains abundant carbonaceous material, and even yields fossil plants that were recognised as identical with some of those in the Carboniferous system. It was at first supposed by De la Beche that these plant-bearing rocks lie below the rest of the Greywacke of that part of the country. Murchison, however, from the evidence of his clear sections in the Silurian territory, felt convinced that there must be some mistake in regard to the supposed position of these rocks, for he had traversed all the Upper Greywacke along the Welsh border, and had found it to contain no land-plants at all, but to be full of marine shells. He induced Sedgwick to join him in an expedition into Devonshire. The two associates, in the course of the year 1836, completely succeeded in proving that the Culm-measures, or Carboniferous series, lay not below but above the rest of the Greywacke of the south-west of England. But what was that Greywacke, and what relation did it bear to the rocks which had been reduced to system in Wales?

The structure of the ground in the south-west of England is by no means simple, and, indeed, is not completely understood even now. The rocks have been much folded, cleaved, crushed, and thrust over each other. But besides these subsequent changes, they present a great contrast in their lithological characters to the Old Red Sandstone on the opposite side of the Bristol Channel. Neither Sedgwick nor Murchison could find any analogy between the Devonshire Greywacke and the red sandstones, conglomerates and marls which expand into the Old Red Sandstone of South Wales, and lie so clearly between the Carboniferous Limestone above and the Upper Silurian formations below. Nor could Murchison see a resemblance between that Greywacke, or its fossils, and any of his Silurian rocks. With their twisted and indurated aspect, the Devonshire rocks looked so much older than the gently inclined Silurian groups by the banks of the Wye, that both he and Sedgwick thought they more resembled the crumpled and broken rocks of North Wales, and they accordingly first placed them in the upper and middle parts of the Cambrian system.[1]

This correlation, however, was made mainly on

[1] *Proc. Geol. Soc.* ii. (1837), p. 560.

lithological grounds. The Devonshire rocks were not without fossils, and considerable collections of these had already been gathered by different residents in the county, but no one had yet endeavoured to make a comparison between them and those of known stratigraphical horizons elsewhere. This task was undertaken at last by William Lonsdale (1794-1871), who towards the end of the year 1837 came to the conclusion that the greywacke and limestone of South Devonshire, judged by their fossil contents, must be intermediate between the Silurian and the Carboniferous formations, that is, on the parallel of the Old Red Sandstone of other parts of Britain.

Such a decision from a skilled palæontologist raised up some serious difficulties, which completely non-plussed the two able geologists who the year before had gone so gaily down to the south-west of England to set matters right there. It seemed to them as if Lonsdale's opinion was opposed to what had been regarded as definitely settled in the stratigraphy of the older stratified rocks. For two years they continued in complete uncertainty as to the solution of the problem. But at last after the examination of innumerable specimens, endless discussion, and inter-minable correspondence, they came to adopt Lonsdale's views. They saw that the abundantly fossiliferous rocks of South Devon contained, in their lower members, fossils that reminded them of Silurian types, while in their upper members, they yielded species that were common also to the Carboniferous Lime-stone. The two geologists therefore recognised in these rocks an intermediate series of strata, containing a marine fauna which must have flourished between the Silurian and the Carboniferous periods. That fauna was not represented in the Old Red Sandstone, which, with its traces of land-plants and remains of ganoid fishes, appeared to have been accumulated under other geographical conditions. To distinguish the series of rocks containing this well-marked facies of marine organisms, they chose the name " Devonian," from the county where these rocks were originally studied and where their true position was first ascertained.[1] The authors claimed that the establishment of the Devonian system was "undoubtedly the greatest change which has ever been attempted at one time in the classification of British rocks." But it was far more than that. It was the determination of a new geological series of world-wide significance, the unfolding of a new chapter in the geological annals of our globe. Soon after Sedgwick and Murchison had finally announced to the Geological Society their reform of the geology of Devonshire, they started for Rhineland, the Harz and Fichtelgebirge, and succeeded in demonstrating that the Devonian system is more extensively and completely developed there than in its original Devonshire home.

I have dwelt on those labours of Sedgwick and Murchison which more especially place their names among those of the founders of geology. But besides these exploits they each accomplished a vast amount of admirable work, and helped thereby to widen the bounds and strengthen the foundations of the science to which they devoted their lives. To enter upon

[1] *Trans. Geol. Soc.*, 2nd ser. vol. v. pp. 688, 701 (April 1839).

the consideration of these further achievements, however, would lead me beyond the limits to which this
volume must be restricted.

Murchison, who had succeeded De la Beche in
1855 as Director-General of the Geological Survey
of Great Britain, held that office until his death in
1871. To the last, he retained the erect military
bearing of his youth, and even under the weight of
threescore years and ten could walk a dozen of miles
and keep a keen eye on all the topographical and
geological features of the surrounding hills. Tall
and dignified in manner, with much of the formal
courtesy of an older time, he might seem to those
who only casually met him to be proud or even
haughty. But under this outer crust, which soon
dropped away in friendly intercourse, there lay a
friendly and helpful nature. Indomitable in his
power of work, restless in his eager energy in the
pursuit of his favourite science, full of sympathies
for realms of knowledge outside of his own domain,
wielding wide influence from his wealth and social
position, he did what no other man of his time
could do so well for the advance of science in
England. And his death at the ripe age of seventy-
nine left a blank in that country which has never
since been quite filled.

Sedgwick was in many respects a contrast to
Murchison. His powerful frame reminded one of
the race of dalesmen from which he sprang. His
eagle eyes seemed as if they must instantly pierce
into the very heart of the stiffest geological problem.
In his prime, he always made straight for the roughest

2 E

ground, the steepest slopes, or the highest summits, and his bodily strength bore him bravely through incredible exertion. Unfortunately his health, always uncertain, would react on his spirits, and times of depression and lethargy would come to interrupt and retard his work, whether with hammer or pen. But even his gloomiest fits he could turn into merriment, and he would laugh at them and at himself, as he described his condition to some friend. His gaiety of spirit made him the centre and life of every company of which he formed part. His frank manliness, his kindliness of heart, his transparent childlike simplicity, his unwearied helpfulness and his gentle tenderness, combined to form a character altogether apart. He was admired for his intellectual grasp, his versatility, and his eloquence, and he was beloved, almost worshipped, for the overflowing goodness of his character.

When in the early part of this century, one discovery after another was made which showed that Werner's so-called primitive rocks reappeared among his Transition and Floetz formations, a doubt began to arise whether there were any primitive rocks at all.[1] We have traced how Murchison and Sedgwick cleared up the confusion of the Transition series and created the Devonian, Silurian and Cambrian systems. In Wales certain schists had been detected by Sedgwick below his Cambrian rocks, but they did not greatly interest him, and he never

---

[1] Thus D'Aubuisson wrote in 1819—"Geology no longer possesses a single rock essentially primitive" (*Traité de Géognosie*, tome ii. p. 197).

tried to make out their structure and history.   Afterwards A. C. Ramsay (1814-1891) and his associates claimed these schists as metamorphosed parts of the Cambrian system.   To this day their true position has not been settled further than that they are known to be pre-Cambrian.

The vast and varied series of rocks, which have now been ascertained to underlie the oldest Cambrian strata, have undergone much scrutiny during the last half century, and their true nature and sequence are beginning to be understood.   The first memorable onward step in this investigation was taken in North America by William Edmond Logan (1798-1875).   Many years before his time, the existence of ancient gneisses and schists had been recognised both in the United States and in Canada.   At the very beginning of the century, the wide extent of these rocks had been noted by W. Maclure, whose general geological sketch-map of a large part of the United States will be referred to on a later page.   In 1824 and afterwards, Dr. J. J. Bigsby (1792-1881) spent much time among these rocks to the north of Lake Superior.   Subsequently the gneisses of the Adirondack Hills were described by Amos Eaton. At the very beginning of his connection with the Geological Survey of Canada in 1843, Logan confirmed the observation that the oldest fossiliferous formations of North America lie unconformably on a vast series of gneisses and other crystalline rocks, to which he continued at first to apply the old term Primary.   By degrees, as he saw more evidence of parallel structures in these masses, he thought that they were probably altered sediments, and he referred to them as Metamorphic. That portion of the series which includes thick bands of limestone he proposed to consider as a separate and overlying group. In the course of years, working with his associates Alexander Murray and T. Sterry Hunt, he was able to show the enormous extent of these primary rocks, covering as they do several hundred thousand square miles of the North American continent, and stretching northwards to the borders of the Arctic Ocean. He proposed for these most ancient mineral masses the general appellation of Laurentian, from their development among the Laurentide mountains. Afterwards he thought it possible to subdivide them into three separate groups, which he designated Upper, Middle and Lower. In the course of his progress, he came upon a series of hard slates and conglomerates, containing pebbles and boulders of the gneiss, and evidently of more recent origin, yet nowhere, so far as he could see, separable by an undoubted unconformability. These rocks, being extensively displayed along the northern shores of Lake Huron, he named Huronian. He afterwards described a second series of copper-bearing rocks lying unconformably on the Huronian rocks of Lake Superior. He thus recognised the existence of at least three vast systems older than the oldest fossiliferous formations. He may be said to have inaugurated the detailed study of Pre-Cambrian rocks. Subsequent investigation has shown the structure of the regions which he explored to be even more complicated and difficult than he believed it to be, and various important modifications have been proposed in his work and terminology by the able geologists of Canada and the United States who have continued his labours. But he will ever stand forward as one of the pioneers of geology, who in the face of incredible difficulties, first opened the way towards a comprehension of the oldest rocks of the crust of the earth.

CHAPTER XIV

The fundamental principles of Stratigraphy having been well established before the middle of last century, this branch of geological science has during the last fifty years undergone a remarkable expansion from four influences. Firstly, it has been profoundly modified by the writings of Darwin; secondly, it has been greatly affected by the introduction of zonal classification among the fossiliferous formations; thirdly, it has been augmented by the rise and extraordinary development of Glacial Geology; and lastly, it has enormously gained by the multiplication of detailed geological maps.

I. Charles Darwin (1809-1882) contributed several valuable works to the literature of geology. But it is not for these that I now cite his name. The two geological chapters in his *Origin of Species* produced the greatest revolution in geological thought which has occurred in my time. Younger students, who are familiar with the ideas there promulgated, can hardly realise the effect of them on an older generation.

They seem now so obvious and so well-established, that it may be difficult to conceive a philosophical science without them.

To most of the geologists of his day, Darwin's contention for the imperfection of the geological record, and his demonstration of it, came as a kind of surprise and awakening. They had never realised that the history revealed by the long succession of fossiliferous formations, which they had imagined to be so full, was in reality so fragmentary. And yet when Darwin pointed out this fact to them, they were compelled, sometimes rather reluctantly, to admit that he was right. Some of them at once adopted the idea, as Ramsay did, and carried it further into detail.[1]

Until Darwin took up the question, the necessity for vast periods of time, in order to explain the characters of the geological record, was very inadequately comprehended. Of course, in a general sense, the great antiquity of the crust of the earth was everywhere admitted. But no one before his day had perceived how enormous must have been the periods required for the deposition of even some thin continuous groups of strata. He supplied a criterion by which, to some degree, the relative duration of formations might perhaps be apportioned. When he declared that the intervals which elapsed between consecutive formations may sometimes have been of far longer duration than the formations themselves, contemporary geologists could only smile incredulously in their bewilderment,

[1] See the two Presidential Addresses to the Geological Society, by A. C. Ramsay, *Quart. Journ. Geol. Soc.* vols. xix. (1863), xx. (1864).

but in a few years Ramsay showed by a detailed examination of the distribution of fossils in the sedimentary strata that Darwin's suggestion must be accepted as an axiom in geological theory. Again, the great naturalist surmised that, before the deposition of the oldest known fossiliferous strata, there may have been antecedent periods, collectively far longer than from the date of these strata up to the present day, and that, during these vast, yet quite unknown, periods, the world may have swarmed with living creatures. But his contemporaries could only shrug their shoulders anew, and wonder at the extravagant notions of a biologist. But who nowadays is unwilling to grant the possibility, nay probability, of Darwin's surmise? Who can look upon the earliest Cambrian fauna without the strongest conviction that life must have existed on this earth for countless ages before that comparatively well-developed fauna came into existence? For this expansion of our geological vision, and for the flood of light which has been thrown upon geological history by the theory of evolution, we stand mainly indebted to Charles Darwin.

II. Although the value of organic remains as a means of identifying strata had been amply proved during the earlier half of last century, neither geologists nor palæontologists were then aware of the extent to which this chronological and stratigraphical test could be carried out in the practical classification of fossiliferous formations. They were content with the broad subdivisions, often to a large extent based on variations of sedimentary material, into which they arranged the geological record. Eventually, however,

it was shown by Oppel[1] and Quenstedt[2] that the
Jurassic series of Western Europe is not only capable
of subdivision into the lithological groups which
William Smith found to be distinguished by their
peculiar fossils, but that in these groups it was often
possible to trace a succession of horizons or zones,
each characterised by the presence of one or more
species of organic remains, which are either confined
to it or are more particularly conspicuous in it ; that
these zones can be followed over Germany, France
and England, and that, though the lithological character
of the strata may vary locally, the same sequence of
genera and species of fossils is on the whole maintained.
These observers found that the Ammonites are especially serviceable in the identification of such zones, on
account of their comparatively limited vertical range.
Thus in the Lias no fewer than seventeen zones have
been distinguished, each of which is known by the
name of its characteristic Ammonite, as the zone of
Psiloceras planorbe, which lies at the bottom, and that
of *Lytoceras jurense*, which forms the top of the series.
The same principle of arrangement was afterwards
found to hold good for the Cretaceous formations,
and it has since been extended through the lower
Palæozoic rocks down even to the bottom of the
Cambrian system.   In the Silurian formations the
most useful fossils for zonal purposes have been
shown by Professor Lapworth to be the Graptolites.
The lowest known fossiliferous platform among the
rocks of the Old and New Worlds is that of the

[1] *Die Juraformation Englands, Frankreichs und Deutschlands*, 1856-58.
[2] *Der Jura*, 1858.

Olenellus-zone, where this distinctive genus of trilobite is found.

This extension of William Smith's doctrine of " Strata identified by fossils " has greatly contributed to the progress of stratigraphy, and has furnished a fresh clue to the interpretation of the structure of districts in which the fossiliferous rocks have been much dislocated and plicated. The general succession of zones appears to be always similar, even in widely separated regions ; but the same zones are not everywhere present nor do the same genera and species always range over the world, though where they do reappear they are believed to keep the same relative order of occurrence.

III. The rapid development of Glacial Geology forms one of the most interesting chapters in the history of modern science. It began within the memory of men yet living, and many of the observers who have most energetically contributed to its progress are still actively at work. The literature devoted to glaciation has grown into a huge bulk, and continues to increase every year. Looking back to the beginning of the investigation we may note that although, as has been already alluded to (p. 314), Playfair, at the beginning of last century, had pointed out the pre-eminent place of glaciers as the agents of transport for large blocks of stone, his acute observation seems to have passed out of mind.[1] Venetz and Charpentier were the first to take up anew this interesting department of geology, to trace the dispersal of the crystalline rocks of the Central Alps outward across the great Swiss plain

[1] *Illustrations of the Huttonian Theory*, p. 348. *Ante* p. 314.

to the flanks of the Jura mountains,[1] and thus to demonstrate the former great extension of the Swiss glaciers. It was reserved, however, for Agassiz to perceive the wide significance of the facts observed, and to start the investigations that culminated in the recognition of an Ice Age which involved the whole of the northern part of our hemisphere, and in the voluminous literature which has recorded the rapid progress of this department of geology.

Jean Louis Rodolphe Agassiz (1807-1873) was born in Switzerland, and rose to distinction by his scientific work in Europe, but he went to the United States when he was still only forty-two years of age, and spent the last twenty-seven years of his life as an energetic and successful leader of science in his adopted home. His fame is thus both European and American, and the geologists of New England, not less than those of Switzerland, may claim him as one of their most distinguished worthies.

We must pass over the brilliant researches into the history of fossil fishes, which placed the name of Agassiz high among the palæontologists of Europe when he was still a young man. What we are more particularly concerned with here is the share he had in founding the modern school of glacial geology. As far back as the summer of 1836 he was induced to visit the glaciers of the Diablerets and Chamounix, and the great moraines of the Rhone valley, under the guidance of Charpentier, whose views as to the former extension of the ice he was disposed to doubt

[1] *Schweizer. Gesell. Verhandl.* 1834, p. 23; *Ann. des Mines*, viii. (1835) p. 219; *Leonhard und Bronn, Neues Jahrb.* 1837, p. 472.

and reject.   But the result of this tour was to convince
him that the phenomena were even more stupendous
than Charpentier had asserted.   In spite of the claims
of his palæontological and zoological undertakings,
Agassiz was so fascinated by the ice-problem of the
Alps that he must needs pursue the subject with all
the enthusiasm and industry of his character.   He
took the earliest opportunity of again investigating the
evidence furnished by the slopes of the Jura mountains, and became so firmly convinced of the truth
and wide importance of the conclusions at which he
had arrived that he determined to publish these to the
world.   Accordingly in the summer of the following
year (1837), when only thirty-three years of age, he
took the opportunity, as President of the Helvetian
Society of Natural Science, to give an address in which
he struck, with the hand of a master, the keynote of all
his future research in glaciation.   Tracing the distribution of the erratic blocks above the present level of the
glaciers, and far beyond their existing limits, he connected these transported masses with the polished and
striated rock-surfaces which were known to extend
even to the summits of the southern slopes of the
Jura.   He showed, from the nature of these smooth
surfaces, that they could not have been worn into their
characteristic forms by any current of water.   The fine
striæ, engraven on them as with a diamond-point, he
proved to be precisely similar to those now being
scratched on the rocky floors of the modern glaciers,
· and he inferred that the polished and striated rocks
of the Jura, even though now many leagues from
the nearest glacier, must have acquired their peculiar

surface from the action of ice moving over them, as modern glaciers slide upon their beds. He was thus led to conclude that the Alpine ice, now restricted to the higher valleys, once extended into the central plain, crossed it, and even mounted to the southern summits of the Jura chain.

Before Agassiz took up the question, there were two prevalent opinions regarding the transport of the erratics. One of these called in the action of powerful floods of water, the other invoked the assistance of floating ice. Agassiz combated these views with great skill. His reasoning ought to have convinced his contemporaries that his explanation was the true one. But the conclusions at which he arrived seemed to most men of the day extravagant and incredible. Even a cautious thinker like Lyell saw less difficulty in sinking the whole of Central Europe under the sea, and covering the waters with floating icebergs, than in conceiving that the Swiss glaciers were once large enough to reach to the Jura. Men shut their eyes to the meaning of the unquestionable fact that, while there was absolutely no evidence for a marine submergence, the former track of the glaciers could be followed mile after mile, by the rocks they had scored and the blocks they had dropped, all the way from their present ends to the far-distant crests of the Jura.

Agassiz felt that the question was connected with large problems in geology. The former vast extension of the Swiss glaciers could be no mere accidental or local phenomenon, but must have resulted from some general lowering of temperature. He coupled with this deduction certain theoretical statements regarding former climates and faunas, which have not been supported by subsequent research.

The main conclusions which the Swiss naturalist drew, so greatly interested him that he spent part of five successive summers investigating the vestiges of the old glaciers, and the operations of those of the present time. He convinced himself that the great extension of the ice was connected with the last great geological changes on the surface of the globe, and with the extinction of the large pachyderms, whose remains are so abundant in Siberia. He believed that the glaciers did not advance from the Alps into the plains, but rather that ice once covered all the lower grounds, and finally retreated into the mountains.

Having arrived at these conclusions from studies in his native country, Agassiz was naturally desirous to see how far his views could be tested or confirmed in a region far removed from any existing glaciers. Accordingly, in the year 1840, three years after his address at Neufchâtel, he had an opportunity of visiting Britain, and took advantage of it to examine a considerable part of Scotland, the north of England, and the north, centre, west, and south-west of Ireland. The results of this investigation were of remarkable influence in the progress of glacial geology. Agassiz demonstrated the identity of the phenomena in Britain with those in Switzerland, and claimed "that not only glaciers once existed in the British Islands, but that large sheets (*nappes*) of ice covered all the surface." [1]

[1] *Proc. Geol. Soc.* vol. iii. (1840) p. 331.

These and the subsequent researches and glacial monographs of the great Swiss naturalist started the study of ancient glaciation. At first his conclusions had been regarded as rank heresy by the older and more conservative geologists of the day. Von Buch "could hardly contain his indignation, mingled with contempt, for what seemed to him the view of a youthful and inexperienced observer."[1] A. von Humboldt also threw cold water upon the ardour of his young friend. But by degrees the opposition waned, and Agassiz had the satisfaction of seeing his most doughty opponents come over one by one to his side. Nowhere were his triumphs more signal than in the British Isles. Buckland (1784-1856), who enjoyed the advantage of being shown the evidence in Switzerland by Agassiz himself, was the first convert of distinction. He signalised his change of opinion by publishing a paper to prove the former presence of glaciers in Scotland and the north of England, followed by another communication on " the glacio-diluvial phenomena in Snowdonia and the adjacent parts of North Wales."[2] Lyell about the same time was won over by Buckland, and likewise hastened to announce his acceptance of the new views by publishing a paper on the former existence of glaciers in Forfarshire.[3] A few years later James David Forbes (1808-1868) gave an account of glaciers that nestled

[1] *Louis Agassiz, his Life and Correspondence*, by E. Cary Agassiz, vol. i. p. 264.

[2] *Proc. Geol. Soc.* vol. iii. (1841) pp. 332, 345, 579.

[3] *Proc. Geol. Soc.* vol. iii. (1841) p. 337.

among the Cuillin Hills of Skye,[1] and Charles
Maclaren found glacier moraines in the valleys of
Argyleshire.[2]

At first, however, the existence of former glaciers in
the valleys of Britain was the main conclusion sought
to be established. British geologists, and indeed geologists generally, were still for many years unwilling to
admit that not only the mountain-valleys, but even the
lowlands of the northern hemisphere were, at a late
geological period, buried under sheets of land-ice.
They preferred to call in the action of floating ice,
without perceiving that in so doing they involved
themselves in far more serious physical difficulties
than those which they sought to avoid.

Important service towards the ultimate acceptance
of Agassiz's enlarged conception of the glaciation of
Europe was rendered by Robert Chambers (1802-
1871), in a series of suggestive papers on the superficial
deposits and striated rocks of Scotland,[3] and in another
contribution (*Tracings of the North of Europe*, 1851),

---

[1] *Edin. New Phil. Journ.* xl. (1845) p. 76. To Forbes glacial
geology stands deeply indebted. He contributed to the *Edinburgh
New Philosophical Journal* an important series of letters from 1842
to 1851. He was likewise the author of excellent papers in
the *Proceedings* and *Transactions* of the Royal Society of Edinburgh,
of three memorable contributions on the viscous theory of glacier-
motion in the *Philosophical Transactions* of the Royal Society of
London (1846) and of two now classic works, his *Travels through the
Alps of Savoy*, etc. (1843) and *Norway and its Glaciers* (1853).

[2] *Edin. New Phil. Journ.* xl. (1845) p. 125 ; xlvii. (1849) p. 161 ;
xlix. (1850) p. 334 ; *Ib.* new series i. (1855) p. 189.

[3] *Edin. New Phil. Journ.* liv. (1852) p. 229 ; *Ibid.* new ser. i. (1855)
p. 103 ; ii. p. 184.

•

in which he detailed the results of a journey made by him to the north of Norway. In later years, by the labours of T. F. Jamieson, A. C. Ramsay and others, the extension of land-ice over the British Isles, and the direction taken by the chief ice-sheets in their movement across the country, came to be regarded as well-established facts in Post-Tertiary geology.

The literature of this branch of the science is now extensive and is increasing every year at a rapid rate. In Europe and in North America the glaciation of almost every region has been studied in great detail. A vast quantity of important fact has been accumulated to fill in the broad outlines traced by Agassiz, but his teaching in all its essential parts has long been generally accepted, and his name is now enshrined as the main founder of glacial geology.

IV. *Geological Maps.*—As the progress of stratigraphical geology has been so largely aided by the production of maps on which the distribution and order of succession of the various rocks can be made visible to the eye, it may not be inappropriate to close a sketch of the foundation and development of this branch of the science with a short account of the first beginnings and early history of geological cartography. It will be remembered that, as far back as the year 1683, Martin Lister suggested that it would be possible to show the distribution of the soils, rocks and minerals of a country upon the basis of an ordinary topographical map. He brought before the Royal Society, and published in the *Philosophical Transactions*, what was called "An ingenious proposal for a new sort of Maps of Country, together

2 F

with tables of sands and clays, such chiefly as are found in the north parts of England, drawn up about ten years since, and delivered to the Royal Society, March 12, 1683, by the Learned Martin Lister, M.D."[1] In this "soile or mineral map" it was proposed that "the soile might either be coloured or otherwise distinguished by variety of lines or etchings, but the great care must be, very exactly to note upon the map where such and such soiles are bounded." By the term 'soil' Lister meant not only the vegetable soil at the surface, but the sub-soil and rocks underneath. "For I am of opinion," he remarks, "such upper soiles, if natural, infallibly produce such under minerals, and, for the most part, in such order." "If the limits of each soile appeared upon a map, something more might be comprehended from the whole and from every part, than I can possibly foresee ; but I leave this to the industry of future times."

Lister's proposal, however, does not seem to have been followed by any practical result for some two generations. In the year 1743, there was published in England what is believed to be the earliest specimen of a geological map, under the title of "A new Philo-sophico-Chorographical Chart of East Kent, invented and delineated by Christopher Packe, M.D." The author sent a letter on the subject to the Royal Society, and accompanied his Chart with a tract wherein he states that his undertaking "is no dream or devise, the offspring of a sportive imagination, conceived and produced for want of something else

[1] *Phil. Trans.* vol. xiv. p. 739.

to do, at my leisure in my study,—but it is a real scheme, taken upon the spot with patience and diligence, by frequent or rather continual observations, in the course of my journeys of business through almost every the minutest parcel of the country : digested at home with much consideration, and composed with as much accuracy as the observer was capable of." The Chart, which he indignantly refused to call a map, is on the scale of rather more than an inch and a half to a mile, and comprises the country around Canterbury. It shows the positions of the valleys and distinguishes the hills by the nature of their component materials, such as chalk, "stonehills" (Lower Greensand) and " clay-hills," lying over the plain of the Weald. As many parts of the valley system are now dry, Packe inferred that they were not hollowed by streams, but by the retiring waters of the Deluge and have remained without change ever since.[1]

The mineralogical maps of Guettard have already been noticed (p. 110). The earliest of these was presented to the Academy of Sciences of Paris in 1746, and the series was continued by the same industrious observer until he handed over the further prosecution of the task to his successor Mounet. The early map of Füchsel (1762) has been referred to in Chapter VII. (p. 198). The first map in which the various geological formations were represented by washes of colour appears to have been one by G. Gläser published at Leipzig in the year 1775 in his *Versuch einer mineralogischen Beschreibung der gefürsteten*

[1] See a paper by Fitton in *Phil. Mag.* vol. i. (1832) p. 447.

452 Early maps in Germany and France

Graftschaft Henneberg, Chursächsischen Antheils. Three years later a more important map, also in colour, was issued at Leipzig in 1778 by J. F. W. Charpentier, Professor in the Mining Academy of Freiberg, to accompany his excellent quarto monograph on the *Mineralogische Geographie der Chursächsischen Lände.* Eight tints are used to discriminate granite, gneiss, schist, limestone, gypsum, sandstone, river-sand, clay and loam ; and there are also symbols to point out the localities for basalt, serpentine, etc.

Palassou, in his *Essai sur la Minéralogie des Monts Pyrénées,* Paris, 1781, gave a series of maps with engraved lines and signs, and also a route-map of the part of France between Paris and the Mediterranean, with the general mineralogical characters of each line of route indicated by strips of colour. He thus distinguished by a green line the granite rocks, by a yellow line the " schists," and by a red line the calcareous rocks. He also indicated the presence of these various formations by different symbols, among which was one for extinct volcanoes, that figures in the Clermont region and also to the west of Montpellier.

William Smith's map, the history of which has been referred to in Chapter XII. appeared in the year 1815 with the following title—" A Geological Map of England and Wales, with Part of Scotland ; exhibiting the Collieries, Mines, and Canals, the Marshes and Fen Lands originally overflowed by the Sea ; and the Varieties of Soil, according to the Variations of the Substrata ; illustrated by the most descriptive Names of Places, and of Local Districts ; showing also the Rivers, Sites of Parks, and Principal Seats of the Nobility and Gentry ; and the opposite coast of France. By William Smith, Mineral Surveyor." The map consists of fifteen sheets on the scale of five miles to an inch ($\frac{1}{316800}$), and measures 8 feet 9 inches in height by 6 feet 2 inches in width. It was accompanied with a quarto memoir or explanation of 50 pages.

While Smith's map was in preparation another large geological map of England and Wales was independently constructed by George Bellas Greenough (1778-1855), an able geologist and a caustic critic of his contemporaries and predecessors.[1] This map was published in 1819. In the memoir which accompanied it the author states that though he knew, as early as 1804, that Smith had begun a similar work, he had been led to believe that the design was abandoned. Accordingly he undertook the task in 1808, and having been encouraged by the Geological Society, of which he was President, to complete it on the scale of eleven miles to an inch ($\frac{1}{696960}$), he proceeded with it, and the map as prepared by him had been more than a year in the hands of the engraver when Smith's map appeared in 1815. Greenough's is a better piece of engraving, and in some respects is more detailed, especially as regards the formations older than the Coal. It shows how much information as to English stratigraphy had become available, partly

---

[1] His qualities are characteristically exhibited in the volume which he published in 1819 entitled *A Critical Examination of the First Principles of Geology*. Every school of writers comes in there for its share of his pungent criticism, and he shows his wide acquaintance with the literature of the science. He was one of the founders of the Geological Society, and as long as he lived was one of its most respected and influential members.

no doubt through Smith's labours, before 1815. Greenough's map was published and taken over by the Geological Society, whose property it became. The second edition, much revised and improved, was published in 1839 and since then the map has from time to time been brought up to date, and is still on sale. But in its present form it differs much from its author's original version. The appearance of this map under the auspices of the Geological Society no doubt affected the sale of Smith's, which does not appear to have reached a second edition, though a much reduced version of it was published in 1820.

In the list of the cartographical achievements of the earlier decades of last century, a place must be found for the remarkable maps and descriptions of Scotland for which geology is indebted to the genius and strenuous labour of John Macculloch. As already stated (p. 261), his account of the structure of the Western Isles, and the excellent maps and sections which accompanied it, had a powerful influence in promoting the progress of the study of igneous rocks, and have long since taken their place as geological classics. The same indefatigable observer, after years of toil prepared a geological map of the whole of Scotland, on the scale of four miles to an inch ($\frac{1}{253440}$)—a most remarkable achievement to have been accomplished unaided by one observer, at a time when means of locomotion were as yet undeveloped over wide tracts of the country.[1]

[1] *A Description of the Western Isles of Scotland*, 1819 ; *A Geological Map of Scotland*, 1840 ; and *Memoirs to His Majesty's Treasury respecting the Geological Map of Scotland*, by J. Macculloch, 1836.

What Macculloch did for Scotland was done even more efficiently for Ireland by Richard Griffith (1784-1878), who, born in Dublin in 1784, devoted his long and active life to carrying out surveys and other investigations for the development of the resources of his native country. In the course of his innumerable journeys into all parts of the island, he accumulated a large body of notes regarding its geology, and from time to time inserted the data upon a map of Ireland. This map was at last ordered by the Government to be reconstructed and engraved on the scale of four miles to an inch, and it was published in the spring of 1839. He continued to make improvements on it as his knowledge of the geology of the country increased, and to embody these in successive editions. If regard be had to its large scale and to the amount of detail expressed upon it, this work must be admitted to be the most remarkable map of a whole country ever constructed by a single individual. Its singular accuracy and breadth of treatment have been amply proved by the subsequent work of the Geological Survey.

Allusion has already been made to some of the pioneer geological cartographers by whom the distribution of the rocks on the European continent was first delineated. The early map of Germany by Von Buch was noticed in Chapter VIII. (p. 251). In France the mineralogical charts of Guettard and Palassou were followed in 1811 by the fuller geological map of the Paris basin by Cuvier and Brongniart (p. 366), and in 1813 by that of Omalius d'Halloy (p. 377), embracing a large tract of the north of France. The first general geological map of the whole of France was prepared as a national undertaking. In the year 1820 a copy of Greenough's map of England and Wales having been sent to the École des Mines at Paris, the desire arose to provide France with a similar compendium of its geology. Accordingly two engineers of the Mines Department, Élie de Beaumont (1798-1874) and Dufrénoy, were, in 1822, sent to England, where they spent six months studying the principles on which the English map had been constructed, and other subjects connected with the project. The map of France, begun in 1825 and completed in 1840, consisted of six sheets on the scale of about eight miles to an inch. This great work, so rapidly carried out, remains as a remarkable monument of the genius of the two geologists under whose supervision it was constructed.

The most important impulse towards the complete and methodical investigation of the geology of wide regions of the earth's surface has been given by the institution of State surveys for the express purpose of constructing geological maps of entire countries, combined with the determination of the character and distribution of useful minerals, and with the formation of large collections of rocks, minerals and fossils. Great Britain led the way in this line of national effort, by inaugurating in 1835, at the instigation and under the personal supervision of Henry Thomas de la Beche, a Geological Survey of the British Isles, together with a School of Mines and a Mining Record Office. The objects of the Geological Survey were to ascertain and depict on maps, as accurately and in as much detail as possible, on the scale of one inch to an English mile (or $\frac{1}{63360}$), the geological structure of the country, together with the position and distribution of the useful minerals; to prepare horizontal sections on a scale of six inches to a mile ($\frac{1}{10560}$), showing the true form of the surface and the ascertained or inferred arrangement of the rocks underneath; to publish various memoirs and monographs in which the geology, palæontology, useful minerals and mineral industries of the country should be fully described, and to form a museum in which the rocks, minerals and fossils of the British Isles should be amply represented by collections of specimens. The first maps issued by the English Survey at once attracted notice as the largest and most detailed maps that had yet appeared of any part of the surface of the earth. De la Beche with much sagacity and energy secured an able staff of professors for his School of Mines, who did much to stimulate the study of geology, mineralogy, palæontology, and natural history. Among these men were Andrew C. Ramsay (1814-1891), Edward Forbes (1815-1854), Warington Smyth (1817-1890), Lyon Playfair (1818-1898), and John Percy (1817-1889). De la Beche was succeeded in 1855 by Murchison, under whom the staff of the Survey was much augmented. The example set by the mother country has been followed among the Colonies and Dependencies of Britain, nearly all of which now have their independent geological surveys. Most civilized countries have also adopted similar organisations, so that now detailed geological maps have been published for a large part of Europe and North America. Even Japan, in adopting the methods of the West, has not omitted to include among them well-equipped geological and seismological surveys. By the detailed style of mapping now in general use the geological structure of the earth is becoming every year more accurately known. International co-operation has likewise been called into requisition. And we are now in possession of a geological map of the greater part of the European continent, prepared mainly by the collaboration of the national surveys of the different countries, under the auspices of the International Geological Congress.

While geology, as shown by the production of Maps and Memoirs, has made such steady progress in the Old World, its advance has been in many respects even more rapid and striking in the New. When we look back upon the history of the science on the other side of the Atlantic the first name that prominently comes before us is that of William Maclure (1763-1840), who has been called the "Father of American Geology." He was born at Ayr in Scotland, and after acquiring a fortune in business in London, he went in 1796 to the United States and finally settled there. Having developed a taste for geology in Europe, he was soon attracted by the comparative simplicity and the imposing scale of the geological structure of his adopted country, and in the course of some years made many journeys across the Eastern States. He recorded on a map his observations of the distribution of the rocks, and in 1809 made a communication on the subject to the American Philosophical Society at Philadelphia. In 1817, having extended his knowledge during the intervening eight years, he presented his map to that Society, and it was then published. This map is of special interest, as the first sketch of the geological structure of a large part of the United States. It is on a small scale—only 120 miles to an inch ($\frac{1}{7603200}$)—but it gives a broad delineation of the general distribution of the larger formations. Maclure was an open-minded adherent of the Freiberg system of classification, for he frankly states that "although subject to all the errors inseparable from systems founded upon a speculative theory of origin, the system of Werner is still the best and most comprehensive that has yet been formed."

The area depicted on this map extends from the Canadian frontier to the Gulf of Mexico and from the Atlantic Coast westward to about the 94th meridian. The formations represented by colour are " Primitive Rock, Transition Rock, Secondary Rock, Old Red Sandstone, Alluvial Rock," and a green line is traced from the north-east of New York State southwards into Tennessee, "to the westward of which has been found the greatest part of the salt and gypsum."

Among the errors of this sketch-map, hardly avoidable at the time, is the inclusion of various important members of the Tertiary series among the alluvial deposits. Further, among the Secondary formations there is classed the horizontal westward extension of the same rocks which, where highly inclined further east, were regarded as Transition. But even with these mistakes, the map must be admitted to be a meritorious first outline of the geology of a vast extent of territory.

In the year 1828 Amos Eaton (1776-1842) gave a fuller synopsis than Maclure had done of the rocks of North America, but misplaced some of the subdivisions.

G. W. Featherstonhaugh (1780-1866), who was appointed "United States Geologist," was employed in making various surveys for the Government, and collected a large amount of material towards the construction of a better geological map of the whole country. Born in France and well acquainted with the rocks of Europe, he was able to institute a closer and more correct parallel between these rocks and their American equivalents than had previously been attempted. Another early pioneer in the geology of the United States was Lardner Vanuxem (1792-1848) whose work on the geological survey of the State of New York deserves special recognition. As one of his important services he corrected the error of taking an inclined position as any reliable indication of the relative age of rocks, and insisted on the paramount importance of identifying strata by the organic remains contained in them. Following this principle, he was able to declare that the Transition rocks of Ohio, Kentucky and Tennessee were shown by their fossils to be of the same age as those at Trenton Falls in New York, and all of them equivalents of some of the Transition rocks of Europe wherein the same fossils had been found.

Later than these early leaders came the group of distinguished men who, by their researches and surveys in Pennsylvania, not only added a series of admirable maps to geological literature, but enriched the science with suggestive memoirs on mountain structure—William Barton Rogers (1804-1882), Henry Darwin Rogers (1808-1866), and J. P. Lesley (1819-1903). Most of the other States of the American Union have also instituted State Geological Surveys, and have produced excellent maps and descriptive memoirs, besides amassing valuable collections of the minerals, rocks and fossils of their respective domains. The central government organised various surveys of the western territories, which did admirable work of a pioneering and prospective kind under such leaders as J. D. Powell (1834-1902), J. S. Newberry (1822-1892), Clarence King (1842-1898) and F. V. Hayden (1829-1887). When it was found in 1879 that some of these explorations were traversing the same ground, a consolidation of the whole geological effort was made, and the Geological Survey of the United States was established. The magnitude and excellence of the work already accomplished by this organisation place it in the forefront of all national geological enterprises.

CHAPTER XV

The Rise of Petrographical Geology—William Nicol, Henry
Clifton Sorby. Conclusion.

I turn now to the Petrographical department of
geological inquiry, as exhibiting the last great forward
stride which the science has taken. We have seen
how greatly geology and mineralogy were indebted to
Werner for his careful and precise definitions. The
impulse which he gave to the study of Petrography
continued to show its effects long after his time, more
particularly in Germany. Methods of examination were
improved, chemical analysis was more resorted to, and
the rocks of the earth's crust, so far as related to their
ultimate chemical constitution, were fairly well known
and classified. Their internal structure, however, was
very imperfectly understood. Where they were coarsely
crystalline, their component minerals might be readily
determined ; but where they became fine-grained, little
more could be said about the nature and association
of their constituents than might be painfully deciphered
with the help of a hand-lens, or could be inferred from
the results of chemical analysis. Hence though not
actually at a standstill, petrography continued to make
but slow progress. In some countries indeed, notably

in Britain, it was almost entirely neglected in favour of the superior attractions of fossils and stratigraphy. But at last there came a time of awakening and rapid advance.

In order to trace the history of this petrographical resuscitation, we must in imagination transport ourselves to the workshop of an ingenious and inventive mechanician, William Nicol, who was a lecturer on Natural Philosophy at Edinburgh in the early part of last century. Among his inventions was the famous prism of Iceland spar that bears his name.[1] Every petrographer will acknowledge how indispensable this little piece of apparatus is in his microscopic investigations. He may not be aware, however, that it was the same skilful hands that devised the process of making thin slices of minerals and rocks, whereby the microscopic examination of these substances has become possible.

In the course of his experiments, Nicol hit upon the plan of cutting sections of fossil wood, so as to reveal its minutest vegetable structures. He took a slice from the specimen to be studied, ground it perfectly flat, polished it, and cemented it by means of Canada balsam to a piece of plate-glass. The exposed surface of the slice was then ground down, until the piece of stone was reduced to a thin pellicle adhering to the glass, and the requisite degree of transparency was obtained. Nicol himself prepared a large number of slices of fossil and recent woods. Many of these were described by Henry Witham in his

[1] See Nicol's original account of his prism in *Edin. New Phil. Journ.* vol. vi. (1829), p. 83.

Observations on Fossil Vegetables (1831), to which Nicol supplied the first published account of his process.

Here then geologists were provided with a method of investigating the minutest structures of rocks and minerals. As it was now made possible to subject any part of the earth's crust to investigation with the microscope, it might have been thought that those who devoted themselves to the study of that crust, especially those who were more particularly interested in the structure, composition and history of rocks, would have hastened to avail themselves of the new facilities for research thus offered to them.

It must be confessed, I am afraid, that geologists are about as difficult to move as their own erratic blocks. They took no notice of the possibilities put in their way by William Nicol. And so for a quarter of a century the matter went to sleep. When Nicol died, his instruments and preparations passed into the hands of the late Mr. Alexander Bryson of Edinburgh who, having considerable dexterity as a manipulator, and being much interested in the process, made many additions to the collections which he had acquired. In particular, he made numerous thin slices of minerals and rocks for the purpose of exhibiting the cavities containing fluid, which had been described long before by Brewster[1] and by William Nicol.[2] In my boyhood I had frequent opportunities of seeing these and the other specimens in Mr. Bryson's cabinet, as well as the fine series of fossil woods sliced so long before by Nicol.

[1] *Trans. Roy. Soc. Edin.* vol. x. (1824), p. 1.
[2] *Edin. New. Phil. Jour.* vol. v. (1828), p. 94.

At last Mr. Henry Clifton Sorby came to Edinburgh, and had an opportunity of looking over the Bryson collection. He was particularly struck with the series of slices illustrating " fluid-cavities," and at once saw that the subject was one of which the further prosecution could not fail to " lead to important conclusions in geological theory."[1] He soon began to put the method of preparing thin slices into practice, made sections of mica-schist,[2] and found so much that was new and important, with a promise of such a further rich harvest of results, that he threw his whole energy into the investigation for several years, and produced at last in 1858 the well-known memoir, *On the Microscopical Structure of Crystals*,[3] which marks one of the most prominent epochs of modern geology. I have always felt a peculiar satisfaction in the reflection that though the work of William Nicol was never adequately recognised in his lifetime, nor for many years afterwards, it was his thin slices, prepared by his own hands, that eventually started Mr. Sorby on his successful and distinguished career, and thus opened out a new and vast field for petrographical investigation.

It is not necessary here to recapitulate the achievements which have placed Mr. Sorby's name at the head of modern petrographers. He, for the first time, showed how, by means of the microscope, it was possible to discover the minute structure and

[1] *Quart. Journ. Geol. Soc.* vol. xiv. (1858), p. 454.
[2] *Brit. Assoc. Reports*, 1856, sections, p. 78.
[3] *Quart. Journ. Geol. Soc.* vol. xiv. (1858), p. 453.

composition of rocks, and to learn much regarding
their mode of origin. He took us, as it were,
into the depths of a volcanic focus, and revealed
the manner in which lavas acquire their characters.
He carried us still deeper into the terrestrial crust,
and laid open the secrets of those profound abysses
in which granitic rocks have been prepared. His
methods were so simple, and his deductions so start-
ling, that they did not instantly carry conviction to
the minds of geologists, more particularly to those of
his own countrymen. The reproach that it was
impossible to look at a mountain through a microscope was brought forward in opposition to the new
departure which he advocated. Well did he reply
by anticipation to this objection. "Some geologists,
only accustomed to examine large masses in the
field, may perhaps be disposed to question the
value of the facts I have described, and to think
the objects so minute as to be quite beneath their
notice, and that all attempts at accurate calculations
from such small data are quite inadmissible. What
other science, however, has prospered by adopting
such a creed ? What physiologist would think of
ignoring all the invaluable discoveries that have been
made in his science with the microscope, merely
because the objects are minute ? . . . With such
striking examples before us, shall we physical geologists maintain that only rough and imperfect
methods of research are applicable to our own
science ? Against such an opinion I certainly must
protest ; and I argue that there is no necessary
connection between the size of an object and the

value of a fact, and that, though the objects I have described are minute, the conclusions to be derived from the facts are great."[1]

Professor Zirkel was the first geologist of note who took up with zeal the method of investigation so auspiciously inaugurated by Mr. Sorby. But some five years had elapsed before he made his communication on the subject to the Academy of Sciences of Vienna.[2] From that date (1863) he devoted himself with much zeal and success to the investigation, and produced a series of papers and volumes which gave a powerful impetus to the study of petrography. This department of geology was indeed entirely reconstituted. The most exact methods of optical research were introduced into it by Professor Rosenbusch, Professor Fouqué, M. Michel Lévy and others, and the study of rocks once more competed with that of fossils in attractiveness. We have only to look at the voluminous literature which, within the last fifty years has sprung up around the investigation of rocks, to see how great a revolution has been effected by the introduction of the microscope into the equipment of the geologist. For this transformation we are, in

[1] *Quart. Journ. Geol. Soc.* xiv. (1858), p. 497. See also Mr. Sorby's Presidential Addresses to the Geological Society for 1879 and 1880.

[2] *Sitzungsber. Math. Naturwiss.* vol. xlvii. 1st part (1863), p. 226. In this paper the author refers to previous occasional use of the microscope for determining the mineralogical composition of rocks by Gustav Rose, G. vom Rath, G. Jenzsch, M. Deiters and others. In England the first geologist who published the results of his microscopical examination of rocks was David Forbes, *Popular Science Review* (October 1867), vol. vi. p. 355.

the first instance, indebted to William Nicol and Henry Clifton Sorby.

In the account which has been presented in this volume of the work of some of the more notable men who have created the science of geology, one or two leading facts stand out prominently before us.   In the first place, even in the list of selected names which we have considered, it is remarkable how varied have been the ordinary avocations of these pioneers.   The majority have been men engaged in other pursuits, who have devoted their leisure to the cultivation of geological studies.   Steno, Guettard, Pallas, Füchsel, and many more were physicians, either led by their medical training to interest themselves in natural history, or not seldom, even from boyhood, so fond of natural history as to choose medicine as their profession because of its affinities with that branch of science.   Giraud-Soulavie and Michell were clergymen. Murchison was a retired soldier.   Alexandre Brongniart was at first engaged in superintending the porcelain manufactory of Sèvres.   Desmarest was a hard-worked civil servant who snatched his intervals for geology from the toils of incessant official occupation.   William Smith found time for his researches in the midst of all the cares and anxieties of his profession as an engineer and surveyor.   Hutton, Hall, De Saussure, Von Buch, Lyell and Darwin were men of means, who scorned a life of slothful ease, and dedicated themselves and their fortune to the study of the history of the earth. Playfair and Cuvier were both teachers of other branches of science, irresistibly drawn into the sphere of geological inquiry and speculation. Of the whole gallery of worthies that have passed before us, a comparatively small proportion could be classed as in the strictest sense professional geologists, such as Werner, Sedgwick and Logan. Were we to step outside of that gallery, and include the names of all who have helped to lay the foundations of the science we should find the proportion to be still less.

From the beginning of its career, geology has owed its foundation and its advance to no select and privileged class. It has been open to all who cared to undergo the trials which its successful prosecution demands. And what it has been in the past, it remains to-day. No branch of natural knowledge lies more invitingly open to every student who, loving the fresh face of Nature, is willing to train his faculty of observation in the field, and to discipline his mind by the patient correlation of facts and the fearless dissection of theories. To such an inquirer no limit can be set. He may be enabled to rebuild parts of the temple of science, or to add new towers and pinnacles to its superstructure. But even if he should never venture into such ambitious undertakings, he will gain, in the cultivation of geological pursuits, a solace and enjoyment amid the cares of life, which will become to him a source of the purest joy.

In the second place, the history of geological science presents some conspicuous examples of the length of time that may elapse before a fecund idea comes to germinate and bear fruit. Consider for a moment how many years passed before the stratigraphical conceptions of Füchsel, Lehmann, and Giraud-Soulavie took more definite shape in the detailed investigations of Cuvier, Brongniart and Smith, and how many more years were needed before the Secondary and Tertiary formations were definitely arranged and subdivided as they now stand in our tables. Remember too that even after the principles of stratigraphy had been settled, a quarter of a century had slipped away before they were successfully applied to the Transition rocks, and a still longer time before the system of zonal classification was elaborated. Note how long the controversy lasted over the origin of basalt, and how slowly came the recognition of volcanic action as a normal part of terrestrial energy, which has been in operation from the earliest geological times and has left its memorials even in the oldest known parts of the crust of the earth. Mark also, in the history of physiographical geology, that though the principles of this branch of science were in large measure grasped by Desmarest, De Saussure and Hutton in the eighteenth century, their work was neglected and forgotten until the whole subject has been revived and marvellously extended in our own day. Again, let me recall how slowly the key that now unlocks the innermost mysteries of rock-structure was made use of. Five-and-twenty years elapsed after William Nicol had shown how stony substances could be investigated by means of the microscope, before Mr. Sorby called the attention of geologists to the enormous value of the method thus put into their hands. Other five years had to pass before the method began to be taken up in Germany, and a still longer time before it came into general use all over the world.

Such instances as these lead to two reflections. On the one hand, they assure us of the permanent vitality of truth. The seed may be long in showing signs of life, but these signs come at last. On the other hand, we are warned to be on the outlook for unrecognised meanings and applications in the work of our own day and in that of older date. We are taught the necessity not only of keeping ourselves abreast of the progress of science at the present time, but also of making ourselves acquainted as far as we possibly can with the labours of our predecessors. It is not enough to toil in our little corner of the field. We must keep ourselves in touch both with what is going on now, and with what has been done during the past in that and surrounding parts of the domain of science. Many a time we may find that the results obtained by some fellow-labourer, though they may have had but little significance for him, flash a flood of light on what we have been doing ourselves.

I am only too painfully aware how increasingly difficult it is to find time for a careful study of the work of our predecessors, and also to keep pace with the ever-rising tide of modern geological literature. The science itself has so widened, and the avenues to publication have so prodigiously multiplied, that one is almost driven in despair to become a specialist, and confine one's reading to that portion of the literature which deals with one's own more particular branch of the science. But this narrowing of the range of our interests and acquirement has a markedly prejudicial effect on the character of our work. There is but slender consolation to be derived from the conviction, borne in upon us by ample and painful experience, that in the case of geological literature, a large mass of the writing of the present time is of little or no value for any of the higher purposes of the science, and that it may quite safely and profitably, both as regards time and temper, be left unread. If geologists, and especially young geologists, could only be brought to realise that the addition of another paper to the swollen flood of our scientific literature involves a serious responsibility ; that no man should publish what is not of real consequence, and that his statements when published should be as clear and condensed as he can make them, what a blessed change would come over the faces of their readers, and how greatly would they conduce to the real advance of the science which they wish to serve !

In the third and last place, it seems to me that one important lesson to be learnt from a review of the successive stages in the foundation and development of geology is the absolute necessity of avoiding dogmatism. Let us remember how often geological theory has altered. The Catastrophists had it all their own way until the Uniformitarians got the upper hand, only to be in turn displaced by the Evolutionists. The Wernerians were as certain of the origin and sequence of rocks as if they had been present at the formation of the earth's crust. Yet in a few years their notions and overweening confidence became a laughing-stock. From the very nature of its subject, as I have already remarked, geology does not generally admit of the mathematical demonstration of its conclusions. They rest upon a balance of probabilities. But this balance is liable to alteration, as facts accumulate or are better understood. Hence what seems to be a well-established deduction in one age may be seen to be more or less erroneous in the next. Every year, however, the data on which these inferences are based are more thoroughly comprehended and more rigidly tested. Geology now possesses a large and ever-growing body of well-ascertained fact, which will be destroyed by no discovery of the future, though it will doubtless be vastly augmented, while new light may be cast on many parts of it now supposed to be thoroughly known.

Each of us has it in his power to add to this accumulation of knowledge. Careful and accurate observation is always welcome, and may eventually prove of signal importance. While availing ourselves freely of the use of hypothesis as an aid in ascertaining the connection and significance of facts, we must be ever on our guard against premature speculation and theory, clearly distinguishing between what is fact and what may be our own gloss or interpretation of it. Above all, let us preserve the modesty of the true student, face to face with the mysteries of Nature Proving all things and holding fast that which we believe to be true, let us look back with gratitude and pride to what has been achieved by our forerunners in the race, and while we labour to emulate their devotion, let us hold high the torch of science, and pass it on bright and burning to those who shall receive it from our hands.

INDEX.

GLASGOW: PRINTED AT THE UNIVERSITY PRESS BY ROBERT MACLEHOSE AND CO. LTD.

Works by Sir Archibald Geikie

F.R.S., D.Sc., etc.

TEXT-BOOK OF GEOLOGY. With Illustrations. Fourth Edition. Revised and Enlarged. In Two Vols. 8vo. 30s. net.

THE ANCIENT VOLCANOES OF GREAT BRITAIN. With Seven Maps and numerous Illustrations. In Two Vols. Super Royal 8vo. 36s. net.

THE SCENERY OF SCOTLAND VIEWED IN CONNECTION WITH ITS PHYSICAL GEOLOGY. Third Edition. Crown 8vo. 10s. net.

CLASS-BOOK OF GEOLOGY. Illustrated with woodcuts. Fourth Edition. Crown 8vo. 5s.

OUTLINES OF FIELD GEOLOGY. New and revised Edition. Extra Fcap. 8vo. 3s. 6d.

GEOLOGICAL SKETCHES AT HOME AND ABROAD. With Illustrations. 8vo. 10s. 6d.

LANDSCAPE IN HISTORY AND OTHER ESSAYS. 8vo. 8s. 6d. net.

THE FOUNDERS OF GEOLOGY. Second Edition. 8vo.

PRIMER OF GEOLOGY. With Illustrations. Pott 8vo. 1s.   [*Science Primers.*

    Box of Geological Specimens to illustrate GEIKIE'S PRIMER OF GEOLOGY. 10s. 6d.

ELEMENTARY LESSONS IN PHYSICAL GEOGRAPHY. Illustrated with woodcuts and ten plates. Fcap. 8vo. 4s. 6d. QUESTIONS FOR THE USE OF SCHOOLS. Fcap. 8vo. 1s. 6d.

PRIMER OF PHYSICAL GEOGRAPHY. Illustrated. Pott 8vo. 1s.   [*Science Primers.*

THE TEACHING OF GEOGRAPHY. Globe 8vo. 2s.

GEOGRAPHY OF THE BRITISH ISLES. Pott 8vo. 1s.

MEMOIR OF SIR A. C. RAMSAY. 8vo. 12s. 6d. net.

MACMILLAN AND CO., LTD., LONDON.

Works on Geology & Mineralogy

GEOLOGY OF SOUTH AFRICA. By Dr. F. H. Hatch and Dr. G. S. Corstorphine. Illustrated 8vo. 21s. net.

GOLD MINES OF THE RAND. Being a Description of the Mining Industry of Witwatersrand, Transvaal Colony. By Frederick H. Hatch (Mining Engineer) and J. A. Chalmers (Mining Engineer). With maps, plans, and illustrations. Super royal 8vo. 17s. net.

THE KLERKSDORP GOLD FIELDS. Being a Description of the Geologic and of the Economic conditions obtaining in the Klerksdorp district, Transvaal Colony. By G. A. Denny. With Plans, Sections, a complete Map of the Klerksdorp district, and a Geological Map of the same area. Royal 8vo. 42s. net.

OBSERVATIONS OF A NATURALIST IN THE PACIFIC BETWEEN 1896 AND 1899. Vol. I. Vanua Levu. Fiji: Its Physical and Geological Characters. By H. B. Guppy. M.B. Illustrated. 8vo. 15s. net.

A TREATISE ON ORNAMENTAL AND BUILD-ING STONES OF GREAT BRITAIN AND FOREIGN COUNTRIES. Arranged according to their Geological Distribution and Mineral Character, with illustrations of their Application in Ancient and Modern Structures. By Edward Hull, M.A., F.R.S. 8vo. 12s.

GEOLOGY AND GENERAL PHYSICS. By Lord Kelvin, D.C.L., P.R.S., F.R.S.E. Crown 8vo. 7s. 6d.

TABLES FOR DETERMINATION OF ROCK-FORMING MINERALS. Compiled by F. Loewinson-Lessing, Professor of Geology at the University of Dorpat. Translated by J. W. Gregory. 8vo. 4s. 6d. net.

A TREATISE ON ROCKS, ROCK-WEATHERING, AND SOILS. By Professor George P. Merrill. 8vo. 17s. net.

MINERALOGY. An Introduction to the Scientific Study of Minerals. By H. A. Miers, F.R.S., Professor of Mineralogy at Oxford. 8vo. 25s. net.

THE DIAMOND MINES OF SOUTH AFRICA. Some Account of their Rise and Development. By Gardner F. Williams, M.A. Illustrated. Royal 8vo. 42s. net.

ELEMENTS OF CRYSTALLOGRAPHY FOR STUDENTS OF CHEMISTRY, PHYSICS, AND MINER-ALOGY. By Geo. Huntingdon Williams, Ph.D. Crown 8vo. 6s.

TEXT-BOOK OF PALÆONTOLOGY. By Karl A. von Zittel, Professor of Geology and Palæontology at Munich. Translated and edited by Charles R. Eastman, Ph.D. Revised and enlarged from the German original. Medium 8vo. Vol. I. 25s. net. Vol. II. 10s. net.

MACMILLAN AND CO., LTD., LONDON.

3

Printed in Great Britain
by Amazon